...blame for his sister's death...

**...Y MONROE: sexy, vengeful, bitter...
determined to solve his sister's case**
Plagued by guilt, this loner has never allowed a
woman close. Then Violet Baker returns, stirring his
passion with her sexy, vulnerable eyes, and heating
his blood with lust. Her visions may lead him to the
serial killer and his sister's murderer, but he must
guard his heart against falling in love...

**THE BONE WHISTLER:
twisted, ruthless...obsessive**
This killer believes his ritualistic sacrifices are
necessary for himself, the greater good...
and for the glory of his Father.

Will his connection to Violet Baker lead her into his
waiting hands, or will it lead to his own demise?
The answer is just *A Breath Away...*

A Breath Away

RITA HERRON

MIRA

*All the characters in this book have no existence outside the
imagination of the author, and have no relation whatsoever to anyone
bearing the same name or names. They are not even distantly inspired
by any individual known or unknown to the author, and all the
incidents are pure invention.*

*Published in Great Britain 2007.
MIRA Books, Eton House, 18-24 Paradise Road,
Richmond, Surrey, TW9 1SR*

© Rita B Herron 2005

ISBN: 978 0 7783 0184 4

63-0907

*Harlequin Mills & Boon policy is to use papers that are
natural, renewable and recyclable products and made from
wood grown in sustainable forests. The logging and
manufacturing processes conform to the legal environmental
regulations of the country of origin.*

*Printed and bound in Spain
by Litografia Rosés S.A., Barcelona*

To:
Karen Solem for believing in this story,
Tracy Farrell and Kim Nadelson for bringing it
to print, Carmen, Stephanie, Jennifer and Jenni
for your constant support, and to my husband,
Lee, for lending his expertise in medical
research to the sinister plot!

PROLOGUE

Crow's Landing, Tennessee

"HELP ME...." Darlene's whispery plea echoed inside eight-year-old Violet Baker's head. *"Please...s-somebody...help me."*

Violet wrapped her arms around her teddy bear, Bobo, rocking back and forth on her bed. Even though the thunderstorm raged outside, she'd heard Darlene's terrified cries in her head all night. Poor Darlene hated storms.

A tree branch scraped the window, and lightning zigzagged across the black sky. Violet rubbed her fingers over her half of the Best Friends necklace Darlene had given her. Violet had a strange connection with Darlene. They'd had it since they were little. Probably because they were both motherless. Nobody in Crow's Landing knew about their connection, though. It had been their little secret.

Until Violet had told her daddy.

He'd spanked her. Said if she claimed she heard things in her head, the whole dang town would think she was as mad as old Miss Laudy. Old Miss Laudy had ended up in a crazy house.

"Nobody needs to know what goes on behind closed

doors," her father had yelled. "And stay away from that family—them Monroes ain't nothin' but snobs."

But Darlene Monroe wasn't a snob. When kids at school teased Violet about wearing Goodwill clothes and standing in the free-lunch line, Darlene yelled at them to shut up. Darlene told Violet secrets and invited her to her playhouse, where they had tea parties. And they dressed up in Darlene's mama's old ball dresses and pretended they were princesses.

"Violet, p…lease. I'm…sca…" The whisper faded, as if Darlene was growing weaker. She was shivering and wet. Cold. All the way to her bones. The smell of a dead animal turned Violet's stomach. There was muddy creek water. And blood.

She had to help Darlene!

She jumped off the bed and peered through the crack in the door. Grammy Baker sat in the old wooden chair in the den. Sheriff Tate stood beside her. His khaki uniform was splattered with mud. Darlene's father, a big man with a woolly beard, paced back and forth, tugging at his chin. Darlene's thirteen-year-old brother, Grady, stared at Violet's door, his dark eyes hard and cold. Accusing. Violet lurched back as if he'd burned her. Did he know about the connection she and Darlene shared?

If he did, he knew she'd told her daddy where to hunt for Darlene. Violet was trying to help. She loved Darlene. Darlene was her best friend in the whole wide world.

Or maybe Grady knew it was her fault Darlene was missing. If *she* hadn't begged Darlene to hurry over to see her new birthday bear, her friend wouldn't have set off by herself. She'd have waited for Grady….

"You didn't find her?" Violet's father asked.

The sheriff shook his head. "We checked the old

schoolhouse like you suggested, but weren't nothing there."

Oh, no. She'd made a mistake. She'd thought Darlene was at the schoolhouse because that's where Darlene had *wanted* to be. Someplace safe.

But she wasn't safe.

Images flashed like photographs in Violet's mind. Dirty water gurgling. Copperheads and water moccasins slithering through the wet leaves. The smell of rotting wood. The well house out by Shanty Annie's. Violet and Darlene had played around it before the scary old woman had run them off. What if Grammy was right about that old haint Soap Sally, who lived in the well? What if Soap Sally had dragged Darlene down inside?

Violet twisted the knob again, her nails biting into the cold metal. But the door didn't budge.

Her daddy had locked her inside!

She swayed and clawed at the door until blood stained the wood. She felt Darlene's pain. Darlene's panic. Her lungs begging for air.

She was so cold and scared. She'd tried to be a big girl and not cry. But she couldn't help it. He didn't like her crying. He yelled at her to be quiet. Then he slapped her. She pressed a hand to her stinging cheek. He had big hands. And mean eyes. She wanted her mommy, but her mommy was dead....

Footsteps clattered as everyone went outside. Violet dragged herself to the window and tried to yell, but her throat closed. Someone was choking Darlene!

She had to stop him. Get the sheriff. But Grady, his father and the sheriff climbed into the police car and roared down the graveled drive.

"Stop!" Violet screamed.

They couldn't hear her. Mud and gravel spewed behind them. Violet collapsed on her knees on the wood floor, heaving for air. Her father wrenched open the door. She lunged forward, gasping. "Tell them, look at Shanty Annie's. T-tell them, Daddy. Soap Sally got her!"

Violet's father dragged her to her feet. "There ain't no such thing as Soap Sally. That's a stupid legend your grammy told you to keep you from the well. Now hush." He shook her so hard her teeth rattled. Bobo skittered across the floor. "I told you not to go around talking crazy like this—it's evil that's got inside you. Pure evil." He turned black eyes on her grammy. "Pack her things and get her out of here tonight. She can't stay here no more."

Grammy nodded. Her hands jerked as she yanked open the bureau drawer. Then she stuffed handfuls of Violet's clothes in a duffel bag as if she feared the devil himself would swoop down and take Violet straight to hell.

Violet's daddy hauled her to the rusty Ford station wagon. She begged him to stop, but he shoved her inside and slammed the door.

Violet beat on the glass. "Daddy, please tell them Shanty Annie's. Save Darlene…."

But he walked away from her. Grammy climbed in, started the engine, then threw the car into gear and tore off. Violet pressed her face against the door, sobs racking her body. Rain pounded the hood and the wind howled, bowing trees and shrubs. The car bounced over a pothole, jarring her head against the window. The house disappeared from sight. Just as they rounded the corner near the sweet gum tree, the voices in Violet's head suddenly quieted.

Another image flashed there.

Darlene. Lying still on the ground. Dead leaves, soggy red clay beneath her. Rain splattered her colorless face. Her eyes were wide open in terror.

Cold. She was so cold. As if ice had frozen her veins.

A screeching sound echoed behind her—the whine of a harmonica.

No, a horrible sound. The whistle of wind blowing through something else. Something Violet didn't recognize. Maybe bone.

She doubled over and reached for Bobo. But she'd left him behind. She'd lost him, too. How could she go on?

Maybe her daddy was right. Maybe she was evil. Maybe that was the reason Darlene had been taken.

Tears gushed out and poured down Violet's face. She would never forgive herself or her father.

It was too late for Darlene....

CHAPTER ONE

Twenty Years Later

HE HAD COME BACK to get her. She heard the sound, breath against bone....

Violet bolted upright from a dead sleep and searched the darkness. She'd known this day would come. That he'd find her and kill her just as he had Darlene.

Shadows from the room clawed at her. A reedy, whistling sound rippled in her ears. What was it? An animal crying? No, it was lower, softer but sharp.

Almost like...like the sound she'd heard the night Darlene died.

Had the sound been in her dreams or was someone really outside this time?

She flicked on the fringed lamp, searching the room, angry that she still hadn't conquered her fear of the dark. Or storms. She had dreamed of Darlene's death a thousand times over the years. And that noise—she'd heard it before, too.

But never like this.

Not like it was right outside, coming nearer.

And this dream was different. In her earlier nightmares, Darlene had remained the same sweet, red-haired child. This time the victim had been a woman.

What did it mean? Was the evil back? Was it inside Violet?

Or was her subconscious aging Darlene so she could see what her friend might have looked like if she'd lived? Violet dropped her head into her hands. Or maybe her grief and guilt had finally robbed her senseless, and she'd lost her mind.

Outside, ocean waves crashed against the Savannah shore. The wind howled off the coast, rain splattering against the roof of the cottage she and her grandmother had rented a few months ago when they'd moved to Tybee Island.

The wind had seeped through the thin panes and weathered wood, causing the whistling sound. That was the logical explanation.

The *only* explanation.

Sweat-soaked and shaking, Violet tugged the quilt around her legs. The clock chimed midnight. The steady crashing of the waves faded into a hypnotic drone. But her heart pounded in her chest like ancient Indian war drums. The last time she'd had a psychic vision or heard voices in her head had been twenty years ago. The day her father had sent her away. The day her best friend had died.

It couldn't be happening again.

Although a few times in a crowded room she'd experienced strange sensations—odd snippets of a stranger's voice whispering in her head—she'd written them off as her overactive imagination. And on a date in Charleston, she'd sensed something dangerous about the man. It was almost as if she'd met him before. As if he'd known more about her than he was telling.

She tossed aside the covers and padded barefoot across the braided rug, then stared through the windowpane at the moonless night. Her fingers toyed with her half of the Best Friends necklace she had shared with Darlene. The rain and fog rolling off the shore obliterated the normally crystal images of the cove and the constellations. Ominous shadows tore at her self-control. It was almost as if someone was watching her.

As if the past had returned to haunt her.

No. Tomorrow marked the twentieth anniversary of Darlene's death. Thoughts of Darlene always dominated Violet's mind at this time of year. Like an obsession that grew stronger, the incessant guilt dogged her like a demon.

Yet as she looked into the inky sky, fear snaked through her and she sensed that it was only the beginning. That just as the tides changed in the ocean, they were about to change in her life.

Just like everything had changed that horrible day when she was eight years old, and she'd stood by and let her best friend die.

"ARE YOU ALL RIGHT this morning, dear?" With gnarled fingers Violet's grandmother gripped the coffee cup painted with magnolia blossoms, and slid into a kitchen chair. "You look tired."

Violet shrugged, pushing away her half-eaten piece of dried toast. "I didn't sleep well."

"Having nightmares again?"

She nodded, her gaze straying to the rain still drizzling in soft sheets onto the beach sand outside. "It's that time of year, I suppose."

Sympathy lined her grandmother's face. "I know it's hard, Violet. Try not to dwell on the past, though."

Violet nodded, resigned. She wouldn't upset her

grandmother by confessing about the voices. She was twenty-eight now, independent and strong. She'd even invested in a gift shop in downtown Savannah, Strictly Southern, determined to plant roots and build a life here. She'd save some money, buy this cabin and fix it up for herself and her grandmother. In fact, she'd already mapped out the first decorating plans: she'd paint the fading, chipped walls yellow; sew some frilly curtains; add a window seat by the bay window so she could bask in the sunlight there to read and draw.

And maybe she would finally escape the ghosts. "I'm going to the shop for a while. Do you need anything?"

Her grandmother pointed to the list on the butcher block counter. "Thanks, dear. I hate that I can't get about like I used to."

"You're doing fine, Grammy." Violet patted her hand, then scraped the dry toast into the trash, a twinge of anxiety pulling at her. The doctor had cautioned Violet about her grandmother's high blood pressure and irregular heartbeat. Occasionally she suffered memory lapses, and her arthritis was becoming more of a problem.

At one time, Violet had told her grandmother everything. Had shared her fears, all her nightmares, the bitter sense of loss that had eaten at her over the years when her father had never called or visited.

"Maybe you'll find a nice young man here in Savannah," Grammy said with a teasing smile. "Get married, make me some great-grandbabies."

"Maybe." Violet feigned a smile for her grandmother's benefit, although she didn't foresee marriage or a man in her near future. If her own father hadn't loved her, how could someone else? Besides, her failures with men were too many to count. The psychologist she'd finally spoken with about her phobia of the dark had suggested she was punishing herself for Darlene's death by denying her own happiness. So she had forced herself to accept a few dates.

But Donald Irving, the man in Charleston, had given her the creeps. When she'd refused to see him again, he started showing up at odd times, calling at all hours of the night. Then the hangup calls...

Her grandmother had become so distraught, Violet had finally agreed to move.

Violet had no plans for marriage or men. She had been a loner most of her life.

And she probably always would be.

"Oh, my goodness." Her grandmother paled. "Did you see this, Violet?"

Violet leaned over her shoulder and stared at the newspaper, her stomach knotting at the headlines.

Twenty-five-year-old Woman from Savannah College of Art & Design Reported Missing. Police Suspect Foul Play.

GRADY MONROE STACKED the files on his desk, wishing he could rearrange his attitude and life as easily. He traced a finger over the edge of Darlene's photo. She'd been so damn young and innocent, just a freckled-faced kid with a heart-shaped face, who'd liked everyone. And trusted them.

But she'd died a violent death.

He pressed the pencil down to scribble the date on the file, his gaze shooting to the desk calendar. The pencil point broke. The date stared back at him, daring him to forget it, the red circle around the fifteenth a staunch reminder of the reason he couldn't.

The single reason he'd studied law himself. Only so far he had no clue as to who had committed the vile crime or how the killer had eluded the police for two decades. The police referred to it as a cold case—a dead file.

The file would never be shut until he found his half sister's killer.

Jamming the pencil in the electric sharpener, he mentally sorted through the recent cases on his desk. Crow's Landing had the usual small-town upheavals. Traffic citations. Domestic crimes. A complaint against a stray dog that might be rabid. Not like crime in the big cities. A man murdered in Nashville two days ago. A drive-by shooting in an apartment complex in Atlanta. And this morning, reports of a woman missing in Savannah.

As if to mock him, the phone trilled. "Sheriff Monroe here."

"Sheriff, this is Beula Simms."

Oh, Lord. What now?

"Get out to Jed Baker's house right away. Your daddy and Jed's at it again."

She didn't have to say at what; Jed and Grady's father had hated each other for years. "I'll be right there." He hung up and snagged the keys to his patrol car. A headache pounded at his skull, the painkillers he'd managed to swallow barely touching the incessant throbbing. He should have left off the tequila the night before, but the approaching anniversary of his half sister's death always brought out his dark side, the destructive one.

And now this call.

Five minutes later, he screeched up the graveled drive

to Baker's clapboard house. His father and Baker were yelling at each other on the sagging front porch. Grady opened the squad car door and climbed out, although both men seemed oblivious that he'd arrived.

"You should have left town a long time ago." His father waved a fist at Jed.

"I did what I had to do and so did you," Jed yelled.

Grady's father raised a Scotch bottle and downed another swallow, staggering backward and nearly falling off the porch. "But if we'd done things differently, my little girl might be alive. And so would my Teresa."

"I know the guilt's eatin' at you, Walt." Jed ran his hand through his sweaty, thinning hair. "We'll both be burning in hell for keeping quiet."

"Hell, I've been living there for years."

"But you don't get it—someone's been asking around." Jed's voice sounded raw with panic. "Claims he's a reporter."

His father coughed. "You didn't tell him anything, did you?"

"Hell, no, but I don't like him asking questions. What are we gonna do?"

"Keep your goddamn mouth shut, that's what."

"I ain't the one who wanted to blab years ago. And what if he gets to Violet?"

"It's always about *her.* What about what I lost?" Walt lunged at Jed, ripping his plaid shirt and dragging them both to the floor. Jed fought back, and they tumbled down the stairs, wood splintering beneath them, before they crashed to the dirt.

The late evening heat blistered his back as Grady strode over to them. "Get up, Dad." He yanked his father off Jed, and the other man rolled away, spitting out dry dirt and brittle grass.

Walt swung a fist at his son. "Leave us alone!"

Grady grabbed him by both arms and tried to shake some sense into him. "For God's sake, Dad, do you want me to haul your ass to jail for the night?"

Jed swiped a handkerchief across his bloody nose and climbed onto the lowest step. Grady's father wobbled backward, a trickle of blood seeping from his dust-coated lower lip.

Grady jerked a finger toward his vehicle. "Get in the damn car before I handcuff you."

His father muttered an obscenity as Grady shoved him into the back seat. He slammed the door and glared at Baker. "Are you all right?

Jed merely grunted.

"You want to press charges?"

"No."

Grady narrowed his eyes, wondering why Baker would allow his dad to assault him and get away with it. But as usual when the two men fought, neither Jed nor his father offered an explanation. Although this time the conversation had triggered more questions than usual.

It was senseless to ask, though. Something had happened years ago that had caused a permanent rift between the men. Something they refused to talk about.

Judging from their conversation, it had to do with Darlene.

And sooner or later, Grady was going to find out exactly what it was. Then maybe he'd figure out who had killed his sister.

A FEW MINUTES LATER, he pulled up to his dad's house. The Georgian style two-story had once been impressive, almost stately with its front columns, but had deteriorated in the past twenty years from lack of upkeep. Paint peeled from the weathered boards, shingles had blown off the roof in the recent storm, and the columns needing painting. A sad testament to his father's life.

"You'd better stay put tonight, Dad," Grady ordered.

His father staggered toward the den, his face ruddy with rage. "You should have left us alone."

"Sleep it off, Dad." Grady slammed the door and jogged to his car. Dammit, just as he'd expected, his father had clammed up, refusing to talk about his fight with Baker or offer an explanation.

His nerves shot, Grady reached for a cigarette, then remembered he'd quit smoking for the dozenth time this year. Rummaging through the papers littering the console, he grabbed a piece of Juicy Fruit gum and shoved it in his mouth instead. The shortest span without his Marlboros had been six days. The longest, six months.

He automatically veered toward the graveyard beside Crow's Landing Church, the daisies he'd bought for his little sister's grave a reminder of the reason he'd started smoking in the first place.

Darlene's death.

Everything in his life could somehow be related to that one crucial event. And the fact that her killer had never been caught.

Twenty years ago today she had been kidnapped. Twenty years ago tomorrow, they had found her dead. He knew his father was in pain. Hell, so was he. Grady had lost his entire family that day.

He'd never forgive himself for it, either.

If only he hadn't stopped to hang out with the boys… If he'd come straight home to watch Darlene, she wouldn't have set off across the hollow by herself to see that little friend of hers, Violet. And she wouldn't be dead.

The small graveyard loomed ahead, shadows of tombstones darkening with age. Some graves were littered with debris, others better tended, a few decorated with artificial flowers. The dank air and smell of freshly turned dirt from a new grave enveloped Grady as he forced his rubbery legs to carry him through the aisles of cement landmarks. It was almost midnight, the day of mourning upon him.

Night sounds surrounded him, plus the crunch of his boots, the snapping of twigs and leaves. He knelt and traced his finger over the curved lines of Darlene's name carved in slick marble, then laid the flowers across the headstone, his gaze straying to her mother's grave beside her. At least the two of them were together; he tried to take solace in that fact. God only knew where his own mother was. She might be dead for all he knew. His father refused to talk about her.

Grady reached into his pocket and removed the bag of marbles he'd purchased earlier at the Dollar General, fingering each colorful ball as he arranged them in a heart shape on top of the grassy mound. A streetlight in the distance illuminated the colors. A green one with swirls of gold flecks looked almost iridescent, like mother-of-pearl, the cascade of bright reds, oranges, purples and yellows a kaleidoscope of colors against the earth.

"Come on, Grady, play Barbie dolls with me." Darlene's childlike voice echoed in his mind. He automatically pressed a hand over his shirt pocket, where he always carried a green marble. He'd refused to play

Barbie with her, though—he'd been too cool. So he'd tried to convince her to play marbles instead. She'd never taken to the game, but she had been enchanted with all the colors, and had started collecting marbles, calling them her jewels.

Damn, if he had it to do over again, he would suck it up and play dolls with her.

He could still picture her angelic little face as she lined her jewels up on the shelf above her bed, those lopsided red pigtails bobbing, the freckles dancing on her pug nose. *"Look, Grady, I'm making a rainbow. The green one looks like my eyes. And this chocolate-brown one looks like yours, and this pretty blue one is like Violet's. And look at this sparkly clear one! I can see through it, just like I can see right through Violet's eyes sometimes.*

Although he didn't understand their friendship, Darlene had loved the homely Baker girl. He'd been shocked when Violet hadn't attended the funeral. But Baker had claimed his daughter had had a breakdown, that he'd had to send her away. And as far as Grady knew, she'd never returned to Crow's Landing. Maybe she'd totally forgotten Darlene.

His life might be different if he moved away, too. He might escape the constant reminders of his past. His father. And his guilt. But he didn't want to escape.

He wanted revenge.

HE PACED AROUND AND around in a wide circle. The moonlight was bright, bright, bright. The light hurt his eyes. Hurt his eyes. Hurt his eyes. But the circle had to be complete.

He raised his arm and tore at the hairs. One, two, three.

No, stop it! he silently cried. He gripped the rocks, inhaling pungent, salty air and the delicious scent of death as he frenziedly twisted his hands over the jagged surface. Then he ground his palms so hard the pointed rocks tore at his skin. The first trickles of blood seeped from the cuts and dripped down his arms. He raised a fist to study the crisscrossed patterns where the streams of blood met, the angle they flowed across, and the thickening at the base of his hand. Snippets of the Cherokee language rolled through his head.

Gi'ga—blood, the force of life. The scarlet color stirred his loins. Excitement sang through his veins. I am the *gi'ga-tsuha'li*. One cut, two cuts, three—

No! He no longer thought in threes. One was his number.

Three was the first pattern. One for his mommy, one for his daddy and one for him.

Then he'd learned about another.

But that one had to die.

He imagined her sweet, baby lamb's face with those big trusting eyes. That day he'd heard another voice in his head, ordering him to stop. He'd known there were more. Too many more. He had to make them all die.

Let them know he was the chosen one.

But his mommy and daddy found out what he'd done. He hadn't been careful. No, he'd been stupid, so stupid, and they'd gotten angry. Finally they'd admitted it wasn't his fault, then they'd called him their little angel. But after that, they'd kept him locked up at night. He despised being shut up. Hated the bare white walls. Had clawed them until blood streaked down, giving them color. Pretty crimson color.

His mommy needed him now, though. Oh, yes, yes, yes. He couldn't let her down.

Laughter bubbled up inside him, erupting like blood bursting from an open vein. Like the dark red substance he drew from the sacrificial lambs before they died. Yes, he was the blood taker, the *gi'ga-tsuha'li*.

He was the good son. The only one who could save the father. And he wouldn't stop until he did.

His favorite childhood song chimed in his head: *"There was one, there were two, there were three little angels...."*

Smiling to himself, he reversed the words. *"There were ten, there were nine, there were eight little angels, there were seven, there were six, there were five little angels, there were four, there were three, there were two little angels, one little angel in the band."*

Yes, when it was over, there would be only one little angel left.

And it would be him.

CHAPTER TWO

"THERE WERE TEN, there were nine, there were eight little angels...."

The childish version of the old rhyme played in Violet's head as she hurried to her shop the next day. It had been playing all night. Except, oddly, the song was playing backward.

Goose bumps skated up her arms, but she didn't understand why. Probably because of the story about the missing woman, Amber Collins.

The story plagued her. Not that the reporter had mentioned angels or the song, but the girl's disappearance had triggered paranoias Violet had struggled to overcome her entire life. One of them, that she would meet Darlene's killer in a crowd and not recognize him. The other, that he knew she and Darlene had shared a connection, and that he would come hunting for her.

She searched the crowd. Was he here somewhere? Watching her? Had someone in town kidnapped the woman? Was one of them a rapist? A murderer?

Amber's picture flashed through her head again. Light blond hair, green eyes. She was only twenty-five. Although Violet didn't remember all her customers, she'd noticed this girl in the shop the day before. Amber had been especially friendly. Once she'd sampled the pecan pralines, she'd bought five tins, claiming she had a bad habit of eating late at night when she was studying. Violet had laughed because she used to do the same thing, her affinity for café mochas and Snickers bars costing her five pounds every exam week.

Shaking off the unsettling feeling that she and Amber would have become friends, Violet crossed the street, frowning at the driver of a black sedan who nearly skimmed her knees with his bumper as he raced through the stop sign. The scents of crawfish étouffée, shrimp and beer oozing from Tubby's Tank House, and the rich aroma of chocolate from Carlotta's Candy Shop, wafted around her. Unfortunately, the stale smell of too much partying and sweaty bodies lingered from the night before, as well, reminding Violet of the seedy side of Savannah nightlife. The side she avoided.

The clatter of glasses and the murmur of voices drifted through the balmy summer air, the sidewalk choked with early morning browsers. A couple of homeless men lay sleeping off their liquor in the trash-filled alley. Pigeons pecked along the Savannah River shoreline, searching for crumbs, the occasional blast of a ship's horn startling them into a skitter. In contrast, the horse-drawn tourist carriages clip-clopped along, adding to the genteel historic atmosphere.

Her grandmother's parting words rang in her ears: "Please be careful, Violet. Make sure no one is following you." She'd shrugged off the warning, knowing her grandmother had been spooked by the report on the missing woman. But she couldn't dismiss the reality that a madman might be stalking innocent women in Savannah.

GRADY DROVE THROUGH the town square, making his usual noon rounds, still contemplating the argument he'd heard between his father and Baker. Why was someone asking questions about a twenty-year-old murder? And why did his dad and Baker want to keep quiet? His father had claimed he wanted Darlene's killer caught....

In fact, her unsolved murder had been an obsession with both Monroe males. The absence of Darlene at the dinner table had not only ended the family Sunday night dinner tradition, it had torn them apart completely. His dad had begun substituting liquor-for-one for the family meal. Booze and anger, a deadly combination that had grown worse over the years.

Grady had borne the brunt of his temper.

Because he was responsible.

The fact that he and Darlene hadn't shared the same mother hadn't made a difference to Grady; the guilt had been the same. And his father had never let him forget that he should have been home watching her the day she'd been kidnapped.

Wiping sweat from his brow, Grady scanned the streets, passing the hardware store, the small bookstore Serena James had opened last year, and the barbershop the Chutney couple manned together. He parked in front of the Redbud Café, cut the engine and headed inside.

The homey scents of fried chicken, meat loaf, green beans and apple pie floated through the ancient establishment. Adobe-colored tablecloths and curtains in turquoise matched the clay-colored laminate tops of the booths and tables. The pale yellow walls held a wide assortment of framed Indian arrowheads, spears and pipes, showcasing the owner, Laney Longhorse's, penchant for preserving the history of the area. She loved reciting tales of the ancient customs, especially the religious tribal dances and traditions. Some of them were pretty damn eerie. As were those bone artifacts displayed on the wall. Her son, Joseph, collected them. Grady wondered if he'd found them or killed the animals first, then hung them to show off his hunting skills.

Kerry Cantrell, an attractive blonde a few years younger than him, offered a flirty smile and sauntered toward him. She'd been throwing out vibes for months. Maybe one day he'd ask her out. Then again, that would piss off Joseph Longhorse, who worked at the diner. The Native American had been chasing Kerry ever since she'd moved to Crow's Landing. He already hated Grady, had since he was a child, although Grady didn't know why. He'd actually tried to stand up for the kid one time, but Joseph had snarled that he didn't want or need Grady's help.

"Hey, Grady. Want some sweet potato pie with that coffee?" *Or a piece of me,* her eyes suggested.

"Pie sounds good." He contemplated her silent offer. It had been a long time since he'd been with a woman. They always wanted more than he could give.

She handed him the dessert, letting her fingers brush his knuckles. "Anything else you want, you just holler, sweetie."

Joseph suddenly appeared through the back door, his shoulder-length black hair tied into a ponytail with a leather thong, his black eyes blazing fire at Grady. Shit, let the man have her. He sure as hell wasn't getting into a fight over a woman. That close call with Luanne years ago had taught him better sense. No woman could understood his obsession with solving Darlene's murder.

Besides, Kerry had that look about her that said she wanted the whole package.

"Kerry, can we get some service over here?" Bart Stancil, a crotchety old man who practically lived on the vinyl bar stool, flicked a wrinkled hand.

Kerry winked at Grady, then pranced toward Bart, coffeepot in hand.

Grady ate his pie in silence, studying the other regulars. Agnes Potts and Blanche Haney, two widow women who organized the Meals on Wheels program at the church, waved at him from their biscuits and hash browns, while a teenage couple cuddled in the corner, feeding each other ice cream sundaes.

Tate, the incompetent sheriff Grady had replaced a few months ago, folded his beefy body over a stool, glaring at him. Tate had bungled Darlene's murder investigation years ago. Unfortunately, the man owned half the town and was now mayor, which meant Grady still had to work with him.

Mavis Dobbins and her son, Dwayne, claimed their usual corner booth. Dwayne was in his thirties now, but he'd had some sort of accident at age fourteen that had triggered a psychotic break. If Grady remembered correctly, the doctors diagnosed him as bipolar. He still lived with his mama. Dwayne laid out three sugar packets for his coffee, then ordered his usual—three eggs, three biscuits, three slices of bacon.

Grady pushed away the remaining pie, his stomach churning. Years ago, when Dwayne was sixteen, Grady's dad had paid him to do yardwork. When Grady had noticed him watching Darlene, he'd threatened to beat him up if he touched her. He'd always wondered if Dwayne had something to do with Darlene's disappearance.

The lunch crowd drifted in slowly, and Grady caught a sharp look from Ross Wheeler. The minister's son, Wheeler was a former teacher who'd lost his job because of complaints of sexual misconduct from female students at the high school. Wheeler had denied the charges, and they'd finally been dropped, but his reputation as an educator had been ruined. Grady had been shocked when Wheeler stayed in Crow's Landing. He still hadn't decided whether the man had been guilty or victimized.

Grady tossed a few bills on the counter, nodding goodbye to Kerry as he walked to the door. Maybe he'd ride up and check out that rabid dog report. Not much else to do today.

Tonight he'd look over the files on Darlene's case. One more time.

Outside, he noticed Laney Longhorse talking to his father. She turned in a huff, then gathered a group of Cherokee children into a circle. Her long gray braid swung around her shoulders as she spoke. "The power of the circle," she said, crooked teeth shining. "Just as the sky is round, and the stars and the moon. The sun comes forth and goes down again in a circle. The seasons form a circle in their changing, always come back to where they were. The life of a man is a circle from childhood to childhood, and so it is in everything where power moves."

Grady nodded, accustomed to her aphorisms, but Tate and a few of the other locals protested her storytelling, especially when she shared Native American folklore with the Caucasian kids. His father was watching her, too, a frown on his face. Odd how some of the town and the natives mixed, while others let prejudices fester like old sores. As did his dad and Baker.

Just as Grady reached his police car, the radio crackled. He pushed the respond button, but static rippled over the connection. He tapped the speaker, frustrated with the inadequate equipment. "Sheriff Monroe. Over."

"Monroe…" More static. "Jim Logan here." His deputy's voice sounded raspy, as if he'd been running.

What's up?"

"I'm out at Briar Ridge. You'd better get over here."

"Trouble?"

"Definitely." Logan paused. "We found a dead body over the cliff."

As VIOLET ENTERED Strictly Southern, she steered her mind toward business. Thankfully, tourists already crowded the gift shop. Children shrieked over the cheap souvenirs, women were gushing over the Savannah cookies and pecans, and teenagers were choosing colorful T-shirts of River Street and scenes from the movie *Midnight in the Garden of Good and Evil.*

"Am I glad to see you, dear," Mrs. Guthrie chirped. "We've been busy as bees this morning. Just sold the last of those lovely notecards of yours."

"Good." Violet removed more notecards of Savannah sights from her bag and arranged them on the display. That steady work, plus her commissioned sketches of the town and historical buildings, had earned her a decent income in Charleston, where she'd lived before. When she'd moved to Savannah, she'd supplied the store with the same type of merchandise, and two weeks ago had bought the gift shop herself.

"These are wonderful," Mrs. Guthrie exclaimed.

"Would you paint a portrait of my granddaughter one day?"

"I'm sorry, but I don't paint people," Violet said softly. Especially children. To draw faces right she had to delve inside people's heads. It was too personal. Too painful. Especially when Darlene's face flashed into her mind.

"That's too bad. I'm sure you'd do a beautiful job." The woman fluttered a hand. "Damon sold the sketches you put in the art gallery. He said one customer wanted to talk to you about showing some of your pieces in Atlanta."

Nerves sputtered in Violet's stomach. "What did you tell him?"

"Don't worry, hon. I know you like your privacy so I didn't give him your address." She removed a business card from her apron pocket. "He left this, though, and asked if you'd call him."

"Sure." Stuffing it in her pocket, she headed to her office, where she spent the afternoon ordering new stock. Around five, she picked up a pack of her grandmother's favorite hickory coffee and shortbread cookies, then walked to the market.

A navy ship had docked on shore and dozens of tourists were lining up to take pictures of the seamen exiting. Violet breathed in the fresh, salty air, focusing on the children's laughter from the park and the sounds of jazz music drifting from the riverbank.

Someone had tacked flyers on lampposts and bulletin boards with the missing girl's picture and a full description. Violet studied one. Amber Collins was twenty-five, originally from Memphis, Tennessee. She had light blond hair, green eyes, was five feet nine inches tall and weighed approximately one hundred thirty pounds. She'd been last seen leaving her dorm room at the college, heading toward the library. She'd been wearing jeans and a blue T-shirt.

Violet hoped they found her alive. The coed was too young to die.

Taking a flyer for her store, she cut across the square, keeping her distance as she passed the graveyard near the parking lot where she'd parked her Civic. She hated cemeteries, had ever since her father had taken her to visit her mother's grave when she was three. It had been a cold winter day in the mountains, and a bristly wind had rustled the bare branches of the trees, heavy with ice from a recent hailstorm. She'd dropped rose petals on the slab of marble, not knowing how to feel as she tried to picture the faceless woman who had died giving birth to her.

Although giant azaleas, neatly trimmed hedges and jonquils flanked the iron gates of this cemetery in Savannah, disguising the morbid interior, the hair on the back of Violet's neck stood on end. Suddenly a whisper broke through the haze. "Help me."

Violet hesitated, wheeled around to stare at the tombstones. She could almost see the ghosts of the dead in the sea of monuments. And she could have sworn someone had just called to her. A woman's voice…

A storyteller from one of the walking ghost tours was spinning a tale for a group of tourists. Slowly, the faces and storyteller's voice faded.

Dizzy, Violet stumbled toward a park bench and dropped onto it. She yanked at the neckline of her shirt as the voice whispered to her again. Images played in her head like an old movie trailer….

HE WAS WATCHING HER, playing out his sick twisted game, dancing around the fact that he was going to kill her with platitudes in that singsongy voice that had grated on her nerves for hours. He enjoyed seeing the terror in her eyes.

And she was helpless to stop from showing it.

She did not want to die.

His olive skin looked pale beneath the harsh fluorescent light. Bluish veins bulged in his arms as he stalked around her. She struggled against the bindings holding her down, but the drugs he'd given her were slowly paralyzing her limbs.

"Your blood is rich and thick, and in some ways perfect," he murmured. "But you aren't the one."

His face loomed like some kind of distorted monster. "I'm sorry, sweetheart," he said in a soothing voice. "I wanted you to be it. I really did."

She moaned and tried to scream, fighting to escape. But a gag captured the sound, and her movements were stilted and slow, only token gestures of the will to survive.

He brushed a tendril of her wiry, tear-soaked hair from her face. "You let me down."

She shook her head violently, silently pleading for him to spare her. But anger darkened his already poisonous-looking eyes.

"It's not my fault. Father needs you. But you can't help us. Don't you see that?" His voice grew edgier, his eyes like marbles cut from ice. "I'm doing it all for him. I shall pray for your soul, and the angels will carry you to heaven. We are all children under one blessed father."

He ran a steady finger over the sharp end of a piece of bone he'd carved earlier. Then he slid the blade of a pocketknife along the jagged edge, scraping and shaving off more brittle bone. The rhythmic sound crawled over her skin. He scraped and whittled, painstaking in his task. Perspiration rolled down her breastbone as he held the bone up to the light and tested its smoothness. Then he raised it to his lips and began to blow.

"The tune of the bone whistle," he said softly. "The song that tells the story of sacrifice. Pin peyeh obe, *my sweetness. Then you must die."*

CHAPTER THREE

A MAN WAS DEAD. Was he a local or a tourist?

Grady flipped on the siren, tore from the Redbud Café and headed toward the ridge. Cutting across town, he took all the side streets because he didn't want any of the nosy townsfolk following. They might interfere with an investigation. If one was required.

He doubted it. The victim was probably some unlucky vacationer who'd wandered too close to the edge and lost his balance.

The Great Smoky Mountains rose in front of him as he veered from town onto Route 5. He sped past rundown chicken houses and deserted farmland, through the valley, then steered onto Three Forks Road to wind up the mountain. Sweat beaded his forehead and he cranked down the window of the squad car, cursing the stifling summer heat and his broken air conditioner. Thick pines and hardwoods dotted the horizon; blinding sunlight reflected off the steaming asphalt. The smell of manure and wet grass filled the air. He shoved his hand through his hair, his throat tightening as it always did when he passed Flatbelly Hollow, where his little sister's body had been found.

The Deer Crossing sign had been vandalized, he noticed, the stop sign from the side road leading to the fishing camp turned the wrong way. The latest graduating class's graffiti defiled the rocky wall of the rising cliff. Moss flanked the embankment, icy water trickling down the rocks like a small waterfall. The air cooled as he navigated up the mountain, the curves so routine he could have driven them in his sleep. Shadows from the yellow pines cast a murky haze over the ground as he parked at Briar Ridge next to Logan's squad car. Paramedics stood on the ledge, organizing the lift procedure.

Logan stalked toward Grady, his sunglasses shading his eyes. "I've already photographed the body and surrounding area."

"Good." Although Grady would take more photos as backup. He peered over the jagged ridge to assess the situation. The man's body sprawled facedown on the ledge a few hundred feet below, his arms and legs twisted at awkward angles. Blood splattered the rocks around his head. He wore plain jeans and a ragged T-shirt, nothing outstanding to distinguish him from any other tourist or a local.

"How did you find him?"

"Hiker called in. He was taking pictures of the mountains and spotted him."

"He still around?"

"Waiting in the car." Logan cleared his throat. "Young kid. Poor guy's pretty shook up."

"Did you question him already?"

"Yeah, said he didn't see any other cars around, hadn't spotted a soul until he came to the ledge and found the body."

Grady nodded and gestured toward the dead man. "You recognized him?"

"No." Logan shoved an evidence bag holding a piece

of paper toward Grady. "But I found this thumbtacked to that pine tree."

Grady pulled on gloves, then removed the note and unfolded it. The handwriting was scrawled, almost illegible, but he slowly managed to decipher the words.

"Sorry. Killed her. Couldn't live with the guilt anymore."

Killed who? Grady read further, his heart thundering in his chest at the name.

Darlene.

Unbelievable. His hands shook as he lowered the note to his side. His hopes for ending the mystery surrounding Darlene's death had finally come true. Full circle, as Laney Longhorse would say.

The dead man had confessed to killing his baby sister.

THE SPANISH MOSS of a giant live oak shrouded Violet in its haven, painting fingery shadows that resembled bones along the sidewalk. Disoriented, she clutched the wrought-iron rail surrounding the tombstones. Her imagination must be overactive. Savannah thrived on ghost stories about soldiers who'd died and hadn't yet found peace. Ones who lingered between realms, tortured and lost, forever searching.

But she had never heard voices from the grave before.

Although this voice hadn't called to her from the grave, she realized. The woman had still been alive. Had the voice belonged to Amber Collins, the missing coed? Had Violet heard her cry for help just before she was murdered?

Had the evil gotten inside her again? Or had she envisioned the images and voice because of the flyer? Because Darlene's murder was on her mind?

Violet glanced at the crumpled paper in her hands and felt paralyzed. People had been reported missing, even murdered in Charleston where she and her grandmother had lived before, but she'd never experienced visions of them.

Pin peyeh obe—what did the expression mean? It sounded like a Native American phrase. But she didn't know any native words, so why would one come to her in her thoughts? And what kind of bone had the man held to his lips?

Her mind spinning, she staggered to her car. Darkness descended as more storm clouds rolled in from the east. According to the weatherman, Hurricane Helena might hit tomorrow. Violet felt as if it had hit today.

Hands trembling, she started the engine and turned onto the island road, wincing as she bounced over the old bridge. A pair of headlights appeared in her rearview mirror, steady but not too close. The car coasted nearer as she crossed the narrow bay bridge and veered onto the side street that led to her cottage.

She clenched the steering wheel tighter, certain he was following her.

GRADY KNOTTED HIS HANDS. Everything had come full circle. Back to the beginning, back to the people in town, the ones they'd trusted. Memories of that grueling search crashed back. The long, endless night before they'd found Darlene. This man consoling Grady's father when they'd finally discovered her small limp body.

Grady turned to the paramedics. "Make sure the autopsy is thorough—tox screens, hair and fiber samples, the works." He gathered the crime scene kit from the car, then snapped more pictures of the area and body, and videotaped the scene. The rescue team lowered a paramedic to the ledge to secure the corpse on a stretcher, prior to transporting him to the coroner's office.

"Why all the fuss over a suicide?" Logan's voice was gravelly as he ran a hand over his sweat-streaked brow.

Grady frowned as he knelt to study the landing. "The first rule of being a good cop—everything is suspicious."

"Right. Sounds like the bastard deserved it. He killed a defenseless child."

Grady cut his eyes toward his deputy, but he couldn't read the man's expression, not with those damn sunglasses he always wore. "What do you know about my sister's death?"

"Not much," Logan said. "Just heard about it in town. I'd think you'd be glad he's dead."

Grady glared at him. They had never talked about personal things before. In fact, once he'd asked Logan about his family, but the man had clammed up and stormed outside. And Grady had certainly never shared anything about his own life.

But Logan was right. He should be happy. Ecstatic. Ready to celebrate.

Yet a nagging feeling plucked at the back of his mind, warning him things weren't quite right. Was it something about the case file? The suicide note? The confession?

Darlene's innocent young face flashed in Grady's head. Her knobby knees, missing front teeth, the strawberry curls he used to tease her about. He pictured her and that homely friend of hers tagging along behind him. Playing dress-up and skipping rope out by that old sweet gum tree. Darlene had always protected her friend. But who had protected her? No one.

Had he really found her killer? It almost seemed too easy….

Deep down he wanted it to be over. Closure meant he could move on with his life. Maybe his father could find his way out of the bottle, too.

Grady fisted and unfisted his hands, blood pounding in his veins. He'd wanted to find Darlene's killer alive so he could exact his own revenge. He hadn't realized how much he'd craved that confrontation, how the urge to make her murderer suffer the way his little sister had suffered had driven him through the years. How much the idea of that revenge had thrilled him.

Fighting for control, Grady scrutinized the ground for foot patterns.

The deputy squatted, then leaned his elbows on his knees. "Find anything?"

"Hard to tell," Grady muttered. "Looks like someone might have moved the straw to cover a footprint or scuffle. Then again, the wind and rain last night could have readjusted the soil." He shifted on the balls of his feet. "I want every inch combed. We'll send the note and any other evidence to the crime lab in Nashville to be analyzed. Did you find his car?"

"Yeah, run into the ditch over there." Logan pointed to a thicket of trees. "Reeks of whiskey."

Grady nodded, then gestured toward the surrounding bushes. "Look for loose or torn bits of clothing. Footprints. Anything to indicate the man might not have been alone. And I want the car impounded and processed." He stood. "I don't want this confession leaked in town, either, not until I have a chance to investigate the case thoroughly." Grady sighed. "For now, this is a suicide, but I'm leaving the case open."

Logan nodded, then began combing the bushes while Grady headed toward the paramedics carrying the body to the ambulance. The man's face was bloody, his clothes smeared with dirt, his broken femur jutting through his ragged pants; it had been severed in two places. His jeans were still damp, indicating he'd probably been there since the night before, but the EMT would give them a better idea of the exact time of death. The fetid odor of lost body fluids hung in the air as Grady checked the corpse for indications of a struggle. A small contusion lacerated the back of his head. If the man had fallen face-first, how had he hit the back of his head? Unless he'd been struck before falling.

Grady frowned, disturbed by his own train of thought. Maybe he'd fallen, then rolled over.

The paramedics loaded the stretcher and the ambulance roared off. Grady had to call his father, tell him they'd found Darlene's killer.

No, he couldn't yet. Not until he was sure. Not until he'd checked out the man's death. Not until he'd notified the next of kin.

He stalked to the woods to search the area. As soon as he finished, he'd visit the coroner's office for a full report, then make that call. Even worse, he had to tell the surviving family that their loved one had taken his own life.

And that he had confessed to a murder.

VIOLET CHECKED HER rearview mirror. Yes, someone was following her. Was on her tail. She wound through the side streets, reminding herself that she shouldn't lead a stranger to her house, then turned right on another side street. Nervous now, she wove through a nearby neighborhood, turned and headed back in the opposite direction. The sedan slowed, then swung into a drive. She sighed in relief. If whoever it was had been following her, he'd realized she was onto him.

Relaxing slightly, she headed back toward her cottage, then veered onto Palm Walkway. The inside of the cottage seemed dark as she parked and exited her car. Crickets chirped in the background. A bird cawed above.

Weary now, she climbed the small steps to the stoop, grateful to be home. When she stepped inside, the house was too quiet. "Grammy?"

Her grandmother was sitting in the wooden chair, pale and listless, the phone clutched in one hand.

"Grammy, what is it?"

Her grandmother's blank gaze showed no sign of response.

"Mrs. Baker…" A man's voice called over the line. "Mrs. Baker…are you still there?"

Violet pried the receiver from her grandmother's fingers and laid it on the counter. "Grammy." Violet gently shook her. "What's wrong? Please talk to me."

"No," her grandmother rasped, in a voice so low Violet could barely discern it. "No, it's not true."

"Mrs. Baker," the man shouted from the phone, "are you all right?"

Her grandmother's face went ashen, and she was trembling. No, she wasn't all right.

Violet grabbed the handset. "This is Mrs. Baker's granddaughter, Violet. Who is this and what did you say to upset her?"

"Violet?" Shock tinged the man's deep voice.

"Yes, who is this?"

"Sheriff Monroe." He hesitated, his voice husky. "Grady."

"Grady?" Darlene's brother?

"I'm sorry…I had to give your grandmother some bad news." His breath whistled out. "Violet, your father is dead."

CHAPTER FOUR

GRADY GRITTED HIS TEETH. He'd never cared for Jed Baker. And when Violet had first left town, years ago, he'd halfway blamed her for Darlene's death. Hell, he'd been a stupid adolescent at the time, battling his own guilt. Using her as the scapegoat had been easy. She was the reason his sister had rushed across the hollow alone. She hadn't been able to tell them where to find Darlene.

But she had been only eight years old.

He stifled the sympathy he felt for her now. If her father had killed Darlene, then he deserved to die, although suicide wasn't nearly severe enough punishment. And if Violet and her grandmother had known her father was guilty and hadn't told…

But what if the coroner did find evidence of foul play? What if his own dad had learned that Baker killed Darlene, and had gone back to finish their fight?

No, that train of thought was too dangerous.

She was so quiet he wondered if she'd fainted. And how old was the grandmother now—eighty? Ninety? "Violet?"

"Y-yes," she said in a choked voice. "How…how did you track us down here?"

"Lloyd Driver, the lawyer who handled your father's papers."

"How…how did my father die?"

Her whispered words echoed all the usual queries he'd expected. The hows and whys, the unanswered questions. "He left a suicide note."

"What? He killed himself?"

"I'm just telling you what I found. I'm having the note analyzed to make certain it's his handwriting."

"What does the note say? Did he give a reason?"

The part he dreaded the most. Violet might love her father, but she'd also cared for Grady's sister. He'd never forgotten the day he, his dad and the sheriff had driven to her house to inquire about Darlene. He'd heard Violet's childish cries through the closed door. And the next day she'd been gone. Later, rumors spread that she was a spooky kid, that she claimed to hear voices in her head, that she might be schizophrenic.

"Tell me," she said, her voice growing stronger. "I *want* to know. I have to know."

He hesitated. "This can wait until you come back for the funeral. I assume you'll want to bury him here. Or…maybe not."

"I…I don't know." Uncertainty laced her voice. "Just tell me what the note said."

He cleared his throat. "Violet—"

"Please, Grady."

Her soft plea twisted his insides. She sounded so young and vulnerable. He pictured those big sky-blue eyes, the innocent little girl who used to tag along behind him with his sister. The scrawny kid Darlene had felt sorry for, because the other kids called her white trash.

What did she look like now? Was she still homely? Did she still think about Darlene? Did she realize today was the anniversary of Darlene's death?

He didn't care. He'd wanted revenge so long he wouldn't let himself.

"From the looks of things, he got drunk and threw himself off the ledge at Briar Ridge, but I'm waiting on an official autopsy report for cause of death. The note said he couldn't live with the guilt any longer." Grady inhaled a calming breath, aware that he was dropping another bombshell, then forced himself to spit it out. "Violet, your father confessed to killing Darlene."

A HEARTBEAT OF SILENCE stretched between them. "What?" Violet clutched the table edge. "Did you tell my grandmother this?"

"Yes. I'm sorry, she insisted."

Violet sank into the chair. Her father was not a killer. He wouldn't have hurt Darlene. Not her best friend. Not the girl who'd defended her.

Bits and pieces of that horrible last day rushed back. Her father's fury when he realized she'd told the town about her connection to Darlene. The nervous way he'd stalked around the house, muttering under his breath that people would think she was a nutcase. That the devil had gotten her.

A shudder gripped her. What did she really know about her father? That he'd dragged her to the car that dark cold night without even kissing her goodbye. That he'd sent her away without a backward glance because he thought she was possessed. That he hadn't contacted her since. That he'd made her feel like some kind of freak.

That he hadn't told the Monroes where to find Darlene in time.

She swallowed to make her voice work, but before she could speak, her grandmother clutched her chest.

"Violet…"

Panic slammed into her. "Grammy, what's wrong?"

Her grandmother doubled over in the kitchen chair, gasping for air.

"Is she all right?" Grady yelled.

She was turning white. No, blue. "I have to call an ambulance!" Violet disconnected the phone and punched in 9-1-1, her heart racing.

"Jed didn't…do it," her grandmother rasped. "Not a…k-killer."

Her frail body jerked, then she slumped against Violet.

WHAT THE HELL WAS happening? Grady hit Redial, his pulse clamoring, but the phone rang over and over. Was Mrs. Baker okay? Had the news killed her?

He scrubbed a sweaty hand over his face and cursed. The scents of death and formaldehyde from the coroner's office came back to him, his sister's child-like face resurfacing. He'd never forget standing beside his father to identify her body. The image of Darlene's glassy eyes. The cuts and scrapes. Dirt and mud and weeds had clung to her pale skin, the signs of rigor mortis already setting in. Signs he hadn't understood at the time. Signs he'd recognized in other bodies since.

He and his father had waited all these years to learn the truth about Darlene's killer. But now to discover he'd been living in their own town, that Violet's father had murdered her. It was almost unbelievable….

But why had Baker killed himself now, twenty years later? It wasn't as if the case had been recently reopened. Unless the anniversary had finally driven Baker mad, as it threatened to do to Grady every year…

Uncertainty nagged at him again. At age thirteen, he hadn't known anything about the police investigation.

But he had read the files since. Hell, he'd memorized them. Tonight he would review them again and see how the police had missed that Baker was the killer. Just as soon as he told his father. A stream of sweat dribbled down his chin.

He hoped his dad didn't already know….

VIOLET CLUNG TO HER grandmother's hand on the ambulance ride to the hospital, as the minutes stretched out. For several seconds back at the cottage, she'd thought her Grammy had died. Then she'd jerked slightly, breathing again as if she refused to give up the fight. As if she knew she couldn't leave this world, not yet. Her granddaughter needed her.

In fact, Violet should have been there to take the phone call. She could have broken the news more gently. She should have protected her, just as she should have protected Darlene.

Violet had tried so hard to atone for that day. She hadn't celebrated a birthday since. And now she might lose the only person who'd been a constant in her life.

The ambulance screeched up to the emergency room entrance. Paramedics jumped into action. A team of doctors and nurses met them at the door, shouting questions and her grandmother's vital signs as they wheeled her through the ER.

"Pulse sixty-five, weak and thready. Respiration thirty, shallow. BP eighty over fifty."

"Dr. Rothchild, cardiology. How long was she out?"

"A couple of minutes." The paramedic glanced at Violet for confirmation.

Violet nodded, running behind, her heart in her throat. The EMTs opened a set of double doors and wheeled her grandmother toward an exam room. One of the nurses threw out a hand and stopped Violet from entering, then pointed to a waiting area with a few stiff chairs and an ancient coffee machine in the corner. "You'll have to wait there, miss."

Violet grabbed her arm. "Please let me know as soon as you find out something."

The nurse offered a tight smile, her expression sympathetic. "I will. Why don't you get a cup of coffee or something. It might be a while."

Violet's stomach was too knotted for her to drink or eat anything. Instead she paced the waiting room, her shoes clicking on the tiles, the conversation with Grady Monroe reverberating in her head.

Your father is dead. He left a suicide note. He confessed to murdering Darlene.

She didn't believe it. Why would he have killed Darlene?

Frustration gnawed at her—it was too late to ask him.

The finality of his death hit her, and a sob welled in her throat. Her father would never make that phone call she'd desperately wanted. Would never walk in the door and take her in his arms or beg her forgiveness for sending her away.

He'd never tell her he loved her.

At least when he was alive, she'd been able to hope that one day he'd reappear and admit the past twenty years had been a mistake. That he was sorry for shutting her out of his life.

Her knees buckled, and she collapsed on the tattered

vinyl sofa, the scents of antiseptic, and death washing over her. Her chest hurt from the pressure of holding back tears. Finally, she could fight them no longer. Sobs racked her as the hands of the wall clock ticked out the seconds, the minutes. Finally her sobs lessened, and anger replaced the pain. Violet stared at the gray walls, the stained coffee table overflowing with magazines. She was massaging her temples when she spotted the newspaper article on the missing Savannah woman.

When Darlene had been in danger, Violet had felt so connected to her. And today she'd thought a stranger's voice had whispered to her on her deathbed. If she had some crazy psychic ability, why hadn't she ever felt a connection to her own father? Why hadn't she known he was in danger or that he was contemplating suicide?

Had he sent her away because he was afraid she might figure out the truth—that he'd killed Darlene?

Violet dropped her head into her hands. The blood vessels in her temples seemed about to explode. She didn't really believe he'd killed her friend, did she?

"Miss Baker?"

She jerked her head up and swiped at her eyes. "Yes?"

"Your grandmother is resting now," Dr. Rothchild said. "She had a mild stroke."

"But she's alive?"

"Yes."

Violet stood on wobbly legs. "Can I see her?"

"For just a moment. She's being moved to ICU."

And her prognosis? She couldn't bring herself to ask.

The doctor jammed his hands in the pockets of his lab coat. "We can release her in a few days, but she'll need lots of rest and physical therapy. You can follow me."

Violet moved on autopilot as they walked to the ICU unit. Seconds later, she hesitated in the doorway, gathering the courage she feared might fail her.

Tubes and needles pierced various parts of her grandmother's thin body. The bleep of a heart monitor sounded over the murmur of nurses' voices and the clink of metal. Violet slowly inched her way to the hospital bed and lifted her grandmother's hand in her own. Her skin felt cold and clammy. She was so frail.

"Hang in there, Grammy," Violet whispered. "You can't leave me, too." Another tear slid down her cheek.

Her grandmother's eyes fluttered open. She tried to speak, but she'd lost her speech and mobility. Panicked looking, she waved a finger. Realizing she wanted something to write with, Violet dug a pen and paper from her purse.

Her grandmother struggled, but finally managed to write, "Take me home."

"I will, Gram," she said softly, "just as soon as the doctor releases you."

"No." She urged Violet closer, then scribbled, "Back to Crow's Landing, to see Neesie. Have to see my family one more time before I meet the master."

Neesie was her grandmother's sister. They hadn't seen her since Grammy had stolen away with Violet that dark, cold night. "You're not dying, Grammy," Violet said in a choked voice, "you're going to be okay."

"Please," she wrote, "prove your daddy didn't kill that little girl."

Anguish tightened Violet's throat at the thought of returning to Crow's Landing. At the mere idea of seeing her father's face again. Of burying him. She couldn't deny her grandmother's plea, though.

But how could she face the town now that everyone believed she was a murderer's daughter?

CHAPTER FIVE

BY THE TIME VIOLET stumbled into the cabin on Tybee Island, she was drained and dizzy with fatigue. Still shell-shocked, she flipped on the overhead light and stared at the vinyl chair where her grandmother had nearly died. The horrible trembling began all over again, stirring pain deep in her soul. She had to gain control.

Or she would never be able to face the people back in Crow's Landing.

The echo of Grady Monroe's voice over the phone line seared through her like a hot poker. Had she heard condemnation in his tone? Did he think she'd known what her father had done? Rather, what her father had *confessed* to doing in that note?

No. Her grandmother didn't believe her father was a killer, and she had never lied to Violet or led her wrong. Besides, even though her father had shut her out of his life, she sensed he wasn't evil.

Would she be able to prove her father's innocence if she returned to her hometown?

"Please, Violet, you have to go…. The hospital will transport me to the facility near there. Go on to Crow's Landing."

Knowing she needed sleep before she began the long drive to Tennessee, she heated a cup of Earl Grey tea and sipped it. She couldn't remember when she'd last eaten, but the thought of food still repulsed her. After some sleep, she'd get her affairs in order and inform her employees at Strictly Southern that she'd be away for a few days.

Shadows claimed the earth-toned walls of the cabin as she crossed the den to her bedroom. The scent of her grandmother's gardenia lotion sweetened the air, reminding Violet of her absence. The hand-made quilt Grammy had stitched, using different fabric scraps from Violet's childhood dresses, lay draped across her antique bed. Hugging the quilt to her as if she was hugging her grandmother, Violet crawled beneath the covers, praying the tea and quilt would finally warm her.

But as she closed her eyes, the image of Darlene's frightened eyes flashed before her, the terrifying plea for help screeching through her head. Another twenty-year-old picture resurfaced with vivid clarity—of her father dragging her to their old station wagon, shoving her inside, then wheeling away from her as she pleaded with him to find Darlene.

Violet curled into a ball, hugging her arms around her middle. She had let Darlene down years ago; could she let her grandmother down now? But what if she discovered the confession was real?

Her father's words echoed in her head: *Nobody needs to know what goes on behind closed doors.* Had he warned her to keep silent so Darlene wouldn't be found in time to point the finger at him?

Had he shut Violet out of his life because of his guilt? Because he'd been afraid she might figure out he was a killer?

GRADY STOPPED BY his office to grab the files on his sister's case, determined to review every inch of them. He had to figure out how the sheriff had missed the fact that Baker had killed Darlene.

First, though, he called Information and requested a listing of all the hospitals in the Savannah area. He tried the two major ones first. A nurse at St. Joseph's informed him that Violet's grandmother had been admitted and was listed in stable condition. Thank God.

Now he had to face his father.

Or was he jumping the gun? Giving his father the illusion the police had found Darlene's murderer when, in fact, they might not have?

Confusion riddled Grady. He'd just been given the answer to the question that had tormented him his entire life—so why didn't he take it at face value? Why was he having trouble believing the suicide note? Because it was too easy, too pat? Because he'd heard his father's argument with Baker?

Or because finding Darlene's killer has consumed you. You've lived for revenge. Without that, what will you do with the rest of your life?

You'll still have the guilt....

Clenching his fingers around the steering wheel, he drove to the Monroe estate, his mind on overdrive. He'd never known his own mother, only his father's second wife, Teresa. He'd wanted to please her and his father so badly.

But he'd failed.

The unkempt yard spoke volumes about his father's downward spiral into depression. Maybe he should have confronted his dad years ago, forced him to discuss the details of Darlene's death. But he'd been a son before he became a cop. The irresponsible teenager who hadn't come home to watch Darlene that day. The boy who'd disappointed his father in the worst way and started the domino effect that had ruined their lives. Discussing details about Darlene's disappearance had been impossible.

Actually, conversation in general had been practically nonexistent between the two men for ages. Any mention of Darlene had driven a deeper wedge between them.

Grady shut off the engine and waded through the overgrown grass to the front porch, wincing as the boards creaked and groaned. After his token knock, he opened the screen door. The faint scent of cigar smoke permeated the humid air, making him crave a cigarette. Inside, the dismal atmosphere magnified the emptiness of the house. Once this place had breathed with life, with Darlene's incessant chatter, the scent of cinnamon bread Teresa had baked. The joy of a family.

"Dad?" He walked across the hardwood floor, listening for sounds of his father. A curtain fluttered in the evening breeze, the sound of crickets chirping outside reminding him of his lost childhood. Of nights when he and Darlene had raced barefoot across the backyard, catching fireflies in mayonnaise jars. Had streaked in front of the sprinkler on hot July afternoons.

He checked the den, then his father's office, surprised he wasn't slumped in front of the TV watching *All in the Family* reruns on cable. Something about Archie Bunker had appealed to Walt's twisted sense of humor, *when* he'd had one.

Hot air surrounded Grady as he walked through the house. A scraping sound coming from somewhere near the kitchen broke the silence. He headed through the double wooden doors, then crossed the room and halted in the doorway to the garage. His father was sitting there—so still that for a brief moment Grady thought he might be dead. The low sound of a knife scraping against wood invaded the stale night air. Grady exhaled. His father was whittling again.

He spent hours carving, scraping away the edges of a raw piece of wood until he achieved the perfect smoothness he wanted. Back and forth, scraping and sawing, watching the splinters and dust fall. Once Grady had even watched him carve a chicken bone into an odd shape, then tell Darlene a story about his creation.

Grady had hated the sound of that carving.

He cleared his throat to alert his father of his presence, then descended the two stairs to the garage. His father's face was craggy, his eyes fixed in concentration, his bourbon beside him.

Oddly, his dad was carving a baby lamb. Did it have some significance?

"Dad?"

As if his father had just realized he had company, his knife froze in midair. The gaze he swung to Grady was not inviting.

"We have to talk," Grady said, ignoring the jab of pain his father's reaction caused.

"Not tonight, Grady. Go away."

Anger flared in his chest. "It's important. It's about Darlene's murder."

A vein throbbed high in his father's forehead. "You realize what day it is?"

He nodded. "Of course. The anniversary of her death."

Pain robbed Walt of all color.

"But it may also be the day we've discovered her killer."

The knife fell to the cement floor with a clatter.

Grady scrubbed a sweaty hand over his chin. "Tonight I found Jed Baker's body on the cliff out at Briar Ridge." He studied his father for a reaction, but detected only the slightest twitch of his eyebrow. "Dad, he left a suicide note confessing to Darlene's murder."

IN THE EARLY DAWN, Violet awoke with a sense of dread, but also with purpose. She ran her fingers over the Best Friends necklace. She had to face the old demons to move on.

Quickly showering and dressing, she grabbed some coffee and phoned the hospital to check on her grandmother.

"She's resting comfortably," the nurse said. "We'll be moving her to the assisted care facility in Tennessee later in the day."

"Please tell her that I'll visit as soon as possible." The nurse assured her she would, so Violet hung up, then left a message with her store manager, telling her she'd be gone for a few days. She left her cell phone number in case they needed to reach her.

After tossing a few things in a suitcase, she headed to the car. It would take several hours to get to Crow's Landing. She didn't want to arrive at midnight. There were too many old memories she'd left behind, too many ghosts.

As she climbed in her car, the anguished cries of the young woman she believed to be Amber Collins seemed to float through the haze. The sound of the bone whistle followed, reminding her of the gruesome murder in her vision.

And now her father was dead, too.

Why was all this happening now? And why did she feel connected to each of these horrid things, but helpless to stop the chain of events from unfolding?

OVER COFFEE the next morning, Grady was still stewing over his father's reaction to Baker's confession. Or his lack of a reaction.

He'd simply turned back to his whittling with a vengeance, as if he wasn't surprised at all to learn Baker had killed Darlene. Or maybe he was, and he couldn't deal with it.

Or maybe he'd known Baker had killed Darlene, and he'd finally exacted his own vengeance.

Grady didn't want to contemplate that possibility, but the argument he'd overheard between Baker and his dad gnawed at him. Determined to get to the truth, he sent the suicide note to the lab to see if it was legitimate. He'd have to get something Baker had written to compare the handwriting.

Rubbing at his aching neck, he poured himself a third cup of coffee and sat down to study the files. First, he pulled up the report of the crime scene and read the details of Darlene's murder. The photograph of her lying in the bottom of that well still tore him to shreds. Her face was deathly pale. Her wild, curly hair frizzed around her face in a tangled mop. Her clothes were covered in dried dirt and sticks and…bugs. Her shorts were tattered, the white cotton shirt ripped, her sneakers caked in mud. Forcing the anguish at bay with deep-breathing exercises, he zeroed in on the ligature marks on her neck. Would they match the size of Baker's hands and fingers? He'd make sure the coroner checked it out. Criminology techniques had changed a lot in twenty years.

Next, he read through the reports chronicling the search party's efforts to find Darlene. Locals had combed the woods behind his family's house, the hollow between the Monroes' and the shack Violet Baker had lived in, all the way to Briar Ridge, where Baker had just been found dead on the overhang. When his father was questioned, a meeting with a town council member had served as his alibi. Baker had an alibi, as well—he'd been supposedly working as a mechanic at a garage that had since closed. The owner, Whitey Simms, had confirmed his presence. But Whitey had passed away ten years ago, meaning Grady couldn't question him now. Not much help there.

He scratched his chin in thought. Had Whitey lied for Baker? If so, why?

A statement from a local citizen, Eula Petro, drew his eye. "Little Violet Baker claimed she heard Darlene's voice calling to her, crying for help. Told her daddy where to look for Darlene."

Grady chewed the inside of his cheek. If Violet claimed to have heard voices telling her where his sister was, had they followed up on what she'd told them? Had she been wrong? Or had the statement been pure gossip?

Ruby Floyd, the woman's older sister, had stated, "The child's not quite right. Might be touched in the head."

Had Violet suffered from a mental condition? Had she ever been treated?

He'd have to do more research to find out.

He read further.

"Search parties explored the northern area of Crow's Landing, covering a fifty-mile radius surrounding the Monroe house, 231 Sycamore Drive. No results. Call from Jed Baker, 2:45 p.m., June 15th. Suggested search parties check Crow's Landing Elementary. Baker claimed his daughter, Violet, and Darlene Monroe were playmates. Search party B immediately dispatched to the area, but turned up nothing. At approximately 10:45 p.m., June 15th, received another call from Baker. Suggested search parties check Shanty Annie's, 913 Flatbelly Hollow. Specifically mentioned the well house. Search party dispatched.

"One hour later, located body of Darlene Monroe in bottom of well. Coroner and sheriff lowered into well to establish death, photograph the body, examine evidence. Body lifted from well at approximately midnight. Transported to coroner's office for autopsy.

"Official cause of death: manual strangulation.

"Noon, June 16th: official press conference revealing the girl's murder."

His gut clenched. Had Violet told them to look in the well? Or had her father known where to find Darlene's body because he'd murdered her and put her there? He might have suggested alternative places to search in an effort to divert the authorities from finding Darlene before he had a chance to strangle her....

Grady grabbed his keys and headed to Baker's house. Killers often kept a token of their victims. Maybe he'd find something inside Baker's place that would give him some answers. At least he could get a sample of Jed's handwriting for the lab.

AS VIOLET DROVE INTO Crow's Landing, a small shudder ran through her at the sight of the big, black metal crow atop the town sign. There was some legend about the bird, but she couldn't recall the story.

Pines, dogwoods and maples lined the country roads, the trees thinning out as she entered the small town. Dust-coated signs that needed painting bore the same names as before, with the exception that the dime store had become the Dollar General, and the Cut & Curl was now Sally's Salon. Did Sally Orion, the chubby blonde she'd known in third grade, own the shop? It didn't matter. Violet hadn't come back to renew old acquaintances, good or bad.

She'd come home to find out the truth.

Uneasiness curled inside her as she passed the sheriff's office and jail. She had always avoided walking past the intimidating adobe-colored, concrete structure. Now it looked old and outdated, but still foreboding. Had Grady called from there when he'd delivered the news about her father? Had he already told the town? Would she see the news plastered all over the Crow's Landing newspaper tomorrow?

The small square still looked the same, although oddly smaller, and some of the storefronts desperately needed a face-lift. Woody Butt's gun shop was on the corner by the hardware store. A small bookstore had opened up, along with a place called the Fabric Hut, but the Redbud Café still stood in all its glory. Laney Longhorse's stories had always fascinated Violet. Was Laney still running the diner?

In the center of the square, a small playground and park benches had been added, although a three-foot-tall statue of a black crow in the center spoiled the peaceful feeling. At least to Violet. What was it about the crows?

Across from the park, the old-fashioned soda shop on the corner remained a perfect diversion for a hot summer afternoon. She could almost smell the cinnamon sticks old Mr. Toots kept inside to hand out to children, and see the thick, old-fashioned root beer floats he decorated with whipping cream and cherries. RC Colas and Moon Pies, along with Nehi's, homemade fudge and boiled peanuts, had been other local favorites. Unfortunately, Violet had never been able to afford the floats or fudge, not until Darlene had used her allowance money to buy both of them treats.

Suddenly Violet spotted the old street sign leading to her father's house. Pine Needle Drive.

She'd thought she might have forgotten the way.

But the turn seemed natural, and she found herself leaving the safety of the town square and heading down the country road. She passed the run-down trailer park in the less cared for section of Crow's Landing where rotting clapboard houses dotted the land, and overgrown weeds, battered bicycles and cars littered the front yards.

The road was bumpy and still unpaved. Although it was too late for kids to be outside playing, she could still picture the poor children who lived here—barefoot, with hand-me-down clothes two sizes too big hanging off their underfed bodies. She had been one of them. But not anymore, she reminded herself. She was strong, independent. She owned her own shop. She had a life ahead of her.

Her headlights flashed across the fronts of houses, and she grimaced, realizing things hadn't changed at all on Pine Needle Drive. One out of three homes had a washing machine or threadbare sofa on the sagging front porch. The old water wells remained, a testament to the fact that some of the houses lacked indoor plumbing.

And then there was her father's place, in much worse shape than she remembered. Overgrown bushes isolated it from the others. Two windowpanes in the front had been broken, the porch steps were missing boards, and some stray animal—most likely a mangy dog—had pawed the front door, scraping the dingy white paint. A cheap orange welcome mat graced the entrance, a mocking touch, while a caned-back chair that needed fixing was turned upside down in the corner. Three old cars that looked desperate for repairs sat to the side of the porch, weeds brushing at a rusty carburetor. Her father's unfinished projects, obviously. As if death had claimed them just as it had him.

The woods beyond echoed with loneliness. But she could almost hear her and Darlene's childhood laughter as they'd raced among the trees, building a playhouse in the pine straw.

Violet cut the engine and balled her hands into fists in her lap. Another, much newer car was parked sideways in the front drive—the sheriff's car.

What was Grady Monroe doing at her father's house?

CHAPTER SIX

VIOLET TWISTED the Best Friends necklace between her fingers as she stared at the door. Should she go inside or drive to the nearest hotel and spend the night, then return tomorrow when she wouldn't have to face Grady? But she had been running from her past all her life.

It was time to stop.

Besides, the sooner she found some answers, the sooner she could return to Savannah and move on with her life. She needed to know that her father hadn't killed her friend.

Gathering her courage, she opened the car door and climbed out, willing her legs to steady themselves as she ascended the steps. Honeysuckle sweetened the air, floating on the breeze. But the musty odor of the tattered welcome mat seeped upward as she stepped on it and raised her fist to knock. Then she caught herself. She didn't need to knock. This house belonged to her. Or at least it had once been her home. In another lifetime.

Footsteps rumbled inside. Grady?

She turned the knob, bracing for his reaction.

GRADY HAD BARELY TOURED the house when footsteps sounded on the front porch. He'd thought he'd heard a car a minute or two before, and had headed toward the front. Who had driven all the way out here to Baker's place?

Someone who knew about his death? Grady's own father, maybe…

He waited for the knock, but it never came. Instead, the doorknob turned. He slid his hand to the gun holstered by his side, then drew his weapon just in case some troubled teen or vagrant had heard about Baker's death and decided to rob him.

The door creaked open. Faint moonlight spilled in from the front porch, silhouetting a human form. Grady inched farther into the den. The low-wattage lightbulb in the foyer showed him it was a woman. She was slight, her pale face in shadows. A tangled web of dark hair floated around slender shoulders. The rattle of her breath broke the tense silence.

"Freeze! Police!"

She threw up her hands. "Please don't shoot."

He stepped forward just as she looked up, and he realized the face looked vaguely familiar. Her accent was familiar, too.

Dear God. It couldn't be.

"Grady?"

"Violet?" Tension crackled between them. She looked so…so different. Not like the homely, sad-faced, big-eyed girl who'd traipsed after him years ago.

More like a…woman. A very *attractive* woman.

Shit, he didn't need this.

"Yes, it's me." Her lower lip trembled at the sight of his Glock pointed at her.

He lowered the gun to his side, his gaze skimming over her, cataloging her features. Yes, she had definitely changed, had grown into a beauty. Not that any one feature was perfect, but she was stunning in an indefinable kind of way. Fragile. Earthy. Natural.

She stood around five-three and was still too slender. But her once scraggly brown hair shimmered with shades of gold, accentuating a heart-shaped face with high cheekbones and a small dainty nose. Her cheeks were pale, yet a natural rose color stained full lips devoid of lipstick. She didn't need it. She had kissable lips.

Damn, if she hadn't developed some luscious curves, too. Grady tried not to linger on the swell of her breasts, tried to stifle the elemental response of his body. Her denim skirt hung loosely on the gentle slope of her hips, and sandals showcased bare toes. Her toenails were painted pale pink.

The whisper of her feminine scent floated to him. That smell and those damn pink toenails made his body stir, waking nerve endings that had lain dormant forever.

For God's sake, this was Violet Baker.

He could not be attracted to her. She had been Darlene's best friend. Her father had confessed to killing Darlene. And Violet might have known.

Besides, he'd heard the rumors about her being strange, maybe crazy.

She cleared her throat, and he realized he'd let the silence stretch way too long.

"What are you doing here, Grady?"

"I…" He halted, not wanting to admit he was searching for evidence to corroborate her father's confession.

She seemed to read his mind, anyway. "Did you find anything?"

"No." He secured his gun back in his holster. "But I haven't conducted a thorough search."

Pain flickered in those expressive eyes—the one thing about her that hadn't changed. They were still huge and an unusual shade of blue, almost purple, the obvious reason her parents had named her Violet. And they still had the power to tug at emotions inside him just as they had when he was a scrawny kid.

He dragged his gaze away. He refused to get sucked in by emotions. He'd waited too damn long to crack this case. Besides, Violet was not a scrawny kid anymore; she was an adult who could take care of herself.

"How did you get in?" she asked.

He gestured toward the door. "It was unlocked."

She frowned as if that surprised her.

He shrugged. "Most people around here don't lock their doors."

The throat muscles worked in her slender neck as she swallowed. "My father always used to. At least he'd latch the screen."

Maybe because he knew he wasn't coming back, Grady thought, but he refrained from pointing that out. "How's your grandmother?"

More pain in her eyes. "Stable. She wanted to be near her sister to recover, so she's being transferred to the Black Mountain Rehabilitation Center today."

He nodded. "Good. I'm glad she's okay."

"She's not okay, Grady."

He let the statement stand in the dank air between them for a minute. "What's wrong?"

"She needs therapy." Her voice took on a hard edge. "But it's not just the stroke. Your phone call upset her."

Another awkward silence fell between them. He had no idea how to reply. Telling her not to blame the messenger seemed pointless. "I didn't expect you to come to Crow's Landing so soon."

She folded her arms beneath her breasts, then tipped her chin up, offering a glimpse of the feisty little girl she'd once been. "I have a lot of things to take care of here."

"Right." The funeral arrangements. "I'll let you know as soon as the coroner releases your father's body." Then she could get out of town. He didn't want her here.

Her hands tightened into fists. "Tell me about this supposed suicide note and the confession. I'd like to see it, too."

Grady shook his head. "I've told you everything I know. And I sent the note to the crime lab to verify that your father wrote it."

"Then I suggest you leave now."

He frowned. "I'm not through here."

"Yes, you are. I won't let you hunt for more evidence to incriminate my father."

Anger flared. "I didn't realize you and your dad were close. You haven't been back here in years."

Violet bit her lip. "My grandmother doesn't believe my father killed—" Her voice broke, her first visible sign of emotion. "She doesn't believe the confession is real," she finished, sounding stronger. "And neither do I."

Could she not even say his sister's name? "Is that the reason you came back?"

She stepped sideways, indicating the door. "Yes."

His gaze locked with hers, and he saw her inner turmoil. She might claim she didn't believe her father was guilty, but she had doubts.

She was afraid her father had killed Darlene.

"Like I said, I'm not finished here," he said baldly.

Her eyelashes fluttered. "Yes, you are. Come back when you have a search warrant."

Her hand trembled as she toyed with a long chain dangling between her breasts. The Best Friends necklace Darlene had bought them. She still wore it.

So she remembered his sister. She *had* cared for her.

Or maybe she wore it out of guilt.

He caught her wrist with one hand, then flicked a thumb along the jagged edges of the necklace, tracing the word *Friends* with his finger. Her breath hissed in. "I'm going to find out the truth, Violet. All my life, I've wanted Darlene's murderer to pay. I'll see that he does."

Both fear and courage emanated from her eyes as she glared at him. "I want that, too."

"Really? What if the killer *was* your father, Violet?"

Ignoring the hurt and uncertainty that darkened her eyes, he released her arm, then stalked outside. But he would be back with that search warrant.

And no matter how much he had to hurt Violet, her grandmother or his own father, he'd uncover the truth and see that Darlene's killer got what he deserved.

And if one of them had covered for the killer…he'd make him or her pay, too.

AS THE DOOR SLAMMED SHUT, Grady's declaration echoed off the dingy walls. Violet shuddered, the empty house closing around her. The mustiness, the echo of abandonment, the stale smells of dirty clothes, booze and old sweat assaulted her. And the familiar smell of Old Spice…

Memories bombarded her, along with the unsettling feeling that she had never quite left this place. Unable to assimilate it all at once, she stood still, willing her body to absorb the shock of homecoming, along with seeing Grady.

Over the years, she'd imagined what he might look like as a man. All the girls had doted on the teenage version, but he hadn't seemed to notice. Any trace of cuteness had disappeared, though, and in its place, a rugged prowess radiated from his every pore. Over six-three, he was big, powerful and muscular, almost frighteningly so. Prominent cheekbones and a nose crooked from being broken dominated his features. And those deep-set eyes were almost hypnotizing. When his callused hands had caught her wrist, heat had rippled between them, charged with frustration and something sexual.

No, she had mistaken that feeling.

The emotion had been anger.

He carried that in spades. An obvious hatred toward his sister's killer flashed in his tortured eyes.

A hatred she understood. But did the killer's face belong to her father?

And would Grady turn that anger toward her now that he realized they were on opposite sides? At least concerning her dad…

She sighed and forced herself farther into the house. Stifling heat and cloying odors of mildew and decay nearly suffocated her.

In the shoe box den, the same plaid sofa lined the back wall, the rust-colored recliner her father had lived in angled toward the ancient TV set, a stack of *Popular Mechanics* magazines stacked beside it. A dog-eared metal antenna jutted upward from the TV in a warped V, proving he hadn't updated the set or his service in twenty years. The beige carpet was stained, the lack of photos a brutal reminder that her father had shut his family out of his life.

She stopped beside the wicker rocking chair and stroked the arm. She imagined her grandmother sitting in the chair, crocheting in the afternoon sunlight, sunshine that turned the tiny room into an inferno in summer. Violet had curled up at her knees and played with her rag dolls while her grandmother watched her soap operas. Now dust coated most of the ancient furniture, and cobwebs hung in the corners. She slowly walked through the kitchen, not surprised to find everything the same, only older and smaller. Newspapers and magazines littered a beige countertop spattered with stains. Dishes encrusted with half-eaten food cluttered the sink. Trash overflowed onto the graying linoleum floor, the stench almost unbearable.

A delivery box containing an uneaten pizza sat on the counter next to a full six-pack of Pabst Blue Ribbon, as if her father had just returned from getting dinner. Odd, but both had been untouched. And the want ad page lay on the table, a red circle around two ads. Why would her father buy an entire pizza and six-pack and be job hunting if he planned to kill himself?

Depressed people aren't exactly rational, she reminded herself.

Her father's room was to the right, but she couldn't bring herself to go inside. On the left, her grandmother's room adjoined Violet's. The crocheted green afghan her grandmother had used to warm her feet at night still lay at the foot of the Jenny Lind bed, the scent of her grandmother's favorite lavender potpourri mellow, yet lingering. Violet grabbed the afghan and hugged it to her, then glanced at her own room. Had her father changed it? Turned it into a study or storeroom for the old car parts he collected? The parts that had meant more to him than she had.

She pushed open the door and was shocked to see the sawed-off iron bed still rooted in the corner, the antique dresser laden with her childhood costume jewelry. Even more surprising, Bobo, her big brown birthday bear, hugged the pillows where she had once slept. Right next to Bobo were her Raggedy Ann doll and the stuffed pony her father had won for her at the county fair. The same pale pink chenille bedspread covered her bed, too, although it had yellowed with age.

Tears pooled in Violet's eyes. Taking a deep breath, she noticed the faint scents of mothballs and wood polish, as if her father had tried to preserve her room. Peculiar, when the rest of the house seemed in such disrepair.

She flipped on the radio her father had given her for Christmas one year. Static bellowed back at her, and she fiddled with the knobs, hoping to find some soft music to calm her. An oldies station came through, so she let it play while she retrieved her suitcase. The floor creaked as she entered the house again. Could she really spend the night in this old place?

Would the ghosts haunt her when she tried to sleep?

Exhausted and drained from the trip, she dragged on a thin cotton nightshirt. But just as she lay down, a newscaster's voice came over the radio. "This late-breaking story in just now, folks. The search for Amber Collins, the missing woman from Savannah, Georgia, has ended tonight."

Violet gripped the sheets. She didn't need to hear the report—she knew what he was going to say.

Amber Collins was dead.

Still, she listened, her pulse racing. "The young woman's body was discovered late this evening on the front steps of a church outside the Georgia state line, in what looks like it might be a ritualist killing. Sources say the coed was strangled. Although no signs of sexual abuse have been reported, one source tells us that the victim was left holding a note in her hand that read, 'For Our Father.' No suspects have been named thus far. Police have refused comment. We'll bring you more information as it becomes available."

Violet pulled the teddy bear into her arms, stroking its ears the way she had as a child. The police hadn't mentioned finding a bone whistle beside Amber's body. Had the killer taken it with him instead of leaving it behind? Or had she simply imagined the whistle?

Maybe her visions weren't real.

But if they were, she needed to alert the police. Would they believe her? Or think she was crazy, the way her father had claimed?

After all, she hadn't seen enough details to recognize the killer or even pinpoint where he'd held the woman, so how could she help?

Her head began to pound, and she lay back and closed her eyes. Why had she experienced this vision about the coed when she hadn't had one since Darlene was murdered? And why were all these other disturbing things happening now—her father's death, the suicide note? It wasn't as if they were related.

Yet, she sensed somehow they were. And that *she* had something to do with all of them.

What about Grady? How would he play into the situation—by proving her father was a killer? By finding the real one?

As she massaged her temples, the reedy sound of the bone whistle grated through the darkness. If her premonition was right, the questions had only begun.

And so had the killings….

ROSS WHEELER'S HEART raced with excitement as he opened the magazine and examined the pictures. The young lovers would take away the pain. Their supple bodies were ripe for picking. Their size didn't matter. They were firm and tender, begging for attention. Begging for him to taste them.

But Father told him no. It was wrong to lust. To satisfy his cravings.

How could sex be wrong when it was in the Bible? Sex was natural, a man's God-given primal need for mating.

But the reverend had different rules for himself. He preached abstinence, while he dipped from the honey pot himself.

Maybe, as God's spokesman, he thought he'd risen above human sins. Shame crept through Ross at the memory of the reverend's condemnation over those sexual misconduct charges. How could the town accuse Ross of such a thing, especially in front of a divine man like his father? Ross was the preacher's son, had been a good teacher, a soccer coach, a deacon himself until they'd ruined his reputation with their accusations.

Worse, his father had believed them….

And to think he'd always done everything to please the man.

Would he ever receive forgiveness?

Bible verses he'd been forced to learn as a child floated through his head, jumbled and distorted versions that made no sense. He'd hated the rigorous memorizing. The daily prayers. The sermons on hellfire and damnation.

His gaze flicked to the pictures again.

His hand slid down his waist, unfastened his belt buckle, pushed it aside. He slipped his fingers beneath the fabric. He was so hard, throbbing like an animal, aching for release, for the sweet fulfillment the young ones promised. He could have it, too. Pleasure lay at his fingertips. All he had to do was look at them, imagine stripping off their clothes and spreading them on the ground for his taking.

His fingers began to stroke his member, closing around the rigid length until it surged to life and droplets of erotic nectar spilled over.

Suddenly heavy footsteps clattered above. Click, clack. Click, clack.

Shit, the reverend.

"Ross!"

He jerked his hand away, grabbed a handkerchief and cleaned himself, frustration and embarrassment burning through him.

Now he would have to repent again, confess his sin to his father and kneel at the altar for hours on end. Damn the reverend for destroying his momentary pleasure.

He gathered his control and went to face the master. Tonight the reverend would be busy sucking up to the televangelist who was coming in to preach at the revival.

Ross would do whatever necessary the next few hours to please them both, but tomorrow night he'd do exactly as he wanted....

CHAPTER SEVEN

GRADY TRIED TO BANISH images of Violet Baker's face from his mind as he and his deputy drove toward her dad's house the next morning. But those startling blue eyes filled with anguish and vulnerability refused to leave him alone. He could still see her standing beside Darlene, looking up at his father with that hungry expression, as if she wanted to fit in, but knew she didn't. That she wasn't wanted.

Damn. Grady wanted a cigarette. But he couldn't give in to the need. Just as he couldn't give in to needs aroused by Violet.

He had never allowed a woman to distract him from his job before, and he certainly didn't intend to do so this time. Not when he was so close to finally closing the chapter on this never-ending nightmare of his life.

He would search the Baker house with a fine-tooth comb and make sure that Baker's confession stuck, so Grady could lay his sister's murder case to rest once and for all.

And this time, with a warrant in his hand, Violet couldn't stop him.

He checked the clock. It was early, but he'd planned it that way. He wanted to search the house before Violet had a chance to clean or move things around. Last night she'd thrown him off guard with her arrival. Today, he wanted the element of surprise on his side.

"I don't know why you're even checking this out," Logan said in his typical dark tone. "Suicide seems cut-and-dried to me."

Grady tried to read his partner's expression, but Logan always wore those dark sunglasses, as if he was hiding behind them. "Yeah, well, I have to cover the bases just in case someone asks questions later. Some folks might not believe Baker is guilty or that he took his own life."

"Hell, who would that be?"

"His daughter." Grady shot Logan a warning look not to probe any further. Had Violet slept well in her childhood bed, knowing her father had killed her friend? Had she suffered any remorse for Darlene?

He scrubbed a hand over his face. He sure as hell hadn't slept. Dammit, had Violet known about her father and kept silent?

Was that the real reason she hadn't returned before now?

VIOLET STUMBLED FROM BED, bleary-eyed from lack of sleep, and groped for the afghan, pulling it around her shoulders. She could have sworn she'd heard someone knocking on the door.

A quick glance at the clock made her grimace. Six-thirty. She hadn't fallen asleep until five. Even then, that woman's cries had reverberated inside her head, tormenting her.

The pounding grew louder. Who would come out here this early? Who even knew she was here? Grady…

"Violet, I know you're in there." His gruff voice resonated with impatience. "You might as well open up."

"Just a minute." Pushing her hair from her eyes, she rushed to the door and opened it. "What are you doing here so early?"

He dangled a piece of paper in front of her. "Search warrant."

She frowned but reluctantly stepped aside. Grady strode in, his big presence filling the small den. Still half-asleep, she found her body tingling traitorously, imagining he'd come for another reason.

Another officer followed on his heels, his gaze skimming over Violet. His attitude said he'd seen the ugly side of life and survived it. Maybe even liked it.

"Deputy Logan." The man tipped a headful of wavy brown hair in greeting, although his taut mouth was unsmiling. And she couldn't see his eyes; they were hidden behind Ray-Bans. They were probably as black as his mood, she guessed, clutching the afghan tighter around her shoulders.

"Go get dressed," Grady growled. "We'll start in the den and kitchen."

Violet simply stared at him. She didn't take orders from anyone. "Excuse me?"

"I said put some clothes on." His icy gaze locked with hers. Any trace of the compassionate boy she'd once known had disappeared.

Heat suddenly blazed her cheeks. Anger at the fact that he had come on a crusade against her father followed. "I…I don't know what you're looking for, Grady, but you won't find it."

He arched an eyebrow. "You haven't tampered with evidence, have you?"

Violet's fingers dug into her arms. "Of course not."

Suspicion flared in his eyes. "Did you know your father killed Darlene?"

Her lungs tightened at the accusation.

"Is that the reason he sent you away?" A strained heartbeat passed. "Did your grandmother know and keep quiet about it all these years?"

His cold tone cut through her like a knife. She staggered backward, then turned and ran to the bedroom to change.

GRADY BRACED HIMSELF for the onslaught of guilt that attacked him at Violet's shocked reaction.

"Playing bad cop?"

He glared at his deputy. "I was just doing my job." And trying to find out the truth.

Or were you trying to hurt her because you hate yourself for being attracted to her? For reminding you of Darlene every time you look at her?

"You going to charge her with accessory?"

Grady pivoted on his booted feet. "She was only eight when Darlene died."

"But she could have come forward since."

He nodded. He had entertained the idea. And he would charge Violet if he discovered she'd lied.

"Let's verify Baker's confession. Look for a handwritten note or bill so we can compare writing samples. Then we'll discuss strategies."

"Right." Logan grunted. "Although she's almost pretty enough to make a man forget the law."

Grady's jaw tightened. He might not want Violet, but he sure as heck didn't like the lascivious way Logan had looked at her. "Stay away from her," he warned. "A good cop never gets involved with a potential suspect. And he never forgets the law."

Logan's mouth twitched as if he was about to argue. Then he seemed to think better of it, turned and went to work.

Grady dismissed the odd reaction. The sooner he finished, the sooner he could get away from Violet. Then he could forget that he'd almost agreed with Logan.

But not at the cost of letting Darlene's killer get away.

VIOLET TREMBLED INSIDE. She would never forget the look of accusation in Grady's eyes.

It had been the same piercing look he'd given her twenty years ago when he'd stood outside her bedroom, waiting for her to tell them where to find Darlene.

Pressing her hands to her temples, she battled another onslaught of tears. She would not cry now. No, she wouldn't give Grady the satisfaction of watching her crumble. Besides, she'd cried a river of tears the past two days, and it hadn't helped. She had to be strong.

After all, she'd expected Grady to blame her for Darlene's death because she'd begged her friend to come over that day. But she'd never imagined he'd believe she would protect the killer.

So why was she defending her father?

Because if he had evil inside him, then maybe she did, too.... Maybe he had been right about her. Maybe that evil was the reason she'd heard the woman's cry.

Confused, Violet yanked on shorts, a T-shirt and sandals, then dragged a brush through her hair and scrubbed her teeth. The itch to run from this house and her father's mess gnawed at her, but she couldn't run away. Not without knowing the truth.

But what if Grady found something in the house? And why hadn't she thought to look around last night after he'd left?

You were too shaken by coming home again. And by everything that's happened.

Steeling herself against Grady's anger, she went to the kitchen to brew coffee. The deputy was searching the den, while Grady was examining the pizza box, his eyebrows furrowed.

"The answer to your question is no, Grady. That confession note was a complete surprise."

He glanced up, a flicker of regret simmering in his dark eyes before his mask slid back into place. "Did you and your father keep in touch?"

"We haven't spoken in years."

He nodded curtly, then scribbled some notes in a small notepad.

"Can I clean up this mess now and make some coffee?"

"Let me dust for fingerprints first."

She stared at him, wondering where the kind boy she'd once known had gone. Had he died the same day Darlene had?

Well, she refused to stand here and watch him tear apart her house. She stalked out onto the front porch, more questions assailing her. If her father had killed Darlene twenty years ago and had brought her to the house, which Violet knew hadn't happened, any evidence would be long gone. So why fingerprint the kitchen if he thought her father had committed suicide?

What exactly was Grady looking for?

GRADY WINCED AT THE SOUND of the screen door slamming, then frowned when Violet's car tore down the graveled drive. As much as she might not want to face the fact that her father was a murderer, he had to know the truth.

She'd claimed she wanted that, too. But would she be able to handle it?

Would he, if he discovered his own father had something to do with Baker's death?

Logan whistled as he scavenged through the desk in the den, bringing Grady out of his reverie with the location of a bill for signature comparison. Other than that, Baker's house offered little in the way of clues, except the fact that Jed had been as depressed and lackadaisical about life as his own father. The two of them seemed so much alike that they should have been friends instead of enemies. But something had torn them apart.

Secrets. What were they?

Grady checked the refrigerator, logging the contents, then scanned the sink and counter. The uneaten pizza in its box, full six-pack of beer and the want ads on the counter disturbed him. Why would a man buy food and beer and job-hunt right before he killed himself?

It didn't make sense.

He copied down the number of the pizza place. He'd check and see what time and day Baker had bought it. That, along with the M.E.'s report on the time of death, might help him piece together the chain of events that had led to Baker's trip to Briar Ridge.

Other details bothered Grady. Why would Baker go to the mountains to kill himself instead of doing it at home? If guilt had triggered the suicide, why wouldn't he have returned to the scene of the crime to take his life?

"Not much in here but some old magazines." Logan gestured toward the desk. "Oh, and there's a couple of photo albums of his daughter. Thought she told you they weren't close."

"She did. Said they hadn't spoken in years."

"That's strange." Logan pointed to three scrapbooks. "There's all kinds of pictures of Violet growing up."

Grady frowned. Had Violet lied to him about not staying in touch with her father?

NEEDING A REFUGE from Grady Monroe and her past, Violet drove into town and parked in front of the Rosebud Café. Without sleep, she desperately had to have caffeine and food.

Hoping no one in town would recognize her yet, she ducked her head and entered the café. It was like entering a time warp. Nothing had changed. The same earthy adobe and turquoise colors, the warm smell of coffee and biscuits, the same Native American artifacts filled the place.

Three elderly women sat at a table sipping tea, a hefty man was hunched over a bar stool, scooping up sausage patties from his plate, and two other men she didn't recognize faced the bar, away from her. She spotted Laney Longhorse behind the counter, her long braid now graying, her skin leathery from the sun. Violet had always been fascinated with the woman. Maybe because she ignored the difference in social status between people instead of dividing them into classes the way the more prominent citizens did. In fact, Violet had felt more at home with the kids from the reservation than she did the white children in town. Except for Darlene.

She slid into a corner booth and studied the menu, surprised to see the same items Laney had always carried. Thankfully, some things never changed. A fairhaired man in his thirties smiled at her from the booth across from her. She forced a tight smile, then averted her gaze.

The older woman ambled over to her, her long skirt swishing against her thin legs. "Hi!" Laney said in her Cherokee accent. "Your order, miss?"

Good. Laney didn't recognize her. "Coffee. And I'll have your country breakfast."

"Comin' right up." Laney studied Violet for a moment, shook her head as if she was trying to place her but couldn't. Then she sauntered off to get the coffee.

Violet dialed the nursing home on her cell phone. The nurse assured her that her grandmother had arrived safely, but was in physical therapy. Her sister, Neesie, was there, waiting to visit.

Determined to avoid eye contact with any of the locals, especially the man who kept watching her, she informed the nurse she'd call again later, then studied the back of the menu. A small inscription described the history of the town's name. Crow's Landing had been named after an old Cherokee myth.

Although eagles were the revered, treasured bird of the Cherokee legends, their feathers used in religious ceremonies, one myth described an Indian boy's battle with a wicked gambler who could change forms. When put to the test, the boy, Thunder, beat the gambler, who had turned himself to brass. The boy planted the brass in the river and hung crows on each side of a pole to ward off the beavers, so they wouldn't chip away the brass and free the gambler.

Violet was pondering the legend when the woman returned. Interesting folklore. The crows were actually protecting the town, not haunting it or looking on, ready to prey.

Laney placed the coffee and food in front of Violet, her squinty eyes assessing. Violet offered nothing. Not yet—she wasn't ready. But she wondered if the woman would know the Native American expression from Violet's vision.

She thanked Laney and sipped her coffee, then took a few bites of her eggs. A tall man with a shoulder-length, black ponytail bustled in from the back. Joseph Longhorse? All grown up?

He had always been quiet, moody, angry. But she'd felt a kinship with him. Not a psychic one like she'd shared with Darlene, but they had connected. She'd been called white trash, while Joseph had suffered the cruel prejudices harbored by a few small-minded people in the town. The Barley boys had been especially ruthless, turning Joseph's Native American name, Strong Legs, into a joke because Joseph had been the shortest kid in the class. Not anymore. Now he was six feet tall, strong and tough. She bet they didn't mess with him now.

Laney returned to her table with fresh butter. "You are not an *asgi'na,* a ghost, are you? No, you are the little Baker girl come back, heh?"

Violet nodded, aware that a few of the other patrons pivoted to check her out. And some still tensed when Laney used Cherokee words.

"Yes, ma'am. I came back to bury my father."

"Oh, my." Laney flattened a weathered hand on her cheek. "I'm so sorry. I hadn't heard of your *edata*'s passing."

The man with the fair hair smiled. Violet leaned toward Laney. "Who is that man, Laney?"

She cast a look over her shoulder, then grinned. "The new doctor. Dr. Gardener. Handsome, huh?"

Violet shrugged, wondering why he was staring at her.

"The young women in town, they are all over him. But he seems to have eyes for you."

"I'm not going to be here long enough to get to know anyone," Violet said, hoping it was true.

A robust man at the bar swiveled on his stool, then dragged his bulk off and stalked toward her. Violet crouched back in her seat at the sight of his face. She would recognize his beady, unforgiving eyes anywhere.

Darlene's father.

"How dare you show yourself in this town again!" His sharp voice rose, echoing off the tile floors, then he slammed his fist on the table in front of her, rattling the dishes. "Did you know your daddy killed my baby girl?"

GRADY HAD BEEN SURPRISED at the number of photos Baker had of his daughter. He'd also been startled at his own reaction of seeing the homely little girl emerge into a shy teenager. Judging from the smile on her face, she hadn't recognized her own beauty.

There had been no pictures of boyfriends, though, prompting his curiosity about Violet's personal past. An area he shouldn't be concerned with at all.

Unfortunately, he and Logan hadn't turned up anything that would implicate Baker in Darlene's murder.

What had he expected? That Baker would have kept a souvenir all these years? Or a hidden file somewhere describing the secrets he shared with Grady's father?

Grady glanced in the small bathroom one last time and frowned. The edge of the faded bath mat had shifted, probably caught on one of their boots. Underneath, the flooring was discolored, an unnatural shade lighter than the rest of the linoleum. He squatted down, peeled back the rug and examined it. It looked as if it had been scrubbed with bleach. Nothing else in the house appeared to have been cleaned in ages. Why here?

He remembered the knot on Baker's head. He could have gotten it from a fall anywhere. Maybe even here. Grady leaned closer, studying the area for bloodstains.

The nagging doubts wouldn't let go, so he retrieved some Luminol from the car and sprayed the flooring. His hunch was right. Traces of blood shone through. He took a couple of samples, hoping he was wrong about the source. Hoping there would be no traces of his father's DNA in the mix.

But the argument between his dad and Baker echoed in his head. *"Some reporter's been asking about Violet,"* Baker had said. Who was that reporter and why would he want to speak with Violet? And why had Baker been afraid of him?

Logan finished, then left for the station. Knowing he wouldn't rest without answers, Grady decided to confront his father one more time. With Baker's body in the morgue and Violet in town claiming her father's innocence, it was time Walt Monroe started talking.

A JOLT OF FEAR BOLTED through Violet at the malevolence in Mr. Monroe's eyes.

"Did you know your daddy killed my baby girl?" the man bellowed.

Violet shook her head.

"Then get the hell out of town."

Violet chanced a look at the other patrons, who all sat gawking at the scene, either too stunned by the confrontation to move or too intimidated by Monroe.

All except Joseph Longhorse.

The Cherokee's black eyes flared with contempt, reminding her of his temper. He started toward her—rather, toward Grady's father.

But the last thing Violet wanted was to make a scene. She especially didn't want Laney's son to suffer at her expense. This was her problem. She'd deal with it.

"I understand how you feel, Mr. Monroe."

"You don't have any idea how I feel, Miss Baker." A blood vessel throbbed in his forehead. "So don't play your little game of innocence with me. It won't work."

"I'm not playing games," Violet said, hating the quiver in her voice as she stood. "I just came here to bury my father. Then I'm leaving town."

"If you know what's good for you, get him in the ground and get out of here today."

Joseph inched toward her, but she threw up a warning hand. Holding her head high, she dug inside her purse, dropped some cash on the table, mouthed a thank-you to Laney, then turned and strode to the door.

She didn't breathe easy until she reached the car.

What had she expected? For Grady's father to welcome her or act concerned about her feelings? And what about the other people in town? Did they believe her dad was a murderer?

Part of her wanted to drive straight out of town, but she had to talk to people, find out if anyone had known her father the last few years. Learn everything she could about him and the life he'd led.

Her resolve intact, she started the car and headed to the cemetery. She had been sent away before Darlene's funeral. And she'd never returned to visit her friend's grave.

It was time she did, and said goodbye.

HE WAS WATCHING HER.

Enjoying the view of her tantalizing skin, so pale beneath the blinding noonday sun.

It was time. Time to choose another one. If his mama knew, she'd stop all the fun. She tried to force the drugs on him, but they made him lethargic. He hated the pills. His sex didn't even swell like it should.

Damn her. Bitch.

She wanted to take away all his fun. Hell, he was doing this for her. And his father...

Always the father.

He was so tired. Tired. Tired. No, he couldn't let himself slip back into the threes.

The drugs would stop that, but he hated them. They robbed him of his pleasure. Made him feel numb, like a dead man walking.

So he didn't take them when she wasn't around. Even then, he held them in the back of his throat and spat them on the ground.

Yes, he could suppress the threes on his own.

One. One was his number. He was the one. The first one. The chosen one.

And one was all it would take for his sacrifice.

But she had to be perfect.

Back in his private lair, he'd already assembled the test tubes and needles, the surgical gloves to keep the conditions sterile. He couldn't take chances. No, this was too important. Mama said he had to have clean hands. He scrubbed them over and over until his skin was raw. Adrenaline surged through his veins as he realized the moment had come.

Time to meet her.

He breathed in the scent of the chase and watched as she disappeared into the deep thicket of hardwoods. The trees cloaked her innocence as if they could save her.

But nothing could protect her now.

Because he was the hunter. The hunter had his trap well prepared. And death surrounded it.

Only he would have to wait until nightfall to make the sacrifice....

VIOLET DROVE STRAIGHT TO the graveyard, her insides churning. She did not want to be here.

She hated graveyards.

Hated the concrete slabs, the monuments, the whispers of the dead...

Yet she had to talk to Darlene.

She parked the car in the shade, remembering the times she and Darlene had met under the sweet gum tree to play.

Playtime was over.

Sliding from the car on rubbery legs, Violet felt the humid air engulf her. She swatted at a mosquito as she picked her away across the lawn, among the graves.

Soon, she would bring her father here to rest. So close to Darlene.

But would he rest? Would he go to heaven or spend eternity paying for the murder of her friend? Or could he linger in some kind of limbo waiting for justice, for someone to prove his confession wasn't real?

As she crossed the ground, which was littered with leaves dry and brittle, the clouds and sky seemed to spin around her. Someone was watching her.

Breathing down her neck.

She whirled around, ready to fight, but grabbed at empty air.

Certain she was losing her mind, she plowed on, listening for footsteps. Leaves and brush crackled beneath her feet. Or beneath someone else's boots. Her vision blurred. Colorless eyes seemed to peer at her through the shadows of the trees behind her. No, the trees were shading her car. They provided safety.

At the edge of the forest, thick rhododendrons grew tangled along the iron gate. To the right, the mountains thrust upward, the sturdy pines guarding the graves like soldiers. A thick vapor curled in front of Violet. Her foot caught on a vine. The ground moaned as if the red clay was sucking at her feet, trying to drag her under. And she was slipping into someone else's mind. But it was so real, she felt as if it was happening to her.

He was coming for her. She heard his muttered cry. Felt the heat in his brutal stare. Sensed his hiss of delight at her fear.

She had to run. Escape. Pumping her legs, she fought for air. Searched for a way out of the dark maze. But the trees ahead merged into a mass of slaty gray. Mist curled beyond them, rising like steam. Fingers of hot air encircled her, choking her.

His breath scorched her neck. He was behind her. Closing in. He would catch her soon and lay her in his pit. Then it would all be over.

God help her! She ran faster. Her arms and legs ached. Her breathing grew sporadic. She had to get away. She couldn't let him catch her.

But she was trapped. She'd reached an impasse. An iron gate blocked her way. Trees too tall and dense to squeeze through. Panic seized her. Which way should she go?

A hand snaked out to grab her. She tried to scream.

Then a voice reached her ears, "It's time to offer your blood. I am the gi'ga-danegi'ski, *the blood taker. I must take it for the father.*

"And then tonight, my sweetness, you must die...."

CHAPTER EIGHT

MAVIS DOBBINS WISHED like hell she could leave Crow's Landing. Wished she could start a new life someplace where no one knew her or her son.

Hell, she knew her boy was trouble. She'd been fighting his evil side for years and was flat out exhausted from it. But Dwayne was hers, and a mama had an obligation to take care of her baby.

Even if her baby was thirty-two years old and half the town thought they were both crazy. Oh, she'd caught the looks at breakfast this morning, just like she noticed them every other morning for the past twenty years. She had to ignore them. Because as much as she hated the town, she also needed it to keep Dwayne safe.

Needed it to keep his secrets.

Guilt over his accident still weighed heavily on her mind. She'd thought he wasn't quite right when he was little. But then again, she weren't no rocket scientist herself, and her old man hadn't had the sense God gave a rooster. Then Dwayne had been acting up one day, fell off the back of his daddy's pickup and hit his head. He hadn't been near normal since.

She'd lost him that rainy afternoon, and soon after, his daddy.

Trying not to dwell on the past, she finished scrubbing the toilets at the Rest Easy Nursing Home outside of town, tossed her rubber gloves in her work bucket, then headed to the phone to check in. Every day she had to leave her boy for a few hours to work. But she was always a nervous wreck until she talked to him at lunchtime. Then again in the afternoon, until she got home and locked them both in for the night.

But it was better than having him locked up somewhere else.

Thank God for Mayor Tate and Reverend Wheeler. The good-old-boy mayor had covered up Dwayne's indiscretions over the years, or she wouldn't be able to walk down Main Street with her head up at all. Of course, the mayor's help had come at a high price, one she hadn't always wanted to pay. But in the end, she had. After all, a mama did whatever she had to in order to protect her child.

God bless his soul, Reverend Wheeler had counseled her through the worst of the crises. He'd given her the faith to accept what she couldn't change. The fact that her son would never fully recover was one of those things.

The fact that she was scared of him and what he might do was another.

Doc Farmer had helped her with the medication. But then he owed her.

She dialed her home number and thumped her foot up and down while she waited. By the fifth ring, she was sweating bullets. Where in the hell was that no-account boy? He knew better than to go out by himself. What if he hadn't taken his medication...?

One of the nurses walked by, carrying a bedpan, and Mavis reminded herself things could be worse. Dwayne could be physically handicapped, too, and wearing diapers, or bound to the bed and needing that bedpan like poor Miss Laudy.

Or she could be old Mrs. Baker, who'd just found out her boy killed a child, and who needed nursing care herself.

Praying Dwayne had just gone out in the yard to play with that mangy dog he'd named Snake, she punched the number again, and wiped sweat from her neck when he still didn't answer. Finally, she slammed down the receiver and hurried over to the desk.

"I'm taking my lunch hour now. I'll be back to do the east wing in an hour."

Willese, the volunteer at the desk, patted her hand. "Everything all right, Mavis?"

"I've got to go home for a minute."

Willese offered a sympathetic look, and Mavis headed to the door, nearly running. *Please don't let him have taken off again.* The last time, just last week, he'd been gone over twenty-four hours. She'd nearly lost her mind. She still didn't know where he'd been and what he'd been up to. But she had an idea, and it weren't no good.

Ten minutes later, Mavis's ancient El Camino barreled down Pine Needle Drive. As she passed the rundown Baker shack, she remembered the rumors in town, that Baker had thrown himself off the cliff, that his daughter was back to bury him. Would Dwayne do the same for her when she kilt over?

Panic stabbed at her. She couldn't get sick and die. Who would take care of Dwayne then?

She screeched into her driveway, jumped out, then shuffled through the grass to the house. It was empty.

Her stomach knotted when she noticed the pills sitting on the table. Dwayne had taken his medication this morning, but now he'd missed a dosage. Even one would throw him off.

She twisted the dishrag into knots in her hands. Where on God's green earth was that boy?

GRADY'S FATHER WASN'T HOME, so he drove into town, his senses on alert for his dad's white Cadillac. Once he'd have known exactly where to find his old man— the town hall. Monroe had once been entrenched in the politics of the small town and had loved the title of mayor—until Darlene's death. Then he'd stopped working, stopped socializing, stopped caring about anything. Not the future of the town, his son's or his own.

A small car whizzed by, and Grady did a double take, thinking it was Violet's. But the car was a VW. Violet had been driving a Civic. Where had she gone? Was she in town?

He scanned the side streets and parking spaces for her car, but didn't spot it anywhere. She didn't have old friends living here, did she?

No, Violet's only friend had been Darlene.

Determined to question his father during the light of day, when he might actually find him sober, Grady took a chance and stopped by the Redbud Café. In spite of his snobbery toward the Longhorse family, his father usually ate at least one meal a day at the establishment.

Grady lumbered inside, scanning the room, curious at the odd looks the locals shot his way. What was going on?

Normally he'd assume his old man and Baker had gotten into another public brawl, but with Jed gone…

Kerry fluttered a wave, then darted toward him. He forced a smile, although the waitress's hopeful look suddenly irritated him. He didn't want anyone expecting anything from him, not ever again. He'd just let them down.

She pumped up her breasts. "Well, Sheriff, what can I do for you today?"

He ignored her innuendo, checked to see if Joseph Longhorse was watching, but didn't see the man. "Have you seen my father?"

Heads snapped sideways and downward. Whispers hushed instantly. Laney Longhorse turned her head away and began slicing an apple pie. Something was definitely up.

"He was here a while ago," Kerry said.

"Left right after he told that Baker girl where to go," Bart Stancil added with a snort. "Thought they was gonna pick up where your daddy and Jed left off."

Grady gritted his teeth. "Did he say where he was going?"

"Probably to follow her and make sure she left town," Kerry offered.

Laney frowned in disapproval. Violet had dragged Darlene along to visit the older woman sometimes. She'd filled their heads with Native American legends that had fascinated the girls. Darlene had tried to tell their father, but Walt Monroe hadn't allowed talk about the ancient legends in his house. Just as he hadn't allowed Violet.

Grady had hated his father's prejudice back then. He'd treated Violet like some kind of leper just because she was poor.

He didn't like his attitude now, either.

Not that *he'd* treated her much better….

What if Violet was an innocent bystander in this whole damn mess? He was the sheriff, responsible for all the people in town.

Any time he'd lost his way over the years, he'd tried to think of Darlene. She was his dose of humanity. The rich kid who hadn't differentiated between herself and a girl no one else wanted as a friend. Peculiar or not, she had loved Violet dearly. What would his baby sister want him to do now? Let their father vent his bitterness and anger toward Violet and run her out of town? Protect her from the truth about her old man?

But what if she had known the truth or she'd learned it over the years and had kept silent? Then she had betrayed Darlene….

Ignoring the knot of emotion festering in his throat, he turned to leave.

Kerry touched his arm. "Don't you want to stay and have some coffee?"

He glanced down at her hand and wished things had been different. But he couldn't give her what she wanted. He just didn't have it in him. "No, thanks."

Then he strode out the door, hoping she'd finally get the message.

As he drove out of town, he told himself his easy dismissal of her had nothing to do with the blue-eyed woman his daddy had tried to run out of town.

She was so cold. She couldn't breathe. Couldn't move. Where had he taken her?

She opened her eyes and tried to see through the darkness. Shadows obliterated the light. She couldn't see, couldn't make out his face. Dear God, she didn't want to die. She was young, she had plans, she had to finish school, get her master's degree. Teach awhile. She had always wanted to work with little children.

And she wanted to get married, wear a long white wedding dress, have babies of her own. See her mother be a grandma. What would her mom do when she was gone? She was all alone....

A tear seeped from her eye and rolled down her cheek. She tried to lift her hand to wipe it away, but her hand was numb. He'd tied her down like an animal. She couldn't move.

Panic rippled through her. She couldn't give up. She had to fight.

She tried to squirm, to escape, but it was useless. Whatever drug he'd given her had robbed her of life. Everything was numb except her mind.

She could still think. Could feel the horror of what he was going to do to her.

Then his hand touched her. Icy fingers pulled at her clothes. The stale scents of sweat and other body odors assaulted her. Nausea rose to her throat, nearly choking her. One button popped open, then another. Cold air brushed her torso. His hands slid lower. Lifted her slightly. Lowered her skirt and began to slide it down her legs. She opened her mouth to scream, but the sound died in the back of her throat.

Finally she gave in to the fear, closed her eyes and prayed for darkness.

Death had to be better than this. She would go to heaven. She had to. She had been a good girl. There would be no pain on the other side.

His fingers brushed across the bare skin of her abdo-

men. Then he dribbled warm water on her belly. A cry tore
from her throat. She only hoped that he made it quick.

And that one day, someone found her killer.

She had to get help.

Violet struggled to clear the vision and orient herself.
She was still in the woods beside the graveyard. But another woman was going to die. She could sense her
fear, see her losing consciousness. Feel the prick of the
man's fingers as he trailed his nails over her skin.

Just like in her vision, she was weighted down. She
couldn't move.

She was suffocating from the darkness.

"Help me."

Violet gasped for air, hearing Darlene's childlike
voice crying out, too. No, this time it was the woman's.

Was it real? Or was she going crazy?

His fingers brushed her bare stomach, and she
jerked.

It was real. He was taunting her. Baiting her. He
wanted her to know what he was doing.

GRADY UNDERSTOOD EXACTLY how it felt to be on the receiving end of his father's hatred. But he had no idea
how Violet would react to it. Especially since she'd suffered enough trauma already the past few days.

He cranked up the engine of the squad car and drove
through town, once again scanning the streets. This
time for Violet. He checked the obvious. The florist. The
funeral home. But he didn't see her car. Other than her
childhood home, Grady could think of a couple other
places she might go. The morgue or the graveyard. Or
maybe the sweet gum tree. Since the coroner hadn't yet
released her father's body, and the sweet gum was near

her house, he hedged his bets and decided to check the graveyard first. He had to pass by there anyway on his way home.

He should just let her be alone. Let whatever his father had said to her stand.

It wasn't as if Grady wanted her to stay around, anyway, or that he could console her. Not until he knew the whole truth.

The squad car took the ruts in the mountain road with no trouble. Perspiration trickled down his neck and dampened his shirt, the open window circulating hot air as the noon sun beat down on the asphalt. He swiped at the sweat and steered onto the graveled road that led to the small church. Violet's Civic was parked near the entrance, empty. She had either come to visit Darlene's grave or her mother's.

He parked, then sat in the hot sun for a minute, batting away the flies, contemplating his next move. He wanted to put this case to rest. To know that Darlene's murder had gone avenged. But too many questions still taunted him.

Violet's doubt over her father's guilt clouded the case even more.

Did she know something she wasn't telling?

Releasing a frustrated sigh, he opened the car door and stepped onto the drive. His gaze scanned the rows of gray granite markers, some graves well-kept, others left to the weeds, as forgotten as the loved ones who lay six feet under. His father had hired someone to tend Darlene's mother's grave or it would be overrun by kudzu by now. And Darlene's... Grady visited it yearly, on the anniversary of her death, but had forced himself not to become obsessive.

Violet was nowhere to be seen.

He squinted at the shafts of sunlight slanting through the trees surrounding the property. A shadow moved in the distance, then retreated. A man with long hair tied back in a ponytail? Joseph Longhorse?

A scream suddenly echoed from the thicket. The shadow darted the opposite direction. Grady started to follow.

But another scream rent the air, and he took off running.

HE HAD TO MAKE SURE Violet Baker left town.

Walt Monroe tapped the end of his pipe, lit the imported tobacco and took a long draw, savoring the rich taste along with the first sip of his afternoon bourbon. The girl had always been trouble. Putting crazy notions in his daughter's young mind, enticing her to the other side of the tracks to carouse with the white trash.

Darlene should have been going to ballet class, preparing for the Sweet Gum Pageant, being primed for the cotillion. He'd known he had to put a stop to her relationship with the spooky little child before Darlene's teens or his daughter would be lost to him forever.

Bitterness blistered his insides along with the smoke and liquor. He had lost her, anyway. And it was half that Baker girl's fault. Hers and her goddamn mother's and father's.

He ran his fingers over the knotty pine branch he'd picked earlier, then angled his knife and began to carve away the rough edges. Even strokes. Rhythmic. Soothing strokes that would turn the raw wood into anything he wanted. Another lamb, maybe.

Thank God Jed was gone. Walt had worried too

many years that the old coot might blow a gasket and spill the truth about what had happened twenty years ago. And that would be deadly.

Enough people's lives had been destroyed. His had changed forever.

But none of it would bring back his baby girl. And he didn't want the Baker bitch around to dredge up old questions. Questions that he'd barely guessed the answers to.

Questions best left unanswered, or they all might end up dead.

GRADY'S HEART POUNDED as he raced over the graves and brittle grass toward the woods beyond the cemetery. That scream sounded like Violet. If something happened to her...

Thick maples, pines and dogwoods encircled the property, shadows clinging to the mossy trunks. He hesitated, listening for another scream as he drew his gun. Which way should he go?

Suddenly Violet came running through the dense brush, her hair tangled and wild around her pale face. He grabbed her, but she screamed again, then flailed her arms at him.

"Violet, stop it!" He shook her, forcing her chin up so she could see into his eyes. "Look, it's me, Grady."

She froze, the pupils of her eyes so dilated he could see his reflection in them.

He stroked her arms, wanting to comfort her. "What's wrong? Who's after you?"

Her chin quivered. She dug her nails into his arms and sagged against him. "You have to save her, Grady. He's going to kill her."

His breath caught as he tucked her close to him. "Who? Someone in the woods?"

A sob rattled out. "No...I don't know." Her voice broke. "But he has her. He's taking off her clothes, touching her. He's going to kill her tonight."

Grady's hand tightened around the cold metal of the gun, and he turned toward the woods, ready to run. "Go to the car. I'll find him."

She clawed at his arm. "No, don't leave."

"I'll be back, Violet, but I have to search the woods. Run to the car and lock the door."

"No, you don't understand," she screeched. "He's not there, but he has her. He's going to kill her tonight!" She looked wild-eyed and crazy, the panic in her voice nearing hysteria.

"Violet, I don't understand." He gestured toward the thicket of trees. "Was someone after you? Joseph Long-horse? Was he in the woods?"

"Joseph was here?"

"Yes, at least I thought I saw him. Was he chasing you?"

"No," she cried. "I mean, I didn't see Joseph. But a man has her."

"Who are you talking about?"

"I don't know her name, but she's a student. He left her alone for a while, but he's going back." She gripped his arm tighter, but he felt the trembling in her limbs. God help him, he wanted to protect her.

"Grady, you have to find him before he takes her blood. Then he's going to kill her, just like the last time."

"What do you mean, the last time?"

She gave him a beseeching look that tore at his soul. "Just like the woman in Savannah."

CHAPTER NINE

VIOLET DIDN'T WANT TO SEE these awful things, didn't want to feel these women's fears and pain.

It's the evil within you.

Was her father right? Did she have a connection to these murders because she carried the devil inside her?

"Violet, what do you know about the woman in Savannah?" The cold, harsh tone of Grady's voice snapped Violet back to reality.

She blinked him into focus, then read the questions in his eyes. He thought she was crazy. Either that or that she might be involved, just as he'd suspected she'd known that her father had killed Darlene.

"I asked you about the murder in Savannah. Did you know the woman who was killed?"

"No…I mean yes, I'd met her…in my shop. But I didn't really know her." Her voice faded. She felt so drained, as if all the energy had been zapped from her.

His cutting gaze pierced her to the bone. "Do you know who killed her?"

She shook her head, emotions gathering in her throat. "I…I saw her, though. I heard her crying for help."

His expression became skeptical. "You mean you witnessed the murder?"

"No." How could she make him understand when she

didn't understand herself? Not why she'd connected to Darlene or these two women, when she hadn't connected to her father. She couldn't read Grady's thoughts, either, except to know that he must suspect that the rumors about her being unstable were true.

Tension stretched between them. The cloying heat was suddenly suffocating. The woman was cold, though, so cold and numb with fear she'd lapsed into a comatose state somewhere between reality and sleep.

Violet needed to rest, too. Her legs buckled beneath her, but she caught herself, hating to show weakness.

"Violet, if you know something about that murder, you have to go to the police."

"Why? So they can look at me like I'm crazy, just as you're doing?" She pulled away and stumbled forward, intending to leave, but he grabbed her arm.

"The police can provide protection."

He sounded almost worried. But no man had ever cared for her, and Violet couldn't believe that Grady did now. Not after her father's confession, and his own father's attitude.

"That's just it—I don't really know anything. Besides, they wouldn't believe me any more than you do." She scrubbed a hand over her face as helplessness washed over her.

"Tell me the truth," he said in a gruff voice. "I'll believe it."

Why did she feel as if he were talking about her father, not the Savannah woman?

"I did. Another woman is in danger," she said softly. "I don't even know her name."

"You don't know where he's taken her?" His voice

was hard again, his eyes slices of black granite in his chiseled face.

"No."

"But you supposedly told your father where to find Darlene."

Again, it was back to his sister. The chasm of darkness that had opened between Violet and the rest of the world so long ago would never close. It had obviously affected Grady the same way, had shaped him into a different man than the kind young boy he'd been.

"Yes, I told my father where to find Darlene," she said in a pained whisper. "But it was too late."

Contempt mingled with disbelief in his eyes, robbing her of a reply. So she turned and ran, her legs wobbling as she picked her way across the graveyard.

She would visit Darlene's grave later, when she could be alone. Grady was no longer the big brother of her best friend. He was a hard-hearted sheriff. A man ready to hang her and her father for his sister's death.

She'd have to find out the truth on her own.

JOSEPH LONGHORSE WATCHED from the shadows of the elm tree, his anger growing like the kudzu that tangled around his *etsi*'s sunflowers, choking the life from them. He did not want Grady Monroe to have Violet.

Monroe was his enemy.

And Violet was his friend. Or she had been once, before her father had sent her away. Though different cultures separated them from birth, a deep connection ran between them, like the river joining the jagged rocks of the two mountain ridges at Black Mountain Peak. Violet was like a wildflower, a patch of color brightening the desolate parched ground that had been his childhood.

Thankfully, she had run from Monroe. Not like Kerry, who was running after him.

Joseph's gaze followed her as she crossed the grave-yard, her chestnut hair dancing in the wind like the mane of a wild mare who'd been tethered all her life. His body stirred, a primitive arousal rising within him that he'd never anticipated feeling for his childhood friend.

She was no longer a child.

He pictured her in that old raggedy, tattered dress that had been two sizes too big, hanging on her frail body when she'd slunk up to his mama's fire. Until her grand-mother had moved in, Violet had gone for days without a good meal. She'd stand at the edge of the forest near their camp, those big eyes peering through the darkness, watching their rituals. He'd caught her looking, heard her stomach growling. And he had taken her hand and brought her into their circle. Somehow he'd known it was right. His *etsi* always roasted enough ears of sweet corn and fried enough cornbread cakes to go around. And later, as they'd gathered in the firelight, she'd told the stories of their people.

He and Violet had forged a silent bond back then. They were both outcasts, shunned by the rich and pow-erful members of the community.

But his mama had dreamed of a better life for him, had insisted he get a white man's education. She'd forced him to attend the classes at the schoolhouse, though he'd begged to stay on the reservation and live off the land. The mountains, the wild animals, the cus-toms of his ancient forefathers lay deep in his soul and blood.

Bitter childhood memories flooded him. Of the kids

taunting his size, his native ways, his skin color, his customs, his mama. They hadn't completely singled him out. They'd made fun of Violet's shabby outhouse, her bare feet and thrift-store clothes, her daddy's drinking. And some had been so cruel they'd tossed out ugly names. The one time he'd defended her, five bullies had ganged up on him and beaten him to a bloody pulp. Grady Monroe had stepped in to save him.

He hadn't wanted Grady Monroe's help. In fact, he'd despised it.

It had only been a reminder of the power the wealthy had, and how little Joseph himself possessed. He did not want to be indebted to anyone, especially a Monroe.

His mother had preached to him not to blame Grady or the other kids in town. Even when some of the old biddies had refused to eat at her café, she had not hated. She'd tried to teach him forgiveness, had even claimed a deep sadness for those who were close-minded.

So he had hated them for her. The Monroes, Mayor Tate, even Doc Farmer. And though the wilderness called him, he had stayed around to protect her.

But he'd sworn that one day the town would pay.

His muscles tight with restrained anger, he raced across the woods and into the mountains.

The comforting balm of nature and his tribal rituals beckoned. He could already smell the blood and feel the excitement of the hunt....

GRADY TOLD HIMSELF to let Violet go. It was better to not get involved with her. She might be beautiful and troubled, but she was the daughter of the man who'd murdered his sister. And she sounded half-crazy.

Or was she?

A headache gnawed at him as he stopped by Darlene's gravesite, knelt and straightened the flowers that had bent in the wind. The marbles were still there, just as he'd placed them. Except for the blue one. Strange. Had it been blown away? Had someone taken it?

"I'm going to find out who did this to you, Darlene, I promise. I won't stop until I do."

Although God knew he hadn't been to church in years, so he had no idea if the man upstairs would listen, he offered a silent prayer before he headed to his car. Then he swung back by his place, picked up the files and drove to his office.

His deputy glanced up from the desk when Grady entered, his eyes hidden behind his sunglasses. The blinds were closed too. For some reason, his deputy liked the darkness.

"Any calls come in?" Grady asked.

Logan shook his head. "A lady named Samson—her cat ran up a tree. Volunteer fire department went out and rescued it."

Grady nodded. "Coroner's report come in on Baker?"

"Not yet."

"Hear anything on that Savannah case? Any more missing women?"

Logan leaned back, crossed his booted feet on top of the desk. "You think there'll be more?"

Grady shrugged. "Just wondering. The ritualistic aspect suggests it might be a serial killer."

"True," Logan said. "Didn't that Baker chick come from Savannah?"

Grady nodded, checking through the messages on his desk. "I believe so."

"Does she know something about the murder?"

Not wanting to incite any more questions, he shook his head. "Not that I know of. Why?"

"Seems like danger's following her."

Grady jerked his gaze toward Logan. His voice had a cynical note, almost as if he knew something he wasn't telling.

Then again, maybe Grady was making too much out of his comment. Looking for suspicion in every corner. He spun around and strode out the door. Hell, he had enough on his hands making sure Baker's confession was real, and chasing down his daddy.

He didn't need Violet Baker's weird rantings. He might be drawn to her, but she was here to clear her father and prove he hadn't killed himself. If Baker hadn't committed suicide, it meant he had been murdered.

Then the finger would be pointed at Grady's father....

As SOON AS VIOLET arrived at her father's house, she locked herself inside and called to check on her grandmother. The nurse assured her Grammy was fine. Unfortunately, she still hadn't regained her speech. Her recovery would take time.

Exhausted, Violet stretched out on her childhood bed. The weight of knowing another woman would die tonight taxed every nerve in her body. But what could she do?

Lie here and wait for another vision? Hope that the woman revealed some detail to help Violet find her?

Why all this now, when she was supposed to be clearing her father's name?

She closed her eyes and tried to control her fear, but the woman's cry echoed in the back of her mind. She was so still now, so cold and alone. Just as Darlene had been.

Violet's body trembled. She had let Darlene and Amber Collins down. She had no idea how she could save this woman, either....

Unable to sleep, Violet got up, cleaned the kitchen, but she was still restless. Her art had always been therapeutic, so she took out her sketch pad. The images she drew weren't pleasant, but they had filled her head... and she had an incessant urge to put them on paper.

When she added the outline of the bone whistle, its eerie sound invaded her peace again, and she shoved the pad away. There was nothing in the drawing that could help the police. No details about the killer's appearance or where he was holding the woman.

Just as there hadn't been anything concrete in her visions twenty years ago.

Frustrated, she decided to focus on her father. Grady and that deputy had searched the house, but maybe she would see something they'd missed.

She headed to the den first. At first glance, her hopes disintegrated. Not much inside the room but dusty, worn furniture. She looked through the kitchen cabinets and drawers, the wooden table where the phone sat, hoping to find a note or letter—anything that might offer information about her father.

Next, she rifled through a stack of auto mechanic magazines on the wobbly coffee table, then leafed through the mail topping the knotty pine desk in the corner. Overdue electric bill, overdue phone bill, overdue water bill... How long had it been since her father had worked?

Finally, she opened a drawer and spotted a photo album. She frowned, wondering if it was something her mother had started when she'd been alive, then lifted it and opened the cover. Surprise rippled through her. The album contained photos of her growing up, mostly candid shots that her father would have no way of having unless her grandmother had been keeping in touch with him all along.

Violet flipped the pages, recalling the events—her middle school graduation, then high school. Several snapshots of her walking on the beach in Charleston, where she'd taken classes. Each time, she'd thought of her father, wished he had cared enough to be there.

Each time she'd been disappointed.

Had he followed her growth through pictures her grandmother mailed him? And if Grammy had been sending him photos all along, why had she never mentioned it? Had her father wanted the pictures, or had her grandmother been trying to solicit his interest?

A horn blasted outside, then another and another. Violet ran to the window and looked out, shocked to see three cars barrel by, teenagers hanging out the windows.

"Get out of town!"

"Child murderer!"

"Crazy lady!"

Eggs and tomatoes flew toward the house, splattering the mailbox and windows. A rock crashed through a windowpane, sending shards of broken glass raining over the floor. Violet jumped back and brushed the slivers from her hair and blouse. Hateful childhood memories resurfaced. She hadn't backed down when she was five and the bullies in town had teased her. And she didn't plan to leave now.

No matter what they did to her.

"I DON'T CARE WHAT happens, what they do to you." Walt Monroe stabbed a chubby finger at Doc Farmer.

"Even if they threaten to take away your license or lock you up, keep your goddamn mouth shut."

Alvin Farmer twisted the end of his white beard, the pains in his stomach growing in intensity. He'd had an ulcer for going on ten years, the beginnings of it starting twenty years ago. He should never have gotten involved with the project....

"Farmer, you aren't thinking about talking, are you?"

God forgive him, but no. He was too much of a coward. He didn't want to give up his pension or the respect of the town. Not when his wife was ailing and needed him the most. Hattie had been so good to stand by him over the years, even after she'd found out he wasn't perfect.

"No. I don't know why you're so worried. With Jed dead, you and I are the only two who have a clue what really happened."

"Not the only two."

Sweat beaded on Farmer's neck and face. True—a few others, like Mavis Dobbins, suspected, but it would be to no one's advantage to tell all now.

"You should be grateful to find out who killed your baby. After all these years..."

Walt ducked his head, his expression forlorn. "You don't get it, do you? What if Jed lied about the confession?"

Farmer gasped. "What?" He yanked a roll of antacids from his pocket, tore off the top and downed two of them. "Good God, you aren't suggesting..."

"That his suicide wasn't real?" Monroe cut him a scathing look that Farmer had seen once before. When Monroe had come to see him about his wife's death, Monroe had claimed she was murdered and that he suspected something odd about Darlene's birth.

"Whether it is or not, it doesn't matter," Walt continued. "What matters is that someone's asking questions, the Baker girl is back and Jed is dead. Let's just pray he took his secrets with him to the grave." Monroe thumped him in the chest. "Just like we're going to do, you hear me?"

Farmer nodded, fear grappling with panic. If the truth ever got out, his reputation, his whole life, would be over. He might end up like Baker. Poor Hattie wouldn't be safe, either.

And Violet Baker—that girl would be six feet under, just like Darlene.

CHAPTER TEN

ON THE WAY to his father's place, Grady spotted his dad standing on the porch of Doc Farmer's small family practice. His father and Farmer had kept up over the years, although Grady didn't remember them being friends.

They had never been antagonistic toward one another before, but today they appeared to be arguing. Grady slowed and parked on the street, studying the two of them. Farmer had begun to turn clients over to the new guy in town, Dr. Gardener, but still saw a few of the old-timers who refused to relinquish their health care to a man they claimed couldn't grow face hair yet. Had Grady's dad enjoyed picking fights so much that he'd decided to choose another adversary? Or was something else going on?

A second later, his father lumbered off the porch steps and headed toward his Cadillac, his head downcast, his gait slow. Grady climbed from his car and cut him off at the corner.

"We need to talk, Dad."

Walt jerked his head up as if startled. "What the blazes are you doing here?"

Grady frowned. "I told you we need to talk. What was going on with you and Doc Farmer?"

"Are you following me, Grady?"

His father's defensive tone heightened Grady's anxiety. "No, but this is important."

"Then call me."

"No."

"Well, we're sure as hell not talking out here in front of the whole damn town."

Grady gritted his teeth. "Then get in the car. We'll have some privacy there."

His father dug in his pocket for his keys, flipped the switch to open the car door, and slid inside. Grady claimed the passenger side, not surprised when his father cranked the engine and turned up the air conditioner. Walt Monroe didn't tolerate the smallest discomfort, not when his money could remove it.

"I stopped by the Redbud Café today and heard you had a run-in with Jed Baker's daughter."

"No run-in," his father said. "I told her she wasn't welcome." He narrowed gray eyes at Grady. "Don't tell me you're interested in *that* woman personally."

Grady stiffened. "You haven't paid any attention to my life the past few years. Don't tell me you care now!"

Anger flared in his father's cheeks. "Jesus Christ. She's the daughter of the man who killed Darlene. You can't be serious."

"I never said I was interested," Grady stated. "But I'm the sheriff—it's my job to keep law and order."

"Then tell her to put her old man in the ground and leave town...or else there'll be trouble."

"What's that supposed to mean?"

His father smacked his lips. "It means we can't put this mess behind us with her around reminding us of her daddy."

Or Darlene.

"You knew Jed Baker as well as the rest of us, Dad. Do you really think he killed Darlene, or that he committed suicide?"

His father shoved a hand in his pocket and pulled out a cigar, then began to unwrap the tip. Just the scent made Grady crave a cigarette, but he popped a breath mint in his mouth instead.

"He said he did. What else can we believe?" Walt muttered. "He had opportunity, and he told us where to find her body. He got rid of his own kid, so she wouldn't figure it out."

Was that what had really happened?

"What was his motive, Dad? If he'd been a pedophile, he wouldn't have just stopped with Darlene."

"He hated me. Maybe he wanted to get back at us for being better than him."

Grady chewed his lip. "Then why not kill you instead of your little girl?"

"Hell, Son, why are you asking me? He was a sick bastard, that's why. You need more?"

Maybe he did. Baker hadn't seemed mentally ill, just coldhearted, in that he'd sent his daughter away and never mentioned her again. But twisted enough to kill an innocent child… Something about that didn't ring true. "What was going on with you and Doc Farmer?"

His father's nostrils flared as he lit the cigar. "Nothing."

"I saw you arguing."

"I told you it was nothing." He gave him a hard look. "I've had enough of your inquisition, Son. Send Violet Baker packing and forget the investigation."

Grady stared at his dad, wondering if he'd heard him right. Something had happened between him and

Farmer, something his father wanted to keep hidden…
just as he'd had secrets with Baker.

Did his father really want to blame Baker so badly
he'd pin guilt on him even if he were innocent? And
what kind of secrets could possibly be so important that
he'd risk not finding Darlene's killer to keep them hidden?

REVEREND BILLY LEE BILKINS glanced out at the throng
of people gathered in the big tent, waiting on the message he'd come to deliver from the Lord. He had his
work cut out for him.

There were secrets in this town. And evil. A darkness
that held hostage the inhabitants, an ugliness mired in
the prejudices of the small-minded locals, and in the
deaths of the Native Americans who'd died brutally on
the land. Their ghosts lived among the burial grounds
in the foothills, shimmering between worlds unknown,
waiting on rectification.

But there was more.

Good people trying to weave their way into the
crowds. They were hidden in the midst of the sprawl-
ing mountains and harder to find, yet wrestling with demons of their own. Good people who needed to be
saved.

People who would be sacrificed or lost without his
help.

Brother Wheeler stepped up to the podium, already
wiping sweat from his brow with a monogrammed
white handkerchief. The heat in the valley was oppressive, the only reprieve the occasional breeze brought
from the mountains encircling them. Wheeler waited
until the last chorus of "Shall We Gather at the River"

faded, then raised his hands in the air, commanding attention as his long robe billowed out like a vampire's cape. "Ladies and gentlemen, boys and girls, we have the special honor of having the acclaimed Reverend Billy Lee Bilkins with us tonight."

Reverend Bilkins smiled and nodded, the words already forming in his head.

"Praise be," several people shouted.

"Amen," others added.

"Glory hallelujah." Brother Wheeler raised his hands again and a hush fell over the excited crowd. "And now, let us listen to the words and meditations he has brought so that they may cleanse us of the sins fraught upon us! Let him cast the devils from our souls and lead us to the way of the God almighty!"

More shouting and words of praise erupted.

Reverend Bilkins stepped forward, smiling broadly, allowing himself to revel in the glory of the moment. He didn't prepare his sermons in advance, didn't write down or practice with tape recorders, but went by the old ways and allowed the words to come to him from the heavens.

A sea of troubled faces stared back at him, thirsty for his healing. They needed him in this town. In fact, he might have to stay longer than he'd planned. Rome hadn't been built in a day.

Evil couldn't be expunged so quickly, either.

He spotted Wheeler's grown son watching from the back of the tent, his eyes twitching nervously. Wheeler would be one of his greater challenges.

In fact, he wasn't sure he could be saved....

"LISTEN TO THE GOSPEL as I speak it," Reverend Bilkins shouted. "Repent, sinners. Bare your evil souls to the Lord, pray for forgiveness, and I can save you now."

Ross Wheeler's eye twitched as he watched Brother Billy Lee stalk across the stage, shouting and clapping his hands, throwing his body around in dramatic gestures as his sermon gained steam. The audience praised and amened every other sentence, hanging on to Bilkins's words as if God had beamed him down in their midst to personally change them.

But Bilkins was simply a show. Playing to the audience, getting them fired up with platitudes. Scaring them shitless with his holy roller litanies of hellfire and damnation. Then he'd be passing his hat, collecting money and feeding his empire—all in the name of glory to the Father.

As big a hypocrite as his own old man.

"I ask you now to look inside your hearts," Brother Billy Lee shouted. "Find the seed that sprouts from evil, pluck it out and lay yourself at God's feet...."

An elderly woman at the back rose and yelled out, "Amen, brother, I'm plucking mine out now." She swayed and thrust her hand over her heart, pulled out an imaginary seed and tossed it forward. The middle-aged woman next to her began to speak in tongues, and a chorus of "Praise be's" echoed throughout the audience.

Kerry Cantrell, the waitress at the Redbud Café, moved up beside him, hugging the edge of the tent as if she wasn't quite sure what to make of the service. "He knows how to fire up a crowd, doesn't he?"

"Yes, he does," Ross said, surprised the attractive young waitress had spoken to him. She barely paid attention to him at the café. She was always flirting with the sheriff, practically flaunting herself to get his attention. Maybe she was getting tired of being turned down.

So tired she'd decided to look elsewhere. Ross laughed at the irony.

She probably hadn't heard yet about his reputation. Or maybe she didn't care.

Not that the rumors had it right.... Not even his father knew the truth.

If it wasn't for the reverend, Ross would have moved on a long time ago. Someplace where no one knew about his tainted name. Someplace where he could start all over again.

Only now he'd found a lover here. A reason to stay.

"I haven't seen you at our church," he said. "Thinking of visiting?"

"Maybe." She thumbed a strand of hair behind her ear. "Truth is, I've never been much of a churchgoer."

"I was never anywhere else on Sunday," he admitted. "Or Wednesday night."

"Must have been difficult being a preacher's son."

She had no idea. And was he mistaken or had her voice turned sultry? Maybe she liked walking on the edge....

"I managed."

"Yeah, but always having to be good. Living under the microscope all the time." She sighed, her breasts heaving.

His breath caught in his throat. His father would like this one. "You sound like you've been there."

"Let's just say my folks had high expectations." She laughed, a soft melodic sound that twisted his stomach. She wanted him. It was almost funny.

But he had other plans tonight.

Yes, the temptation was too strong for him to resist. He'd been thinking about his lover all day. He couldn't wait any longer.

It was time for him to slip from the crowd, to become invisible and find his pleasure.

VIOLET HAD NEVER FELT so alone. At least when she'd moved, she'd had her grandmother. But, here, in her father's old house, all she could do was stare at the dingy walls and remember the events that had brought her to this homecoming.

She couldn't bear the memories any longer.

The solitude felt like a vise choking her. She checked outside to make certain no more kids were driving by to harass her, then hurried to her car. Where should she go? It was already late, the evening shadows reminding her that the woman who'd cried out to her for help didn't have much longer. If only she could see where the killer held her….

Shivering and needing a safe haven herself, she drove toward the Redbud Café. Maybe Laney could explain the meaning of the Native American expression.

A few minutes later, she parked. Laney wasn't in the café but in her apartment above it. Violet felt more at home at Laney's than she had at her own father's. Laney welcomed her inside with open arms and handed her a cup of herbal tea as if she was expecting her. Violet settled onto the faded patchwork-covered sofa, admiring the familiar Indian artifacts, rugs and simple crude furniture. Something peaceful emanated in the air around Laney, a kind of satisfaction with herself and her soul that Violet wished she possessed.

Although it was hot outside, and the apartment had

no air-conditioning, the room felt cool and comfortable. "Where's Joseph?"

Laney shrugged. "He needs to be alone," she said. "It is his time to commune with the earth. Enjoy the hunt."

"He's proud of his heritage, isn't he?" Violet said.

Laney smiled and nodded, draping her long braid across her shoulder. "It is a miracle he is, but yes. If we forget who we are, then we are nothing."

Violet frowned, studying the tea. Who exactly was she? The daughter of a killer? A woman possessed by evil, able to see other's pain but unable to stop it?

"It is hard for you here," Laney said, more as a statement than a question.

"Yes." Violet sipped the tea, giving herself time to relax.

But the woman doesn't have time. You need to hurry or she'll die, just like Darlene.

"I think I'm cursed, Laney." She closed her eyes as the querulous admission rushed out.

Laney didn't react, simply rested a hand on top of Violet's. "Why would you think that, child?"

Violet opened her eyes, expecting to see the condemnation she'd seen from Grady and his father, but found only compassion and wisdom.

"Tell me, dear, and you'll feel better. Together we can solve this."

Together? Violet had been alone so long she didn't know how to lean on anyone else. Besides, saying the words out loud made them sound even harsher.

"You came to me for help. I cannot give it if you are silent."

Violet twisted her hands in her lap. "Do you remember when Darlene Monroe was kidnapped?"

Laney's mouth pinched with sorrow. "No one in this town will ever forget."

"I heard her crying for help that night," she said, the truth spilling out. "Laney, I told my father where to find her."

"Yes, I heard that."

"But he was too late and Darlene died." Violet searched the woman's gray eyes. "Do you think my father killed her?"

Age lines creased Laney's mouth as her lips formed a frown. "No, I do not believe he is a murderer."

Relief surged through Violet, but she still had so many questions. "Then why would he leave a confession?"

Laney shrugged. "I can't answer that, Violet."

"Do you believe he killed himself?"

Laney thought for a long moment before answering. "Your father was a very unhappy and lonely man. I think he pined for you after you left."

"But he sent me away," Violet said, choking back emotions. "Did he talk about me?"

"Not in so many words, although I could read the pain and loneliness in his eyes."

That pain had probably been disappointment. Or shame at having a misfit child. "He never contacted me after that, never came to see me. It was as if he had thrown me out of his life."

"There are some things we don't understand," Laney said in a soft voice. "But time will give us the answers."

Violet shifted restlessly. She didn't have time. The other woman was dying.

"You have blamed yourself for Darlene's death,"

Laney said. "It wasn't your fault, dear. And your sight is not a curse, but a gift."

"How can it be a gift if Darlene died, anyway? If I was too late?"

"Maybe you were not meant to save her, but to be with her so she didn't die alone. Your presence made her journey into the afterworld less frightening."

Violet's fingers tightened around the cup. She'd never considered that possibility. "But it's happening again."

The rocking chair creaked as Laney leaned forward. "You've had other visions?"

Violet stood and paced across the wooden floor. A collection of bones drew her eye, causing a chill to slither up her spine. She'd seen Joseph carve an animal bone when she was small....

"I had a vision of a woman dying in Savannah," she whispered, quelling the image. Joseph was her friend, not a killer. "Her name was Amber Collins. And then tonight, I had another one of a different woman." Violet described the visions and her frustration over not seeing enough details to identify the killer or where he held his victims. "What does the expression *pin peyeh obe* mean?"

"Look to the mountain.'" Laney slowly waved her arm in an arc as if she were pointing over the horizon. "Look as if you're standing on top—there one can see things in a broader perspective, perhaps that of generations to come."

"The bigger picture." Violet pressed a finger to her temple, a throbbing pain taking root as she contemplated the message. "I still don't understand why the killer used it."

"He said this to the woman?"

Violet nodded.

"You believe he is Native American?"

"I have no idea. But he's going to kill her tonight," she finished in an agonized whisper. "Unless I do something to stop him."

HIS PULSE ACCELERATED as he studied her blood, regret and excitement warring against one another. She wasn't the one.

His father would be disappointed.

But he would offer her up, anyway.

He raised the needle, tapped the tip, then stalked toward her. A slow smile curved his lips. She was so beautiful. Young. Supple. Primed for life.

But imperfection tainted her blood.

And his father deserved perfection. He had to have it. Nothing else would do.

She cried out. A weak, pathetic screech of a sound that rippled up his spine. He approached slowly, murmuring soothing words in the native language. The white of her eyes widened into big moon-shaped globes. The irises glistened with tears, offering him a clear reflection of himself.

The one who should have been.

"No…please," she whimpered. "Please, don't do this. Whatever you want—if it's money, whatever…"

"No money," he said softly. "Just your blood, my dear. But it isn't right."

He slowly injected the solution into her veins, watching as panic captured her in its clutches.

"Pin peyeh obe," he whispered. "I am the blood taker, and now you must die…."

VIOLET LIFTED ONE HAND from the steering wheel and tried to drag in air, but she was suffocating. Her limbs felt heavy. Panic paralyzed her.

Dear God, he was doing it—killing another woman. She felt the pressure of his fingers tightening around her throat. The mind-numbing fear. The realization that her life was slipping through his fingers.

"No, God, why…" She had to fight it, make it home. She could see her father's house in the distance.

The fingers squeezed harder. She coughed. Couldn't breathe. Lost control of the car. Tires squealed. Then she was sliding. Skidding on the asphalt. She tried to right the vehicle. It bounced over a pothole and hit the ditch. Then she slammed into the guardrail and screeched to a stop. She jerked forward. The seat belt slammed her back against the seat.

She gasped, but her windpipe closed. Darkness replaced the streetlight's glow. Sucked her into its clutches. Unable to fight any longer, she dropped her head forward against the steering wheel. Then she fell into unconsciousness.

Just as she did, the reedy sound of the bone whistle echoed in the darkness….

CHAPTER ELEVEN

TOMORROW GRADY WOULD talk to Doc Farmer himself, maybe even his wife. Supposedly his father had been at a town meeting when Darlene had been kidnapped years ago. Maybe if Grady reviewed the circumstances and events of that day, he'd get a clue as to what had really happened. And surely the M.E. would have the report on Jed Baker by then. His specific time of death would be helpful, too.

Then Grady would find out if Baker had had any friends twenty years ago that might attest to his character.

His police radio went staticky, then cleared. "Sheriff, it's Logan. There's been an accident on Pine Needle Drive. That Baker woman ran her car into a ditch."

Grady's gut tightened. "Is she all right?"

"I don't know. She looks like she might have hit her head, but she's semiconscious. I've called the paramedics."

"I'll be right there." Grady spun his squad car around and made the turn to the Baker place, scanning the streets as he always did for anything amiss. His hands gripped the steering wheeler tighter at the sight of the profanity spray painted on the driveway and mailbox. Broken eggshells and tomatoes littered the front porch, and a window had been shattered. Had Violet been home during the vandalism? Could whoever it was have caused her accident?

He spotted lights from Logan's car ahead and sped up, his pulse accelerating at the thought of someone in town hurting Violet. Seconds later, he jumped from his car and ran to the ditch.

"She's coming to," Logan said.

Grady pushed past his deputy and leaned inside the car. Her head had lolled forward, and she was leaning against the steering wheel, her arms draped across it. His heart pounded faster. "Violet?" He gently brushed her hair back, checking for head injuries. Already a knot was forming on her forehead, a small gash trickling blood down her cheek. He removed a handkerchief, pressed it to the cut, then stroked her back. "Violet, can you hear me? Are you all right?"

She moaned and shifted slightly, her arms slipping down to her sides. Finally she raised her head and looked up at him. Shock glazed her eyes, and something else—fear? Sorrow?

"What happened?" He rubbed her back again, his breathing erratic as he waited. "Are you okay?"

Tears spilled from her eyes. "It's too late," she whispered. "She's already dead."

He stared at her, not comprehending for a moment. Was she was talking about his sister? "Who, Violet? Darlene?"

She shook her head, her bottom lip quivering. "The other w-woman. He strangled her just like he did Amber Collins."

WHILE GRADY CALMED Violet, Logan stared into the darkness, a puzzled expression on his face. Grady understood the feeling; he had no idea what to make of Violet's assertion.

A siren roared closer, and the paramedics wheeled up, then jumped from the ambulance. "What do we have?"

"Head injury," Logan said.

Grady stepped aside to let the EMT check Violet.

What had just happened? If Violet had been psychic, why hadn't she been able to save his sister? Had Darlene's death traumatized Violet in such a way she'd lost touch with reality, as rumors suggested? She'd seemed coherent the first night she'd arrived, had even seemed defensive and confrontational.

"Ma'am, let us take care of that cut." The EMT blotted the blood with a gauze pad. Finally he and his partner helped her from the car toward the back of the ambulance and treated the wound. Grady watched them check her for more serious injuries, then try to coax her into going to the hospital.

"I'm fine." Violet looked up at Grady. "I don't need to go to the hospital."

He leaned forward. "At least let me call the new doctor in town."

"No. I'm fine."

"Are you sure?" Grady massaged her neck. "You hit your head pretty hard."

She nodded, her skin ghostly white. Then she reached for him, her slender fingers gripping his arm. "Please, just take me home. If I'm not feeling well tomorrow, I'll get rechecked."

He chewed his cheek, remembering the graffiti and ugly slurs painted on her father's driveway. Something about the way she was holding on to him, almost pleading, as if she trusted him to believe her, twisted at his gut. He didn't want to want her. But he did. "Someone vandalized your house."

"I know," she said softly. "I was there when it happened."

Anger bolted through him. "Did they hurt you? Did someone cause you to have this accident?"

She shook her head. "It was the vision. I felt him choking me...."

Grady grimaced. Why was she talking such nonsense? Was she trying to distract him from her father's death? "Maybe you need help, Violet."

She pushed away and stood. "I'm not crazy, Grady. I don't need a shrink—I need to go home."

The paramedics glanced at Grady. "We can't take her in if she refuses treatment."

Logan hooked his thumbs in his belt. "You want me to drive her home, watch her for a while?"

The thought of his deputy alone with Violet set Grady's teeth on edge, although he didn't know why. Maybe because she held a part of his past, maybe even the answers to the truth about what had happened to his sister.

Or maybe because he was attracted to her. Although God's knows, he wasn't going anywhere with it. She was practically *his* little sister.

Except his feelings toward her weren't brotherly at all.

Violet backed away, her look of distress cementing his decision.

"No," he said. "Follow us, take a few paint samples, and see if we can figure out who vandalized her place."

"It was just a bunch of kids," Violet said.

Logan nodded. "Probably be hard to trace, but

maybe a neighbor saw something." He glanced at Violet. "What kind of car were they driving?"

"It was too dark to tell." She shrugged. "But I'm sure they didn't mean any harm."

Grady frowned. Maybe. Sometimes teenagers got off on vandalism, but he didn't like the timing or implications of their act, especially knowing his own father had warned Violet out of town earlier in the day.

What if someone had put them up to their nasty tricks? Or what if someone came back and crossed the line from defacing her property to a more personal attack?

Violet could be in danger.

VIOLET SWAYED, hating the dizziness and exhaustion draining her. But she couldn't seem to gather her strength. Grady caught her, steadying her. Heat mingled with embarrassment, reddening her cheeks. Still, it felt so good to be near Grady. So safe.

"I don't want to leave my car," she said, righting herself. "I'll need it tomorrow."

Grady's gaze met hers as if he'd felt the connection between them. He glanced at the dented front end. "I'll have it towed and repaired."

"Thanks. If it's drivable, just have it taken to my father's," Violet said. "I don't want to be without it. I can have body work done later."

"I'll call it in," Logan offered.

Grady nodded and urged Violet toward his car. "I'll see you at the Baker house."

Violet allowed Grady to help her, although he obviously didn't believe the story about her vision.

Not that she blamed him. She didn't understand it,

either. She'd never known anyone else who had psychic abilities. It wasn't like this gift ran in her family.

But what she'd seen had been very real. And once again, she'd been too late to save the woman.

Why had God given her this sight if she couldn't help stop the terrible things she saw? And why connect with these particular women?

It was almost as if she was connected to the killer himself.

MAVIS DOBBINS HAD NEARLY worried herself sick. She twisted the dishrag into knots, squeezing cleaner on the surface of her battered counters and scrubbing them for the hundredth time. When she got nervous, she cleaned. Ridding her house of germs would make the other dirty things go away. She only wished she could erase the ugly slate of nasty deeds from her life like she did the dust and grime at her fingertips.

It was okay, though. As long as Dwayne hadn't done gone and made some mess that she couldn't clean up.

A pesky fly buzzed in front of her sweaty face, then lit on her arm. Her stomach pitched. She'd heard that flies regurgitated wherever they landed. Sickened by the thought of their guts on her skin, she snatched the fly-swatter, lifted it and flattened the insect with one swing. Its innards splattered, seeping onto the stained counter surface she'd just scoured.

Blast it, she had to clean it all over again.

She poured another round of cleanser on her brush and began to scrub. The sound of a motor rumbled outside, and her heart jumped to her throat. Dwayne.

Thank the good Lord he was home.

She couldn't relax, though, until he walked inside the

house and she saw his face. Just by the set of his eyes, she'd know if the boy had been up to no good.

She switched off the overhead light, throwing the room into shadows. Footsteps shuffled outside. Then three stomps. Right, left, right again. The screen door screeched open, then the wooden one.

Dwayne's head was ducked, and he was mumbling something in a singsongy voice that sent her nerves skittering again. She gripped the scrub brush and folded her arms, waiting.

His head slowly came up. That devilish smile was on his lips. Trouble.

"Where have you been, boy?"

He shrugged. "Out."

"I asked you where."

He rolled his shoulders. "I'm grown now, Mama. You don't have to check up on me."

She flicked him with the flyswatter. "I asked you a question. Don't give me no disrespect."

He pursed his lips in a pout. "The mountains. You know I like to walk at night."

Yes, he did. He sometimes got lost in the sounds of the night. But sometimes…no, she wouldn't think that.

"Let me see your hands."

"Uh-uh." He shoved them behind him and backed up, ready to run.

"Listen, here, Dwayne, I've sold my soul to keep you out of trouble. And here you go running off to God knows where, skipping your medicine. Then hiding from me." She yanked his hands up to examine them. Dirt and bits of leaves were lodged beneath his fingernails. The smell of damp earth clung to his hair and clothes. But another smell, something almost rancid, permeated his clothing. And…drops of blood dotted his hands and stained his fingernails. Had he been at his old habits again?

She jerked her head up. "Do you want to be locked up again at night? Or maybe you want me to send you away?"

"No, Mama, please…" His voice broke again, that of a child. His knees sagged, too, and he clung to her like a kid, lost and afraid. "I'll do anything, just don't shut me away."

Just like always, that puppy-dog look got to her. "Then scrub those hands, take your pill and go to bed. If you skip your medication again, I'll lock you in."

He nodded, dropping his shoulders forward. Back to being obedient. She handed him the scrub brush, then pushed him toward the sink and turned on the hot water.

A few minutes later, when his hands were red and nearly raw, but clean, she made him sit down, then handed him a glass of water. "Take your medicine now like a good boy."

"Yes, Mama." He placed the pill in his mouth.

"Now, go get undressed. Hand me your clothes before you get in the bath, so I can take care of them."

"Wash them good, Mama. Make them smell good."

Yes, she had her obedient little boy back now. "I will," she promised. Although she'd burn them instead, just in case he had been up to no good.

He hugged her and loped into the bathroom. Seconds later, he squeezed the door open just enough to toss out the stench-filled garments. She carried them outside to the old metal garbage bin where she burned her trash. A bad feeling settled over her as she lit the rags and watched her son's clothes go up in flames.

He wasn't getting any better. In fact, even with his medication, his spells seemed to be getting worse. His obsessive-compulsive tendencies had come back. His mood swings were more frequent.

She was really afraid now.

Afraid that one day he just might be the death of her....

SPECIAL AGENT NICK NORTON had a bad feeling. The minute he received the call from the locals in Nashville, he suspected they had a serial killer on the loose. Trouble was, the murderer hadn't started in Tennessee, but in Georgia. And from the description, the second victim looked nothing like the first.

"M.O. is the same as the Collins girl who died in Savannah, Georgia," Detective Clarence Hendricks said.

Norton took one look at the victim lying on the church steps and nodded. "It appears that way, but we'll have to see what forensics tells us."

"Judging from the ligature marks, I'd speculate she died of strangulation," the M.E. said. "No signs of sexual abuse, but I'll perform tests to make certain."

Norton nodded again, studying the way the woman had been positioned. Her clothes had been removed, and she was wrapped in a sheet. A note, identical to the one left with Amber Collins, was found beside her saying, "*Pin Peyeh obe,* for the father."

"We'll get our profiler on this," Nick said. "The note indicates our killer is some kind of religious fanatic."

Detective Hendrix grimaced as the crime lab finished taking pictures. "Don't serial killers usually pick a certain type of victim? All blondes or all brunettes?"

"Usually. The relationship, whatever it is, normally

has something to do with a person from their past—often their mother, especially if she's an abuser. Sometimes the victim represents a former lover or wife who abandoned the perp." He cracked his knuckles, a habit that helped him think and relieve stress. "We'll have to dig deeper to find the connection between these two women. That is, if we are in fact dealing with a serial killer."

"A serial killer?" Bernie Morris, a reporter from the *Nashville Nighttime News* trotted up, microphone in hand. Norton glared at him and swept his hand for the locals to keep the man and his camera crew back. "Come on, Detectives," Morris screeched, "if we're dealing with a serial killer, the public has a right to know."

Norton bolted forward and jerked him by the collar instead. "No one said anything about this being a serial killing, so don't you dare report that and start widespread panic."

"I heard you say it." Morris thrust his patrician nose up with an air of bravado. "And you have no right to keep it from the press or the people."

"We're trying to conduct an investigation here," Norton snarled, "and we can't do it with you interfering. Now, when or if we determine what happened, we'll release a statement."

Morris tried to push forward again, but at Norton's sudden gesture, two locals hauled him backward, guarding the taped crime scene area with weapons drawn.

"I'll get this story," Morris shouted.

Norton ignored him. He hated reporters, always had. One had interfered and nearly gotten his partner killed before. Another had nearly cost him a collar on a child molester.

He wouldn't let this jerk mess up this case.

This poor woman—victim number two, as everyone would start calling her—deserved to have some privacy. And he needed to find the person responsible for her murder. Time meant everything.

If they were dealing with a serial killer, the psycho was probably already choosing his next victim.

CHAPTER TWELVE

VIOLET SHUDDERED, unable to think of anything except this last woman. If only she could tell them where the killer chose his victims or even why he was choosing them. And if she could just see his face….

Grady remained quiet, seemingly oblivious to the tense silence between them as he drove her back to her father's house. What was he thinking? That she was crazy? That she'd make up a bizarre story about hearing and seeing things to get attention?

She didn't know why it meant so much to her that he believe her, but it did.

As he pulled into the drive, he frowned at the vandalism. "I wish you'd gotten the make of those cars."

She shrugged. In light of this recent woman's murder, the vandalism seemed petty. "Don't worry about it, Grady. I'm sure the kids had their fun and games and I doubt they'll return."

His gaze shifted toward her. "You don't know that, Violet."

The air crackled with tension. His grim voice slid over her nerve endings, triggering a disturbing mixture of feelings. Discomfort that he thought she might be in danger. And an aching need… What would it be like to have a man like Grady actually care for her?

"It's my job to protect this town," he said, heat rippling between them. "I take my job seriously."

Right. His job... She was just another citizen.

His fingers curled around the steering wheel. They were long, wide, rough with calluses, but so masculine they sparked her senses to arousal. She imagined those big tough hands stroking her, giving her comfort, maybe even pleasure. Bringing her to life in a way she'd never experienced.

"How long are you staying in Crow's Landing?" he asked, oblivious to her train of thought.

Violet fidgeted with her hands and opened the car door. She was such a novice at reading a male's psyche. He obviously didn't feel this attraction. And he probably didn't want her around asking questions. He and his father were satisfied they had Darlene's killer, and were ready to close the case. She was only a painful reminder.

"I'm not sure, but I refuse to let anyone run me off."

The deputy pulled in behind them and began to assess the vandalism. Something about Grady's assistant made her uncomfortable, but she couldn't put her finger on anything specific. She closed the door, aware that Grady disagreed with her intentions, then steered a wide berth around Deputy Logan as she and Grady walked up the sidewalk.

A muscle ticked in Grady's jaw. "You should consider staying at a hotel, at least until that window gets fixed."

She shook her head and unlocked the front door. "Forget it, Grady. I'm not running." *Not this time.* "I came here for the truth, and I intend to find it."

His gaze locked with hers, his dark eyes full of turmoil. She understood that feeling.

"Even if it gets you hurt?" Grady asked.

A long, weary sigh escaped her. "The truth can't hurt any more than thinking my father might have killed Darlene."

GRADY FELT A PANG of sympathy for Violet. Even after being here and facing the town, she still intended to defend her father.

Part of him wanted to pull her into his arms, hold her, protect her from the harsh truth, from the people in town like his dad who didn't want her around. Another part of him wanted more. To slide his hands over her delicate skin, through that long dark hair, and kiss the pale flesh at her throat… To skim off her clothes, turn that pained look in her eyes to one of rapture, and let her wrap her legs around him while he sank deep inside her.

But he wasn't sure she was stable. Besides, she'd come here to defend her father. They were on opposite sides. "How do you think you'll find out anything? The police worked on this case for months and came up with nothing."

Her lips parted a fraction, indecision flashing in her eyes. "I don't know, but there has to be someone in town who knows the truth."

"Do you think you might know something about the killer, something you forgot?"

"I told my father and grandmother everything I knew back then," she said, emotions tinging her voice. "I tried to help them find Darlene, Grady."

She sounded so lost, he barely resisted dragging her into his arms. "I meant that maybe you haven't tapped into all your memories. Maybe subconsciously there are details you've forgotten."

"You mean like repressed memories?"

"It's possible."

She rubbed at her forehead as if probing her brain for the past, and he silently cursed himself for pushing her when she'd just suffered an injury. Her head was probably pounding. Her complexion was pale, her eyes gaunt as if she hadn't slept in days. And he had felt her fragile body sway in his arms a half hour earlier.

"Why do you ask that?" she asked in a low voice.

"You were only a child, Violet. Sometimes children are so traumatized by a crime that they block out details."

Her shattered look rose to meet his eyes. "You think I saw my father kidnap Darlene, maybe even murder her, and that I've repressed that memory?"

He shrugged, uncertain. "It's a theory," he said cautiously.

"No…I don't believe it." She dropped her hand, her expression anguished. "But if I have repressed memories, then being here might jog them back to the surface."

It also might put her in danger. The thought of someone hurting her disturbed him more than he wanted to admit. "You need to get some rest," he said, his voice more gruff than he'd intended.

She started to argue, and he realized she wasn't quite as fragile as he thought. She had to be gutsy or she would have never driven back to town to face the past after her father's confession. But Grady cut off her arguments, anyway. "Look, I promised the paramedic I'd make you go to bed. If you don't rest, I'll take you to the hospital."

The phone rang, preventing a reply. She hesitated, then answered it. "Hello?"

Grady waited, wondering who would be calling Violet. Did she have a special someone back home? A boyfriend, lover?

"Hello?" Her voice sounded agitated.

He lifted his eyebrows in question.

"Hello."

She bit her lip, then dropped the phone in its cradle. "They hung up."

A knot of apprehension tightened Grady's belly. First vandalism. Now hang-up calls. He didn't like it. "Go on to bed and I'll watch out. I'll make sure Logan questions the neighbors, then we'll get someone out here to clean up that mess outside."

"What?" She swung her gaze toward him, her voice a startled whisper.

"I said I'd get someone to clean up—"

"No, not that. You said you'd stay and watch out."

"That's right."

Her eyes flickered with panic. "Not all night?"

He thought he'd detected heat between them moments earlier, but her discomfort at the idea of him staying suggested the opposite. "Yes, Violet, all night."

"But…why?"

He ticked the reasons off on his hand. "First, the window is broken, so anyone could climb in. Second, your house was vandalized tonight. And third, I told the paramedic I'd wake you up every few hours and check on you. We want to rule out a concussion."

A strained heartbeat passed. "You don't have to do that. I'll be fine."

"Yes, I do. I'm the sheriff." He gripped her arms, turned her and gently shoved her toward the bedroom.

"But, Grady—"

"It's my job to protect the citizens and enforce the

law." He paused at the threshold of her bedroom, the scent of some kind of potpourri drifting outward, eliciting a momentary lapse in his thoughts while a vision of Violet stretched out on her bed flitted through his mind. He quickly banished it. "I'm not about to leave you here alone tonight, Violet. Not until you get some damn good dead bolts on this shack and that window fixed. Now go rest before I carry you to bed myself."

Her shocked look twisted his insides. He hadn't meant the threat as an invitation for sex, but somehow his traitorous body had reacted, anyway. She backed away, looking panicked, then slipped into the bedroom, closed the door in his face and locked it behind her. Obviously she didn't like the idea of him taking her to bed, or even entering her room. Her attitude rankled, although he had no right to want her so badly. She was innocence itself compared to the black mark left on his soul after Darlene's death.

Or was she as innocent as she seemed?

Confused, he turned away from the door, reminding himself that he was the sheriff, here to do a job, not the boy she'd known as a child. She wasn't the bedraggled, lost little girl, either. She was the daughter of the man who'd confessed to killing his sister. She'd come here to prove her father's innocence. And Grady wanted nothing but to see the killer pay no matter what the costs. Even if it hurt Violet.

And he'd damn well better remember it.

VIOLET HAD TO WASH the stench of death off of her. Although the killer hadn't actually touched her personally, she could still feel the pinpoints of pressure from where he'd strangled the other woman. Where was she now?

Had he left her body on the steps of a church, as he had Amber Collins's? Had the police found her yet?

Had her family been told?

Violet stood beneath the hot spray of water and closed her eyes, willing away the fear and the memories. Where the killer's hands had dirtied her body with evil and violence, Grady's strong fingers cleansed her. In her fantasy, he stroked her gently, massaging away the terror and bringing her body alive with warm, delicious sensations. Sensations she'd only fantasized about before.

Maybe because every man she'd met she'd compared to the version of the grown-up Grady she'd carried in her mind. The real one was so much better. Stronger. Tougher. Harder. Sexier.

Darker.

And even though they stood on opposite sides of the fence where her father was concerned, he'd assigned himself her protector.

But he had stayed to guard her because he was a cop. A decent lawman who protected the people in the town. Not because he wanted a personal relationship with her.

Or maybe he'd stayed hoping she'd remember something to incriminate her father.

The tingling, erotic sensations she'd experienced moments earlier faded, an icy chill engulfing her. In spite of the oppressive heat in the unair-conditioned house, she turned off the water, stepped from the shower and wrapped herself in a thick terry-cloth robe, huddling inside it to ward off the cold that gripped her. Seconds later, she picked up a comb and studied her reflection in the mirror. She had mousy, wavy hair and a plain face. But her grandmother had always told her that her eyes were beautiful—the windows to the soul.

What did Grady see when he looked at her?

Darlene's childhood friend? A homely child who'd worn hand-me-downs to school? A misfit who was unstable?

The evil her father had seen?

Or could he possibly look beyond to see the woman yearning to break free and take her first taste of love?

Love? What did she even know of the concept? The only people she'd ever loved had deserted her. Except her Grammy. And now her grandmother needed care that Violet couldn't provide.

Her feelings for Grady were simple attraction. Normal hormone surges that had been late to bloom. At least they proved she wasn't a cold fish after all, as one college date had called her.

But why now? Why had Grady awakened these dormant feelings and desires when no other man before him had?

Because you're scared and vulnerable. Because he represents one of the few happy childhood memories you have—your childhood crush on him. And your friendship with Darlene.

Although that memory was marred in pain, as well.

And Grady would always see her as part of that pain, especially after her father's confession.

Tomorrow, she'd visit more people in town, learn everything she could about the past. It was the only way she could move on with her life and leave Crow's Landing. Then she would return to Savannah, work in the shop, resume her artwork. Forget Grady.

Her head throbbing, she turned off the bedroom light, crawled into bed and closed her eyes. But darkness surrounded her, bringing with it the eerie sound of the woman's cry, and the sound of the killer blowing through that piece of bone.

A bone whistle.

The same sound she'd heard right after Darlene had died.

GRADY HAD FORCED HIMSELF to go outside and confer with Logan. His libido had taken a roller-coaster ride when he'd heard the shower kick on. For some reason, Violet's big sad eyes had gotten to him tonight. And so had her slender lithe body.

He couldn't afford the distraction.

"Did you ask the neighbors if they saw anything?"

Logan nodded. "Not much luck. Mrs. Corn lives next door. She's almost ninety, has a hearing aid and is just about blind."

"Great."

"Levelle Hubbard on the left side was visiting her great-aunt. I got an earful about her ailments."

Grady chuckled. "I can imagine. She's always in to see Doc Farmer. I think he gives her sugar pills to satisfy her hypochondria."

"The rest of the street was the same. No one heard or saw anything specific." Logan checked his notepad, where he'd jotted down details from the interviews. "Rowdy Paul's thirteen-year-old son avoided eye contact. He might have been in on the vandalism."

"Or hell, maybe he had a stash of cigarettes," Grady said. "Or he'd slipped one of his daddy's beers, and he thought we were onto him."

Logan made a clicking sound. "That's possible. I'll check around town about the paint, but I wouldn't hold my breath."

"Thanks. Maybe we can get a crew out here tomorrow to clean it up."

Logan pinched the bridge of his nose, a habit Grady had noticed him doing a lot. "Taking a personal interest in the Baker woman?"

Grady harrumphed. "No, but those kids might come back. If they do, I'll put a stop to their nonsense."

"I could stay," Logan offered.

Grady shot Logan a warning look. "No, I'll do it. I want to question her more about her father, anyway. See if there's something she remembered that might help confirm Baker's confession."

"Pretty screwed up family, huh?" Logan said in a low voice.

"Yeah." Just like his own. "Violet's father sent her away after my sister was killed," Grady admitted. "I want to know why."

"I heard it was because she was crazy."

Grady gritted his teeth, still uncertain what to make of Violet. He told his deputy he'd see him the next day, then went inside. Knowing he couldn't sleep, not with Violet lying in the neighboring room, he flipped on the news.

"This late breaking report on the *Nashville Nighttime News.*" The camera zeroed in on a reporter outside the local police department. "This is Bernie Morris reporting to you live where police are investigating the murder of a woman found tonight on the steps of a small Baptist church outside of town."

Grady craned his neck and turned up the volume.

"Although police are keeping details to themselves for the moment, early speculations suggest that the woman was killed in the same manner as the young coed from Savannah, Georgia. They're offering little comment, but details suggest that police may be look-ing for a serial killer."

Grady stood, his nerves pinging. He waited for more information, but the reporter claimed the police would issue a statement the following day.

His mind spinning, Grady walked toward Violet's room. At least she'd unlocked the door. He gently eased it open, then stood and stared at her, shifting uncomfort-ably at the sight of her slender body enveloped in the handmade quilt. She looked so innocent lying there, yet so fragile. And sexy. One bare, slender leg had slipped from beneath the quilt. Her long hair was spread across the pillow. Her lips were parted. She looked almost se-ductive and too damn tempting.

But her earlier words raced through his head: *"It's too late. He killed her, just like the woman in Savan-nah."*

He dragged his gaze from her bare feet. Spotted her open sketch pad. Walked over and stared at the outline of a woman's body, a grisly image filled with anguish and darkness.

Bizarre. She'd insisted she'd had a vision on the same night another woman had died. *Before* she had died.

Could it be possible? Could Violet really have seen visions of this murder? And if so, had her connection with Darlene been for real, too?

LOGAN'S HEAD POUNDED as he drove to the old place he'd rented high on top of Black Mountain. He needed some place dark to hide. But it would have looked sus-picious if he'd told the sheriff the truth.

He parked in the thicket of underbrush, then paused and inhaled the fresh night air and sounds of the wild. This property had called to him just as the woods had done lately, arousing natural urges that he sometimes had to fight.

Something was happening to him. Changing him.

It had started years ago. He knew that now. Only he hadn't understood it.

He bypassed the towering old clapboard house and moved toward the woods. The sliver of moonlight was lost in the pines. He removed his shades, grateful for the black emptiness that swallowed him up. A wolf's howl echoed from the recesses of the canyon. Another answered.

He stretched his hands in front of him. Flexed and unflexed them.

He was awed by the power they held. And shocked by what he had done with them.

The hands of death. They belonged to him. They held powers he didn't understand yet. Powers he had to control.

Thankfully, no one in Crow's Landing knew his secrets.

He crawled into the cavern where he slept at night. Water trickled down the sides of the cave. An inky blackness obliterated the light, offering peace. The sounds of the night creatures echoed off the jagged walls. Cool air brushed his body as he undressed.

Then he stretched out on the sleeping bag on the dirt floor and stared up at the rocky ceiling. He had come here for a purpose, and he wouldn't leave until he'd accomplished it.

The ache behind his eyes throbbed harder. A reminder of his secrets.

Secrets that set him apart from the others.

Secrets he must keep hidden forever.

CHAPTER THIRTEEN

VIOLET JERKED AWAKE, her skin tingling, the Best Friends necklace cold against her throat. She'd been dreaming about Grady. Grady lying beside her. Grady touching her. Grady undressing her. His hands gliding along her naked skin. His fingers gently teasing her thighs apart....

Shaken by the images, she slipped on her robe and padded to the kitchen for coffee. Grady was sitting at the table, hovering over his laptop, a serious scowl on his face. His icy look made her tremble.

He'd been kind, almost gentle, when he'd awakened her during the night to see if she had a concussion. But now he was back to stone.

She tightened her robe and reached for a coffee mug. He obviously hadn't dreamed of being with her as she had him. "I wasn't sure you'd still be here."

"I told you I would."

"And you always do what you say?"

He leaned back and ran a hand over his face. Thick dark beard stubble graced his strong jaws. His hair was rumpled, his clothes disheveled. He looked tired. Wary. He probably resented her putting him out of his own bed. "Yeah, I do."

She hesitated. Told her body not to react. Not to remember the warmth of his hands on it. "Then you're the first man I've met who does."

His dark eyebrow rose a notch. "You don't like men?'"

She poured her coffee and added sweetener, realizing she'd walked into that one. "Let's just say I don't trust them."

"Because of your father?"

His voice was low, gruff, almost intimate. But he was fishing for information to incriminate her dad. So she simply shrugged. "Chalk it up to a list of bad experiences."

He gave her a long scrutinizing look, glanced back at his screen, then to her. She circled the table to see what he was researching, but he closed the laptop. Had he been looking at information on her?

Or was she being paranoid?

"We have to talk."

"If you're asking more questions about my father, I don't have any answers."

Sighing, he stood, grabbed himself more coffee, then leaned against the counter. He was so tall he towered over her, his shoulders seeming even more massive this morning in his wrinkled denim shirt. With fatigue lining his face, he should have looked unapproachable, but his brown eyes had turned smoky, sexier even, his unshaved face giving him a renegade appearance. She itched to reach up and dab away the trickle of perspiration on his cheek.

He sipped his coffee, then cleared his throat. "Another woman was murdered last night."

Her breath hitched. The vision resurfaced. Violet swayed, wishing she could sink into his arms and let him banish the images.

But she'd never relied on anyone, and Grady was the wrong one to ask for comfort or favors.

Instead, she claimed one of the wooden chairs. "Just like the woman in Savannah."

"The newscaster said the M.O. is similar."

"My God." Violet dropped her head forward, cradling it between her hands. "I hoped I was wrong."

He didn't comment. He simply let the tension mount between them until she finally looked up at him.

"You don't believe me?"

"I don't know what to believe."

That was fair enough, but his comment still hurt. "What was her name?"

"Connie Allen. She was twenty-five, just graduated from Vanderbilt. Planned to get married next week." He hesitated. "I saw those drawings you did."

Violet jerked her gaze to his. Did he think she was sick for putting those ugly images on paper?

It didn't matter. The poor girl. She was just like Amber. She was young, had her entire life ahead of her. "Who would do such a horrible thing?"

"I was hoping you could tell me. Since you supposedly connected with this woman, didn't she tell you who'd kidnapped her?"

"It doesn't work that way."

"Then how does it work?"

"I really don't know, Grady. This whole psychic thing is all new to me." Anger, confusion and a fierce need to make him believe her hardened her words. "I didn't ask for this to happen. And other than Darlene, it never has before." She paced across to the window, stared at the big yard where she and her friend used to play. She could almost hear the creak of the old swing.

"I wish to heaven it wasn't happening now. I have enough to worry about with my grandmother in the nursing home and my dead father accused of murder."

He sipped his coffee, his intense perusal unnerving her more.

"If you think I want to see these women die, to hear them cry out for help and know I can't do anything, you're wrong." She wrung her hands. "Darlene and I were friends—I could maybe understand that connection. But I didn't know these other women."

Another long silence stretched between them. "Why do you think you're connecting with them then?" he finally asked.

"I have no idea. Laney said it's a gift, but how can it be if I can't use it to stop the murders?" The pure desolation she'd felt the night she and her grandmother had fled Crow's Landing haunted her. "Do you have any idea how much I wanted to find your sister? How much I loved her?"

Emotions choked her, and she swung away from Grady, unable to allow him to see her pain. Seconds later, she felt his hands stroke her arms. Then he turned her to face him.

"I know you loved her," he said, his voice gruff. "That's why we have to make sure her killer pays. No matter who it is."

Violet nodded, seeing that the emotions in his eyes were as tumultuous as her own.

"My father thought my vision was evil. That I was evil."

"No, Violet." Grady's voice softened. "There's nothing evil about you." He pulled her against him. She leaned her head on his shoulder for the briefest of moments, savoring the feel of his comforting arms around her. He stroked her hair, and she breathed in his scent, remembering the thirteen-year-old boy who'd played marbles with Darlene. The teenager Violet had had a crush on. Now a virile man. She wanted to stay in Grady's arms forever.

But in her heart, she knew that they were still at odds. He wanted to pin the crime on her father, and she didn't want to believe her dad was a murderer.

Today, she had to find some evidence to prove Grady wrong. And figure out who was killing these women.

IT WAS WRONG to get too close to Violet, but Grady hadn't been able to resist pulling her into his arms. She seemed so lost, so upset over his sister's death, that childhood memories suffused him. Her and Darlene skipping rope under the sweet gum tree. The two of them playing dress-up. How they followed him out to the pond where he used to go fishing. The stubborn way Violet fought back against the bullies who'd teased her about being white trash.

She wasn't white trash, couldn't help being part of the family she'd been born to any more than he could.

Were Violet's so-called visions real? Or had she invented them because she was ill, or to divert attention from her father?

Grady pulled back slightly, studying her big blue eyes, trying to find sanity. He wished like hell he wasn't so drawn to her. But the way she trembled in his arms made him feel alive for the first time in forever.

"Tell me everything you saw and heard in this vision."

Her eyes widened. Then she glanced down at her

hands. She'd been clinging to his shirt, but she slowly eased out of his arms. He missed the contact immediately. Felt the heat try to draw him back.

And told himself not to give in to it.

Hell, maybe she'd trip up, and he'd catch her lying.

Instead of reaching for her, he removed a pad from his pocket, ready to take notes. Anything to occupy his hands.

She tucked a strand of her unruly hair behind one delicate ear. "Both times, I heard the woman whispering, 'Help me.' It's like I'm looking through their eyes, feeling their fear. They were so afraid, Grady. They were both aware they were going to die." Her voice broke, and she took a deep breath to settle her emotions. "And they couldn't move to stop him."

"He tied them up?"

"Yes. He drugged them, too."

Grady jotted down her description. "What does he look like?"

"I can't see his face, but he's pacing. He was holding a hypodermic needle. He injected the woman with something, then carried her someplace dark and left her for a while."

"He returned later?"

"Yes, around midnight. That's when he k-killed her."

"How does he do it?"

"He strangles them," she said, her voice a throaty whisper. She stared out the window now, her expression faraway. "But first he bathes them as if he's performing some kind of cleansing ceremony, then he wraps them in a sheet."

Grady stifled a reaction. The sheet matched the description he'd read on the police report, but she could have guessed that. "Can you hear anything in the background that might indicate where they are? A railroad train, cars, a boat?"

She shook her head. "No, I don't think so."

"Does he talk to the victims?"

Violet's gaze swung back to him. "Yes. He speaks in a singsongy kind of whisper. Then he murmurs a Native American phrase."

Grady frowned, his attention piqued. In the police report he'd just read, they'd mentioned a phrase the killer left in a note. That information hadn't been made public yet. How could Violet know? "What is the expression?"

"He writes the phrase on a piece of paper and adds, 'For the father.' Then he plays this whistle he's carved from bone and tells them it's the song that tells the story of sacrifice." Violet shivered, the sound echoing in her mind. "It's so eerie, then he says, '*Pin peyeh obe*, my sweetness, you must die.'"

"*Pin peyeh obe?*" Grady scratched his chin. It was the same expression as in the police report. Although they hadn't mentioned anything about a whistle carved from bone. An image of his father's whittling came to mind. No, the idea was crazy…his father wasn't a killer. "Do you know what the expression means?"

Violet nodded. "I asked Laney Longhorse."

"You told her about this?"

"Yes, I had to know the meaning."

"And what did she say?"

"It means look to the mountain." Violet rubbed her arms to ward off the cold. "From a mountaintop, you can see things in a broader perspective. You must look at the future and generations to come."

Grady tried to make sense of the phrase in the context of a murder, but he couldn't grasp the relevance. Still, how had Violet known the killer had used that expression?

Should he go to the FBI and tell them what she'd seen?

Yeah, right. They'd think *he* was crazy. Besides, she hadn't really seen anything specific enough to be helpful. If the visions were real, why was she connecting to the victims?

Did she know the killer personally?

"ALL EVIDENCE POINTS to the fact that we're dealing with a serial killer." Special Agent Norton passed out identical files to the members of the recently formed task force seated around the conference table. The chief of police in Nashville had joined the group, along with two detectives from the Nashville PD, two locals from Savannah who'd flown in for consultation and a profiler from the agency. They all were going to work together to find this maniac—if, indeed, they established that they were dealing with a serial killer.

He gave each member time to review the details in the files. "So far, we haven't found a connection between these two women, but I have agents exploring that now." He turned to the Savannah police officer, Barton. "Do you have any leads on the Collins woman's murderer?"

Barton shook his balding head. "So far, the boyfriend's story checks out. He appeared genuinely distraught over her death. The vic was five-five, light blond hair, green eyes, last seen by her roommate leaving her dorm room the evening she went missing. Unfortunately, we have no real clues. She was well-liked, friendly, faithful to her boyfriend, even attended church." He made a disgusted sound. "Not an enemy in the world."

"She had one," his partner said.

"Unless he's choosing his victims at random," Chief Humberstone suggested.

Nick nodded. "It's possible."

The profiler, Special Agent Adams, cleared her throat. "It is, but let's keep searching for the connection. Usually these guys have a method behind the madness. This guy has taken the time to bathe the vics and wrap them in a sheet—that indicates a more personal connection, or at least that he's conflicted about what he's doing."

"Conflicted means he's emotional?"

"It means he's trying to protect or preserve them for someone, even if he hates them himself."

"Interesting." Nick chewed over the information. "How about the second victim?"

"Connie Allen," Special Agent Adams said. "Five-seven, brown hair, blue eyes, graduated from Vanderbilt with a degree in international studies, engaged to be married next week."

"The fiancé?" Nick asked.

"Completely devastated," Chief Humberstone said. "Had to give the poor guy a tranquilizer."

Norton frowned. "He's not faking it?"

"I've seen a lot of fakes. This guy's the real thing. And he has an alibi—he was in Atlanta on business."

Norton nodded. This wasn't going to be easy. "Still, check out his relationships with the family, see if he has any priors, other girlfriends who might tell a different story."

"Will do."

"My agents are checking out other possible connections, everything from Internet chat groups the women had visited to health clubs, vacation spots and family members." Norton turned to Special Agent Adams. He'd heard she was good, but hadn't realized how attractive.

Shit, he needed a damn woman like her distracting him. She was a do-gooder who believed in all that behavioral crap. And she was married at that. But she messed with his libido, made him want to forget his own personal problems and the ugliness of the case and crawl between the sheets with her. Not that she was interested, or that he would encroach on another man's territory, even if the couple was having problems...

Besides, he had his own dark secrets, reasons he couldn't get involved, reasons a relationship would never work.

"Agent Adams, do you have anything to add?"

She crossed her legs, and every man in the room eyeballed her. "Have we discovered anything missing from the victims yet, something the killer might be taking as his treasure?"

"Nothing with the Collins woman," one of the Savannah officers stated.

"Not on the second vic, either," the detective said. "She was wearing a hunk of an engagement ring, but he didn't even bother to take it."

"Keep looking," Nick said. "These guys almost always keep some kind of trophy."

"Have you worked up a profile yet?" the chief asked.

"I'll need more time to do a complete one," Agent Adams said, "but my preliminary analysis suggests our guy's in his mid-twenties, maybe early thirties, probably Caucasian, although the Native American phrase indicates he might have an ethnic background. Either that or he's obsessed with Native American rituals. He's also a religious fanatic or one of his parents was. It's possible he might have studied religion, as well." She indicated the picture of the bone found beside the victim. "This whistle looks like it was carved from a crow's bone. If my memory proves correct, historically the bone whistle was used in religious ceremonies. Native men were practically tortured—"

"The sun dance," Norton said. "I thought those ceremonies were banned years ago."

Adams shrugged. "You think our killer adheres to the rules?"

He shook his head, his stomach churning. The dance had been so violent that it had been eliminated, although some natives had continued to practice behind closed doors. If this guy belonged to some cult practicing that ritual, they had a real sicko on their hands.

"Anything else, Adams?"

She shrugged. "Just that he's a hunter. We may not know how or why he's choosing his victims, but he has a purpose. He's methodical, maybe psychotic or obsessive-compulsive. He could be on meds, but he's not taking them. And he derives great pleasure from the hunt."

Norton smiled, his natural competitiveness kicking in. "Then let's turn things around. We'll let him become the hunted."

AAH, THE THRILL of the hunt…

Joseph Longhorse believed in the rituals of his forefathers. He had completed the necessary hunt, made the sacrifices required, then entered the sweat house he had built years ago. Even though he'd scrubbed his hands, he could still smell the blood on his skin.

When he was a boy, he had been given the special privilege of being admitted to the *asi* on occasion to tend the fire. There he had listened to the stories and learned of the secret rites of his people. Following tradition, he built the fire, then placed a flat rock in front of it—and near it, a pile of pine knots. When the fire burned down to a bed of coals, he lit two of the pine knots and laid them on the others in a crosswise pattern. They blazed a light that shone bright in the darkness. He fed it until daybreak.

Weak but rejuvenated, he left the camp at dawn and walked through the mountains, inhaling the fresh air and scents of nature that aroused his primal being. As he made his way back down to his mother's home, he gathered herbs and berries to add to the growing mounds she used in her special teas and medicines.

In spite of the prejudices still harbored by some toward his people, knowing his mother had her own rituals and passed her stories down to the children in town cemented his closeness to his roots. A man could never forget from where he came.

His path had been chosen for him before his birth. Joseph did not intend to stray from it. No matter what it cost him.

He thought of Violet Baker's return to town and wondered, though…how would the people in town react to her now? Had their prejudices against her died, or were they still as alive as the ones that festered toward him?

Her father's confession would make it even more difficult for her in Crow's Landing. Some people forgave easily. Others never did.

She would need a friend.

Maybe his path had taken a detour…a fork in the road that he had not foreseen.

Yes, Violet needed a friend. They had connected long ago as children. She did not see him as the shunned one as some did. She saw him as an equal. He would go to her now. Offer his friendship, his shoulder.

He inhaled deeply. The hunt had revived him, temporarily satisfied his need for blood and vengeance. It had restored his calm.

Until the hunt called him again…

HOW COULD VIOLET have known about the native phrase? Grady wondered. Was there a piece of bone left beside each victim?

Grady's cell phone rang and he answered it, grateful for the reprieve. He was getting way too caught up in Violet Baker. "Sheriff Monroe."

"Sheriff, it's Logan. First off, the writing sample matches Baker's confession. Second, the M.E. phoned…the autopsy report on Baker is ready."

Grady grimaced, hating to have to tell Violet. "Is he going to fax it to the office?" Grady asked.

"Yes, but he wants to see you in person."

Had he found something suspicious? "Okay, I'll swing by his office now." He hung up and turned back to Violet, deciding to wait until after he'd spoken with the M.E. before divulging that the confession was real. "I have to go. The coroner completed your father's autopsy. He'll probably release him, so you can start planning his funeral if you want."

Her face paled. "All right, but I want to see the autopsy report."

"Violet—"

"I have a right to know exactly how he died," she said, her voice stronger. "Please don't deny me this, Grady."

In spite of his own reservations, her soft plea got to him. He gestured toward her robe.

"Then go get dressed. I want to talk to him as soon as possible."

She nodded and rushed to her bedroom. He tried not to imagine her peeling off that robe, but an image of her creamy pale skin glowing in the early morning light came to him unbidden, anyway. Her hair was such an unusual russet color. What color would her nipples be? Coral? Darker?

Dammit. He banished the image, poured himself more coffee and paced across the room. Sweat trickled down his cheeks, the heat ignited by Violet adding to the temperature. Outside it was already close to ninety.

He hoped the coroner had discovered something that would corroborate Baker's suicide note and confirm he was Darlene's killer. Yet Grady couldn't help wondering how Violet would react if he did confirm her father was a murderer. Would she be able to cope with the knowledge that her dad had killed Darlene, especially when Violet seemed to be struggling with guilt over these other women's deaths?

And what about those women? He wasn't a shrink, but he refused to rule out the possibility that Violet had created these visions out of guilt over their deaths and Darlene's murder....

Violet stared out the window as they drove to the coroner's office, the silence between her and Grady a staunch reminder that they were both hoping for different outcomes to the autopsy report. An image of her father's face had been frozen in her mind since he had thrust her into the old station wagon and sent her away.

Seeing him again, now in death, would be a harsh reality that she wasn't ready to face. When he'd been alive, she'd held on to hope that one day they might be a family again, that one day he'd love her and forgive her for bringing this so-called evil into their lives.

But now...

Grady parked in front of the office, killed the engine, then slanted his gaze toward her. "Are you sure you want to do this?"

"I have to," she said, attempting a brave voice.

Looking resigned, he nodded and climbed out. She didn't wait for him to come around, but opened the door and pushed herself up from the car, willing her legs to be steady. A few minutes later, they were seated in an outer office.

"Miss Baker?" Dr. Robert Claven, the medical examiner, seemed startled to see her.

"Yes." She shook his hand, aware that the tension had just cranked up another notch, adding to the cloying heat in the already stifling quarters.

He offered her a tight smile, then turned to Grady. "You want to come back to the morgue?"

Grady nodded.

Violet started to follow.

"Miss Baker, maybe you should stay here," the doctor said. "At least for now."

"But—"

"Let me talk to him first," Grady said. "Then if you want to see your father, we'll arrange it."

"I want to know what's in the report," Violet said.

Grady and Claven exchanged concerned looks, then Grady nodded. "I'll share it with you after we go over it," Grady said.

"You'll tell me the truth?"

"Yes." His voice dropped. "You haven't seen your dad in years, though, Violet. You don't need to see him like this, not on the morgue table."

The image that passed before her eyes was gruesome. "All right." She sank into one of the hard chairs in the outer office. She just prayed Grady told her the truth, not the abridged version. And if she sensed he hadn't, she'd force herself to read the report.

She'd just have to brace herself for whatever it held.

"OKAY, DOC, what's going on?" Grady approached Baker's body with trepidation. The acrid smells of death assaulted him, amplified by the chemicals Claven had used in the autopsy and the stench of removed body parts. Harsh lights accentuated the older man's ghostly face and the bluish tint to his skin.

It was better Violet hadn't seen this. It nearly turned Grady's stomach every time he went through it.

"Tox screenings proved Baker was inebriated."

"That's no surprise." After all, Grady had seen him drinking earlier that evening, when he'd been arguing with his own father.

"And you were right. The contusion on the back of his head didn't come from the fall off the cliff."

"How can you tell?"

"The angle of the wound and the position of the body on the ledge." He shifted the corpse, pointed to the knot on Baker's head. "This was caused by some kind of blunt trauma to the head, an object maybe."

"Like a rock?"

Claven shrugged. "Or maybe an ashtray or a household object. The blow to the head was what killed him, not the fall." Claven crossed his arms. "In fact, he didn't die up on Briar Ridge. He was moved there afterward."

Grady's stomach knotted. "What are you saying?"

Claven frowned and tugged the sheet lower to reveal bruises on Baker's chest. Maybe defensive wounds. "The bottom line—in my opinion, Baker didn't commit suicide, Sheriff. He was murdered."

CHAPTER FOURTEEN

THE MINUTE VIOLET SAW GRADY emerge from the morgue, she sensed something was wrong. He avoided her gaze, speaking in hushed tones to the coroner. She rose, determined to get some answers, no matter what they were.

"Grady?"

He gestured for her to wait, then shook the doctor's hand. "Thanks, Dr. Claven."

"I'll have your father moved to the funeral home, Miss Baker. Then you can see him."

She nodded and waited for Grady to join her. Claven fled back to his office, and Grady approached her.

"What happened?" she asked.

He hesitated, then cleared his throat. "First, the confession note was in your father's handwriting."

Violet staggered back. "But Claven's report says that your father didn't commit suicide."

"What? I don't understand."

"He died of blunt trauma to the head."

She gasped. "You mean someone forced him to write the note, then murdered him?"

Grady nodded, his expression dark. "It appears that way. Claven thinks he was moved to Briar Ridge after his death."

"Then someone pushed him over the ridge to make it look like he committed suicide." Violet pressed a shaky hand to her mouth. "But why would someone kill my father?"

"I don't know," Grady said. "But I intend to find out."

He started toward the door, but Violet grabbed his arm, heat flooding through her at the touch. "You know what this means? If the suicide note was a phony, then the confession might have been, too."

Grady's anguished expression indicated he'd already considered the possibility. He didn't like it, but he had thought of it. "And if he didn't kill her," Violet said, "that means the real murderer is still out there."

She remembered the eerie sound of the bone whistle following the women's murders, the same sound she'd heard years ago when Darlene had lost her life.

Could the killer possibly be the same man? And even if he was, did he have anything to do with her father's death?

GRADY NEEDED AIR. He didn't like Violet's assumption, but he couldn't dismiss it. Darlene's killer could still be out there.

Damn. A week ago, Crow's Landing had seemed like a safe, sleepy little town. The only hint of violence had been the lingering memories of his sister's brutal murder twenty years ago. But now he had another crime to solve. He didn't like the number of suspects that instantly came to mind in Jed Baker's murder.

His father topped the list.

Darlene's killer was also a possibility, although Grady couldn't fathom why he'd kill Baker. Unless

Baker had known something he wasn't telling. Yet why wait twenty years to off him?

Maybe Baker knew who the serial killer was. Maybe it was someone in town....

His father and Baker's fight returned to nag Grady. They'd both been worried about secrets being revealed. Had someone shut Baker up so he wouldn't spill them?

If so, who? What the hell had his father been involved in?

Maybe Walt and Jed had somehow figured out who'd killed Darlene, but why wouldn't they have told the police?

There were too many unanswered questions.

And only one way to find out—confront his dad again.

Grady stalked outside. Violet followed, not speaking until they'd settled into the car. He started the engine and headed back toward her house. He'd go by the station next, and afterward, talk to his old man.

"Tell me everything you remember about Darlene's disappearance," he said.

Violet pressed a finger to her temple, fatigue lining her features. He'd forgotten about her car accident.

"Are you all right?" he added.

"Yes." She dropped her hand to her lap and wrapped a fold of her skirt in her fingers. "It was my birthday," she said in a small voice. "I was so excited because I'd gotten this new stuffed bear."

She paused. His insides twisted again as he imagined that little girl. Violet had had so few possessions she would have been ecstatic over a present.

"All I could think of was that I wanted Darlene to see it. I...I wanted her to come over." Her voice trailed off with a quiver. "I didn't think about her safety, though. I was so selfish."

He grimaced at the catch in her voice, and slid his hand over hers. "You were just a child, Violet. You don't have to explain that or blame yourself. If it was anyone's fault, it was mine."

"No, Grady."

"Yes." He cleared his throat. "I was supposed to come home and watch her that day. But I stopped to goof off with the boys."

She squeezed his fingers. "You were just a kid, too, Grady. You didn't know."

But I was responsible. He shook inside, unable to discuss it. "What else happened?"

Violet sighed, emotions rattling out. "When she didn't get to the house, I called again, but there was no answer. I kept calling and calling…."

"He must have kidnapped her in the field between your place and ours. He might have even followed her when she left our house." Grady's mind ticked back to his original suspects. Dwayne Dobbins had worked for his father, tending his lawn. Even if Dobbins's mother had known, she'd cover up for him. And Ross Wheeler had been a young man then. If the allegations against him were true, Ross could have abducted her.

Violet shuddered. "She was so scared. I could feel it."

He swallowed, then steered the car down Pine Needle Drive. "Do you think it was someone Darlene knew?"

Violet closed her eyes as if trying to see the images again. "I…I don't know."

"When did you connect with Darlene?"

"We always seemed to sense things about each other. When she was sad or mad, I knew it. And when I was upset with Dad, she'd just automatically call. I can't explain it. But it was nothing like that night," she said softly.

"You didn't realize when she was first abducted?"

She shook her head. "I don't know why, but I wish I had." She released a shaky breath. "Maybe we could have reached her in time."

Did he really want to pursue this line of questioning? Having two unsolved murders was taxing enough, but dealing with Violet and her so-called visions... "What else do you remember?"

"I heard her crying. She kept whispering for me to help her, that some man had her." Violet clenched his hand in a death grip. "She was so cold, Grady. It was dark and I could hear water dripping...it was raining. But I didn't know where to look."

Yes, it had been raining that night. He'd watched the droplets splatter the car windshield as he and his father had driven the streets in town, searching for Darlene. The rain had reminded him of big fat teardrops, the ones stuck in his throat. He'd been so scared himself, had felt sick to his stomach because he should have been home to watch his little sister. But he'd tried not to show his emotions. His father hated it when he did. Had even backhanded him once for crying.

His mouth was dry. "Did you hear the voice of the man who kidnapped her?"

"No. I just heard Darlene crying. She wanted her mommy." Violet paused, brushed at a tear that rolled down her cheek. "But she knew her mother was gone. And she was trying not to cry. He slapped her when she did."

A muscle ticked in Grady's jaw. "Did you see his face at all?"

"No."

"And he didn't say anything?"

She shook her head. "No…but I heard a sound. At first I thought it was a harmonica."

"He was playing an instrument?"

"No, I think he was blowing through a whistle."

His gaze shot to hers. "What?"

Her eyes widened, looked frightened. "I'm almost sure it was the same sound that I heard after that woman died. It was so eerie," she whispered, "it sounded like breath against bone. Maybe some kind of whistle made from bone."

Grady tensed. Dear God, it couldn't be. Was it possible the serial killer who had just struck in Savannah and Nashville was the same man who'd killed his sister?

But the latest victims were women, not children. Why would the killer have changed his M.O.? No, it had to be a copycat, someone who knew about Darlene's murder and wanted to throw off the cops.

But what if it was the same man? Why had he waited so long between murders? Where had he been for the past twenty years?

WHEN GRADY PULLED INTO Violet's driveway, the ugly graffiti mocked her, reminding her of the way the kids had taunted her as a child. Her car was there, too. It had a dented front fender, but at least she would have transportation without having to rely on Grady. She had been doing too much of that already today.

Grady angled his head toward her as he parked. "Will you be all right?"

She nodded. "What are you going to do now?"

"Go to the station and check out some lab reports I'd requested."

"You think my father might be innocent?"

He gave a noncommittal shrug.

"You knew him better than I did, Grady. You saw him around town. Did he have any enemies?"

He hesitated, averted his gaze and stared at his hands, which he'd wrapped around the steering wheel. "He kept to himself," he said quietly. "But he'd been drinking a lot the last few years."

"Didn't he have *any* friends?"

Grady shrugged. "I didn't keep tabs on him, Violet."

She reached for the door handle, wondering why he was being so evasive. Or was he just angry because his tidy case against her father was no longer neat?

She clutched his arm, not quite ready to be alone again. "You'll let me know what you find out?"

He slowly turned to search her face, the memories of Darlene a lifeline between them. Their eyes connected. Emotions, heat, the need for comfort rippled between them. And there was more, that simmering, burning chemistry that drew her to him like a moth to a flame. But if she gave in to this need, she might never let him go.

"I'll let you know," he said gruffly.

"Thanks." She climbed out and walked up the path to her father's old house, contemplating what she would do with it when she returned to Savannah. The mere thought brought a small surge of relief, but also a pang of sadness. She would never see Grady again. Never have a chance to experience the hunger that she saw in his eyes.

More lonely than ever, she opened the door and went inside. Knowing her father hadn't killed himself would offer a small measure of comfort to her grandmother. But Violet couldn't relay the news that he'd been murdered without upsetting her, too.

She'd hold off a little longer. Until Grady had found out who had killed him.

This afternoon, she had to plan a funeral. Maybe someone at the funeral home would know something more about her dad.

GRADY ENTERED THE STATION a few minutes later. The blinds were closed, and his deputy was sitting in the shadows.

Logan glanced up from the telephone, then ended the conversation. "Yeah, I'll make sure someone's there for extra security."

"What was that all about?"

"TV crew's going to be here to tape the tent revival tonight, that televangelist Billy Lee Bilkins." He frowned. "They're worried folks may be so excited they'll get out of hand."

"That guy puts on a show, all right. I imagine he'll draw a crowd."

"He's a damn lunatic, if you ask me," Logan said. "Those televangelists just con people out of money."

Grady agreed halfheartedly, although the deputy seemed a little adamant, even moodier than usual.

"What did the M.E. say about Baker?" Logan asked.

Grady dropped the file in front of him. "Baker didn't kill himself. He was murdered. Most likely at home, then he was dumped at Briar Ridge to make it look like a suicide."

"You're kidding!"

"I wish to hell I was."

Logan skimmed the contents. Seconds later, he cocked his head. "Do you have any idea who the perp is?"

"Not yet." The only person he could think of was his old man. And Grady wasn't ready to share that information.

Logan stood. "You could ask his daughter. Isn't she supposed to be psychic or something?"

Grady didn't know what to believe anymore. "She claims she doesn't know anything about her father."

"But she had some weird connection to your sister?"

"That's what she says." And dammit, after today, he was beginning to think it might be possible.

The phone rang, and Logan snagged it. Angling away from Grady, he lowered his voice. Seconds later, he stalked to the back room, looking sullen. What was eating at him? Grady had half a mind to follow and ask him, but the work on his desk took priority over Logan's foul temper.

He turned his attention to the Fed Ex folder—the lab reports he'd requested. He'd had the coroner take hand prints from Baker so they could compare them to the marks found on Darlene's neck. It was a long shot but it might prove something. He opened the envelope and removed the contents, then read the report. Baker's hands were all wrong. Granted, it had been twenty years, but the man's size hadn't changed much.

Which meant he hadn't killed Darlene.

Back to square one.

Logan stormed back in, took his seat and shredded a pencil in the sharpener. Remembering Violet's comment about the bone whistle, Grady searched the file on Darlene's murder but saw no mention of a piece of bone beside her body. There also had been no note, which, so far, was a trademark for this new serial killer. And Darlene had been found at the bottom of a well, not on the steps of a church.

But still, Violet seemed so sure about that bone whistle. Perhaps the rescue team had missed something. Maybe there had been a piece of bone but they hadn't recognized it as anything significant. After all, the incompetent Tate had been in charge of the case. Or it could still be there.

No, Grady was grasping. And after twenty years, the bone would probably have disintegrated or been buried so deep in the muddy bottom of the well, they'd never find it or be able to trace it back to Darlene. He checked the crime scene photos again, but didn't spot the bone sliver.

Frustrated, he booted up the computer, then accessed the police database to see if anything new had been posted about the serial killings, or if any recent murders might have occurred similar to Baker's. The FBI profiler had posted an initial report, so he skimmed it, the Native American phrase and religious implications troubling him. Wheeler and his father instantly came to mind, and then Reverend Billy Lee Bilkins. Hmm. Any woman would trust them if they approached.

A lot of Tennessee communities had Native American residents. Crow's Landing certainly had a few of its own. The Longhorse family, for one.

Joseph. The man had always seemed intense, angry, bitter toward the Caucasians. Not that he hadn't had a right. In fact, he'd hated Grady growing up, although Grady hadn't understood the reason. He assumed it was because he was from the wealthy side of the tracks, that Joseph associated Grady with the other snobby kids who'd teased him. Had he hated Darlene back then? Had she somehow shunned him and made him angry enough to kill her?

"Pin peyeh obe," Grady murmured, thinking about the phrase.

"Look toward the mountain," Logan said.

He snapped his head around. "What?" He hadn't realized he'd spoken aloud. "How do you know what it means?"

Logan shrugged, not quite meeting his eyes. "My great-great-grandfather was part Cherokee," he admitted.

Grady studied Logan's features. Now that he looked, he could see traces of a Native American heritage. Logan was dark-skinned. He had high cheekbones. Dark eyes.

Logan chuckled without humor. "In fact, my old man named me Logan because it means friend of the white man."

Grady's mind cataloged the knowledge. Logan had been in trouble before, but his records were sealed. He seemed particularly antagonistic about the televangelist. And he had secrets. Maybe Grady needed to find out more about his deputy and his past.

He'd definitely check out Joseph Longhorse, too. Then he'd question Mayor Tate and see what he remembered about Darlene's case.

After that, he'd confront his father.

NERVOUS ADRENALINE HAD kicked in, after Violet visited the funeral home and chose her father's casket, so she went home and cleaned her father's house from top to bottom. She'd even gone to the dollar store, found slipcovers for the furniture and bought a new set of kitchen curtains. Anything to liven up the place. She'd have to ask her grandmother what she wanted to do with it. Maybe they'd sell it.

The low hum of elevator music drifted toward her as she reentered the funeral home later. Moving on shaky legs toward the room where her father lay, she tried to prepare herself. She'd imagined seeing her father a million times over the years, but a raw ache clawed her insides at the sight of him stretched out in the casket.

His brown hair had thinned, his skin had turned a yellowish tint—probably from drinking too much—and wrinkles had softened his angular jaw. Age spots marred the once smooth surface of his crossed hands. When she hadn't found a suit in the closet, the funeral director had offered to have the church send one over.

"He looks at peace now," Melvin Pearce, the funeral director, said as he moved up beside her. "Finally at peace."

Maybe he was, but she certainly wasn't. How could he have died and left things unresolved between them? Why had he never contacted her? Tears pricked her eyelids, but she blinked to stem them. She refused to cry over a man who'd virtually abandoned her.

But she was helpless to stop the memories from bombarding her. When she was four, washing her father's old pickup truck together. Having a battle with the water hose. When she was six, sitting on his lap. He'd never been one to listen to music, but he'd loved one particular song back then. What was it called? "The Men in My Little Girl's Life." He'd hugged her and she'd thought he'd always be the only man in her life….

Then she'd met Darlene and their friendship had changed everything.

"Why do you say he's finally at peace?" Violet asked. "Did you know my father well?"

"Not well," Pearce admitted. "But anyone could see he was miserable. Turned to the bottle after you and your granny left."

"He sent us away," Violet said, the pain cutting through her again. "And he never tried to see me again."

Pearce's balding head reddened. "I'm sorry, I thought it was the other way around."

Violet dragged her eyes from her father's face and stared at him. On her tenth birthday, a day she refused to have a party or celebrate, she had shown her work in her first art show. She hadn't cared if she'd won or not. She'd just hoped her father would come to see her pictures.

He hadn't.

She'd vowed then to forget her art. To forget him. But her art was therapeutic, and eventually she'd picked up a paintbrush, charcoal and a sketch pad.

"Is that what he told people?" Violet asked. "That my grandmother and I didn't want to come back?"

"No…it's just that he seemed so lonely all the time. I assumed your grandmother wanted you away from your father's drinking."

Footsteps sounded behind them. "There's Reverend Wheeler now." Mr. Pearce went to meet him, then ushered him over and introduced him. The preacher was in his late fifties, with thick, curly dark hair. A younger man who resembled him stood beside him. His son, Ross. A faint memory surfaced—Ross had been nearer Grady's age. She hadn't liked him when she was little.

She didn't think she did now, although she had no real reason for her snap judgment.

"Do you have anything special you'd like me to say or incorporate into the service?" Reverend Wheeler asked.

"Not really." Violet backed away, wanting to escape both men's presence. Reverend Wheeler's scrutinizing gaze made her uneasy. And his son's intense look was even more nerve-racking.

"Just something simple," she said. "Maybe a song or two."

"Do you know your father's favorite hymn?"

The question took Violet off guard. She didn't know anything about her father, not even if he'd attended church. "No, just pick something. I...I have to go."

She turned and fled, Ross Wheeler's probing look trailing after her. Something about the man was eerie. Maybe even evil.

But how would she know? Unless she was evil, too, just like her father had said.

"What can I do for you, Sheriff?"

Grady ignored the sardonic edge to Mayor Tate's voice. It was no secret the two men didn't like each other.

"I just came from the M.E.'s office. Jed Baker didn't commit suicide—he was murdered."

Tate's normally calm demeanor shifted slightly, for the briefest second. "And what does that have to do with me?"

"Nothing really. But I have reason to suspect his

murder might be related to my sister's death twenty years ago."

Tate pulled at his chubby chin. "He left a confession, right?"

"There was a note, but if the suicide note was a fake, the confession might be, too."

Tate frowned. "Looks like you'd want to let that case die."

"I do," Grady snapped. "But I want the real killer to pay."

"Listen, Monroe, I did everything I could back then to find your sister's killer. Your daddy knows that."

"I'm not saying you didn't. Just indulge me."

Tate drummed his fingers on his desk, which was piled a mile high with papers. "All right. What do you want to know?"

"You questioned Baker about Darlene's disappearance?"

"He had an alibi—it's in the report."

"Was there anything that indicated he might have been lying?"

Tate scrunched his mouth in thought. "The fact that he kept telling us places to look made me wonder, but Whitey Simms was a good man. There's no way he'd lie or cover up for a child killer."

"You questioned Dwayne Dobbins and his mother?"

"She swore her boy was with her all night. I never could prove no different."

But Mavis Dobbins would lie to protect her son, and they both knew it. "How about Ross Wheeler?"

Tate frowned. "He was a teenager then. We didn't question him, although the reverend joined in the search."

Grady contemplated that information. "Was he involved with the search the entire time?"

Tate hesitated, as if thinking back. "No, he came after the revival ended that night. Led the town members in a prayer."

"Did you find anything at the scene that seemed out of the ordinary?"

"Hell, boy, the whole damn thing was out of the ordinary. It was the only murder we'd ever had."

And Grady had been haunted by it since. He reached inside his pocket, craving a cigarette so bad his mouth watered. "I know, but think back. The killer didn't leave a note, a souvenir of some kind?"

Tate snapped his fingers. "The only thing we found was a sliver of bone in Darlene's hand. We figured she picked it up when she was trying to claw her way out of the well."

Grady's blood ran cold. He forgot the cigarette. Darlene had been found holding a sliver of bone just like these recent victims? Maybe the killer had put it there. "Did you keep the piece of bone?"

"You'll have to ask your daddy. He was the one who found it."

CHAPTER FIFTEEN

VIOLET TOLD HERSELF she was being paranoid about Ross Wheeler, but the man had unsettled her just as Donald Irving, the man she'd briefly dated in Charleston, had. She considered driving over and seeing Laney again, but decided to call and check on her grandmother instead, then drop by Lloyd Driver's office. The lawyer had left a message that she should come for the reading of her father's will.

She dialed the nursing home and spoke to a nurse. "How is she today?"

"Resting," the woman assured her. "And she's beginning to regain mobility in her right arm."

"How about her speech?"

"It hasn't returned yet, but don't let that upset you. It takes time for stroke patients to heal. We can't push her too hard."

"I know." Violet felt suddenly bereft and very much alone. Tomorrow she would bury her father; she couldn't lose her grandmother, too. "Please tell her that I called, that I love her. I'll try to get over to see her next week."

The nurse assured her she would, and Violet hung up. Maybe by next week she'd know something more definitive.

She drove past the Redbud Café, then into the town square and checked the addresses. Five minutes later, she was seated in Driver's office. He was middle-aged, his face parched by the sun, his hair almost completely white. He shook her hand and introduced himself, then got straight to business.

"The will is pretty self-explanatory, Miss Baker," he began. He skimmed through the opening paragraphs, then hit the highlights. "Your father left the house to your grandmother."

"Good." Although the place needed some work, at least he hadn't forgotten his own mother. "Did you know my father well, Mr. Driver?"

"I'm afraid not. We ran in different circles."

Right. The price of his suit indicated that.

"He drew this document up years ago." He scratched his neck, almost apologetic. "Unfortunately, he didn't have any investments, not even a checking or savings account, so there's nothing else there."

She wasn't surprised. But as she returned to the house, she contemplated the fact that her father hadn't kept a checking account. Had he kept cash in the house? Hidden somewhere, maybe? If so, she could give it to her grandmother.

Earlier, when she'd been searching for a burial suit, she'd noticed a small metal box in his closet. Curious now, she went to the bedroom, took it off the shelf and noticed the lock had been broken. Probably by Grady and his deputy. Although Grady hadn't mentioned finding anything.

Receipts and check stubs filled the box, but it was empty of cash. A small red ribbon lay curled inside.

Another memory returned—her and Darlene tying ribbons in each other's hair. Had this red ribbon been hers? Had her father saved it all these years?

Then a receipt from a local mental hospital caught her attention.

She studied it, shocked to see the bill was for patient services—for her mother. When had her mom been in a mental institution?

Her heart pounding, she dug through the box and found other similar receipts, all dated about the same time—when she was two years old. That couldn't be.

Her mother had died in childbirth. At least that was what her father had told her.

She read the receipts again. There had to be a mistake. Maybe the bill was for her grandmother....

Unable to believe his deception, she phoned the hospital to check the information. Pretending that she wanted to donate money to honor her mother, she asked for verification on the dates and her mother's name. Seconds later, the clerk confirmed it.

Violet hung up the phone, stunned. Why had her father lied to her?

Reeling with questions, she nearly jumped out of her skin when the telephone trilled. She stared at it dumbfounded for a minute, then finally answered it. Maybe it was Grady with some answers. "Hello?"

"Get out of town and stop snooping around," a low voice whispered. "Or you're going to end up just like the others."

Violet's fingers tightened around the handset. "Who are you? What are you talking about?"

The phone went dead in her hands, the dial tone roaring in her ears.

SWEAT DRIBBLED DOWN Grady's back as he drove toward his old homestead. Hell, yeah, he'd ask his father about the bone. That piece of bone might connect his sister's murderer to the serial killer stalking the South today.

He searched his memory banks for his father's reaction the night Darlene had disappeared—had he given any indication he might know who'd kidnapped her? The details were so foggy….

Only thirteen at the time, Grady had been battling guilt over not coming home to watch her. And then his father had turned to him with accusing eyes, placing the blame on his shoulders. Search parties had been organized. The town had been in an uproar. And the calls from Baker had started, suggesting places for them to search.

Had Jed Baker led them on a wild-goose chase? Had Walt suspected Baker all these years, or did he know something else he wasn't telling?

Struggling with unanswered questions, Grady opened the car door and jogged up the porch steps, knocked, then let himself inside. The house was dark, quiet, the emptiness swelling like a vise, closing around him. Echoes of Darlene's childlike voice drifted from the walls, an image of her racing down the steps materializing like a ghost. He hated this house, the memories. The ache of wanting his father to be proud of him. The fear that his dad would abandon him just as his mother had.

"Dad?"

There was no answer, so Grady walked down the hall, knowing somehow he'd find his father in the same place he had the last time he'd visited. His workshop.

Seconds later, the familiar sound of a knife scraping wood seared his consciousness. Had his father ever whittled a whistle out of bone?

For God's sake, what was wrong with him? His father had not killed his little sister. And he certainly wasn't a serial killer.

"Dad?"

The knife paused, his father glanced up, then back down. He was carving another lamb. The sight of the carving gnawed at Grady. Weren't lambs some kind of religious symbol? The sacrificial lamb...

"What do you want?" Walt asked.

"The truth about what was going on with you and Baker."

His father's hand shook slightly, but he resumed his carving. "What truth?"

"You two had a secret. I heard you arguing the night before he died. What were you afraid of?"

His dad shrugged, his cotton shirt wrinkling at the shoulders. Grady noticed suddenly that his father had lost weight. He appeared almost gaunt, his clothes hanging off of him. "You know why I hated him."

"Because you thought he steered you wrong in finding Darlene?"

He nodded.

"There's more."

His father's hand hesitated again, then he lifted his eyes. They looked like flat pieces of glass. Devoid of any emotion except bitterness.

"I spoke to the M.E., Dad. Baker didn't commit suicide...he was murdered."

A flash of panic filled his father's face before it slipped back into impassivity. "And you think I care?"

Anger churned Grady's stomach. "Tell me you didn't kill him, Dad."

A small smirk twisted Walt's lips. "Get out, Grady."

"Not until you answer me."

"I didn't kill him," he said coldly. "But I'm not sorry he's dead."

Relief tried to break through Grady's worry. "You argued with him the night he died."

"I argued with him every time I saw him."

"But that night there was something different," Grady insisted. "Baker was scared and so were you. Had you figured out who really killed Darlene?"

"You said Baker left a confession?"

"But I don't think he did it, and neither does Violet," Grady said in a low voice.

"Is that what this is about? You've taken that crazy, white trash girl's side." His father stood now, his craggy features strained. "Or are you in her pants?"

Grady balled his hands into fists. He'd never wanted to hit his father so badly in his life. "I'm not on anyone's side," he said. "But I'm trying to get to the truth, and I think you're hiding something. You don't believe Baker killed Darlene, either."

"Believe what you want."

Grady glared at him. "What the hell kind of answer is that? I thought you wanted to see Darlene's killer pay."

"I do." His father sighed, sounding defeated. Once again, he resumed his carving. "I did."

"Then tell me about the piece of bone you found in Darlene's hand."

His father's head jerked up. "What?"

"Tate told me Darlene was holding a piece of bone when you found her. Do you have it?"

His father blinked as if he was trying to remember. Or think of a lie.

"For God's sake, Dad, if you do, why wasn't it filed as evidence? It might be a vital clue."

"It was nothing," his father said. "Just some bone sliver she picked up trying to fight her way out of that well."

"Maybe, maybe not." Grady sighed. "Besides, I thought Darlene was already dead when the killer put her in the well."

His father paused, rubbed at his forehead with the back of his arm. "We didn't know, not for sure."

Emotions froze Grady's throat. He imagined Darlene lying in the well. Frightened. Alone. Hurting. Was that what Violet had seen?

"Just tell me what you did with the bone."

"I threw it away. I couldn't stand to think about—" His father choked, then reached for his bourbon. "Drop this, Grady. Let it go before someone else dies."

Grady locked his fists tighter. Had his father just threatened him or had he meant his comment as a warning?

AFTER THAT PHONE CALL, Violet couldn't stay at the house alone. Her nerves on edge, she drove back to town. If she didn't learn anything here, tomorrow after her father's funeral she'd visit the mental hospital.

When she arrived at the diner, the sun had faded, as if it, too, had drawn its last breath. A crotchety-looking old man she heard someone call Bart occupied the same bar stool he had the last time she'd been there. Two elderly women were laughing over thick pieces of apple pie, and another half-dozen people she didn't recognize filled the booths.

She claimed the only vacant one, wondering where the pretty young waitress she'd seen before was. Joseph Longhorse was talking to a man in khaki slacks and a navy shirt, although she couldn't see his face.

Reverend Wheeler and his son walked in and took the table across from her. A knot of anxiety pinched her belly. Another man in an expensive black suit joined them—Reverend Billy Lee Bilkins. She'd seen him preach on TV but didn't care for his overly dramatic hellfire and damnation sermons. And she'd heard he took half of each offering to feed his own ostentatious lifestyle.

Laney strode toward her with a wave, and Violet relaxed. "What can I do for you today, dear?"

Violet ordered a bowl of homemade vegetable soup. "Laney, I have to ask you something."

The woman's pensive eyes narrowed. "You're still troubled by your gift?"

"Yes, and I found something unusual in my father's house." She inhaled deeply, then explained about the bills for the mental hospital. "Did you know my mother?"

The older woman shook her head. "No, I'm afraid not."

Violet glanced around the diner. "Who in town did know her?"

"Doc Farmer. He was a young man then, just starting his practice."

Laney nodded. She should have thought of him right off. "He also might know my mother's medical history."

A TV blared from the bar, and Violet's gaze flew to the reporter on the screen. "Yes, folks, it appears we have a serial killer in the South. So far, this man has murdered two women, the first victim a coed in Savannah, the second, a young woman in Nashville. FBI profiler Special Agent Amelia Adams states that the killer is a male in his twenties with a strong religious upbringing. It's also possible he has Native American roots. If you have any information that might help find this killer, please call your local police."

Violet shivered. Loud voices broke out, and she and Laney both turned to see the Barley boys in a heated argument with Joseph. The other man angled his head slightly, and Violet saw his face.

A cold chill slid up her spine.

It was Donald Irving, the man who'd practically stalked her in Charleston. Had he followed her here?

"My boy." Laney tsked. "He has such a temper."

"Those Barleys have always had it in for him," Violet said.

The heaviest of the men—Chuck, if Violet remembered correctly—turned and bellowed, "Did you hear the earlier news report, folks? A serial killer is on the loose, and the police suspect he's an Indian." He pointed toward Donald. "And this here's Bernie Morris, a reporter from the Charleston paper. He thinks the killer might be here in Crow's Landing."

Several of the townspeople gasped. The two white-haired women huddled together in the corner. Violet stared at Donald Irving in shock. He was a reporter? And his name wasn't Donald, but Bernie?

He'd lied to her. Or was he lying now?

"Hell, we always knew he was trouble," Chuck's brother, Leroy, yelled. "Now he's killing women."

"Maybe we ought to take care of him ourselves," Chuck shouted.

They jumped on Joseph with thrashing fists, grunting obscenities. Laney stepped forward to break up the fight, but Violet held her back, afraid the men would hurt her.Bart Stancil scooted off his stool to get out of the way. The white-haired women squealed and ran toward the door. Two teenagers gawked as if they were enjoying the show.

Reverend Billy Lee Bilkins jumped up and raised his hands. "Lord God, please come down and bless these people. There's evil in this town, take the devil out of here."

"Joseph!" Laney shouted.

"I called the sheriff," a lady in a pink suit said.

Deputy Logan and Grady strode in, grabbed the Barley boys and hauled them off of Joseph.

"Stop it!" Grady yelled.

Chuck swung around, trying to escape. "But he might be that serial killer!"

Grady dragged the man toward the door and shoved him through it. "Get out before I arrest you. And don't come back until you've cooled down."

Logan booted the brother out the door. Laney hurried to Joseph to make sure he was all right. She knelt and helped him stand, then pressed the napkin to his bloody mouth. He sank into a bar stool while Laney rushed to get ice.

Violet hovered nearby, and Joseph caught her hand. "I am all right." His hawklike eyes bore into hers, and for a brief moment, she thought she saw hunger flare. He closed his fingers around hers. "I am glad you're back, Violet."

Grady cleared his throat. "What's going on here?"

"Nothing," Violet said, then realized he was talking about Joseph. "The Barley boys are idiots. They jumped Joseph."

"Longhorse?"

Joseph glared at Grady. "I don't need your help, Sheriff." He squeezed Violet's hand. "Come on, let us go somewhere and talk."

Violet hesitated, but Grady reached out and took her arm. "Not now. I need to talk to Violet."

Violet's gaze darted back and forth between the men, noting the tension.

Did Grady have new information about her father's death? About Darlene's or the other women's murder? If so, she had to know.

"We have to discuss my father's burial," she said softly.

Joseph's eyes dropped downward, his mouth tightening. "All right, I'll see you later. We are not finished, Violet." He released her hand and stalked from the diner, leaving Violet to wonder what he'd meant. And what he really wanted.

GRADY HAD NEVER HAD a possessive streak over a woman before, but for some reason seeing Joseph Longhorse's hand on Violet had triggered a monster inside him. He'd wanted to finish the beating the Barley brothers had started.

But he had no good reason.

He and Violet were not involved. For God's sake, she thought she had psychic visions, and he had his hands full trying to sort out these murders.

"What did you need?" Violet asked.

He latched on to her arm. "Let's sit down."

She gestured toward her booth, her adrenaline waning. "Do you have a lead about my father's murder or Darlene's?"

He braced his hands on the table. "Darlene was holding a piece of bone in her hand when she was found."

Violet gasped, her eyes glazing over for a second. Then she'd been right about the sound. "I don't understand."

"Neither do I," Grady said, "Not yet. But I will." He cleared his throat, started to reach for her hand, then seemed to think better of it and paused. "Violet, if you are somehow connected to this killer, you have to be careful. You might be in danger."

She chewed her lip. "I received a threatening call earlier."

"From whom?"

"I don't know."

"We'll get a trace put on your phone." He clenched his fists, then cleared his throat and glanced toward the door where Laney's son had exited. "Stay away from Joseph Longhorse."

Her gaze met his, surprise registering. "You can't suspect Joseph of killing Darlene or my father?"

"I don't know what to think yet, but we can't discount the fact that there's a maniac out there killing women. Longhorse not only has a temper, he has some kind of grudge against me and my father, too." His voice dropped lower, his fear for Violet unleashing something primitive inside him. "And he fits the profile of this serial killer."

"But—"

"Just promise me you'll be careful, Violet, and that you won't let down your guard around him."

"All right," she whispered hesitantly. "But keep an open mind. Except for the Native American part, there are other people in town who fit the profile."

He nodded. "I'm aware of that. Believe me, I'm checking them out, as well."

She bit down on her lower lip. He itched to reach up and wipe away the indentation of her teeth on the soft flesh. To draw her into his arms, kiss her and reassure her that everything would be all right. To make Joseph Longhorse realize that Violet was not a woman to be had.

Except maybe by Grady.

Jesus, where had those thoughts come from?

Logan cleared his throat. "Sheriff?"

Grady glanced up and met Logan's questioning look, then saw the deputy's eyes shift to Violet. "What is it?"

Logan gestured behind him to a corner booth. "There's a reporter here from the Charleston paper. He says he wants to talk to you," Logan said. "I'll check around outside. Make sure the troublemakers are gone."

Grady nodded. "I wonder what this reporter's doing in Crow's Landing."

"I think he's here because of me," Violet said.

"What do you mean?" Had she told someone else about her visions?

Violet released a shaky breath. "I met him in Charleston. He wouldn't leave me alone. I'm afraid he followed me here."

"He was stalking you?"

"I thought so," Violet said. "But maybe he was just being a pest and wanted a story. He lied and told me his name was Donald Irving, not Bernie Morris. Or maybe he's lying now."

Those protective instincts surfaced again along with Grady's suspicious nature. What kind of story had this reporter expected to get from Violet? And why had he lied about his name?

Even without his deceit, a stranger showing up when a serial killer was on the loose was good enough reason to doubt the man and his motives. "Then I'll go find out who the hell he really is and what he wants."

THE CLOCK WAS TICKING. Time to take another.

Violet Baker.

No, she was way down on the list. Although the prospect of being so close to the one who'd known his original conquest exhilarated him. But he had to go in order.

Order meant everything.

He left the town square, smiling as he thought of the commotion at the diner. The tension in the town was high. Tempers were flaring.

The scent of fear was upon them.

He meticulously gathered his supplies, adrenaline pumping through his veins. Maybe this one would serve his father.

Kerry Cantrell.

A sense of desperation mingled with worry. But if she was perfect, what would happen? Would they make him stop?

The other names on his list flashed into his mind. Seven more. His mouth salivated. He couldn't stop.

He wanted to draw the blood from each of them. Watch the life flow from their pretty pale necks and place them on the altar for his father.

Then he would be the only one left. The Cherokee word rolled off his tongue. *"Suye'ta"*—the chosen one.

And they would sing him into glory. Just as it should have been.

CHAPTER SIXTEEN

GRADY STARED AT Bernie Morris's proffered hand, sizing him up. Morris had longish brown hair, a patrician nose, expensive clothes and an uppity air about him. Some women might find his face attractive. But Morris's frame seemed wiry to Grady, his green eyes suspicious. Grady immediately disliked the weasel and didn't trust him.

He also noticed several scars on the man's arms that looked questionable. An accident, maybe? Something seemed suspicious about the nicks and cuts, as if they might have been self-inflicted. He'd guess a suicide attempt. But slicers usually chose the wrist area and made a longer gash instead of small puncture wounds up and down their forearms. Unless these had been tentative attempts, and he'd been working up his nerve to kill himself. He looked like a coward.

"Sheriff Monroe, Bernie Morris."

Grady frowned and refused his handshake. "I heard your name was Donald Irving."

Morris glanced toward Violet, and every cell in Grady's body sprang to alert. "What are you doing here?"

"I'm an investigative reporter."

"And why would that bring you to Crow's Landing?" His gaze latched on to Morris's. He took some pride in seeing the man squirm.

"I'm following the serial killer story."

"The serial killer didn't strike here."

"Not yet."

Grady froze. "What does that mean?"

Morris shrugged. "Nashville's not that far away. He might be hiding here now, choosing his next victim."

"That's true." Grady altered his voice to a menacing pitch and gave the man a pointed stare. "Gives us reason to be suspicious of any newcomers."

Morris's eye twitched at his insinuation. "Don't be ridiculous."

Grady crossed his arms. "You're the stranger in town. Why shouldn't we suspect you?"

Morris's eyes bulged. "Because I write about crimes. I don't commit them."

Grady's patience snapped. "Or maybe you commit murder, then write about it to glorify yourself and get attention."

Morris coughed, his face turning ruddy. "That's ridiculous."

"Listen, buddy," Grady said, "if you have information about those murders, you need to turn it over to me."

"When I have proof, I will. In fact, I suspect Violet Baker knows something about them."

"What makes you say that?"

"She was in Savannah when the first woman died. She was also here twenty years ago when your sister was murdered."

Grady twisted Morris by the tie. "What do you know about my sister's death?"

Morris's eyes shifted sideways. "That Violet Baker isn't who she says she is." His gaze flickered with accusations. "In fact, I doubt even she knows the truth. And if my guess is right, neither did your sister."

"What the hell do you mean by that?"

"You're the detective, you figure it out." Morris jerked away and strode toward the door. Grady stared at his back, his mind spinning.

VIOLET'S FINGERS WORRIED the Best Friends necklace. Whether or not the reporter's name was Morris or Irving, she still didn't like him. Seconds later, the images in the room blurred. A slow numbness crept over her. The lights in the diner became fuzzy. Her head swam.

She lowered her head into her hands and closed her eyes in an attempt to regain her equilibrium. The air was trapped in her lungs.

It was happening again.

The noise in the diner bounced off the walls, magnified by the shrill cry in her head.

"Help me. Please help me…."

A wave of nausea washed over Violet. She stood and stumbled forward. She had to get air. Go outside. Try to connect with this woman so she could save her.

And she couldn't do it with half the town watching her.

Perspiration beaded her forehead. The room swayed and pitched, growing fuzzier. Someone spoke, called out her name. But she rushed on. The lights swirled in a kaleidoscope of colors, faded into black.

She dragged in a huge gulping breath and felt her way toward her car. She barely managed to unlock the door before she collapsed inside.

"Help me, please help me."

She closed her eyes and tried to make a connection. "Tell me where you are, who you are, so I can find you."

"He's going to kill me." A sob wrenched the air. *"I don't want to die."*

Gripping her stomach to suppress the nausea, Violet gave in to the images. Maybe if she could connect with the woman more, see the killer through the frightened woman's eyes, she could save her.

Or maybe she could connect with the killer....

A wall of blackness engulfed her, a haze of fear and panic surrounding her. He stretched his hands out in front of him. They were long. Thin. Covered in surgical gloves. He reached for the needle. Raised the tip. Tapped the hypodermic. Then he removed a small vial and placed it in a rack filled with test tubes.

"Gi'ga-tsuha'li," he murmured. *"I am the blood taker. It is time."*

The woman screamed again. Violet watched in horror as the needle pricked her arm. Unable to stop him, she stared hollow eyed as the blood slowly seeped from her veins into the test tube. She was fading, nearly incoherent now. She glanced at the row of vials. Other ones filled with blood.

He was adding hers to the collection.

What did he want with her blood? She tried to speak. To ask him. But her windpipe closed. Speech was impossible.

He hovered above her. Soon his hands would close around her neck, choking.

And it would all be over....

Violet tried desperately to pull herself from the grisly image before the sound of the bone whistle added to the terror.

GRADY STORMED OUT of the café, Morris's words dogging him. What had he meant? That Violet didn't know who she was and neither did his sister? Violet was Jed Baker's daughter. Darlene was his father's child. And Teresa's.

A gloomy darkness cast shadows around the town, the low hum of evening traffic a backdrop to tension clogging the sultry summer air. He scanned the parking lot until he spotted Violet's car.

His chest clenched when he saw her sprawled across the front seat. Her eyes were closed, her head thrown back as if she'd passed out. Panic seized him as he yanked open the door.

"Violet?" He pressed a hand to her neck, breathing in relief when he found a pulse.

He gently stroked her hair back from her forehead. "Violet, are you okay?"

She stirred slightly, reaching for him to help her sit. He eased one hand beneath the back of her head, the other around her waist. She swayed, blinking as if to focus.

"What happened?" he asked gruffly.

She clung to his hand, steadying herself. "I saw the killer. He has another woman."

Grady quickly glanced around the parking lot, searching the shadows. "Was he here? Did he attack you?"

She shook her head, her tangled hair swaying around her. "No, but he…he's going to kill her. I can feel it."

Grady scrubbed a hand over his face.

She angled toward him, her eyes imploring. She was trembling uncontrollably. "He takes a vial of their blood…it's his souvenir."

Grady studied her face, searching for a clue to the truth. She appeared to totally believe what she was saying.

And if she was telling the truth, really seeing visions of the murders, maybe she could help him find the killer.

"DO YOU SEE WHERE he has her?"

She shook her head. "No…it was like I was looking through the woman's eyes. She doesn't know where they are. But she saw his hands. He had on gloves, and he was taking her blood." Violet's voice broke. "Then he was carving that bone whistle."

Grady's expression turned somber. "I'll drive you home."

She nodded. She didn't think she could drive, anyway.

He gently eased her over to the passenger side and slid in beside her. Grateful for his nearness, she closed her eyes, rested her head against the seat and let the sound of the engine lull her into relaxing. But images of the vials of blood returned to haunt her. Why would a killer draw his victim's blood? Was it just some kind of strange perversion?

And he'd been putting the vials in some kind of order…as if that was significant. She wondered if there had been names on the vials. Maybe if he labeled his next victim's test tube in advance, she could read the name, warn the woman.

A few minutes later, Grady parked at her father's house and came around to her side. She fumbled for her purse and found her key, holding on to the door as she pulled herself from the car. Grady slid an arm around her waist and helped her stand. She started to argue, but he took her hand and led her up the sidewalk and steps.

The scent of cleaning chemicals assaulted her as they went inside.

"Are you all right?" Grady asked.

She shook her head. "No, how can I be all right?" Her voice cracked. "Why can I see these things if I'm not able to stop them?"

"It's not your fault, Violet." His husky tone surprised her. Added to her guilt.

"You don't understand. I feel so helpless. It's like I'm standing there watching but not doing anything to prevent the murder."

He reached for her. Rubbed his hands up and down her arms. "You should rest."

She swung around, shaking her head, her emotions raging. "I don't want to see these things. I didn't ask for this… I don't want it."

He pulled her into his arms, cradling her against the hard wall of his chest, and rocked her back and forth. Violet resisted, but he soothed her with a whisper. Finally, she relaxed against him, clung to him, savored his strong arms.

"It's terrible," Violet murmured, struggling for some tangible detail that might help catch the killer. "I can hear them, just like I heard Darlene, then I…I can't do anything. I…have to watch them die."

"We'll figure it out," Grady promised. "But it's not your fault, just like Darlene's death wasn't."

A sob built in her throat, then bubbled over.

He stiffened, seemed to pull away slightly. Then a second later, his arms tightened back around her. "Tell me what happened between you and your father."

Her throat clogged. She'd never confided in anyone about that night. She wasn't sure she could now.

Grady pressed a kiss to her temple, then another into her hair.

Violet inhaled his masculine scent, clung to the steel band of muscles in his arms, felt herself come alive as his chest heaved with breath beneath her own. He murmured sweet assurances to her, stroking the hair from her damp cheeks, drying her eyes with the pads of his thumbs.

The mood shifted. Changed subtly. Heat radiated from his touch, his breath became a fiery whisper—part comfort, part need, part desire.

"Violet?"

"I can't talk about it," she murmured. Then she looked up into his face, saw the questions lingering in his gaze. Hunger flared in his deep brown eyes.

Life was so short, Violet realized. One woman might die tonight. Another one might tomorrow.

She could be next.

Life and death were only a breath away.

As soon as the thought came to her, she knew it was true. She might be one of the killer's victims. Maybe that was the reason for this connection.

She didn't want to go through life running anymore. Afraid of her shadow. Afraid of letting a man get close enough to touch her. She didn't want to die without experiencing love.

Grady could erase the unbearable fear, if only for a little while.

As if he understood her silent reply, he bent down and claimed her mouth with his own, setting her on fire.

FLAMES OF DESIRE LICKED at Grady, surging through his loins. Violet needed him tonight. He needed her....

Yet he still paused. She held the key to extinguishing that fire with a simple no, but she didn't speak. Instead, she parted her lips in a slow seduction and invited him inside. It had been dark for so long in his life. He had been alone. Struggling with the same guilt that ate at Violet.

He tasted honey and sweetness and spice all mingled together, an innocence blended with erotic desire. It swept over him in waves, splintering his resistance. Her throaty groan stroked the hot coals of hunger to life.

The past few days faded, the years of anguish and isolation, the emptiness. She threaded her fingers in his hair, and he wove his hand through her long tresses. His other hand explored the soft nape of her neck, then slid lower to pull her against him. She felt delicate and small, fragile like glass, yet malleable in his hands, as if his touch made her bend to his desires. He thrust his tongue deeply, sipping at her lips and stroking her back until her breasts swelled against his chest. Her nipples felt like pinpoints of pleasure as they brushed against him. He trailed kisses lower, tasting the softness of her throat, the hint of her body wash in the curve of her breasts, the sultry essence that belonged only to Violet.

He had never wanted a woman the way he wanted her.

But she was Violet…his little sister's friend.

Reality intervened, but his hunger didn't wane. Instead, he realized that their pasts had drawn them together in the darkness, just as the heat rippling between them had given him light.

His hand brushed her breast, and his body surged with the ache to fill her. He lowered her to the sofa, slid down beside her, cradling her in the V of his spread thighs, and began to caress her through the soft cotton blouse.

"Grady…"

Her sultry response was all he needed. He reached for the buttons of her shirt, flicked the first one open, dropped a kiss onto the bare skin exposed by his invasion. But a trilling sound cut into the moment. He flicked another button, ignoring the sound. He was too close to having Violet. To assuaging the ache.

Again a trill. Another. Another.

His cell phone.

She stiffened in his arms. He froze and muttered a curse. Listened again. Knew he had to take it. He couldn't escape his job. A woman's life might depend on it.

He kissed Violet once again, hard, long, a promise that they weren't finished, then reached for the mobile unit.

"Sheriff Monroe."

"Sheriff, it's Logan. We might have trouble."

Grady gripped the phone tighter. "What kind of trouble?"

"Laney Longhorse said Kerry Cantrell is missing." He paused. "I've asked around and no one's seen her."

Grady's pulse missed a beat. "Maybe she just took the night off."

"No, she called earlier to say she was on her way in to the diner. I checked out her place. Looks like someone broke in. There was a struggle."

Grady glanced at Violet. She looked exhausted, but sexy. Her half-dazed eyes, full of desire and now fear, met his. Part of him wanted to crawl over beside her, finish their lovemaking. Shut out the world.

But he couldn't.

He had the same bad feeling in his gut he'd had the night Darlene turned up missing. He had to organize a search party, look for Kerry Cantrell. He only hoped Violet had been wrong.

That Kerry wasn't already a victim....

"I'M GOING WITH YOU," Violet insisted.

"No. Logan will pick me up." Grady moved away. It was back to business. "You're too exhausted, Violet. You need rest."

Unfortunately, he was right. She could hardly move. She would only slow him down, be a liability.

Sensations he'd aroused still tingled through her body. Disappointment followed. Fear replaced the pleasure. She had to be strong. "You'll be careful?"

He halted at the door, stared at her long and hard, then nodded. "Lock the door behind me. And don't let anyone in."

She shook her head, following him across the room. "I won't. But come back...tell me when you find her."

His jaw tightened. He had to search, had to know for sure.

Had to find the body.

"Kerry's the one I saw," she finally whispered. "Check the churches," she added, her heart breaking again at the thought of the pretty young waitress being defiled in public.

He nodded, then bent down and kissed her again before he jogged outside.

Violet closed the door, then staggered to the bedroom, drained, defeated. She stretched out, ready to wait the grueling hours. But when she closed her eyes, the shadows moved in, eating at her sanity. Just like the killer's hands. She felt the scarf sliding against her skin, his hands squeezing....

Seconds later, she jerked upright, stale air and the scent of danger engulfing her. She wasn't alone.

The air shifted. A faint pungent odor filled her nostrils. She could feel someone's presence. The killer's.

He was staring back at her, and he was only a breath away from touching her...

SOMEBODY WAS WATCHING HIM.

He pivoted, searched the darkness, listened. Had someone found him?

Silence met his questions, the answering stillness in the air confirming that he was alone with the dead woman. Her bulging eyes told him she'd prayed for a savior until the last minute.

Her limp, drained body proved her savior hadn't heard her.

Her blood told him she wasn't the one.

Still, as he laid her gently on the altar, he felt the exhilaration of having served his father. But he also sensed someone else's presence. That had happened to him only one other time.

With Darlene Monroe.

He'd read that the Baker girl had some kind of psychic connection with Darlene. Had she somehow climbed into Kerry Cantrell's head to watch him?

If so, he hoped she'd enjoyed the show. It wouldn't be the last.

In fact, he vowed to make it better for her each time. Until she lay in his arms and he drew her blood, then laid her at the altar. The last little lamb.

His final sacrifice to his father.

CHAPTER SEVENTEEN

IT TOOK GRADY less than an hour to organize a search party. But déjà vu flooded him, memories of the night Darlene disappeared rushing back.

News traveled quickly in a small town, the main barriers being the distance between homes and the lack of technology—some people still didn't have the Internet, and cell phones hadn't taken the community by storm as they had in metropolitan areas. People here were country born and bred, liked the old ways and weren't in a rush to get anywhere, much less into the future. Others simply couldn't afford it.

A few locals began the search in town, while others formed small groups to check the foothills of the mountains and get word to residents on the periphery. There were so many places to search—vacant chicken coops scattered among the hills and valleys, abandoned cabins and outbuildings tucked away in the middle of nowhere, two or three storage warehouses, old farm silos, barns and bins, even a dozen small caverns that would make a good place to hide.

Grady kept hope that Kerry would be found safe and alive, but with every passing hour, his hopes faded. The other women had been found around midnight.

It was already twelve-thirty.

He and Logan had begun with the churches, leaving someone to watch each of the two in town while they drove to the smaller country churches on the outskirts. The first one, the small Presbyterian church on Route 9, was empty, save for a vagrant they found sleeping on a front pew.

"Don't run me off," the old man whined. "I ain't hurtin' nothing."

"Come morning, find a new place," Grady said.

"Why are you out here, anyway?" the old man snapped. "The preacher knows I come, and he don't mind."

Logan explained about the serial killer and the missing woman in town.

The old man shivered. "Maybe I will find some other place. I don't want to be here if some maniac comes up." He rose and staggered outside, disappearing into the woods.

Grady and Logan headed to the Church of God in the foothills. The sounds of the night echoed in the strained silence as they swung onto the dirt road that led to the wooden church. Clusters of oaks and pines surrounded the chapel. The location was so isolated, Grady wondered how the attendees ever found it. But the people who belonged were a tight group, all finding housing in the lower half of Crow's Landing, all reveling in the simplicity of the setting. A wolf cried in the distance as they climbed out. Logan scanned the darkness as if checking for bobcats or bears.

"If this killer isn't from the area, I don't see how he'd even know about this place. Doesn't he usually leave the victims so they can be found easily?" Logan cleared his throat. "I thought part of the sickness was showing off and not getting caught."

"Usually." Grady grunted and walked up the steps, checked inside. Nothing. Logan combed the property, but he, too, came up empty.

Maybe Violet had been wrong. Maybe Kerry would appear back in town, and everyone would laugh about how they'd exaggerated her situation. She'd probably had a secret rendezvous with some new lover.

"Should we check the one at the top of the peak?" Logan said.

Grady nodded and once again took the wheel. His stomach knotted as they climbed the mountain, memories returning of that night twenty years ago when they'd ridden the roads hunting for Darlene. They'd found her at Shanty Annie's, the old well house, not a church, though.

But that piece of bone still bothered him.

Ten minutes later, he wound along the dirt road toward Black Mountain Church. The wind whistling through the window tried to cool the air, but only shifted the heat around him. He was sweating, his palms damp, his heartbeat accelerated. He parked the car, his hand on his gun, his instincts alert as he and Logan scanned the woods. Ten steps toward the white wooden church and he saw her.

She was sprawled facedown on the front stoop, as if she'd been left there for the gods, her neck twisted at an odd angle, a sheet wrapped around her.

"Christ." Logan removed his sunglasses. "It's Kerry."

VIOLET STARED INTO the darkness, the feeling that she'd actually seen into the killer's mind plaguing her. Why would she connect with a madman?

A board creaked in the front room. She searched the shadows. She wasn't alone.

Someone was in the house now. Was it the killer?

Shoving the covers away, she reached for her cell phone, then tiptoed to the den to listen, blinking to acclimate her eyes to the darkness. Moonlight softened the corners of the room. The desk in the corner had been disturbed. Drawers hung open.

A shadow flickered. Moonlight splintered across the room, illuminating him.

She backed toward the door and opened her mouth to scream. He lunged toward her and covered her mouth. Violet kicked and swung her fists, but he gripped her tighter.

"Be quiet. I'm not going to hurt you."

She froze, the blood roaring in her ears. The reporter.

"I just want to ask you some questions."

She kicked at him, but he jerked her arm so hard she buckled.

"Don't push me, Miss Baker."

Deciding to play along, she nodded.

"Now, if I release you, promise not to scream."

She nodded again, deciding she'd have to choose her moment.

He released her mouth and she gasped. "What are you doing here? I could have you arrested for home invasion and assault."

"I told you I just want to talk."

Her gaze shot to the door. He was blocking it. "How did you know where I lived?"

"It's my job to investigate things."

"Then why did you lie to me in Charleston?"

"Because I didn't think you'd talk to me if you knew the truth about who I was."

"You're right." Their eyes met, locked. His smile held an evil glint. He liked knowing she was scared.

"Why are you following me?"

"Looking for information. I think you're the key to my story. And I might be able to help you."

"I don't see how that's possible." She glanced around. "You told Sheriff Monroe you were following the serial killer case."

"I am, and I think it's linked to you."

Violet inhaled to steady her breathing. "What makes you think that?"

His thin lips spread into a grin. "I've heard about your gift. And I understand that you tried to save Darlene Monroe twenty years ago."

"How do you know that?"

He wheezed a breath, the sound echoing in the tension. "I grew up outside of town here. I remember the stories."

"So," Violet said, her temper flaring, "you want to write about the crazy girl?" She stalked by him, tried to punch in 911 on her phone.

He hesitated, then grabbed her again and yanked the handset from her. "No, I want to find out the truth, just like you do. I haven't pieced everything together, but there's a research center, a hospital near here. There was talk of some unusual experiments going on twenty years ago, ones some of the townspeople knew about, ones they covered up."

Violet stared at his hand, willing him to remove it from her arm. He finally released her. She met his gaze again. "What are you talking about?"

"Your father's murder. Darlene's. They had something to do with your mother."

"My mother died when I was born."

"No, she died when you were two. She was in a mental institution."

Violet gaped at him in shock. "Where did you hear that?"

"I told you I've done my research. But I've only scratched the surface. Whatever this secret is, it could be big, and I'm going to blow it wide open."

Violet folded her arms. But she was so desperate for answers, she had to listen. "Go on."

"I suspect your father was murdered because he knew too much."

Violet racked her brain for a reply, but so far the reporter seemed on target. "How do I know you didn't kill him? And that you're not here to kill me, too?"

"If I wanted to kill you, I would have done it already."

She hesitated. "If you are telling the truth, what happened twenty years ago? And why would someone kill my dad over it now?"

He ran a hand through his scraggly hair, mouth twitching. "I'm not sure yet, but I'll find out." He slanted a cold gaze at her. "But it seems too coincidental that you were connected to a little girl's murder, and now this serial killer."

Violet's heart pounded. How could he know she was connected to both of them—unless he was the killer?

"WE HAVE TO FIND this killer." Grady's gut pinched as he photographed Kerry Cantrell's body. No woman deserved to die like this. To be left naked, wrapped in a sheet, treated like some sacrificial animal.

He radioed the other search parties to relay that they'd discovered Kerry, although Grady insisted he not reveal their location. The last thing he wanted was for half the town to show up in a panic and contaminate the crime scene.

Then Logan scribbled details about the body's position and the scene as Grady recited his findings. Finally Grady read the note. The same native expression had been written as a farewell to Kerry. And Violet had known about it. There was also a sliver of a bone beside the body.

The bone whistle.

"People in town are going to panic when this gets out," Logan said.

"I know. Her disappearance has already created some hysteria." Guilt over his dismissal of Kerry's interest in him added to Grady's temper. "We'll have to do what we can to control the crowds, especially those Barley boys."

Logan nodded, then strode to the edge of the woods, searching for footprints.

Within an hour, the Nashville CSI unit barreled up to Black Mountain Church, along with the FBI. Grady braced himself for the posturing he expected over jurisdiction and who had priority on the case. The FBI didn't think much of small-town law enforcement. They probably thought he was inept, too.

Special Agent Nick Norton, who was spearheading the task force, introduced himself along with a female profiler, Special Agent Adams. Agent Norton scowled at Logan. "What are you doing here?"

Logan's hand balled into a fist. "I'm the deputy in town."

Norton cast his eyes toward Grady for confirmation, and Grady nodded. "You two know each other?" he asked.

"We met on another case," Agent Norton said in a clipped tone.

Logan rocked back on his heels, his gaze unwavering. "Have you touched or moved anything?" Agent

Adams asked, breaking the tension between the men and bringing them back to the task at hand.

Grady frowned, curious about Norton and Logan's history, but that would have to wait. "No. We may be small town, but we know how to do our jobs."

Agent Norton raised an eyebrow. "Good, we'll need your cooperation."

Agent Adams studied Kerry's body and began to assess the scene while the crime scene techs began to work.

"She was left like the others?" Grady asked.

"Identical," Agent Norton said. "Even the note is the same."

"Have you traced where the killer bought the sheets he wraps the victims in?" Logan asked.

Norton didn't bother to look up. "Not yet, but we're working on it. What's the victim's name?"

"Kerry Cantrell," Grady said. "She's a local, worked as a waitress at the diner in town."

"Was she from around here?"

He shook his head. "She moved to Crow's Landing about a year ago."

Norton jotted down notes, recording their conversation. "Married?"

"No."

"Boyfriends? Lovers?"

Grady hesitated. "Not that I know of."

"She's attractive. You mean there was no one?" Norton asked again.

"That native was interested in her," Logan said, piping up. "Although Kerry turned him down. She was interested in the sheriff."

Grady glared at his deputy, but Special Agent Norton perked up.

"When was the last time you saw her, Sheriff?"

Grady crossed his arms. "Yesterday at the diner."

"I assume you have an alibi for the last few hours."

He gritted his teeth. "You've got to be joking."

"Listen, Monroe, you know the drill. Play the game so I can eliminate you, and we'll get along fine."

The muscles in Grady's neck bunched. He'd been on the verge of telling them about Violet's vision. Shit. If he did that, they'd think he was nuts. "As a matter of fact, I was in town all day. Half the citizens saw me. I've been with my dad, then the mayor, then my deputy and I rode in together to break up a fight at the diner."

"And this native?"

"Joseph Longhorse is his name. His mother owns the Redbud Café. He was involved in the fight." Grady explained about the reporter and the panic he'd created, along with the hysteria over the profile reported on the news. "The Barley boys are prejudiced bullies. They never liked the Native Americans in town and have been ruthless to Joseph Longhorse for years. The profile gave them an excuse to go after him."

"But he does fit the profile." Norton made a clicking sound with his teeth. "Then I say we talk to Mr. Longhorse. Find out just how angry he was that Miss Cantrell rebuffed him."

Grady nodded reluctantly. He might not get along with Longhorse, but he didn't see him as a killer. Then again, the man did hike off into the woods for days. He liked to hunt. He had some peculiar customs, a lot of anger bottled up. And he collected those damn bones.

But even if he'd hurt Kerry, why would he have killed those other women?

Unless he was simply copycatting the murder to make it look as if the serial killer had killed Kerry.

THEY HAD FOUND HER BODY.

A sense of elation warmed his blood as they scurried around with their cameras and notepads. Kerry Cantrell had been so easy. So ready to fall into his hands.

So far from perfect that he had almost spat in her face.

And her blood…oh, it held secrets.

Secrets that she had kept from her lovers. Secrets that labeled her as damaged goods. Such imperfections made her so wrong for his father that he had been tempted to leave her completely naked and exposed. She didn't deserve the cleansing ritual or the soft sheet he had wrapped her in to cradle her in death.

But his mother had taught him to be clean. To wash the blood away, scouring the evil from deep within as the dry flakes of dead skin fell away.

And his father was the blessed one. The one who spoke of sin and repentance. Of redemption and life everlasting.

He saw Violet Baker's eyes in his mind and smiled, thinking about the test tubes. He had so carefully printed each of their names on the labels.

She was last on his list.

His body hardened at the thought of taking her. Of watching her blood seep into the test tube. He could hardly wait to tighten the tourniquet around her arm.

And to feel the silky softness of her throat as his hands closed around it….

CHAPTER EIGHTEEN

THE KILLER'S HANDS were closing around her neck.

Violet raised her fingers, massaging the tender skin, wishing she could run away. But she couldn't move. Couldn't escape. Couldn't leave these other women to die.

Bernie Morris's questions had spiked her curiosity about her past even more. Was he right? Had something happened twenty years ago between her mother and father and Darlene's parents? Morris had hinted it had something to do with a research center. But her father had never been into research. Although Darlene's mother had once been a nurse...

She needed to talk to Grady.

Unable to sleep, she fought the choking sensation and once again drew the images she'd seen. When she finished, she stared at the woman's face, knowing it was Kerry.

Frantic, Violet paced the floor, praying she was wrong, that Grady would find the waitress alive. He'd been searching for hours. But she could see the woman's face now, pale with death, her fingers closed around the sliver of bone. The killer had carved it while Kerry had been forced to watch.

Then Violet saw the blood again. Long fingers lined

up the test tubes in a row, one by one. Three tubes of blood now. Three women he had killed.

But he had more. She saw the test tubes. Tried to read the names.

The reporter's comment returned to taunt her. Something about a research center. Where was it? Nearby?

She struggled to make out the room where the killer was, but she couldn't see specific details to draw it. It wasn't a hospital room and it wasn't sterile. No, it was darker. More like a bedroom in a house. But, it wasn't his bedroom. It was a secret hiding place. Someplace in the forest. A place no one knew about.

The killer had taken the blood with him there. They were his trophies. She drew the test tubes on the sketch pad, outlined the labels.

She had to read the names. See who was going to be next. Try to save her.

But the killer's fingers traced over the labels, obliterating her view. It was almost as if he knew she was watching. As if he was teasing her.

He turned them around and around, then held them up to the light, toying with the blood and watching it swirl. Finally, his fingers traced along the bottom of the case. Another empty test tube sat waiting. Then another. And another. She counted seven more.

His finger rested on the final one. He traced his finger around the edge of the label as if savoring that last tube. His souvenirs.

A smile spread on his lips. Then laughter erupted. Eerie, sinister laughter.

He slid his finger to the left.

She saw the name.

Violet Baker.

Dear God, he knew she could see him. And he wanted her to know she was on his list.

THE KILLER WASN'T THROUGH. He had only begun.

Grady knew it in his soul. He just wished he could pinpoint the man's identity before he claimed another life.

Violet.

Fear burned through his lungs as her face filled his mind. No, he wouldn't let anyone hurt her.

He drove like a bat out of hell into town, wanting desperately to stop by her house. But he couldn't, not with Special Agent Norton on his tail. Still, he saw her lights on, reassured himself she was safe at home. He would see her later.

Even though it was well past 3:00 a.m., there were lights burning in several houses. Grady could feel the tension rippling through the community.

Undoubtedly word had spread that Kerry's body had been found.

Occasionally he noticed a curtain part slightly, as if the owner had to peek out to make sure a madman wasn't stalking outside. Thankfully, the town didn't know yet that the police suspected Kerry's death was the result of a serial killer, a man Special Agent Norton and his task force were now calling the Bone Whistler.

But Grady had other problems. First, what to do about Violet and her so-called visions. He still hadn't informed Norton of the oddity.

And now two murders had occurred in Crow's Landing within the span of a few days.

Were they connected or not?

Exhausted but too wired to sleep, Grady scanned the streets, searching for potential trouble. He checked the

Redbud Café to make sure the Barley boys hadn't gone mad and organized some kind of lynch mob, then breathed a sigh of relief to find that things were quiet.

Special Agent Norton parked behind him. With trepidation, he led the agent up the back stairs to the Longhorse apartment above the café. He hated like the devil to wake Laney at this ungodly hour, but Norton insisted on questioning Joseph tonight.

As a cop, Grady knew the agent was right. As a local, he despised what their suspicions would do to poor Laney. And what if Joseph turned out to be guilty?

Norton raised his fist and knocked. They waited several seconds, then footsteps sounded. A minute later, Laney checked the peephole and opened the door.

"Sheriff?" She ran a hand over her long braid. "What's wrong?"

"I'm sorry to disturb you this late, Laney." Special Agent Norton cleared his throat and Grady introduced him. Laney's expression immediately turned wary.

"I guess you heard about Kerry," Grady said.

She nodded, tears glistening in her gray eyes. "It's awful. Poor thing…she was such a sweetheart. I can't believe she's dead."

He nodded. "We have to talk to Joseph."

"You don't think my boy had something to do with Kerry's death?" Her eyes widened. "Grady, you've known Joseph all your life. You can't possibly think such a thing."

"Ma'am, we just need to talk to him," Norton said.

She twisted the neckline of her robe. "I…he's not home."

Grady frowned. "Laney, we're not here to arrest him, we just want to ask him some questions."

"Go get him, ma'am."

Laney pursed her lips. "I told you he's not here. That's the truth." She gestured toward the door, opening it wider. "If you don't believe me, check for yourself."

Grady started to back away, but Norton pushed inside. "I certainly will."

Grady and Laney exchanged a troubled look, then Grady followed Norton as he strode through the five-room apartment. The agent was looking for evidence, anything in the open that might link Longhorse to the murders. Norton froze when he noticed the bone collection on the wall.

"Does that belong to your son?" he asked.

Laney nodded, still clutching the neckline of her robe. "They're from different animals he hunts. He uses some of them in our traditional rituals."

Norton glanced at Grady, then back to Laney. "Where is your son, ma'am?"

"He was upset after that fight," Laney said. "When he gets that way, he goes off into the woods to be alone, sometimes to meditate, sometimes to hunt. But he always returns by dawn."

Norton nodded. "Then we'll be back then."

Grady followed him out the door. As soon as it closed, Norton said, "Let's get a search warrant. I want it in my hands when we return at dawn."

Grady remembered the sliver of bone his father had found in Darlene's hand. Was it possible Joseph Longhorse had put it there just before he'd killed her?

ROSS WHEELER KNELT at the altar, offering silent prayers that his father accepted his mere offerings and forgave him his sins.

His own earthly father would not be so forgiving.

Not if he discovered what Ross had done after the prayer meeting the night before, when Reverend Bilkins had spoken.

Especially if he discovered his visit to Kerry Cantrell.

His eye twitched, but he struggled to control it as a hard, firm hand pressed down on his shoulder. His father. Had they not been in church, the good reverend would have lashed out with more force. The scars beneath Ross's thin shirt burned from his shame—evidence of his father's previous punishments.

"Where were you earlier, Son?"

Ross pasted a sugary, kiss-ass smile on his face. He'd learned to play his father's game well. At least most of the time.

Unless his father could smell the evidence of his sins still on him.

He'd scrubbed and tried his best to wash it away, but those closest to the Lord sometimes knew things that others didn't. And the scent had seeped beneath his fingernails…. "I heard Reverend Bilkins speak, Father. I was most moved by his words."

His father nodded. "I didn't see you in the front row."

"I stood among the crowd, hoping to be moved by the spirit in the spectators. There was an energy there tonight, Father, an energy that lifted the crowd to new heights."

"An energy you do not feel when I speak?"

Ross winced. His father didn't like playing second fiddle to anyone, even a famous televangelist like Brother Billy Lee Bilkins. Ross rose, brushed the seams of his slacks so they hung perfectly, then smiled at the reverend. "No one moves me as you do, Father. I simply meant to compliment your taste in choosing Brother Billy Lee to join you at the pulpit for this revival."

His father's eyes narrowed, flaring with suspicion as he studied his son's eyes. "You heard the Cantrell woman is dead?"

"Yes, Father," Ross said quietly. "They found her body up at Black Mountain Church."

"We must pray for this town, Son," his father said, pushing him to his knees again. "Pray to extinguish the evil forces that live among us."

Ross nodded obediently and closed his eyes. But in his prayers, his mind wandered. He saw Kerry as he had last seen her.

No one must ever know he had been there....

GRADY COULD BARELY stand to think about what the killer had done to Kerry before he'd finally strangled her. What he might do to another....

Violet.

While Agent Norton arranged for a search warrant for Longhorse's place, Grady drove by her house. He hated to disturb her if she was sleeping, but when he'd left, she'd been so worried about Kerry that he doubted she'd be able to rest. She was probably up waiting, wondering....

Besides, he had to verify that she was safe himself, that the killer hadn't come after her.

Tomorrow he'd get that tracer put on her phone. They'd catch this maniac before he hurt Violet.

Although it was nearly 4:00 a.m., her porch light was still burning. Grady scrubbed a hand over his bleary eyes as he parked and walked up her drive. He knocked softly, then called her name.

"Violet, it's me, Grady."

Seconds later, the door squeaked open. Violet looked pale and worried, the harsh light of the porch accentuating the dark circles under her eyes. She needed sleep. Rest.

Comfort.

He didn't know how he knew that but he did.

Or maybe he needed to be comforted. Hell. It didn't matter.

Unable to stop himself, he stepped inside and pulled her into his arms. He was too damn tired to remember all the reasons he shouldn't. She felt fragile and small and so damn sweet and tender he was afraid he might crush her. But he clung to her for a second, anyway, dropping his head forward into the crook of her shoulder, breathing in her scent.

"You're okay?"

She nodded against him, her hands tentatively reaching up to grip his back. "You found her?"

He nodded. "I'm afraid so."

She let that sink in for a moment. "She was on display just like the others?"

"Yes," he said gruffly.

Violet rested her head against his chest and released a weary sigh. "It's not going to stop, Grady."

He squeezed his eyes shut, knowing she was right. Then realization dawned. He raised his head. Searched her face. "You saw something else?"

"He's putting the victims' names on the vials of blood."

His breath locked in his throat. "Do you know who the next victim is?"

"No, but there are seven more. His finger covered up the names. All except one."

He frowned, his eyes narrowing. "Whose name did you see?"

She hesitated. Bit her lip. Tried to turn away.

"Violet?" He slid a thumb to her chin and tipped her jaw up so she had to look at him. "Whose name was it?"

She picked up the sketch pad and showed it to him. "Mine."

Violet gave a start as Grady released her. He paced across the room like a wild animal, shouting expletives. "Son of a bitch. We have to stop this goddamn maniac...."

"I tried to see more," Violet said. "But it's almost like he knows I'm watching, as if he's taunting me."

Grady halted, looked up at her. His expression was skeptical, then almost believing.

"Did you see anything else?"

"He raised the test tubes and studied the blood." She shivered. "He gets off just looking at it. He wants it to be perfect, but it's not. If only I knew what he meant by that."

Horror darkened her face, and Grady went to her again, then pulled her onto the sofa. He slid an arm around her, cradled her against him. "I told you my dad had found a piece of bone in Darlene's hand."

She squeezed his fingers, ached for his warmth. She had been cold and alone so long. "I don't understand how this is all connected, but it has to be."

"Unless someone knows who killed Darlene and is toying with us, making it look like the murders are connected."

"They are connected," Violet said with conviction.

"The town is going to be in a panic over this," Grady said. "The FBI was already here. I'm meeting one of the special agents in half an hour to question Joseph Longhorse."

Violet shifted, her eyes questioning. "You don't believe Joseph did this?"

Grady shrugged. "I don't know what to think yet. We went by his house, and he wasn't home. Laney said he was out in the woods alone. And he was pissed when Kerry turned down his advances."

"He used to comb the woods when he was a kid." Violet twisted her fingers together. "But that doesn't make him a murderer."

Grady stiffened. He should have guessed Violet would defend Longhorse. "He's a known hunter, Violet. He goes into the woods for days at a time and performs some of those barbaric rituals. And he has a collection of animal bones on his wall."

A shudder gripped Violet. The sound of the bone whistle echoed in her mind. Joseph did have a dark side and a lot of anger. But he had been her friend. Or was he just pretending?

She'd always felt drawn to him. She was drawn to this killer, too....

Could Joseph be the murderer they were looking for?

VIOLET WAS SO SHAKEN, Grady insisted she lie down for a while. She needed rest.

Today at noon she would bury her father.

He promised to see her at the funeral, then left to meet Special Agent Norton. The profiler accompanied Norton, quiet and thoughtful. Grady wondered if she could see into the killer's mind.

Laney Longhorse was dressed in a native smock,

waiting on them at the door. Joseph had not returned. Laney twisted her fingers together, looking more agitated than he'd ever seen her.

"We need to have those bones analyzed," Norton told Adams.

Laney started to protest, but Grady calmed her. Apparently his job here was to play mediator.

Although so far forensics hadn't found any DNA of the killer on the victims, Agent Adams began to collect the bones while Norton searched Longhorse's bedroom and retrieved a few items of clothing and hair to compare for DNA. He also confiscated two hunting knives, a book on Native American ritualistic ceremonies and some miscellaneous articles Laney explained were used for special potions.

"You cannot take all that, can you?" Laney asked.

"The warrant mentions anything that seems suspicious," Agent Norton said.

Laney's chin snapped up. "My boy did not kill anyone. He is a good man."

"But our people are the first ones they run to for questioning, am I not right, Mama?"

Grady glanced up to see Joseph standing at the screened door, a bow and arrow slung over his shoulder, his face smudged, his jeans and bare chest dirty and sweaty.

"Where have you been, Longhorse?" Grady asked.

His dark eyes were devoid of emotion. "Following the ways of my forefathers." Special Agent Norton stepped from the shadows of Longhorse's room. "As in performing the sun dance?"

Longhorse shrugged. "I believe in the ancient customs, as does my *etsi*."

"How about the law?" A menacing expression tightened Norton's face. "Do you believe in that?"

"The law of the universe," Longhorse said. "To follow the sun, the earth, the wind and fire." He dropped his bow and arrow onto the floor. "Now, what is this about?"

"Kerry Cantrell," Special Agent Norton said.

Longhorse turned and glared at Grady.

Norton seemed to detect the tension. "Did you see Kerry last night?"

"No."

Laney shook her head sadly. "There was a search party, Son. Kerry is…they found her. She's dead."

A momentary flicker of Longhorse's eyebrows reflected surprise. Sorrow. Or maybe he was faking it. Maybe the look was regret for getting caught.

"Did anyone see you overnight?" Norton asked.

Longhorse squared his shoulders, met Norton's steady, scrutinizing gaze with a flat look. "No one but the creatures of nature."

"Then you have no alibi?"

"I did not know I was going to need one."

They spent the next few minutes with Longhorse talking in circles. The federal agent's patience waned quickly. And poor Laney looked fit to be tied.

Grady was straddling the fence, uncertain what to believe about Joseph Longhorse.

Agent Adams reentered the room. "I think we've covered things for now."

Longhorse raked his eyes over her. An interested look crossed his face—the look of a man attracted to a woman.

Grady had seen him stare at Violet the same way. A primitive male look.

He hadn't liked it then, and he didn't like it now. And this time it wasn't because he wanted Agent Adams for himself.

He jerked upright, shocked at his own thoughts.

Then again, Grady was a man. Even though he'd first slated Violet as off-limits, there was something about her that was getting under his skin.

Longhorse's attitude was getting to Grady, too. He'd never understood the native's animosity toward him. Perhaps Longhorse's anger against the world was beginning to reveal itself in other ways.

Some very sick, sadistic ones…

After all, he was a hunter. Had Darlene been his first taste of human blood? If so, why had he waited so long to taste it again?

CHAPTER NINETEEN

VIOLET HAD COME TO tell her father goodbye. But what could she say to a man she had barely known?

A cold clamminess covered her skin as she stood beside his casket. She felt his hand in hers as he had walked her to the bus stop her first day of school. Saw the Big Bird lunch box he'd bought for her peanut butter and jelly sandwich. The chocolate chip cookie. The old bike he'd taught her to ride. The day he'd caught her when she'd fallen from the tire swing.

But then he was shoving her in the station wagon. Telling her grandmother to take her away.

Maybe he'd loved her once, before the evil had possessed her.

"I don't understand why you never contacted me, Dad," she whispered, "but at least I know you didn't kill Darlene. Grady's going to find out who did and who put you here."

Reverend Wheeler approached with his son beside him, and Violet knotted her hands. Ross Wheeler's presence added an edge to the already tense atmosphere. She slipped to the front row of the small chapel. Thankfully, Ross claimed the pew on the opposite side. With all that had happened in the past and now the news of this serial killer and Kerry Cantrell, she wasn't surprised that the church was nearly empty. The anxiety in the town was thick. Residents were hiding inside their houses, locking doors that had never been locked before.

Her father's lawyer drifted in, out of respect, she was certain. An elderly couple who lived down the street from her joined the small group, and the town busybody, Beula Simms, tottered in. Probably to gather gossip about Jed Baker's lunatic daughter.

Laney Longhorse slid into the seat next to her and placed a wrinkled hand over Violet's. Violet met her gaze, sensing the turmoil in the older woman's eyes. She hated knowing Laney had suffered through the ordeal of watching her son being questioned for murder. But as always, Laney held her head high, her constant strength and courage an inspiration to Violet. Then Joseph padded up the aisle and joined them, his quiet presence both reassuring Violet of their childhood friendship, but unnerving in the intensity with which he now watched her.

Violet glanced at the pews behind her in search of Grady. She'd thought he would come, as he'd promised....

Then again, why would he? Their fathers hadn't exactly been friends.

Footsteps sounded behind her, though, and she froze. Grady's father strode into the church and took a seat, his hands clasped, his eyes boring holes into Violet. She supposed he wanted to make sure her father wouldn't rise from the dead.

She darted her gaze away from him and clung to Laney's hand.

"Do not let him intimidate you," Laney whispered.

"He is a troubled man. He has lived with much guilt himself."

The reverend read a Bible passage, then spoke in a soothing voice. His words of comfort fell over Violet, echoing through the near empty room, a testament of how sad and devoid of friends and family her father's life had been. How could one eulogize someone who had no one, a man some still believed guilty of murder?

Finally, the pianist played "Amazing Grace." Then six strangers, whom Violet assumed were church deacons, entered and carried her father's casket out the back door to the small graveyard beyond the church. When she'd spoken with her grandmother earlier, Violet had assured her she would bury her father beside her mother.

Both had taken their secrets with them.

Outside, the afternoon heat felt scorching, a cloying humidity hanging in the air. Storm clouds loomed above, the sun hidden behind them. Thunder rumbled, and a streak of lightning zigzagged across the treetops just as it had the day Darlene died.

Joseph and Laney flanked Violet as the preacher offered a prayer. When he finished, she turned and saw that Grady had arrived. His gaze met hers. Regret, questions, heat flared.

Then his eyes cut toward Joseph and his jaw clenched. Joseph responded accordingly. The two men were like lions moving in a circle to fight over prey.

Beula Simms tottered toward Violet and patted her hand. "I'm sorry about your father, dear. Will you be staying in Crow's Landing now?"

Violet swallowed. "I...I'm not sure. For a little while, until my grandmother gets better."

"I'll have to go visit her sometime."

Surprise caught in her throat. "I'm sure she'd like that."

Grady's father barreled toward her. Grady reached out to stop him, but Walt Munroe jerked away. "Miss Baker, if you know what's good for you, you'll leave town today. I told you once, nobody wants you here."

"I'm not leaving until my grandmother is better."

"Dad?" Grady gripped his father's arm.

"She's nothing but trouble," the older man said. "Stay away from her, Grady, or you'll end up in the ground like her old man."

A sudden noise came from the trees behind her. Violet pivoted and noticed Bernie Morris rushing toward her. Behind him, a photographer wielded a big camera. A local news anchor trotted beside him.

Violet shrank back toward Laney. "Miss Baker, we'd like to do a live interview," Bernie shouted.

The news anchor, a thirtyish woman with bottle-blond hair, curved ruby-red lips in a wide smile at her. "Is it true that your father confessed to murder?"

Grady stepped in front of the camera. "Miss Baker has no comment."

A clap of thunder nearly drowned out his reply. The first drops of rain splattered the parched earth.

"Who are you?" the female reporter asked.

"Sheriff Monroe."

"Monroe? Were you related to the little girl who was murdered twenty years ago?"

A muscle twitched in Grady's jaw. "That's correct. We have an ongoing investigation into her murder, as well as Mr. Baker's death, therefore neither I nor Miss Baker are at liberty to discuss the matter."

"But Mr. Baker killed himself," the woman said.

"There's new evidence that says otherwise," Bernie said. "How do you feel knowing your father was murdered, Miss Baker? Don't you want to do something? Avenge his death somehow?"

The clouds opened up and rain began to pour. Violet pushed against the man to reach her car. "I'm not sure what I can do, Mr. Morris. The police are handling things."

"But you're psychic." Morris gestured toward the camera. "Miss Baker has visions. She did twenty years ago when she connected to Darlene Monroe, and I believe she knows things about this serial killer, too."

Violet gasped. The newswoman shoved a microphone in her face, and Grady lunged forward. "Turn off that damn camera." He grabbed the mike. "And keep this off the air."

"It's too late for that," the woman said, huddling beneath her umbrella. "We just went live."

Grady's father suddenly disappeared into the woods. The rain was pouring in sheets now, running down Violet's face. The mound of fresh earth covering her father's grave was turning into a muddy mess.

An image flashed—of Darlene lying in the rain, red mud swirling around her.

Violet shoved away, nearly knocking the reporter over as she crossed the remaining distance to her car. Joseph Longhorse followed, but she didn't wait.

Now everyone would know about her visions, that she'd connected to the killer. The police and FBI would be banging on her door. The town would be gossiping even more that she was crazy.

And the killer…it would give him all the more reason to come after her.

Would Grady be in danger, too? His father's warning echoed in her head. Maybe he was. If so, she needed to stay away from him....

GRADY GRABBED MORRIS'S shirt, twisting the neck so tight the reporter's legs buckled. "Stay away from Violet," he ordered. "Or I'll put you in jail for harassment." Furious, he released him so roughly Morris hit the ground. Then Grady stalked off.

The reporters dashed toward their cars. Joseph Longhorse had cornered Violet at her Civic. Although they hadn't found enough evidence to arrest Longhorse, Grady refused to leave the man alone with Violet. He headed straight toward them.

Longhorse pivoted, glared at him, then walked back to his mother.

Grady caught the door to Violet's car as she climbed in. "Are you all right?" he asked her.

She nodded. But she was soaked and trembling. Mud had splattered the hem of her linen dress, although she seemed oblivious to the fact.

He ached to hold her. "I'm sorry I was late, but I arranged a tracer on your phone, then added dead bolts to the house and repaired that window. I'll follow you home now."

"No." She shook her head and started the engine. "I need some time alone."

He hesitated, swiping at the rain running off his face. "Are you sure?"

Before she could answer, his cell phone rang. He checked the number. Shit. Special Agent Norton. "It's that FBI agent," he said. "I have to take it."

Violet shifted the car into gear. "I'll talk to you later."

Looking frantic and pale, she spun away from the graveyard.

Grady answered the call. "Sheriff Monroe here."

"Monroe, what the hell is this about some damn psychic being connected to our killer? Are you withholding information?"

Grady muttered an oath. He couldn't believe Norton had already seen the footage. "Listen, I can explain."

"Good. I want to talk to the woman, too."

"But—"

"Special Agent Adams and I will meet you at your office in half an hour."

Norton hung up without waiting for a reply. Grady cursed again. As much as Violet wanted to be alone, he couldn't ignore the federal agent's request.

He had to get her and make that meeting. Once they explained Violet's visions and details of the past, it would just be a matter of time before Norton questioned Grady's father....

VIOLET HAD JUST CHANGED out of her drenched clothes when Grady appeared at her door. He looked fierce and sexy, all male hardness and strength. His black hair hung in wet swathes around his bronzed forehead; his eyes were smoky and full of anger and something else—hunger. A charged moment passed between them. It was as if she felt his need, as if he wanted to throw her down on the floor and take her. She wanted that, too. Wanted him to erase the grief and fear she'd been living with for days. Wanted him to make her come alive and burn with feelings. To sate this desire that simmered between them.

But if her visions threatened Grady's safety, she

couldn't allow him any closer. And his own father hated her, had implied that she was endangering his son.

Grady's gaze raked over her, bold and assessing. He didn't reach for her, though. Instead, he stood erect, his eyes alight with turmoil.

"Grady?"

"Violet, Special Agent Norton saw that damn interview with Morris. Norton and his partner insist on seeing us immediately."

The first tendrils of panic rose within her stomach. "No, Grady, I can't." She wrapped her arms around herself. "What will I tell them?"

"The truth," he said matter-of-factly. "Bring your sketch pad, too. There might be something there that could help them." He gestured toward his car. It was still thundering and raining outside.

She didn't want to go out in the storm again. She especially didn't want to face the FBI today.

"They're meeting me at my office in a few minutes."

Resigned, she gathered the sketch pad, dragged on a raincoat, then followed Grady to his car. The ride over was silent, the air fraught with dread.

After the introductions, she was seated at a long table in a small back room at the sheriff's office. She felt as if she was facing an inquisition.

Special Agent Norton was tall and intimidating. His air of authority commanded attention. His partner, Agent Adams, was a feminine version, although Violet detected a slight moment of compassion when she shook the woman's hand.

Norton folded his arms and propped himself, half sitting, half standing, at the edge of the table. "Miss Baker, is it true that you have psychic visions?"

"Lately I have had some odd experiences, yes."

"You said lately?"

"In the past few weeks. The only other time…" She hesitated and picked at a loose thread on her shirt.

"Go on," Norton said.

"When I was eight years old, I shared a special connection to another girl." She explained about Darlene and her death. "Until recently I hadn't experienced a connection with anyone else."

"And why do you think that changed?"

"I have no idea," Violet said. "At first, I thought it was because it was the anniversary of Darlene's death. But I wasn't connecting to her. I was seeing visions of a woman crying out for help."

The agent traded a skeptical look with his partner.

"Can you describe these visions?" Special Agent Adams asked.

Violet nodded, closing her eyes to collect herself. Grisly images bombarded her. "They started while I was in Savannah. I heard this woman crying out for help. Then I saw a man's hands strangle her. And later…later a young woman turned up missing."

"Amber Collins?" Agent Norton said.

"Yes, she'd been in my store the day before."

"And you've seen visions since?" Agent Norton asked.

Violet nodded. "Of the two other women who died."

Again Agent Norton and his partner traded looks. "Describe exactly what you see," he said.

Violet hesitated and glanced at Grady. He nodded for her to continue. She spread the sketch pad on the table, then pointed to the drawings. Both agents' expressions changed. Sharpened with interest. "He ties them up, then draws their blood into a syringe," she said. "Sometimes he calls himself the blood taker, sometimes the chosen one. He keeps it—the blood is his souvenir."

Norton cleared his throat while Agent Adams jotted down some notes.

"Anything else?" Agent Norton asked in a harsh voice.

Violet was trembling inside. "He always leaves the woman with a note that says, 'For our father.' Then he says, *Pin peyeh obe,* my sweetness, you must die."

Agent Adams's eyebrows rose a fraction of an inch. Norton's mouth flattened into an angry, thin line as he turned to Grady. "Have you disclosed details of the serial killer case to this woman?"

"Absolutely not," Grady said. "I would never do that."

"Miss Baker?" Norton snapped.

"No, you asked what I saw, and I'm telling you." Violet shook with fury. She had expected skepticism, but not for him to suspect she was a fraud, or to blame Grady.

"Then how does she know these details?" Norton asked.

Violet stood, reeling with anger. "I told you, I saw them." She reached for her raincoat. She'd had enough. "I didn't ask to see these things, Agent Norton. I don't *want* to see them, either. They just come to me."

"Is there anything else you can tell us?" Agent Adams asked. "Do you see the killer's face? Has he mentioned who his next victim will be, or how he's choosing them?"

Violet searched her expression and found a genuine openness. "There is one more thing. He carves a whistle out of bone," she said. "He makes the women watch him carve it, then he blows through it when they die."

Agent Adams jerked her head toward Norton, then back to Violet. "Miss Baker, if you believed you were seeing details pertaining to these murders, why didn't you come forward?"

Violet chewed her lip. "First of all, I didn't think anyone would believe me. And I didn't see any details that would help. But then… I finally told Sheriff Monroe."

She turned to Grady. "You knew this?"

He gave a short nod.

"Then why did you keep this information from us?" she asked.

Grady cleared his throat, keeping his eyes turned away from Violet. "Because I wasn't sure *I* believed it."

A pang of hurt squeezed Violet's vocal cords. She had to leave. Get out of this room.

She'd thought Grady of all people would back her up.

"Wait, Miss Baker," Agent Norton called.

"There's nothing else I can tell you." She rushed toward the door, exhausted and filled with a myriad of emotions.

Grady stalked after her. "Violet, wait."

"We're not finished with you, Sheriff," Agent Norton snapped.

Grady shot him a threatening look. "Just a minute."

"Go on, Grady," Violet said. "I'll get your deputy to drive me home."

She flung the door open and left, her heart in her throat as she realized she had fallen for Grady, a man she'd trusted with her darkest secret.

A man who hadn't believed her.

"CLOSE THE DOOR, Sheriff." ·

Grady squared his shoulders, bracing himself for an inquisition.

"All right, spit it out. We want everything. The story on your sister's murder, this man Baker's, and anything else you've been holding back."

"I'm not sure they're all connected," Grady said, meeting Agent Norton's gaze.

"But you suspect they are?"

He shrugged. "It's possible."

"Violet Baker knew things that no one could have known," Agent Adams interjected. "Are you sure you didn't let something slip? Maybe she got a look at your files."

"No, this is the first time Violet has even been to the jail since she returned to Crow's Landing." Grady hesitated. "And I didn't report it because I didn't know what to think at first. Even now I wonder if she's on the level."

"The details on all the cases?" Norton snapped.

Grady nodded, then laid out everything he'd uncovered so far.

"No suspects in Baker's death?"

"No one concrete." He explained about Darlene's case, relayed his suspicions about Dwayne Dobbins and Ross Wheeler, and explained their background. But he managed to omit that his father and Baker had argued the night before Jed Baker's death.

"It was interesting that Violet Baker knew about the bone whistle," Agent Adams said.

"That's one reason I think the crimes are connected. I just recently discovered that my sister was found holding a sliver of bone."

Both the agents looked as perplexed as he had been. "The M.O.s are certainly different," Agent Adams commented. "And a serial killer usually doesn't wait twenty years between crimes."

"Unless he's been in jail or a mental institution," Grady said.

Agent Adams nodded.

"We've already been checking priors along with the mental institutions and recent paroles," Agent Norton said.

"The blood angle is interesting," Agent Adams murmured. "So far, we hadn't determined what the killer was taking for his trophy. I wonder what it is about the blood."

"You mean you believe Violet?" Grady asked.

A faraway look settled in Agent Adams's eyes. "Let's say I've seen a lot of strange things, Sheriff. I have an open mind and will look at any possibility that might help us crack this case."

Agent Norton still seemed unconvinced. "Let's get the forensics reports and compare the victims' blood," he said. "See why he might be interested in taking blood samples."

"It may just be a part of his sickness," Agent Adams said. "But it may indicate our guy's in a medical field."

Grady chewed the inside of his cheek, thinking of Farmer. But he couldn't see the older man killing women....

What the hell were they missing?

SOMEONE WAS FOLLOWING HER.

Violet sensed him on her tail as she drove toward the mental hospital where her mother had been. She made a series of turns as she circled the mountain, and checked in her rearview mirror constantly, but she couldn't pinpoint any specific car.

Maybe she was just being paranoid. Spooked by all

that had happened. More than ever, she wanted to get to the bottom of her father's murder and Darlene's. She had a feeling solving them might lead them to the serial killer.

What had that reporter said? That the murders had to do with her mother and father and Darlene's parents.

After she'd gotten home, Violet went to question Dr. Farmer about her mother, but he wasn't around. His wife had seemed nervous, too, as if she didn't want to talk to Violet.

No telling what the poor woman had heard about her....

Wetting her dry lips with her tongue, Violet turned onto Black Mountain Road, bypassing the small church where Kerry Cantrell's body had been found. Whether Grady or that special agent believed her or not, she had to help find this killer. She just had no idea how he was connected to her past.

But he was. The feeling grew stronger and stronger.

Maybe the secret was at the sanitarium where her mother had died.

She pulled into the parking lot and gripped the steering wheel. Black Mountain Mental Hospital. What had happened to her mother here?

Five minutes later, she was seated in an office, facing the director of the facility. Judging from the fine lines around her mouth, her graying hair and the stack of paper coffee cups on her cluttered desk, she was in her late fifties and had a serious caffeine addiction. "I'm Irene Gailstorm. What can I do for you, Miss Baker?"

"I need some information about my mother." Violet recited her mother's name and the dates she had been hospitalized.

"Hmm. What kind of information do you want?"

"Well, recently my father passed away, so I guess I'm feeling very much alone." Violet pieced together the story she'd invented. "I'm sure my father wanted to protect me, so he told me she died in childbirth. I was shocked to find she'd been here and didn't die until I was two."

"Oh, my." The woman worried with her gold loop earring. "I'm sure he did want to protect you, dear."

Violet tensed at the lie. "Right. You see, I've recently gotten engaged, and I'd like to know anything you can tell me about her condition. You understand?"

"You mean you're worried her illness might be hereditary, something you could pass on to a child?"

"That's right."

"Hmm. With both your parents deceased, I suppose it wouldn't hurt." She clicked on the computer to access the files. "Actually, those files are so old they've been archived into the basement. I'll have to get permission to let you see them."

"Is the doctor who treated my mother still here?"

"I'm afraid he passed away."

Violet sighed. "Do you remember my mother or his diagnosis?"

The director pulled off her glasses, swinging them in one hand. "Actually, I do. It was a strange case. She had a reaction to some medication when she delivered you, and she was brought in afterward. She was suffering from delusions and never responded to treatment. Then one night she got hold of another drug and overdosed."

Violet struggled to maintain her composure. She hated to think of her mother alone, locked away, dying.

"Thank you." Her mind logged the details. Had her mother self-medicated and overdosed herself? Or, in light of all the recent revelations, could she have been murdered?

Violet had to see those files.

She slipped through the halls and found the staircase, checking over her shoulder to make sure she didn't get caught. The wing housing the files was old and out-dated, the staircase dark and musty. She shivered and fought her nagging fear of the darkness, once again sensing someone was following her. She glanced over her shoulder and saw a shadow, which disappeared down the murky corridor.

A clerk sat behind the metal cage, talking on the tele-phone and filing paperwork at the same time. Violet ex-pected security, but the shabby facility hadn't bothered to update it. The small lock on the gate to the rear had already been opened by someone else and hadn't been refastened securely, so she eased it open and tiptoed in-side.

The room resembled an old warehouse, with boxes of labeled files stacked on metal shelves. She wandered up and down the aisles until she located a box marked with the correct year, plus the initials A to F. After pull-ing over one of the metal stools, Violet climbed up and dragged the box off the shelf. She had just sat down to examine it when a shadow loomed over her abruptly. Vi-olet caught her breath and swung around, just as some-thing hard slammed against her head. She saw stars, then slumped to the floor.

Through the haze of semiconsciousness, the pungent scent of smoke drifted toward her. The room was on fire.

And she was going to die in the blaze.

CHAPTER TWENTY

DWAYNE DOBBINS REACHED in his pocket, removed the matches and lit another cigarette as he wove through the woods of Black Mountain. A giggle escaped him as the flame caught, then he raised the match and watched it burn down to his fingers. When he felt the heat scald his fingertip, he inhaled, then blew out the flame and dropped the match to the ground. Another drag and he started walking again, whistling as he went.

His mama would be mad with him, but he didn't care. He was a grown man now. He oughta be able to do what he wanted. She couldn't keep treatin' him like a kid.

But she did. She got mad about everything. Mad when he tracked dirt on her clean floor. Mad when he didn't take his pills. Mad when he didn't run straight home from his job, cuttin' grass out at the cemetery. But he liked it there. Liked to sit with the gravestones. Like to pretend they were tall towers reaching up toward the sky. Toward heaven where the great father lived. He could climb up the sides and reach up and touch him.

Just like a real angel.

Yes, he tried to be good for that father, just like Reverend Wheeler said on Sundays. Wheeler's son understood. He tried to please his father all the time, too. But Wheeler was naughty.

So was Dwayne. He liked girls. Only his mama didn't know about it. She thought he was just a kid with a little itty bitty moron brain.

But he was a man now. And he had man urges. His hand fell to his crotch, and he grinned. His mama couldn't stop that. Couldn't keep him from wantin' what other men wanted. Like that pretty Violet Baker. He'd liked her when she was little and scrawny. Her and that girl Darlene.

Too bad Darlene hadn't liked him back.

He'd liked Kerry Cantrell, too....

But she hadn't liked him. She'd looked at him like he was an idiot. But he was big and strong. Some day he'd show them all.

Maybe he'd show Violet how strong he was. He'd watched her today at the graveyard. She'd looked so sad and lost. Lonely. Just like he felt sometimes. The two of them had connected.

That's why he'd followed her.

He had to impress her.

But then that fire had broke out. And he'd knowed he had to get out of there fast. They'd blame him. Then his mama would really be mad. She might find his matches and his Marlboros and take 'em from him. She might even send him away this time.

He finished the cigarette, tossed it to the ground and stomped out the stub. Then he beat at his shirt to knock the smoky odor from the material. If Mama smelled the smoke on his clothes, she'd punish him. He'd be scrubbin' his skin until it fell off in layers. Sometimes he could feel the bones pokin' through when she used the brush on him.

He should have brought a change of clothes.

But he hadn't thought that far ahead.

Oh, he weren't as stupid as everyone thought. His daddy said so. His daddy was good to him. He let him drive his old truck. Left it parked at the junkyard so Dwayne could get it whenever he wanted. But he'd had to leave it there instead of driving it home.

He wanted to see his daddy again tonight. But his mama had no idea he'd met him. She said his daddy was no account. But she'd run him off. It was her fault Dwayne didn't have a father. So he had to sneak away to visit.

Oh, there was so much she didn't know. So much she'd punish him for. Especially if she knew the secrets he shared with his daddy. But he'd keep those secrets with him forever.

He'd do anything to please his father.

AS SOON AS GRADY LEFT his office, he drove to Violet's, but her driveway was empty. Irritated that she'd left with his deputy, he rode through town to see if he could find her. Tension crackled through the downtown area. No longer were women strolling with their babies in the park or people chatting and visiting on the sidewalks. The streets were empty, the citizens safely locked in their houses, behind closed doors.

He radioed Logan. His deputy sounded out of breath when he answered.

"Where the hell did you take Violet Baker?" Grady asked.

"To her house," Logan said. "But she was acting suspicious, so I followed her. She drove up to the Black Mountain Mental Hospital."

Grady frowned. "Why did she go there?"

"I don't know," Logan said. "But a fire just broke out, and they're evacuating the place now."

Grady snapped the siren on and raced out of town toward the mountain.

WALT MONROE WATCHED the west end of the mental hospital erupt in flames, and thought *good riddance*. That Baker girl shouldn't have been asking questions. Dammit, he'd warned her to leave town. To let the past rest.

Nosing into stuff that had happened twenty years ago wasn't going to do anything but get her killed. Along with the rest of them.

Teresa's pale face flashed into his mind. Sure, her death had been ruled an accident, but he knew better.

Regret for his own indiscretions played heavily on him.

Maybe if he'd been a better husband, more understanding, more faithful, Teresa wouldn't have done what she had. She wouldn't have gone back to work. She wouldn't have taken a job at that hospital. She wouldn't have been desperate. And she wouldn't have contemplated leaving him.

And if he'd had better control over her, she wouldn't have talked.

That mouth had gotten her killed. And all because she'd wanted to avenge the Baker woman's murder. Those no-account white trash hadn't mattered. But he hadn't been able to make her see that.

Just like he hadn't been able to convince Darlene to stay away from Violet. Damn tenderhearted women.

He felt for the piece of bone in his pocket and ran his fingers over the jagged surface as he watched the fire truck race up to the building. Orange flames already licked the sky, and smoke billowed upward, a fog of black. The fire department would save the wing where the patients were, but hopefully, the files on the Baker woman would all be destroyed.

Then nothing could link the woman's death back to Teresa's. Unless Doc Farmer decided to talk…

AT THE SIGHT of the thick funnel of smoke curling into the sky, Grady felt his heart slam against his ribs. Chaos had erupted. The lawn was filled with emergency workers and nurses unloading patients and running back to help evacuate more people. EMTs and doctors checked patients, calling out orders and vital signs. Nurses were scattered through the throng, assisting wherever they were needed.

The firefighters jumped into motion, spraying water on the section of the hospital that was on fire. It seemed to be contained at the moment in the west end, but the structure was so old the fire would spread quickly. His heart pounding, Grady searched the exterior, then waded through the crowd looking for Violet.

Five minutes later, he still hadn't found her. Was she inside? Trapped somewhere? Or had she escaped and already left?

He spotted Logan assisting an orderly with a gurney, and raced toward him. Another fireman helped a heavy woman in a white uniform toward the ambulance. She didn't appear burned, but was gasping for air and obviously needed oxygen.

Grady waved his arm and got his deputy's attention. "Where's Violet?"

Smoke and sweat coated Logan. "I don't know. I haven't seen her."

"Did you follow her inside?"

"Yeah, she went to talk to the director. I heard them discussing old records."

Grady grabbed one of the nurses. "Where do you keep the old records?"

She pointed to the blazing fire. "In the basement in that wing."

Jesus. Grady ran toward the building to get help. Violet might be trapped inside.

VIOLET STIRRED, her head aching, her eyes blurring. She tried to sit up, but choked on the smoke curling inside the room. It was thick and heavy. Perspiration trickled down her face. No, it was blood. She wiped it away. Someone had hit her over the head.

Had whoever it was set the fire, too?

A sob welled in her throat as panic tore through her. Wood crackled and hissed around her. Flames inched up the wall on the far side, rippling along the floor. Heat scorched her back, the acrid smells of burned wood and hot metal filling the air.

She tried to scream for help, then crawled toward the door and felt it. It was slightly warm; not hot yet. Maybe she could still escape.

Weak but determined, she covered her mouth to stifle the smoke and yanked on the door. The handle wouldn't budge.

A shelf of files behind her erupted into flames. Sparks spewed and scattered as ashes scattered along the floor. She yanked and pulled again, but the door wouldn't open.

Think, Violet, think. You have to save yourself. No one even knows you're here.

Frantic, she glanced around for something to break

the small window at the top, but saw nothing. Fire sizzled and blazed toward her, eating the paper and files in seconds. A rag and a bottle of cleaning chemicals sat nearby. Oh, God. The chemicals would add fuel to the flame.

She moved them out of the path of the blaze, but realized that gave her only a few more seconds. The fire was spreading way too fast. The entire back section was a fireball. Soon the rest of the room would be engulfed.

The small metal step stool she'd used earlier had been shoved in the back corner. She grabbed it and slammed it against the window. Glass shattered and exploded. She dragged in air and screamed again. Someone had to hear her. She couldn't die. Not yet.

Not before she found her father's killer.

Not without holding Grady and kissing him one more time.

"I HEAR SOMETHING. That way." Grady rushed down the stairs, the firemen on his heels. Although they'd tried to hold him back, he'd managed to bypass them and lead them to the basement. Broken glass littered the concrete floor in front of him. A shout erupted from behind the door. His heart pounded.

"Help!"

He raced toward the door. Tried to open it. It was locked. Hot.

A fireman rushed up behind him.

"She's in there!" Grady yelled.

"Stand back!" The fireman raised an ax and slashed at the door. Wood splintered. He swung again and a fist-size opening appeared above the doorknob. Another blow and it broke completely. Thick gray smoke poured out. Fire hissed at their feet.

"Violet!" Grady tried to push his way in, but the fireman restrained him. "Violet!"

A cry sounded, then she stumbled out. Grady grabbed her as she collapsed against him. Her forehead was bloody. She was coughing and choking. The fireman placed a mask over her face, and she gulped in air.

A different fireman dragged a hose down the stairs. Another joined him and they started dumping water on the flames.

Grady lifted Violet into his arms and ran up the stairs, taking her to safety.

His lungs ached as he rushed down the smoke-filled hallway and into the fresh air. Outside, a surreal scene met their eyes, but a certain order had taken over the madness. Grady scanned the lawn for the nearest paramedic, then hurried forward. When he reached the ambulance, he eased Violet onto a stretcher.

She pulled at the mask. "I'm all right." She coughed again, running a finger over the bruise on her head.

The orderly pushed the oxygen mask back in place. "Keep this on for a few minutes."

Grady examined her head, then motioned to the paramedic. The man nodded, reached for gauze and antiseptic to clean the wound and check for the severity.

Grady took her limp hand and searched her face. "Are you hurt anywhere else, Violet?"

She shook her head.

Relief welled in his chest. He stroked her cheek with the pad of his thumb. "What happened?"

Violet's chin trembled as her big blue eyes met his. Her voice came out a whisper. "Someone tried to kill me."

AFTER THEIR CONSULTATION with Violet Baker and seeing those drawings, Special Agent Norton reviewed the forensics report with renewed fervor. He hadn't believed the woman, but he couldn't figure out how she'd described the details of the Bone Whistler crimes that the police hadn't revealed unless she'd been informed by the sheriff or witnessed the murders herself.

And he believed Monroe when he'd claimed he hadn't told her.

Agent Adams had recounted other cases where psychics had helped the police crack cases, and seemed to think the Baker woman was the real thing.

Norton suspected she was a nutcase. Maybe she'd somehow hacked into police files. Either that or she'd slept with Monroe, and he hadn't even known when she'd accessed his files.

Norton worked with details. Concrete evidence. He didn't believe in hocus-pocus or ghosts or psychic abilities. In fact, he didn't believe in anything intangible.

Turning back to the file, he contemplated what he knew so far. His research into Monroe's past had confirmed the sheriff's story about his half sister's death and the subsequent investigation.

But Monroe had been holding back. Keeping something from him.

Parents were always main suspects when children turned up missing. The sheriff hadn't once mentioned that his father had been a suspect in his sister's disappearance.

And then there was that deputy. Logan's past was questionable at best. His wife had disappeared last year. Logan had been a major suspect. And there were other things about the man that were odd. Like the fact that he practically lived in the dark. And he'd had some genetic tests run....

Norton definitely had to do more digging on the man.

Agent Adams entered, a slight scent of rose water drifting through the door with her. Norton's libido kicked up, his body responding. He ignored it. This attraction to her was simply male hormones. Sexual chemistry. He could find someone else besides a co-worker to sate that need. Especially a married one.

So why hadn't he lately?

"What does the report say?" Agent Adams asked.

As usual, she was oblivious to his thoughts. "We've found a connection between the victims."

Adams moved closer, one hand snaking out across the scarred wooden table as she read the report with him. Her wedding ring sparkled in the light.

"All the victims share an unusual genetic trait," Norton said, thinking of Logan. "The first victim had a gene for a rare disease and should have been dead by now. But a mutated gene has reversed the disease's effect."

"Interesting." Adams's dark brown eyes rose to meet his. "The other victims share this same unique quality."

Norton shifted, reading her mind. Those damn test tubes Violet Baker had claimed the killer collected. Could this genetic disorder be the criteria he was using to choose his victims? And if so, why would he choose someone with an abnormality and draw their blood?

"According to the specialist at the M.E.'s office, the trait had to be passed down through the birth father."

"But these three women weren't related. They certainly didn't share the same parents growing up."

"That doesn't mean they couldn't have the same father."

Their eyes connected. The possibilities registered.

"We need to check the sperm clinics," Norton said. "And any nearby scientific research facilities."

Agent Adams nodded. "And we have to question Violet Baker again. Maybe there's more she can tell us."

VIOLET'S HEAD WAS spinning. While the paramedic checked on another patient, Grady stood beside her, his hands clenched, his jaw tight. Through the haze of smoke, she saw the new doctor in town. He was rushing around from one patient to the next, soothing their fears, administering wherever they needed him. One of the EM's pointed out his assistant, Finley, also. Violet shivered. The guy seemed creepy.

Then she spotted Grady's deputy. He stood with his hands on his hips, his face taut, as if he was transfixed by the grisly image of the fire. What was he doing here?

Grady brushed a strand of hair from her cheek. "We're going to take you to the hospital overnight—"

"No." She pushed away the oxygen mask and sat up. She didn't want to be in the hospital. She wanted to go home with Grady.

"Violet, you've been injured. You inhaled smoke," he said. "Let them admit you."

She reached for his hand, squeezed it. "Please, I want to go back to my father's." She saw the deputy approaching, and a chill skated up her spine. "Did he come with you?"

Grady twisted his head sideways, hesitating. Before he could answer, Logan reached them.

"Are you all right, Miss Baker?"

Violet swallowed. Remembered that eerie feeling that a car had been behind her on the road. "Did you follow me here?"

Logan cast his eyes toward Grady, then back. "I was worried about you, ma'am. I just wanted to make sure you were safe."

She bit her lip. She didn't believe him.

Grady's cell phone rang, and he stepped to the side to answer it. "Sheriff Monroe here."

Grady's mask fell back into place. "All right. We'll be right there." He pocketed the phone, then turned to her. "Are you really feeling okay?"

Violet nodded. Although she couldn't explain the reason, she wanted to escape Logan. "What's wrong?" she asked.

"That was Special Agent Norton. He wants to see both of us at the office ASAP."

"Should I come, too?" Logan asked.

"No. Stay here. Find out what caused that fire."

Logan squinted at the now dwindling blaze. "You think it was arson?"

Grady glanced at Violet, then nodded. "Someone knocked Violet out before the fire started. Alert the fire marshal to check for evidence of assault as well as arson."

Logan gave a clipped nod, his expression unreadable. "I'll get right on it."

Violet gripped Grady's arm as he helped her stand. They argued about her driving, but she insisted, so he walked her to her car. "Has something happened, Grady?"

"Agent Norton has the forensics report. He said they found a connection between the women."

Violet fastened the seat belt, brushing dirt from her jeans. "Maybe they're getting close to the truth."

"Or we are."

Violet met his gaze. Emotions clouded his eyes. Anger. Fear. Questions. That was the reason someone had tried to kill her—they *were* getting close to the truth.

"Why did you come out here, Violet?" Grady asked.

She shivered. Glanced back at the smoky, charred remains of the wing that housed the files. "I was looking for information on my mother."

He angled his head to study her. "What are you keeping from me?"

She explained about the receipts. "My father lied to me about my mother. She didn't die in childbirth, Grady. She died here." Hurt welled inside her. "The story was that she had a reaction to the anesthesia when she was pregnant, then had a psychotic breakdown. Two years after she was admitted here, she overdosed."

Grady's eyes sharpened. Then sympathy lined the edges of his mouth as he captured her hand in his. "Maybe your father didn't want you to know that your mother had emotional problems."

Violet shook her head. "No, there are just too many strange things that happened. I think she was murdered."

SOMEONE HAD TRIED TO KILL Violet.

Grady still couldn't get past that fact. A feeling of impending doom tightened his chest. They were on the cusp of learning something significant about the Bone Whistler murders, and his instincts told him it all pointed back to Darlene's killer.

And then there was Violet. Almost killed tonight. Trapped in that fire. The image would give him nightmares forever. He...was starting to care for her. Too much.

When Darlene had died and his father had written

him out of his affections, Grady had sworn he'd never get close to another living soul. His mother had abandoned him. His father hated him. And every woman since had wanted something he couldn't give.

His heart.

Now it throbbed and ached, the shell he'd built around it shattering into pieces. Violet was going to be hurt again before this was over. He knew it in his soul.

And he didn't know how to prevent it. Because something about the tone of Norton's voice had alarmed him. What had they discovered?

"You didn't see who attacked you?" he asked.

"No." Violet shifted restlessly. "Someone followed me up the mountain."

"You didn't tell anyone in town where you were going?"

"No."

Grady contemplated the facts. Logan had followed her. Logan had a Native American heritage. He'd known the expression *pin peyeh obe.*

But so did Joseph Longhorse. And Grady had seen Longhorse at the graveyard that day. Longhorse carved bones and hung them on the wall like prizes. Longhorse had been shunned by society, especially by Walt Monroe.

"Why do you think your mother was murdered?" Grady asked.

"I don't know."

A long silence stretched between them. He let it linger, hoping she'd elaborate.

"But my father lied to me about her being alive, so he could have lied about everything."

Her silence registered. She wondered if her father had killed her mother.

Grady covered her hand with his again. To offer comfort. His own skin tingled in response. His sex hardened.

"I don't understand all this, Grady."

He willed himself to be a gentleman. The last thing Violet needed was a pawing man demanding something from her. But God, he wanted to pull her in his arms and feel her, just to make sure she was still here, alive. "For what it's worth, I don't think your dad killed her."

"Maybe he knew why she was murdered," Violet whispered.

Or who had murdered her.

The unspoken accusations echoed in her voice. Maybe her father had known. Maybe it had something to do with his own father's argument with Baker. And her father's death.

Twenty minutes later, Grady parked by his office, hopped out and rounded the hood to assist Violet from her car. She'd already opened the door, and met him halfway, the courage in her eyes admirable. He slid his hand to the small of her back as they entered, silently offering his support. He had no idea what was coming. But he knew it might change their lives forever.

VIOLET'S STOMACH fluttered with nerves as she took a seat across from the federal agents. Agent Norton shot her a scathing look. He obviously thought she was a freak.

She steeled herself not to care.

Catching this killer was the only thing that mattered. Not the man's coldhearted, judgmental attitude.

Only Grady's opinion counted. But he'd told Agent Norton he hadn't believed her....

Her gaze drifted to Grady's, her instincts warning her not to count on him. But she couldn't help it. She was so tired of being alone. She needed Grady on her side.

"What's this all about?" he asked.

Special Agent Norton gestured toward the file. Agent Adams folded her arms and leaned a hip against the desk.

"We received the forensics report and found some interesting facts," Norton said. "First of all, the killer injects the victims with a drug called Pancuronium bromide. It paralyzes the body."

"So we should look at suspects with medical backgrounds," Grady stated.

"Or someone with access to medical supplies," Agent Adams said. "With the Internet these days, anyone could access information on what kind of drug to use to cause paralysis."

Agent Norton nodded. "We also discovered the connection between the victims," he said in a matter-of-fact tone. "Apparently, each victim had a special genetic trait inherited from her father."

Violet frowned.

Grady leaned forward. "I didn't think the victims were related."

"It appears that they are, genetically. The first woman, Amber Collins, had a gene for a rare disease. She should have died at an early age," Norton explained, "but the gene mutated and reversed the disease's effect. Our specialists tell us this is traced to past experiments—the gene had been given to the birth father in gene replacement therapy to cure an autoimmune disease."

"And all the women have this gene?" Violet asked.

"Yes," Agent Adams said. "We're having more extensive bloodwork done, but there are definite similarities."

"Had each of the victims received genetic treatment?" Grady asked.

Agent Norton cleared his throat. "We believe the victims were all products of one sperm donor."

The images of the test tubes of blood the killer collected flashed in Violet's mind. The names on the labels. Her own printed and waiting. "You think that's the reason the killer draws their blood?"

Agent Adams nodded.

Violet's head was reeling. Then *she* might possess this gene…. She might be a product of a sperm donor. Perhaps she was not her father's child….

"There's more," Special Agent Norton said, glancing at Grady. "Before you arrived, we traced the births to the clinic where we believe the women were impregnated."

"Where?" Grady asked.

"From the same clinic where your mother worked, Sheriff Monroe."

Grady tensed. Violet put the pieces of the puzzle together. They had been looking for a connection between Darlene's death and the recent killings.

Violet caught her breath. Had Grady's stepmother been involved in this experiment? Could Darlene have possibly been born from this sperm donor? If so, that meant Grady's father was not Darlene's.

The reporter's words reverberated in her head. *It all goes back to your mother and father and Darlene's….*

CHAPTER TWENTY-ONE

QUESTIONS BOMBARDED Grady. If the victims shared a sperm donor father, then they were technically half sisters.

His mother had worked at the clinic where these women had received in vitro fertilization—had she known about the treatments? And if these victims were related through a sperm donation, could Darlene have been a product of the donor, as well?

If so, did his father know?

"This puts a new spin on the case," Special Agent Norton said. "We need to explore that research facility and anyone with a medical background. I'll get someone to check out all the employees."

"And you need to find a list of all those women who received donations from that sperm donor," Grady said. "Check to see if my half sister was one of the offspring."

Norton nodded.

"Warn the agents to tread lightly here," Special Agent Adams advised her colleague. "Some of the parents may not be aware they received this donation. It's possible the women were duped into thinking they were receiving their husband's sperm, and that the husbands have no idea their offspring aren't their biological children."

"We'll check with the research facility first," Norton agreed. "But this opens up an entirely new set of suspects. If one or more of these women did know about the sperm donor and withheld the information from her spouse, and later the husband discovered his child was not legitimately his, he might have been upset enough to retaliate."

"True," Agent Adams said. "Although why kill the offspring? Why not kill the wife? Or go after the original donor or the doctors who performed the in vitro? They were technically the ones who betrayed the men, not the offspring."

"There's something about the abnormality in their blood," Violet said, gaining everyone's attention. "He's infatuated with the blood, but he's upset that it's not perfect."

"What do you think he's looking for?" Adams asked.

Norton hissed dismissively.

Violet ignored his reaction. "I don't know yet. But he's still searching for the perfect specimen for his ultimate sacrifice. He has seven more test tubes ready."

"Can you tell who the next victim will be?" Agent Adams asked.

"No, but he's following a definite order. I can't figure it out."

"Being orderly fits the profile," she said. "But he's not going alphabetically. So far it's Collins, Allen, then Cantrell."

Grady contemplated the new revelations, not liking the questions they triggered in his own mind. They'd been searching for a connection between the past and present. If Darlene was a product of this sperm donor, they'd found it.

Teresa had died in a car accident when Darlene was

small. His father and Jed Baker had secrets—had they suspected Darlene wasn't Walt's child?

Agent Adams's theory about the fathers echoed in Grady's head.

Had Teresa's death really been an accident? If his father thought she'd had an affair… Grady had seen his dad and Doc Farmer arguing. Could Farmer be involved?

Grady's stomach convulsed at the disturbing train of thought. Although he had suspected his father played around on the side, Walt had been jealous of Teresa. Grady had heard them argue more than once, his father accusing her of flirting with someone in town, of not being satisfied with him. He'd been afraid she'd abandon him, as Grady's mother had.

"We're still wondering why you've connected with all the victims," Special Agent Adams said, looking at Violet.

Violet's face had turned ashen. "My name is on one of the killer's test tubes."

Grady shuddered. Agent Adams's eyes widened in response.

"You believe you're going to be a victim?" Agent Norton asked.

Violet nodded. "You think it's possible that I might have been one of these sperm donor babies?"

For a long moment the air was charged with tension.

"It's possible," Norton finally replied.

"Then I should be tested," she stated.

Both agents murmured in agreement.

Grady contemplated the significance. If Darlene was a product of the sperm donor and Violet was, too, that meant she and Darlene were half sisters. Then he and

Violet were related.... No, that wasn't possible. He and Darlene had different mothers. Now he realized they might have different fathers, too.

If Violet and Darlene were related through blood, that could explain Violet's psychic connection to her and to the other victims. It might also explain Violet's theory that her mother had been murdered. And if Violet's father had known and decided for some reason to come forward with the information, that might be motivation for his own murder.

SHOCK WAVES RIPPLED through Violet's whole being. Darlene might be her half sister. No wonder they had connected. But if she had been a product of a sperm donor, then the man she'd believed to be her father all these years was not her biological one.

Was that the reason her father had sent her away? He thought she was some kind of freak, because she didn't belong to him. Was that the reason he hadn't loved her?

Was it possible he'd discovered the truth and killed her mother out of anger?

No. Violet couldn't believe it. Besides, he was dead now. He couldn't be involved in these other killings. Maybe he'd discovered the truth and planned to tell, so someone had murdered him to keep his secret hidden....

Deputy Logan knocked and stuck his head in. "Turn on the TV, Sheriff. That reporter's on. You won't believe what he's saying."

Grady cut his eyes toward Violet, then the federal agents flipped on the small set in the corner of the sheriff's office.

"Earlier today a fire broke out at the Black Mountain Mental Hospital outside of Crow's Landing. Police have confirmed arson." The camera panned across the chaos on the lawn, flickered over to where Violet sat on the gurney. "A local psychic who is helping the FBI with the recent serial killer case, now called the Bone Whistler, was at the scene. According to the director here, Violet Baker was searching for information on her mother, who died at the hospital. My own research shows that the Baker woman was directly tied to a nearby research facility that may be linked to the Bone Whistler murders. Police are looking at Ross Wheeler, a local teacher who was also implicated in a scandal involving child molestation charges. Other suspects include a local Native American, Joseph Longhorse, and Dwayne Dobbins, a psychotic young man with a history of violence.

"Interestingly enough, I've recently learned that Ross Wheeler, son of the prominent Reverend Wheeler, was the product of a sperm donation that originated at this very same research facility."

Norton turned accusatory eyes toward Grady, then Violet. "How the hell does he know all that?"

Rage darkened Grady's eyes. "I have no idea. But he should be arrested for interfering with an official investigation." The sheriff stood and paced, his boots clacking on the hardwood floor. "Maybe he's our killer. He's been in every city so far where there was a murder. And he sure seems to know a lot."

"We should investigate him," Agent Adams agreed. "I'll get someone on it right away."

"Have you talked to this reporter, Miss Baker?" Norton asked. "Is this some kind of ploy to get attention for your hocus-pocus?"

"No. The last thing I want is publicity." Or to be tied

to Ross Wheeler. Could he possibly be related to Darlene and the others?

"That's right," Grady said, his voice gruff. "Going public is only going to put Violet in danger."

Violet hugged herself. She'd seen Ross Wheeler in the crowd at the hospital. Had he been following her? Had he tried to kill her to keep her from finding out the truth? Or could Grady be right—could Bernie Morris be the serial killer?

"SHIT. DAMN. FUCK." Doc Farmer slammed the remote control down, his blood pressure boiling. He had to get out of town. Do it now before this whole damn thing blew up in their faces.

He booted up his computer, located the necessary files and trashed them.

Slightly relieved, he phoned the airport in Nashville and booked a one-way flight for two to the Caribbean. First they'd take that vacation Hattie had been babbling about for ages. Yes, he'd get out while the getting was good. While his wife still admired him.

His palms damp, he grabbed his briefcase and started tossing papers in it. His will, insurance forms, the bonds he'd saved for retirement. Then he opened the safe behind his desk, removed the cash he kept stashed inside and stuffed it in one of the pockets. By the time his wife got home, he'd have them ready to go. He'd tell her he'd planned the trip for a while, that he'd wanted to surprise her. It would be like a second honeymoon.

Swiping at his bald spot, he closed the briefcase, then started up the winding staircase to pack suitcases. The doorbell rang midway. He halted, his knees nearly knocking together. It was probably Walt, who must have seen the news report and panicked. God, he didn't know if he could calm the man or not. He might have to give him an injection. Just like the night Teresa Monroe had died. And then Darlene....

The doorbell rang again, then again. It had to be Monroe. The impatient bastard. Trying to calm his own erratic nerves, Farmer hurried down the steps and opened the door. Instead of Walt, it was Monroe's son.

Damn. What was the sheriff doing here?

"Evening, Sheriff, what can I do for you?"

Grady strode in, his feet practically pounding the parquet flooring. "I want some answers, and I want the truth."

Farmer inhaled sharply, reached inside his pocket for an antacid and popped it in his mouth, then led Grady to his office and closed the door. As much as he wanted to throw the man out, this was the sheriff. But if Hattie came home, he didn't want her to hear their conversation.

"Years ago, you worked with the Black Mountain Research Hospital, right?"

Acid burned his stomach. But he couldn't very well deny what was public knowledge. "Yes, a while back. What's this about, Son?"

"My family. The fertility clinic."

He had obviously seen the news report. That little scum-sucker reporter had just opened a dangerous can of worms. But Farmer wasn't offering up any confidences and getting himself killed.

"And?"

"Tell me the truth. Was Darlene my father's child or was she the product of a sperm donor?"

Farmer propped one hand on his aching stomach. "Don't you think you should ask your father this?"

"This is an official call. I'm asking as a part of an ongoing investigation," Grady said.

"You know I can't divulge patient-doctor information."

"My sister was part of some experiment there, wasn't she?" Grady snapped, ignoring Farmer's comment. "She was a product of a sperm donor. Did my father know?"

Grady was getting way too close to the truth. "You need to ask him," Farmer said. "As I told you, my medical files are confidential."

"Did Teresa know what she was getting into?"

"Sheriff—"

Grady grabbed Farmer by the collar, but the door in the foyer slammed, and Farmer jumped aside. "My wife is home now. You should go, Sheriff."

Grady cursed, told him he'd be back, then left. Farmer wiped his forehead with his handkerchief, gripping his stomach. Then he picked up the phone. He had to warn Monroe before he got out of town.

Then he never wanted to hear from the man again.

DR. GARDENER, the young doctor who'd replaced Doc Farmer in town, approached with his lab technician, Joe Finley. "We finally meet, Miss Baker."

Violet nodded, remembering the way he'd watched her at the diner. This man, with his nice green eyes and friendly smile, was handsome enough to have any of the women in town. Why would he be interested in her? The plain Jane, poor country girl…

"I've discussed your situation with Special Agent Adams," Dr. Gardener said. "You need a complete workup, right?"

Violet nodded. "We believe I might be connected to the victims in the Bone Whistler murders."

"Is it true you have psychic abilities?" Gardener asked.

Violet searched his face for condemnation, but thankfully found only sincere interest, so she nodded. "It appears that way."

The lab tech's eyes bulged as he watched her, unnerving her slightly. Finley was wiry, and appeared nervous as he assembled the supplies to take her blood. The glass vials clattered in his hands as he removed them from the box.

"Well, we'll find out what you need to know," the doctor said.

"You're new in town, aren't you?" Violet murmured.

"I've been here a few months," he told her. "But it's been slow getting people to accept me."

"Laney Longhouse said all the young women speak highly of you."

"The younger generation is more accepting. The people who've lived here for a while still want to see Dr. Farmer. They're accustomed to his way of practicing medicine."

"I'm sure they'll come around," Violet said, although she, as much as anyone, had borne the brunt of their judgmental attitudes.

"Are you ready?" The lab technician's voice squeaked slightly. Violet frowned, wondering if he was new to the area, too, then chided herself for looking at everyone with suspicion. It was likely that the killer had medical training, though. A doctor, lab tech, orderly, paramedic...

"Finley volunteers here," Gardener said. "He'll take care of you while I check on another patient."

Violet nodded, then sank into the hard vinyl chair. When she received the results from this test, she'd know for certain if the man she'd thought was her father really was her blood relative. Did her grandmother know the truth? If not, what would this do to her? Or would it really matter? Her grandmother loved her...no matter what.

"Make a fist." Finley smiled, but Violet felt the hair on her nape bristle when he touched her. His fingers were long, his nails clipped short, she noticed, as he rolled her arm sideways, examining it. "You have thin veins, don't you?"

She swallowed. "I guess so."

"Yes, you do." His lip twitched. "It makes it harder to find a good vein, but don't worry. I'll get it the first time." He patted her arm. "Drawing blood is my specialty. I've had lots of practice."

She nodded, but stiffened as he reached for the tourniquet. His voice had grown deeper, his eyes intense, as if he derived pleasure in his job. *I am the blood taker....*

"You know, I feel like we've met," he said in a low voice. He wrapped the tourniquet around her arm and tightened it, his fingers lingering slightly before he released her. The pockmarks on his face were emphasized by the harsh lights.

"I don't think so." Although his voice sounded strangely familiar. Low. Grating. Almost singsongy. Like the killer's.

Or was she imagining things?

He inserted the needle, and her blood began to flow through the tubing. The victims of the Bone Whistler had watched this same scene as they died.

She would be facing the killer soon. Watching him do the same thing to her. But other women were going to die first.

Unless she figured out the killer's identity.

"MAY GOD TAKE DOWN that little bastard!"

Ross Wheeler startled at the sound of his father's fury. He'd prayed that the reverend hadn't seen the news report, but he'd known that was one prayer that wouldn't be answered. Half the town had probably viewed it by now. Knowing the way the old biddies gossiped, the other half would know its contents within an hour.

He slid the cabinet door closed to hide his treasures, and locked it tightly. It wouldn't do now for his father to see what he had collected. No, it wouldn't do at all.

Another string of expletives scorched the walls as the reverend stormed down the steps toward him, and Ross barely resisted the urge to run and hide. He could go into the woods. Back to his secret place. The place where he had seen Kerry.

And his father...

"Son, did you talk to that son of a bitch reporter?"

Ross shook his head, careful to maintain his obedient look.

The reverend jerked him up so hard, his knee hit the edge of the cabinet. He bit back a yelp. Any reaction would only make his father madder. "Are you lying? You know what the Lord will do to you if you lie to me."

"I haven't talked to him, Father."

"How about that crazy lady?"

Violet Baker. He shook his head adamantly. No, he hadn't talked to her. But he wanted to. He wanted to do other things to her, too. To find out what she knew about these women dying.

"Then how the hell did he come up with that nonsense? I'm going to sue the living daylights out of him for saying you aren't mine. That's a lie. Is he trying to ruin my reputation?"

"I don't know, Father."

Beady, angry eyes glared back at him. But Ross managed to maintain his obedient, docile expression. Finally, satisfied with his compliance, his father slung him backward. Ross fell onto the couch, teeming with anger inside.

"I'm calling my lawyer right now," the reverend said. "There's no way that weasel is going to get away with telling those lies and maligning my character."

Ross began to shake as his father climbed the stairs.

He tried so hard to be perfect. But he'd never meet his father's standards.

And a lawyer wouldn't do any good with Bernie Morris. Morris was too greedy. Not just for money, but for fame—fame at any cost. Just like Brother Billy Lee.

Just like Ross's father.

He stroked his sex, safe with his secret for now. But he had other work to do. And it was time to get started.

Then he'd come face-to-face with Violet Baker. If she really was psychic, she might expose his secrets. He couldn't let that happen....

BY THE TIME Grady reached his father's house, he was livid. He'd told himself repeatedly that Walt hadn't been aware of the sperm donor, but as his mind ticked over all the odd things that had happened, he couldn't make himself believe it. The awkwardness and hatred between his father and Baker. The argument between Walt and Doc Farmer. The way he'd never mentioned Teresa again after her death. The fact that the night of her accident, the police hadn't been able to locate him for hours.

If his father had been involved in Darlene's death, or had known the killer's identity all these years and hadn't spoken up, Grady would make him pay. It didn't matter who her biological father had been.

And now Violet was in danger again because she was trying to help find this crazy killer.

It wasn't fair. They had all lost so much. Darlene. Violet. Him. And all because of these secrets.

He pushed open the door without even knocking, and barreled in. "Dad?"

His father didn't answer.

Grady stormed through the kitchen to the workshop, but it was empty. Surprised, he spun around and headed to his father's office. Walt hadn't used it in years, but just might be there now. Seconds later, Grady cursed when he found it empty.

He flew up the steps to his father's bedroom, halting at the sight of the closed door. Was his dad inside, sleeping off another drunk?

Grady didn't care. He pounded on the door, then charged in. "Dad?"

His father was rummaging through a lower drawer of his bureau. He jerked upright, gripping something in his hand. Grady's mouth fell open, his heart racing when he recognized the object.

It was a whistle. A whistle made of bone.

CHAPTER TWENTY-TWO

GRADY STARED AT THE BONE whistle in horror. His father had claimed to have gotten rid of it. He'd lied to Grady.

But he'd kept it all these years…why? Because he thought it might help him find the killer? Or had he kept it as a trophy?

"It's not what it looks like, Son."

Grady jerked his head up. His father hadn't called him son in years. Why now? To make up for the lies? Hell, he was too damn old to fall for it. "No?"

"No." His father's sallow face was blanched, his eyes puffy and red. The alcohol was killing him. Or the guilt.

"Then why the hell did you lie to me about keeping it?"

"I don't know." He ran a shaky hand over his face and sank onto the bed. The covers were rumpled, the sheet hanging askew. "I guess I thought it was sick of me to have kept it."

"Sick because it was a trophy?"

His father's lips compressed into a narrow line. "Is that what you think, Grady? That I killed my own daughter?"

"But she wasn't your real daughter, was she, Dad?" Anger hardened Grady's voice. "You found out that Teresa had used a sperm donor and you couldn't stand it.

You were jealous so you killed her. Then one day the truth got to you and you killed Darlene."

"No…" Walt dropped his head into his hands, rocking back and forth. "No, that's not the way it happened."

Grady inhaled, reining in his temper. He had a job to do, and if it meant arresting his own father, he'd damn well do it. For Darlene's sake. For all the other victims. For Violet.

"What I don't understand is how you could have been so cruel to me. Why you blamed me and made me live with this guilt all these years."

"I told you it didn't happen the way you said. I never laid a hand on your mother or Darlene."

Tense minutes stretched between them. Anger, distrust and painful memories had created an unbreachable gap. "I wish I could believe you, Dad. But you've lied to me before. Why should I accept your word now?"

"Because he is your father."

Grady snapped his head sideways as Laney Longhorse entered the room from the adjoining bathroom. He watched in utter shock as she went to his father and laid a hand on his shoulder. "The truth must come out now, Walt. It's time for Grady to know everything."

DARKNESS WAS FALLING as Violet let herself inside her father's house. It would take time for the results of the bloodwork to come back. Although deep down, she already knew the answers.

It all made sense. If she'd been a product of the sperm donor, and she and Darlene shared some genetic abnormality with the other victims, their blood connected them all. Hopefully, the FBI would retrieve a list of all the recipients of that sperm and be able to locate the other possible victims before the killer struck again.

An eerie quiet enveloped the room, allowing childhood memories to flood back. She struggled to remember the good moments, but the image of her father shoving her into that station wagon always stood at the forefront of her mind. When had Jed Baker discovered she wasn't biologically his? Had that realization tainted his feelings for her?

And if he wasn't her father, then who was? Who had donated the sperm? Had the donor discovered the abnormalities in his genes and decided to kill the offspring because they weren't perfect?

She flipped on the lamp, halting at the sight of a small brown package on the kitchen table. It hadn't been there when she left.

Suddenly panicking at the realization that someone had been inside the house again, she reached for some kind of weapon to protect herself. A kitchen knife in hand, she listened carefully as she tiptoed toward the den. Empty.

What about the bedrooms?

Inhaling sharply, she held the knife in front of her and slowly padded toward her room, listening for an intruder. The floor squeaked beneath her shoes. A fly buzzed somewhere in the corner. Dust motes floated in the air in front of her.

She peeked inside her bedroom. Nothing. Her grandmother's room was also empty.

And then her father's. No one. The faded chenille spread still hung crookedly. The sheer curtains, yellow with age, were in place.

Breathing a sigh of relief, she headed back to the kitchen and picked up the box. It weighed next to nothing. Fearing the worst, she held the package to her ear and listened to make sure there was nothing ticking inside. No sound. Not even a rattle. It was wrapped in plain brown paper with no postmark or return address. "Violet" had been spelled with letters cut from a newspaper. She'd leave the letters in place for the police in case they could trace them. But she had to know what was inside.

Her hand trembled as she tore the edge of the brown wrapping. Her imagination went wild. Movie clippings flashed in her head. Sometimes killers sent body parts. Fingers, toes…

The paper fell away. A small jewelry-size box came into view. She sucked in a sharp breath as she opened it.

Her heart squeezed at the sight of the object. Emotions clogged her throat. It was half of a Best Friends necklace. She felt the jagged edges of her own. This was the other half.

Darlene's.

GRADY STOOD STONE STILL, trying to recover from the shock of seeing Laney Longhorse here with his father. "What's going on?"

His father gestured for him to sit down, but he couldn't. Not here in his father's bedroom. "Answer me, Dad."

"I…made some mistakes in the past, Son. But I kept this bone, hoping someday I'd be able to use it to find Darlene's murderer."

"If you wanted that, you should have given it to me."

"I was trying to protect you."

"I'm a cop, Dad. It's my job to study evidence, connect the clues to solve crimes." Grady rocked back on his boot heels, impatient. "For God's sake, that piece of bone could be vital to this serial killer case. We think they're all connected."

"I'm aware of that," Walt said.

"And you know all about that research clinic, that Teresa conceived Darlene through a sperm donor."

"Yes, but at first Teresa didn't realize it wasn't my sperm. And when she found out, well, that's why *they* killed her."

"Who, Dad?"

His father hissed. "I don't know names. She called me as she was leaving the clinic that day. She was upset, mumbling something about sperm donors and some kind of experiment and the Baker woman. She'd discovered that Darlene wasn't mine, but they warned her to keep silent." He hesitated, his breathing wheezing out. "Then she had an accident. Just like that Baker woman, she ended up dead."

"Why didn't you report your suspicions, Dad?"

His father squeezed his eyes shut, then opened them. Anguish blackened his pupils. "Because I had no proof. And I was mayor. I didn't want word to spread that Darlene wasn't my child."

Grady shook his head in disgust.

"And then we lost Darlene and I had no proof," he said, reaching for a match and a cigar. "I was worried if I said something, whoever killed Darlene would come after you."

"You didn't come forward to protect me?"

"That's right."

Grady leaned against the doorjamb. "If you wanted to protect me, you wouldn't have blamed me for Darlene's death."

"I was so screwed up by then," his father admitted, lighting the cigar. "Tate was beatin' at my door with questions, and I felt guilty. Teresa would never have gone back to work if she hadn't found out I was sleeping around. And she wouldn't have wanted a baby so bad. She thought..." he hesitated, suddenly clamming up.

"She thought having a child would hold him forever and make him love her," Laney said. "And your father didn't hurt your sister or Teresa. At least not physically. He tried to do right by both of his children."

"And how would you know all this?" Bitterness edged Grady's voice.

"Because I was with him the night of Teresa's accident."

Grady gaped at them both. He'd always suspected his father of having affairs, but with Laney? Joseph's mother? Jesus, if Joseph knew, no wonder he hated Grady and his dad.

Grady was shaking inside. He couldn't believe all the secrets. "How long has it been going on?"

His father rubbed a hand over his chest. "A long time. I'm ashamed to say I never had the courage to go public."

Grady gritted his teeth. "And you were together the night Teresa died? What about when Darlene was killed?"

Laney nodded.

"There's more, Son." His father stood slowly, as if summoning his courage. "Laney was the first woman I ever loved. But we didn't think it was right to be together back then. My career, our family name…"

His father's words began to register.

"So I let him go," Laney said. "I wanted your father to be happy. I thought I was doing the right thing for him. For both of you."

Grady staggered backward. "What are you saying?"

His father slid an arm around Laney's thin shoulders. "Grady, Laney is your mother."

MAVIS DOBBINS HAD TO protect her son. No matter what it cost her. Even if she had to kill that dang, stupid reporter.

She tossed her apron over the kitchen chair and headed toward Dwayne's room to check on him. She hadn't worked all these years to have some no-account, scrawny-ass man nosing into her and Dwayne's past, throwing their dirty laundry on the lawn for everyone and his neighbor to tromp on. It was all she could do to support herself working at the Rest Easy Nursing Home, what with Dwayne hopping from one piddly job to another. And she owed old man Tate and that doctor a bundle already. Now that Morris feller had reported that filth about her boy. Next thing she knowed, he'd be digging into old police reports and bribing Doc Farmer to talk.

That bastard would sell his own young 'un for a dollar.

And if Morris ever got ahold of Dwayne's medical records…

"Dwayne!" She beat on his door, almost taking it off the hinges in the process. But the boy had locked it. What in the world did he do in there all by hisself?

"Open this door before I get me a crowbar and tear it plumb down."

Silence.

"Dwayne Dobbins, do you hear me? I said open this danged door." She banged on it with her fists, the wood vibrating beneath her splotched hands. "Hellfire and damnation, I'm gonna take a stick to you if you don't answer me."

More silence.

Like a pressure cooker ready to explode, she ran to the garage, grabbed a sledgehammer and hurried back. She'd teach him to lock the door. He couldn't lock it if he didn't have one.

She raised the sledgehammer and slammed it into the thin wood, watching it splinter. Again and again she swung it, until the doorknob fell off, rolled across the floor. Then, on a full-blown tear now, she pushed inside the room.

It was empty.

A pack of matches lay on his nightstand, a newspaper spread on the denim coverlet. The picture showed the fire up at Black Mountain Mental Hospital.

Her heart jumped to her throat. What in God's name had her son been up to now?

VIOLET TWISTED her Best Friends necklace between her fingers, remembering the day Darlene had given it to her. She'd been so happy she'd felt like crying.

Tears dribbled from her eyes now. Tears for Darlene, the best friend she'd lost.

The killer had sent the necklace to her. He'd kept it all these years. And he knew where Violet was. The necklace was meant as a message.

He was coming for her soon.

Was that the reason she would be last? Because Darlene had been first? Start this killing spree with Darlene and end with her?

A tingle traveled up her back. Violet froze, sinking onto the couch as another vision rose from the darkness.

He was on the hunt again. She could feel it. He was prowling, looking for his next victim.

She had long blond hair. Hair that looked like a silken web flowing down her slender back. Hair the color of sunshine.

He liked sunshine. So much better than the darkness. It had been so dark when he'd been locked up. And cold. And lonely.

She wouldn't like it, either.

He sighed, his body humming with adrenaline as he imagined her eyes widening in fright as she faced death. He could almost feel her body, stiff and unbending as he laid her on the altar. He could see her blood. Dripping. Dripping. Filling the tube.

All for the father.

She turned, angling her head as if she sensed him in the crowd. No. Only Violet Baker could do that.

He couldn't wait to take her.

Those big, baby-blue eyes would cry out, plead with him to stop. But he'd remind her that it was too late.

She was the final sacrifice. The last little angel.

And if she was as perfect as he expected her to be, his father would bow to him as the favored. Just as it should have been all along.

"Can you see me, now, Violet? Can you look into my eyes and see yourself as I take your blood?"

Violet dropped her head into her hands and moaned, terror ripping through her. Yes, she could see him. But where was he?

"No." Denial, shock, betrayal spread through Grady. Laney Longhorse was not his mother. She couldn't be. She'd been in town, nearby, all these years. His mother had left town....

His mind retraced the years. Years he'd felt abandoned. Years he'd tried to please Teresa and his father, and been unable to do so. Years when he'd blamed himself for Darlene's death.

Years he hadn't known he had a half brother and mother living a mile away.

He had to work to find his voice. "How could you lie to me all this time?"

Laney reached for him, but he jerked back. "I did it for you, Grady. I wanted you to have a good life, the kind of life your father could give you. You've seen how hard it's been for Joseph. It would have been that way for you."

"At least Joseph knew his mother loved him," Grady growled. "I thought mine had abandoned me."

"But I never did. Not in my heart."

Grady's stomach churned. All the birthdays he'd wanted his mother to show up for. The Christmases. The times he'd tried to imagine what she must look like. "I suppose everyone in town knows the truth, but me," Grady said bitterly.

"No." His father reached for him, but Grady backed away. "I told everyone your mother was someone I'd met in Nashville."

"And I didn't move into town until later," Laney said.

"What about Joseph?" Grady asked. "Is he your son, Dad?"

Walt blanched, but Laney answered instead. "No. I met his father a couple of years later. He was a stranger who came through town."

Grady had to get away. He couldn't deal with this now. Avoiding Laney's pleading, tear-filled eyes, he turned to his father. "Give me the bone whistle."

"What?" Walt shook his head. "But why? What are you going to do with it?" Panic laced his voice. "If you give it to the FBI now, they'll think I'm guilty."

Grady glared at him. He didn't know what he'd do. But his father might get rid of it. Grady couldn't let that happen.

"It might help me track down Darlene's real killer, Dad, and the person who killed Teresa and Violet's father. And for God's sake, what about all these other women? Don't you care about anyone but yourself?"

"We both care about you, Grady," Laney said in a calm voice. "Your father kept quiet to protect you."

"He kept quiet to protect his political reputation."

His father dropped his head forward, cigar ashes falling to the floor. "My political career was over when I became a suspect in Darlene's murder."

"Parents are always suspects when there's a missing child," Grady stated.

"And now the FBI is looking at Joseph," Laney said.

Laney pressed a hand to her face and shook her head. "Joseph is innocent. I swear it, Grady. He is not a killer."

Grady stared at them both in disbelief, took the bone whistle from his father and placed it in his shirt pocket. Then he turned and stormed out the door without another word.

He had to get away. Think about what they'd done to him. Find out the truth.

His cell phone rang before he reached his car. Shit. He checked the number. Violet. Emotions hung thick in his voice as he answered, "It's Grady."

"Grady, I just had another vision. The killer is hunting for his next victim."

His hand went to the bone whistle in his pocket. "Did you see anything specific, something that might help us know where he is?"

"No." Her voice broke. "But when I got home, there was a package waiting for me. It was the other half of my Best Friends necklace. Darlene's half. I think the killer sent it to me."

VIOLET PACED THE FLOOR, trying to connect with the woman. But either she had temporarily escaped the killer's clutches, or he had caught her and she was unconscious. Maybe if Violet tried harder, she could read the killer's thoughts. Maybe he'd reveal the victim's name.

She slumped onto the sofa, leaned back and closed her eyes, willing the worst to happen. Willing herself to see inside his head. But there was nothing but darkness. A cold, pervasive emptiness that clawed at her, sucking at her energy. Like a tunnel filled with quicksand, it dragged her deeper and deeper. She couldn't escape. She couldn't move.

Then she was looking into his eyes again.

They smiled at her. Blue. Just like her own.

Suddenly they disappeared behind a wall of black. He was playing with her. But the scent of death surrounded her. Strong. Acrid.

A knock sounded, and she nearly jumped out of her skin. Grady.

She ran to the door and flung it open. Grady's shoulders were slumped, his hair rumpled, his jaw clenched. His eyes blazed with emotions. Something was wrong. He looked more haggard than she'd ever seen him.

"I called and warned Agent Norton about your vision," Grady mumbled. "Did you see anything else?"

Violet shook her head. "No. Nothing specific." She showed him the package that had arrived. His expression turned darker as he bagged it and the wrapping to test for evidence.

"This confirms there's one killer. The feds are working on that list of medical personnel and the sperm donors and offspring." His shoulders slumped even more.

"Grady, I'm so sorry. Did something else happen?"

A sardonic chuckle rumbled from him. "Other than the fact that a serial killer is about to strike again, and I don't have a damn clue who it is?"

She nodded, then he crushed her against him. Her heart was beating frantically.

"I just found out my dad had an affair years ago," Grady said.

She pulled back and looked into his eyes, saw the pain and anguish. "I don't understand."

"He claimed my mother abandoned me."

She nodded, her heart breaking for him. She, of all people, understood that sick feeling. They had both felt abandoned. No wonder they had been drawn together.

"But he lied to me. All these years, he lied." His voice thickened with raw pain. "My mother's been living in Crow's Landing all along. Just a mile from me."

"What?"

He nodded, released her, then turned and paced across the room. His movements were jerky, his breathing erratic. His need palpable.

When he faced her again, a storm brewed in his eyes. "My mother is Laney Longhorse."

Violet stared at him in shock. "Oh, Grady! Why… why didn't they tell you?"

"They said they wanted to protect me." His voice was laced with bitterness. "But he was protecting his damn reputation. He was a fucking politician. And he'd screwed a native woman. He didn't want to lose voters."

Violet's heart ached for him. "I—I'm sure Laney wanted to tell you, Grady. She—"

"She gave me up, Violet. She left me with *him,* a man who didn't want me around." He began to pace again, his boots clicking on the floor. "Do you know how many times I lay in my bed and wondered what my mother looked like? Wondered where she was? Why she couldn't have loved me?" His voice rose, tormented. "I always wondered why he hadn't kept any pictures of her. Why he never tried to find her."

Violet felt his pain, sharp and raw. It was just how she'd felt, all those times she'd ached for her own father.

She had to go to him. Do something. Say something.

"Grady, I'm sure Laney wanted you. She probably thought she was giving you a better life—"

"How could it be better when I thought she didn't love me? When my father blamed me for Darlene's death? When I…" He gripped the edge of a chair, dropped his head forward, his big shoulders shaking with repressed emotions.

Violet couldn't stand it anymore. She walked toward him. Lifted a hand. Stroked his back. He felt hot. Tense. Then he turned. Tried to contain his emotions, but pain darkened his eyes.

She reached up and cupped his jaw in her hand. "I understand, Grady. But Darlene's death wasn't your fault. Your father had no right to blame you. I...I know, I've struggled with that guilt all my life."

"They lied to me, Violet...."

"I know. I'm so sorry." Tears pushed at her throat. But she wouldn't cry. She had to comfort Grady. He needed her right now.

She offered him a watery smile. His hand grasped hers and cradled it. His palms were clammy, his face tortured. "I should go."

She wet her lips, unspoken emotions rippling between them. The fear she'd felt earlier rushed back. Her own need pulsed in her words. "No, Grady, please don't leave."

He shook his head. "You don't deserve this, Violet. You were right to stay away from this town. You should leave now, go somewhere so you'll be safe."

"Leaving won't make it go away, Grady," she said in a weary voice. "Believe me, I carried the pain and loss with me wherever I was."

He turned again. Then he raised his head and looked into her eyes. Emotions lay there between them. Hunger. Desire.

She reached for him, and he crushed her in his arms. Then his big powerful body shuddered against her. She forgot her own anguish and fear. She wanted to make his hurt go away, though she had no idea how. But she had to hold him.

Her pulse pounding in her throat, she cupped his face and pressed her lips to his. His mouth met hers. The sound of raw need he emitted set her body on fire.

She'd never been held by a man like this. Had never trusted anyone to get close. Had never wanted to tear away all her walls and let herself be this vulnerable.

But Grady was different. He was strong. Tough but fair. Caring but driven. Dependable. Trustworthy.

And he needed her now almost as much as she needed him.

A guttural groan tore from his mouth as he pulled away. "Violet...I...should go."

"No." She shook her head. Liquid heat flared inside her belly as his eyes raked over her, possessive, needy.

She answered him with the same hunger. His hand slid to her back, jerking her against his body. It was hard. Powerful. Ready. Any resistance she might have had shattered like glass. They had both been through so much. But they could soothe each other in the darkness.

Violet wanted to do that while she could. Just in case they didn't have a tomorrow.

CHAPTER TWENTY-THREE

GRADY ORDERED HIMSELF to walk away. To collect himself. He should be doing something more to solve the case.

But the federal agents were on it now, and there was nothing he could do until he got their reports. At the moment, he felt worthless. As if he were falling apart at the seams. As if being in Violet's arms would hold him together.

At least, by being here, he could protect her.

Her lips parted in invitation, and a surge of wanton possessiveness overcame him. He tasted sweetness and innocence, and the undeniable yearning of a woman who knew how to give. Her unselfishness touched him. Her tenderness spiked the heat in his blood. Her quietly whispered hunger fueled the need that had become a desperate, incessant urge.

He had wanted her for so long. Ever since the moment he'd seen her in her father's house that morning, wearing nothing but that flimsy, cotton nightshirt.

Telling himself it was all wrong had made no difference. Tonight wasn't about wrong or right, but about soothing the ache that had been building in him for so long. The emptiness and hunger that he sensed Violet felt herself.

Blinded by his own selfish needs, he walked her backward to the sofa. He slid his hand into the tangled tresses of her long dark hair and wound them around his fingers. Seduced by her sultry femininity, he inhaled her own special scent. She felt small, fragile and needy, and he wanted to protect her as much as he wanted to throw her down and grind himself inside her.

She parted her lips, and he slipped his tongue inside, tasting, exploring, memorizing each tiny sound she made as his sex throbbed between them.

Her breath bathed his neck when he broke the kiss. He lowered his mouth to the nape of her neck and suckled the fragrant skin there. His hands moved over her shoulders, her breasts, her hips, down to pull her more snugly into the V of his thighs. She was softness against his hard planes, gentle against the fierce driving force of his raging desire.

"God, Violet, I've wanted you ever since I found you at your father's house that first night."

"I want you, too, Grady. Don't let go."

He smiled against her hair. The dam of frustration broke with her softly spoken plea, his resistance splintering. Intoxicated by the flame of desire in her eyes, he traced a path back up to her neck, lifted the straps of her top and slid them down her shoulders. His lips followed his fingers, the shell she wore falling to the floor around her feet. She kicked off her sandals, and he breathed in the earthy scent of her body as her breasts spilled over the lacy bra.

While her clothes were simple and conservative, her undergarments were daring, hinting that beneath all that gentle calmness and strength lay a passionate woman. One who had been deprived of loving. And she was only a breath away from him now.

"You're so beautiful."

A shy smile spread on her lips. "Grady, I'm not."

"Not ready?" He raised a brow, the heat enveloping them.

She blushed. "No, it's not that. I'm…not very experienced," she whispered.

Her throaty admission only heightened his desire, making his resolve to pleasure her more intense. "Baby, just tell me if there's anything you don't like."

"I can't imagine not liking anything you'd do, Grady."

"God, Violet." He dropped his head against hers, amazed at her confession. He had always been reluctant to get involved, afraid he didn't have enough to give.

He wanted to give Violet everything within his capacity. Whether or not it was enough, he didn't know. But he'd damn sure die trying.

His heart pounding, he unfastened the button and zipper of her skirt, then watched it fall to the floor, as well. A pair of pale blue lace panties hugged her heat and accentuated the delicate flare of her hips. He breathed in the sight of her, his erection straining inside his jeans. She glanced down and noticed. A purely feminine smile spread on her mouth. Then she reached out and tentatively touched the bulge. He groaned, his sex jumping. Murmuring his name, she cupped his face again, kissing him with the fervor of a wanton lover.

Grady forgot restraint and slowness. There would be time for that later. All he knew was this urgent need to brand her as his. To stamp himself all over her and let her assuage his pain, banish this dreadful feeling of loneliness.

He shucked off his shirt, his nipples stiffening as her hands raked over the coarse hair on his chest. Then she was in his arms. Against him. Close. But not close enough.

He cupped her breasts in his hands, lowering his head to taste her there. Then he stripped off her bra and panties and planted kisses all over her body. She moaned and writhed as he eased her onto the sofa, then crawled between her thighs.

Brushing himself over her femininity, he watched her face twist with excitement, saw her eyes glaze with passion as he lowered his head and drew her nipple into his mouth. He tasted, explored, suckled until she bucked and clawed at him. He thrust his sex against her heat, loving her other breast the same way, then fingered her nipples as he kissed her belly and rolled his tongue along her inner thighs.

"Grady?"

"Shh, let me have all of you, Violet." Aching to be closer, he slid his hands under her hips, brought her to his mouth, drinking in her sweetness as his tongue savored her moistness. She shivered, gripping his arms, moaning wildly. He couldn't release her. Instead he made her a prisoner to his desires as he sated himself with her taste. Finally, her body bucked, the sensations gripping her eliciting an inferno of need in him. Taking her pleasure as his own, he kicked off his jeans and underwear, slipped on a condom and rose above her. He thrust himself inside her with a low throaty moan.

She hugged him tighter, her hot sheath enveloping him, her innocence humbling. He slowed, not wanting to hurt her. But she gripped him and urged him to move faster, deeper. His resistance fled. He buried himself inside her, filling her until their bodies were one, until sensations overpowered him.

As his own release exploded, he dropped his head into her neck and called out her name, claiming her innocence as his, forever.

"I DON'T WANT TONIGHT to end," Violet whispered.

Grady braced himself on his hands above her. "Neither do I." His dark gaze skated over her, searching. "Are you okay? I didn't hurt you, did I?"

She wet her lips and smiled. "Do I look like I'm in pain?"

He shook his head, a damp strand of hair curling on his forehead. "You look like a woman who's just been loved."

A giggle escaped her as she brushed the strand of hair into place. "I think I could be in love with you, Grady." In fact, she always had loved Grady, she realized. The reason she'd never let another man take her to bed. She had been waiting for him.

He froze, studied her face. His mouth twitched as if to smile, but his eyes were dark with turmoil. The last thing she wanted to do right now was pressure Grady.

"I—"

She pressed a finger to his lips. "You don't have to say anything. Just love me again, Grady. And this time I want to pleasure you," she whispered.

Grady nuzzled her neck again. "Oh, baby, don't you realize you did? I enjoyed every minute." His voice grew low, throaty. "But I've never been good with words. I…I don't know what I can offer, Violet."

"I'm not asking for promises, Grady." His sex surged toward her, though, proving he wanted her again. She rubbed her belly against him. "I just want tonight. To be in your arms. For you to hold me so I can love you." When the case was over, she'd return to Savannah. And he'd stay here, go on with his life.

Regret warred with desire in his eyes, but she traced her fingers down his length, teasing the tip of his erection. Sensing the power she had, she began to stroke him, her own body growing moist at the passion enflaming his eyes. He groaned and pushed himself into her hand, lowering his head to take her nipple between his teeth. When he tugged it into his mouth, sensations flooded her. "Oh, Grady."

He flipped her over so she sat astride him, and he thrust inside her. Violet could never have imagined acting with such abandonment. But the minute he cupped her breasts in his hands and stroked her flesh with his torturous fingers, she came apart. She didn't need experience. She only needed to act on her own primal instincts.

And to be with Grady.

GRADY HAD ALMOST FALLEN asleep on the couch with Violet cradled in his arms when someone started pounding on the door. He was disoriented and groggy, for the first time in weeks, maybe years, feeling sated, comfortable and warm. So warm and happy that he didn't want to open his eyes. He didn't want to deal with whatever god-awful police business he'd have to handle today. He didn't want to remember the reasons he'd come here… he only wanted the bliss of lying in Violet's arms.

The knock sounded louder.

Damn. It might be something important. After all, Violet had said earlier that she'd had another vision.

She jerked upright, her bare breasts swaying in the dim light.

The knocking came again.

"Dammit." He reached for his jeans. "I'm coming!" He shrugged them on, then grabbed his shirt, but the bone whistle he'd taken from his father fell from his pocket onto the floor.

Violet gasped.

He turned to her, ready to explain. But the horror in her eyes stopped him cold. And the accusations… She was looking at him with fear in her eyes, as if she thought *he* might be the Bone Whistler.

Violet scrambled off the couch, reaching for the faded afghan and wrapping it around her. "Grady?"

He picked up the whistle. "It's not what you think," he said, realizing he'd used the exact wording his father had just before he'd delivered his lies.

The pounding intensified and Logan yelled Grady's name, just as he yanked open the door.

Special Agent Norton stood on the stoop, along with Logan.

"What the hell are you doing?" Grady asked.

Both men glanced at his state of undress, then past him to Violet. Grady couldn't deny the obvious.

"We've arrested your father on suspicion of murder," Norton said. "I thought I'd give you the courtesy of telling you myself. I didn't realize you were busy…."

Grady bit his tongue. How could he explain taking Violet to bed? He'd needed her. He glanced at her pale face and saw the wheels of doubt turning in her head. She thought he'd used her, that his father was guilty and he'd covered it up. After all, Walt Monroe had threatened her. He might have been responsible for the vandalism on her house. Her accident. The fire…

Grady broke out in a sweat. "Why did you arrest my father? Do you have new evidence?"

Agent Norton nodded. "Your father and Jed Baker had a fight the night before Baker died, a detail you neglected to tell us. And we also learned your father had a bone whistle similar to the one found at the crime scenes."

Norton's gaze fell to the item in Grady's hand, his flat look indicating his conclusion. He suspected the same as Violet—that Grady was covering for his dad.

"We also know that he lied about his whereabouts the night your sister was murdered. He has no alibis for the nights any of the women were killed. And we found DNA placing him in Kerry Cantrell's room."

"His DNA?"

"Yes, it was on file from when your sister was missing."

Shit.

"There's more," Logan said in a harsh tone. "The reporter who ran the story yesterday was found dead at the edge of your father's estate."

Grady hissed, cursing beneath his breath as he zipped his jeans. "I'll be right there." He cleared his throat. "Can you give me a minute?"

Agent Norton offered a clipped nod and spun on his heel toward the door. Logan was watching with an odd look, as if he resented his boss bedding a possible witness. Hell, Grady had known better, too. He just hadn't been able to stop himself.

Or maybe Logan had wanted Violet for himself. Well, he damn sure wouldn't have her.

As soon as the door closed, Grady turned to Violet. "Let me explain."

"Did your father have that bone whistle?"

He refused to lie to her. There had been too many secrets already. "Yes, he took it from the crime scene and kept it. I…I didn't know he had it, not until last night, when I went by his house."

"You knew he might have killed Darlene and my father and all those other women. And he threatened me." *Yet you were ready to cover for him.*

He heard the hurt and pain in her voice and reached for her, but she pushed his hand away, wrapping the afghan tighter around her shoulders—those shoulders he had kissed and caressed moments earlier. "No, Grady. I understand, I really do. Even though he lied to you, you're loyal to your father." A wealth of sadness laced her voice. "I guess I can't blame you."

"It's not like that, Violet. I still want to find the truth."

Her look of distrust tore at him. He did want to find the truth, didn't he? But after knowing his father had lied about his mother, could he believe anything the man said?

Agent Norton banged on the door. "We're leaving."

"Stay here," Grady told Violet. "After we meet, I'll send Logan back to be with you until I can return."

Hurt and confused, Violet simply stared at him as he gathered the necklace and wrapping paper, then walked out the door.

THE BITTER TASTE of distrust filled Violet's mouth as Grady left. Their earlier lovemaking seemed shameful now.

Had Grady suspected his father all along? Had he played up to her to see how much she knew? Earlier, he'd suggested she had repressed memories. Had he woven his way into her life, encouraged her trust, to make sure she didn't remember?

A silent war waged within her.

She'd thought she was in love with Grady. Would he be so vile as to deceive her?

No…she didn't believe it.

Your own father sent you away. Why would Grady love you?

Trembling, she paced the room. Even if Mr. Monroe was guilty and Grady hadn't known about his father's involvement, would he defend him? Let his feelings for his dad come between them? After all, he'd slept with her without telling her the truth.

It was only one night, Violet reminded herself. Grady hadn't made any promises.

The telephone rang, jarring her from her troubled emotions. She stared at it for a moment, wondering if it was the killer. Wondering why she hadn't had another vision tonight. Where was he holding the woman?

The phone trilled again, and she stumbled forward and grabbed it. "Hello."

"Miss Baker, this is Dr. Sternum at the rehab facility. It's about your grandmother."

Violet swayed dizzily. "What? Is she okay?"

"Yes, but she's asking for you now. She's agitated and disoriented. It might help if you'd come by."

Guilt suffused Violet. She'd promised she'd visit, but she'd gotten so tied up in solving these murders, in alleviating her own guilt, in Grady, that she had neglected her grandmother. The only person who had ever really loved her.

"I'll be right there." She hung up the phone and ran

to the bathroom to clean up. She had to wash off the scent of Grady's lovemaking so she could forget him. If Grady's father was the killer, and in jail, maybe these visions would stop and she could go back to Savannah tomorrow.

Remembering Grady's promise to send his deputy back to guard her, she decided to forgo a shower. She didn't trust Deputy Logan. He'd been at the mental hospital the day she'd been attacked and nearly died. What if he had knocked her unconscious and set the fire? As a deputy, he could easily approach women without frightening them. Even Grady trusted him.

But Violet's instincts warned her to be wary of him. It was eerie the way he always kept his eyes hidden behind those Ray-Bans. Death and darkness surrounded him. And there was something else…something she couldn't pinpoint.

There was no way she'd get in the car with him or ask him to take her to the rehab facility.

SHE WAS ALONE. And she was coming to see her grandmother.

Perfect. Ross Wheeler had known Violet Baker would run to granny if she thought her grandmother needed her. And he had done a good job of impersonating a doctor. He was right proud of himself.

He bowed his head and said a prayer, asking forgiveness for what he was about to do. But he had to do it for his father. Violet Baker had stirred up too much trouble in town. She had to be dealt with now.

He knew exactly where he was going to take her, too. Yes, Violet had messed up his life with her stupid psychic visions, just like that idiotic reporter had with his lies. Morris was gone now, but Violet...she could expose his secret if she saw into his mind. Or into his lover's. That worried him most.

He couldn't let it happen. Not now, when his father thought he had the obedient son he wanted. And when he had finally found the love of his life.

VIOLET SHOVED THE CAR in gear, backed from the driveway and headed out of town. Heavy clouds rumbled with thunder, threatening another summer storm and adding to the blackness of the night. These country roads needed better markings. She could barely discern the white lines in the middle as she rounded the corner near Flatbelly Hollow.

A streak of lightning zigzagged above the treetops. The back of her scalp prickled. She glanced in her rearview mirror to see if someone was following her. Distant headlights flickered. She sped up, not willing to take any chances. But just as she took the curve near the old dirt road leading to the fishing camp, a deer ran in front of her. She braked and swerved to avoid hitting it, but her car raced forward. She braked again, but the vehicle only jerked and skidded into a tailspin. She pumped the brakes again. They weren't working!

Panic charged through her. She was sliding, out of control! There was nothing she could do to stop it! She braced herself for the impact as the car slammed against the guardrail and bounced off. It flipped and rolled over, again and again. She screamed as glass exploded. Blood filled her mouth, and her vision grew blurry. She was losing consciousness.

No, she had to get out. She could smell gas leaking. The car was going to catch on fire.

Then someone was at the window. Trying to open the door. Grady.

No...Ross Wheeler.

She reached for his hand. Swiped at the blood trickling down her lips. Let him help her crawl through the shattered window.

Her head spun. Darkness swirled around her. She was so dizzy she couldn't see. Then the car exploded in a fiery inferno. Metal spewed, pelting her.

Then the world went black, and she sank into nothingness.

CHAPTER TWENTY-FOUR

GRADY WAS WORRIED about Violet. He hated leaving things unsettled between them, but he had to take care of business. Not that he owed his father anything, but Grady wasn't convinced his dad was guilty of all these crimes.

Only of lying to his son all his life. And withholding information that might have led them to the truth years ago. Grady wasn't sure he could ever forgive him for that.

"Go back and guard Violet's house," he told Logan.

"Can't I help here?" the deputy asked.

"No, I've got it covered." Besides, he needed time to himself, to gather his thoughts, to check information on all the other suspects, especially Dwayne Dobbins and Ross Wheeler.

Logan left, jingling his keys, and Grady strode into his office, where Agent Norton was waiting.

"I know you have my father, but I thought we were looking at people with medical backgrounds. Have you got that list from the research facility where all these in vitro fertilization treatments took place?"

"Not yet. My other agents are on it," Norton said.

Grady nodded. They spent the next hour interrogating his father. Grady watched silently as Agent Norton and Adams grilled him. His father boomeranged from one emotion to another, everything from guilt to fury. He finally confessed knowing of the sperm donor, then admitted he'd had suspicions about Teresa's death, as well as Baker's and Violet's mother's.

"As God is my witness, I didn't kill any of them." Walt pressed a shaky, freckled hand to his chest. "You have to believe me, Grady. I kept quiet because I was afraid for you."

"What about your hair fibers being found at Kerry Cantrell's?"

"I…I don't know how they got there," his father said. "Someone must have planted them."

"You didn't have an affair with her?" Grady asked.

His father stretched his hands in front of him. "No. I…I've been faithful to Laney the last few years."

Unlike with his wife.

Grady shifted his gaze to Agent Norton. "Is it possible the hair was planted?"

He offered a noncommittal shrug. "It's possible."

Grady assimilated that information. Who would want to plant evidence against his father? The real killer, maybe. Joseph Longhorse…he certainly hated them both. He must have despised Walt for sneaking around with Laney all these years. And he'd probably thought Grady had a great life.

"What about Dr. Farmer?" Agent Norton asked. "Our files indicate that he worked at the research center. Did he know about the sperm donor?"

"He recommended people to the fertility clinic," Walt admitted. "Some of the women had no idea they were receiving sperm other than their husband's."

"We've confirmed that through our interviews," Agent Adams added.

"We need the names of everyone involved," Norton said.

"I don't know names." Walt scrubbed his face, looking weary and too old for his years. "Farmer might, though."

"We sent someone for him," Agent Adams interjected. "But apparently he's left town. I've put out an APB on him."

"Damn," Grady muttered. "I should have seen that coming."

"You can't keep me here," his father argued.

"Yes, they can," Grady said. "We have to check your story."

Walt glared at him and sat back down, twisting his hands in his lap. "You know I didn't kill anyone, Grady."

Grady gave him a blank stare. The reporter had been shot, meaning the M.O. was different from the Bone Whistler victims. But if it was the same killer, he could have panicked, thought the reporter was onto him, and decided to get rid of him, the same way he had Violet's mother, Teresa and Jed Baker.

Frustrated, Grady stalked to his office and grabbed the data coming in by fax. Unfortunately, the records for Logan were sealed. But his deputy had medical training. He'd been at the mental hospital the day Violet had almost died in that fire.

And Grady had sent him back to Violet's.

Dear God. If Logan was the killer, Grady had put her right into his hands.

His pulse jumping, he dialed Logan's cell phone, but got no answer. He phoned Violet's, but there was no answer there, either. Hopefully, she was lying down or in the shower. Or maybe she just didn't want to talk to him.

Unable to sit still, Grady put in a call to the police department where Logan had previously worked, but the sheriff was out, so he had to leave a message. He'd try Violet again in a few minutes.

Forcing himself not to jump to wild conclusions, he flipped a page and skimmed the file on Dwayne Dobbins. Apparently, the man had gotten in trouble for some petty crimes. Shoplifting. Vandalism. Abuse of animals. Hmm, wasn't that a sign of a more serious psychosis? The bone whistle had been carved from a dead animal.

He read further. Dwayne had set fire to an old warehouse, although the crime had been deemed an accident—he'd dropped a match after lighting a cigarette. Interestingly enough, Mayor Tate had covered up the incidents. How much had Mavis Dobbins paid for that to happen?

Could Dwayne have set the fire at the Black Mountain Mental Hospital? Even if he had, was he smart enough to carry off these serial killings and not get caught?

Grady doubted it.

He was still waiting to see if the feds turned up anything on the medical personnel at the hospital. So far, Gardener and Farmer looked clean, although Farmer had sent patients there for treatment and knew about the sperm donor recipients. The doc had probably gotten a kickback.

He turned to the report on Ross Wheeler. Sexual harassment and two counts of sexual misconduct with a minor. Both charges dropped. Had the girls been paid off, or decided they couldn't suffer through the abuse of a trial? He skipped to the next part. Wheeler was applying for jobs in Nashville. And Savannah. So he had been in both cities recently.

Special Agent Adams poked her head in. "Got a minute?"

"Sure."

"We found another man's DNA in Kerry Cantrell's bedroom. This time from semen. We're running tests now."

"Run it against Ross Wheeler's," Grady said.

"Right. And I'm going to get a search warrant for his house."

BITTERNESS TIGHTENED Joseph's muscles. His mother had finally confessed the truth to Grady Monroe about her and his father. Joseph would never forget the day he'd discovered that Grady was his half brother. Grady had been eleven, Joseph eight at the time, the apple of his mother's eye. Then he'd seen his mother with Walt Monroe. He'd been disgusted. Sickened. Furious.

Still reeling from shock, he'd overheard them arguing. Discussing Grady. His mother had cried, saying she missed her Grady. Wanted to tell him the truth. Was worried about him growing up without a mother.

But Grady had everything.

Joseph was the one who had nothing. A father he'd never know. A mother who pined for her other son, the son she'd given up so he could have a good life.

Joseph had run into the woods that day, had searched for peace. Had wondered if his mother had had an affair and gotten pregnant with him to replace the son she'd lost. But he'd never found peace. Only solace in the hunt.

And now he wanted to talk to Violet. He shifted the old pickup into gear and drove along the mountain road toward her house. He'd seen her hanging out with Sheriff Monroe a lot. Was Grady screwing Violet the way his father had Joseph's mother?

Walt Monroe had screwed his mama all Joseph's life. He didn't want to see Grady doing the same to Violet.

Ahead, an orange blaze lit the sky. He hit the brakes, staring as plumes of smoke rose toward the heavens. Fire shot upward like a big yellow ball. The scent of metal burning assaulted him as he approached. The car was a Civic, just like Violet's.

Was she inside?

His pulse pounding, he swerved to avoid the glass and parked on the embankment as a black Cadillac spun away from the scene.

Joseph jumped out and sprinted toward the burning vehicle. Heat scorched his face and body as he neared, the flames shooting sparks onto the asphalt. He peered inside and yelled her name, but no one answered. He didn't see a body.

Panicked, he ran to the other side and checked the back seat. Nothing.

He muttered a prayer of thanks to the heavens above. Maybe Violet had been thrown from the car, and she was still alive.

"Violet!" He shouted her name over and over, and was heading into the bushes to search when a police car rolled up, blue lights flashing. The sheriff's deputy jumped out.

"What's going on?" Logan asked.

"I just drove up and found this accident."

"Is anybody hurt?"

"I don't know. It's Violet Baker's car, but she's not inside."

Logan reached inside the car for his radio. "I'll call it in. Then we'll search the area."

GRADY POUNDED ON Wheeler's door as Special Agent Adams shifted beside him.

"His father's a preacher. He fits the profile," she said while they waited.

"He was also accused of sexual misconduct by some students he taught. He hasn't been able to get a job anywhere since."

"I imagine he has some anger and hostility built up," Adams stated.

Grady knocked again, and finally footsteps approached. Reverend Wheeler opened the door, straightening his suit jacket. A frown creased his thick brows at Grady's presence, then transformed completely at the sight of the female agent.

"Reverend, this is Special Agent Adams of the FBI."

The smile froze in place. "What can I do for you?"

Grady pushed through the door. "We have a search warrant."

"What?" The preacher's nostrils flared with shock.

The televangelist, Reverend Bilkins, pushed to his feet and stepped forward. "What's wrong, Brother Wheeler?"

"It's some mistake," Wheeler screeched. "It has to be."

"Is your son here?" Grady asked.

"No, but I'm calling my attorney right now."

"Go ahead," Grady said. "Meanwhile step aside."

"Where's your son's room?" Agent Adams asked.

The reverend ran his palm over his forehead, sweating. "Downstairs. The basement."

Grady gestured for the federal agent to go first, then he followed her down the stairs. The minute he stepped inside Wheeler's room, a weird feeling crept over him. "It's immaculate."

"Obsessive-compulsive tendencies," Agent Adams said as she cataloged the items on his wooden desk. "That behavior fits the profile of our killer. Remember what Violet said—he's following a definite order, looking for the perfect blood."

The mention of Violet's name caused a pang of regret in Grady's chest. He wanted to go back to her, to explain and hold her. Reassure her that he hadn't meant to keep things from her. But he had a job to do. To protect her, he had to find this killer.

Agent Adams searched through a desk drawer, while Grady opened the closet. Wheeler's suits and shirts were all hanging neatly, the pants in one row, the jackets another. His shoes were lined up, polished and new, organized on a shoe rack. Grady spotted a tall metal locker in the corner. He reached to open it and found it locked.

"Did you find any keys in that desk?"

Agent Adams turned and jangled a ring holding two small keys. "There's a nice stash of porn in here," she said. She held up one of the magazines. "But he likes them young."

Grady glanced at the nude photos of the preteens and felt sick. Oddly, most of the magazines featured men, not women. "Makes me wonder about those allegations about him."

"He uses condoms," she said, indicating two boxes of ribbed ones on the bottom shelf. "I guess he's into cleanliness, or worried about disease."

"Yeah, what a guy." Grady inserted the first key and tried the lock. It didn't work, so he inserted the second. Bingo. The metal door screeched open.

Grady's blood rushed to his head. There were more pictures. But instead of porn, photographs of the Bone Whistler victims were taped inside.

Violet's photo had been placed in the center.

VIOLET FADED IN AND OUT of consciousness. She was in a car. Moving. The ride was bumpy. "Where are you taking me?" she asked.

"Shh. Rest now. You should see a doctor."

Her head was throbbing. She tasted blood. And she was trembling. Unable to keep her eyes open, she leaned against the headrest in the front seat. She must have hit her skull when the car rolled, she was so dizzy and dis-oriented. Her vision was blurred. Flames clawed at the car.

No, the flames were gone. There was only darkness.

Another vision was coming on. Instead of fighting it, she tried to embrace it, get into the woman's mind. Maybe she'd see something to save the woman this time. Recognize some clue as to where he'd taken her.

The woman's cry screeched against the quiet. Her eyes were frightened, glassy with shock. Needles of numbness plucked at her skin. The medication the killer had injected her with was paralyzing her. He had left her for a short time.

But he was coming back.

"Help me."

The room was so cold. Like a refrigerator. The walls

*were dark, the shades drawn. No light. She was scared.
So scared she couldn't move.*

She didn't want to die.

*The drip-drip-drip of water floated through the haze.
The stench of alcohol. Antiseptics. His smell, musk and
sweat and cleaning soap. He had washed his hands
over and over. Scrubbed them until they were raw.*

*He had the needles lined up. The tubes ready for her
blood. He had already taken one vial.*

What did he plan to do with it?

*He'd frowned when he looked at her. Said hers
wasn't the right one. It wasn't perfect. Then he had
laughed. Murmured that he was sorry.*

*Sorry she wasn't the chosen one. But he would give
her to his father, anyway.*

*She knew what that meant. She had read the paper.
She was going to die. Then he would wrap her in a sheet
and leave her on the steps of a church.*

*And they would never find him. They didn't know
where to look.*

*The cops had it all wrong. He was walking among
them.*

It was someone they all trusted.

GRADY'S PHONE TRILLED. He checked the number, then
glanced at the staircase as the elderly Wheeler, Reverend Billy Lee Bilkins and Lloyd Driver, the lawyer, descended the stairs.

"It's my deputy," he told Agent Adams, indicating for
her to handle the gentlemen.

She nodded, and he answered the call. "Monroe here.
Where the hell have you been? And where's Violet
Baker?"

"I'm out on Highway 40. I found Violet Baker's car in a ditch. The firemen are here now, hosing it down. It burned to a crisp."

Jesus. His heart stopped. "Violet?"

"She wasn't in the car. I thought she might have been thrown, but I've searched the area and haven't found her. Joseph Longhorse was here when I arrived."

Grady's mind gyrated. What was happening here? Had Longhorse kidnapped Violet? Or worse… "Put him on the phone."

"Sheriff—"

"I said put him on the damn phone." He heard rustling, then Logan's voice muttering to the native.

"Joseph Longhorse speaking."

"What happened to Violet?"

"I don't know, Sheriff. I was driving out to see her when I spotted her car on fire."

"Listen to me, Longhorse, if you've hurt her or touched one hair on her head, I'll hunt you down—"

"You are barking up the wrong tree, as they say," Longhorse said, cutting him off. "I would never hurt Violet. I care for her."

Grady thought he detected sincerity in the man's voice. Then again, Longhorse had always hated him. And now he understood the reason.

"I know the truth about Laney and my father now," Grady said in a gruff voice. "And I see why you might want revenge on me, but—"

"Even so, I did not and would not hurt Violet. You're wasting time accusing me, Sheriff. When I arrived, I saw a black Cadillac rushing off."

Grady cursed. Ross Wheeler drove a black Cadillac….

CHAPTER TWENTY-FIVE

"I BROUGHT HER TO YOU." Ross's eye twitched. "She's in my car. I covered her with a blanket—"

"I told you to never come here." His hands began to shake. Irrational anger clogged his mind. Ross was messing up the order. Everything had to be in order. He'd planned to escalate his timetable, but he wasn't ready for Violet. Not yet.

"But I had to. Don't you see?" Ross screeched. "She's psychic. She was going to expose us." He paced beneath the awning of the building, eyes scanning the surroundings to make sure no one had followed. His head bobbed up and down.

"I had things under control, Ross. Now it's all wrong." The scent of fear washed over him. Tried to trap him just like it did when they locked him away. He could hear the metal doors slamming, the key turning in the lock.

"But that reporter!" Sweat rolled down Ross's hairline and into his eyebrows. "You saw that article. He told lies about me. And he was onto you. He would have exposed everything. Then you and I couldn't be together."

His mind raced, the old familiar zing of panic hitting him. He couldn't think. What to do. What to do. What to do. He pulled at the tiny hairs on his arms. Prick. Prick. Prick.

No, stop it. You don't think in threes anymore. It's one. One is the number.

He was the one. The chosen one.

As soon as he got rid of the others.

Only Ross wanted him to think about the two of them. Two. A couple. He didn't know how to be a couple.

He never should have gotten involved with Ross Wheeler.

Ross's fingernails dug into his shoulder blade. "I did it for you. I know you wanted her. Go ahead and finish this so we can run away and be together." Panic made his eyes bulge. His breathing sounded erratic. "I'll pack tonight. We can leave at midnight. Get away before the sheriff connects us to that reporter."

His heart fluttered like a jumping bean. "What do you mean about the reporter?"

"I had to take care of him," Ross squealed. "I had to. I couldn't let the reverend find out about us."

The truth zapped him in the gut. "You killed Morris?" He groaned, the sound erupting like that of a baby. Ross was messing everything up. It wasn't supposed to happen this way. A film of sweat broke out all over his body. He was not a killer.

No, he was a blood taker.

Sacrificing the lambs for his father. Ridding the world of the imperfect. The ones that were never meant to be.

Ross jerked at his arm. "Come on, we have to put her in your car before they come looking for her."

Thoughts crashed in his head. Noises collided. Violet was way down on the list. His next lamb was already waiting. He had to go back. Take care of her.

He could see her eyes looking up at him. Terrified. Waiting.

His panic ebbed slightly. Adrenaline surged through him.

Maybe Ross was right. He had to escalate his activities before the police found him. And timing was important for his father….

It wouldn't hurt to take Violet back with him now. It might even make things sweeter. She could watch him sacrifice the others. And while she waited, he'd tell her exactly what he planned to do to her.

Laughter bubbled in his chest. If Violet really was psychic, then she probably already knew….

GRADY WAS LOSING his mind. Violet had to be all right. He couldn't live with her death on his conscience. Not after he'd just found her. Not after he'd held her in the darkness and buried himself inside her.

He turned to Reverend Wheeler. "Where's your son?"

Wheeler gripped the bed rail. "I don't know."

"Don't lie to me, Reverend. A woman's life could be at stake. Where is he?"

"I told you I don't know."

Anger knotted Grady's throat. "And I suppose you didn't know anything about these." He gestured toward the women's photos.

"No…"

"That's pretty incriminating," Agent Adams said. "Your son has photos of each of the Bone Whistler victims."

"We should pray for him," Reverend Billy Lee Bilkins said. "Lord have mercy on his soul. I knew evil possessed that boy the minute I laid eyes on him."

"He didn't do anything wrong," Reverend Wheeler argued. "He might not be perfect, but my boy wouldn't hurt a fly, much less a woman."

Grady tossed a stack of porn magazines toward him. They skidded across the bed, one flying open to reveal a picture of two nude men engaged in sex. "I suppose you weren't aware of your son's interest in young boys, either."

Reverend Wheeler jumped back, a gurgle of shock erupting from deep in his throat. "Where did you get that?"

"It was hidden in your son's desk," Agent Adams said. "But if Ross likes men, why was his DNA on Kerry Cantrell's sheets?"

"It wasn't Ross's DNA, it was the reverend's," Grady said, putting two and two together. "He was sleeping with Kerry, not Ross."

Agent Adams nodded in quick understanding, but Wheeler shook his head violently, one hand on his heart, the other on his stomach as if he was going to be sick.

"What's wrong, Reverend? It's okay for you to screw young girls, but you didn't want your son having sex at all, right? Especially with men. You defended him when those young girls accused him of sexual misconduct, or did the paper have it wrong? Was it boys he abused?"

"My son…no, it's not true."

"As God is my witness, I knew that boy needed to be saved…." Brother Billy Lee's voice rose in a loud chant.

Reverend Wheeler cradled his head in his hands and moaned. "It's not true. Ross wouldn't do this to me. He wouldn't ruin my career like this…it's a lie!"

"Like it's not true that Ross was the product of a sperm donor?" Grady asked.

"No!" Wheeler's head flew up. "That was a lie, too. A mistake. My son is mine. That reporter had it all wrong. I have proof."

"What kind of proof?"

"His birth certificate. Bloodwork we had done when he was small. He has a clubfoot just like I do." Wheeler whipped off his Italian loafer and sock.

"You could be lying to throw us off," Grady said.

Wheeler cried out in frustration, then grabbed one of his son's shoes. "Look, he has special shoes to compensate."

Agent Adams looked at Grady in question. Grady let that sink in. If Morris had been mistaken and Wheeler wasn't one of the children spawned from the sperm donor, it alleviated some of the suspicion from him. But everything else pointed to him.

"Where did he go?" Grady asked again, this time more harshly.

Wheeler shook his head. "I don't know...."

It was useless. The man was in shock. Grady called Logan to issue an APB on Ross Wheeler, and filled the deputy in on everything they'd learned so far.

"I asked around town about Farmer," Logan said. "Someone said he stopped by Mavis Dobbins's house."

Grady grabbed his keys. "I'm on my way there now." Agent Adams hurried behind him. While he started the engine, he phoned the hospital to see if Violet had been admitted.

His heart sank when he was told she hadn't. Then he asked Agent Adams to go back and meet his deputy at the station. He wanted her to watch Logan, just in case they were wrong about Wheeler, and his deputy was involved.

PINPOINTS OF PAIN stabbed through Violet's numbness, and yet the urgent whisper of danger coaxed her from sleep. She struggled to open her eyes. Where was she? Dark walls closed around her. The humidity was suffocating. A sense of doom washed over her. The cloying smell of death...

"Help me. Please. I can't move."

Violet tried to turn toward the sound. Was it in her head? Was she having another vision?

Her eyelids felt weighted down as she blinked and tried to focus. A sound rumbled in the distance. Thunder? A train, maybe?

Something white drifted into her view. A jacket. A lab coat. She must be in the hospital. Yes. She'd had an accident. But someone had rescued her. Taken her to his car. Then they'd driven. He'd said he was going to take care of her.

She was going to be fine. Maybe Grady would come.

No. Memories drifted back through the fog. Grady had left her to defend his father. His father hated her. They had both lied to her. Grady had that bone whistle....

"Relax, Violet, I'm going to take care of you."

Violet tried to nod, but her head felt heavy. A small pinprick of pain jabbed at her arm, and she squirmed, but couldn't lift her hand. A metallic taste filled her mouth. Her lips were dry. The room spun, a kaleidoscope of colors circling above her like angel wings fluttering in the wind. Then darkness carried her away into the abyss.

A faint voice cried out for help, but Violet couldn't respond. Maybe if she kept her eyes closed and slept, it would go away. She wouldn't have to watch another woman die.

No, she had to wake up. It was the only way she could help.

But the darkness was too strong. Pulling her under. Replacing the light with shadows. Calling her name. She was at the graveyard with Darlene. She saw her friend's arms outstretched, waiting. The others were there, too. They looked so peaceful.

Then there were more, floating in the distance. Looking to her for help. They weren't ready to die.

Darlene hadn't been ready to die, either....

HE WATCHED HER SLEEP. Felt a connection he'd never felt before. His entire body tingled. She had seen into his eyes. She knew him. Saw him taking the others.

It was her blood. She was going to be the one. The perfect one. The one who would serve his father.

He had to hurry.

But what about the others? He had to maintain his order. Order was everything.

Still, his father was calling him. Urging him to hurry. Time was running out. Death beckoned—sometimes his best friend, sometimes his enemy.

Pin peyeh obe. Look toward the mountain. The bigger picture. What was more important? His father knew. He had started it all. And he would be there in the end, when the rest of them were gone. His father would live on forever.

But then there was Ross—the only person he'd loved besides his father. Ross wanted him to go away with him. He'd be free. Never have to be locked up again.

Stop the hiding. Stop the running. No more dark hallways. No more cold rooms. No more keys turning in the lock.

But his father came first.

The big picture. Finish the sacrifices.

There were ten, there were nine, there were eight little angels. There were seven, there were six... One little angel in the band.

Yes, when they were all gone, he would be the one.

"MISS DOBBINS, have you seen Dr. Farmer?"

Mavis ignored Grady's direct gaze, poured water into the steam iron and dropped it onto the pair of coveralls stretched taut across her ancient ironing board. "Ain't seen him in forever."

The heat in the small cramped house swirled around Grady. The scent of cabbage and sausage cooking grated on his stomach. So did Mavis Dobbins's attitude.

Grady had lost his patience. First, the woman wouldn't open the door. Then she'd ignored his questions. And she refused to tell him where her son was. On the way to her house, he'd thought back to his teenage years, the allegations about Ross Wheeler, the problems with Dwayne Dobbins. It had occurred to him that perhaps Dwayne had been sexually abused, possibly by his former teacher Ross Wheeler. As an already unstable teen, anything he'd said might have been overlooked. Either that or Mavis didn't want more trouble for herself or her son. And what if Dwayne had been a male born from the sperm donor? There could have been more than one male, too.

"Listen, we have reason to believe Farmer knows something about the serial killer who's been murdering innocent women. And now Violet Baker is missing, and so is Ross Wheeler."

"That Baker girl is crazy, always has been," Mavis said. "Don't go bringing my boy and me into her nonsense."

"I didn't mention Dwayne," Grady said, catching her slip.

Mavis's lower lip trembled. But instead of commenting, she ran the iron over the coveralls, pressing them as if she could iron out all of her troubles with the vengeance of her strokes.

"Mrs. Dobbins," he said, "we know Doc Farmer stopped by here."

Mavis's wary look warned him to tread lightly.

"Listen, I'm not here to question your reputation as a mother, but if you know where Farmer was going, you have to tell me."

A groan sounded from the back room. Mavis's eyes darted in panic. A thump followed. Someone was back here.

"Is that Dwayne?"

Mavis blotted at her forehead with the back of her hand. "What if it is?"

"I have to talk to him. See if he knows where Ross Wheeler is."

"He don't know nothing," Mavis said.

Grady started toward the room.

"It's not what it seems," Mavis said as Grady pushed open the bedroom door.

Dwayne was lying in the fetal position on her bed, a toy rabbit hugged to his chest. He was rocking back and forth. The room smelled faintly of urine and smoke.

"How long has he been like that?" Grady asked.

"All night," Mavis mumbled. She squared her boxy shoulders defensively, then shoved her hands in the pockets of her tattered apron. "He wouldn't take his medicine lately. Has been sneaking off. I thought he might be getting into trouble setting fires again. Doc Farmer upped his medicine before he left town."

"He's been in bed since?"

"For the past day and night," Mavis said. "He'll calm down soon. It's got to get back in his system. Get regulated."

"Where did Doc Farmer go?" Grady asked.

Mavis hesitated, then shuffled over to Dwayne to calm him. "He said something about a vacation. A cruise ship, maybe."

Grady punched the number for Special Agent Norton. "Check the airports. Farmer is supposedly going on a cruise, so cover the lines to Miami and any other cruise ship point."

As much as he felt sorry for Dwayne Dobbins and his mother, and wondered at the trouble she'd spoken of, he'd have to explore that later. Right now, he headed to the door. They had to talk to someone at that research center. See if they had names for all the recipients of the sperm. And they had to hurry.

If the killer had Violet, their chances of finding her alive grew slimmer by the minute.

GRADY DROVE LIKE A MANIAC around the mountain. Thunderclouds rumbled above the edges of the thick evergreens. Light rain drizzled down, fogging the windshield. He turned on the wipers and defroster and swore, forcing himself to slow down around the dangerous curves. Agent Adams called when she arrived at the jail, but Logan hadn't shown up. And he wasn't answering his radio.

Grady cursed again, his gaze skimming down the steep, rocky incline to the canyon below, then called Norton. He wished to hell he knew where Logan lived, but he didn't have a clue. The man had been too damn secretive. And Grady had been so absorbed in Darlene's case he hadn't really paid attention.

"I'm meeting you there," Norton said.

"I just hope this isn't a wild-goose chase." But what else could Grady do? They had an APB out on Wheeler and Farmer. Agent Adams was searching for his deputy. And other agents were checking into two lab assistants that seemed suspicious. If they learned the name of the donor and other offspring, it might lead them to the killer. At least they could warn the other possible victims.

And what if the killer was the donor? Maybe one of the recipients discovered that his or her mother had been duped and threatened to expose him. He might kill the recipients to protect himself.

"This research center's the key," Norton said. "Do you think Wheeler has Violet?"

"I think he's connected," Grady said. "But something doesn't fit. He doesn't have the medical background to carry out the murders."

"But anyone could research on the Internet which drugs to take."

"True. And with his staunch religious upbringing and his father's rigorous rules, he fits the profile," Grady said, praying they were on the right track.

"He does seem obsessive-compulsive. Orderly. Violet said order meant everything to the killer."

Grady bit his lip. Did Norton believe Violet now? "But what order? The victims' names haven't been alphabetical."

"Not by last names," Norton said. "That's it—he's dismissing their last names." He paused a second, as if a new realization had dawned. "Since the women were all spawned by the same sperm donor, he's discounting their last names. Technically they're siblings, children of one father."

"Jesus Christ almighty." Grady slapped the steering wheel. "In his note he says, 'For our father.' He isn't referring to God the Father, but to his own—the sperm donor."

"The killer is one of the offspring."

"A male," Grady said. "He couldn't stand the thought that his father had other children. He wanted to be the only one."

Norton grunted. "But Wheeler's DNA didn't show a genetic abnormality."

Grady hit the accelerator. "So if the killer isn't Wheeler, then who the hell is it?" He remembered Norton's reaction to his deputy. "Logan. Shit, tell me what you know about my deputy!"

Norton cleared his throat. "I met him when we were investigating his wife's disappearance."

Grady released an expletive.

"Logan was a suspect, although we never found any definitive evidence that she'd been murdered. For all we know she might have simply left him."

"You didn't think I had a right to know this?"

"It was a need-to-know basis. Besides, technically he was cleared. No body, no crime."

"But you think he might be our killer?"

"I can't say. He did contact this genetic center about testing, but I haven't been able to uncover the details."

Grady nearly howled with agony. Violet's face flashed in his mind. They had to save her before it was too late. "If he's our man and you kept silent, I'm holding you responsible."

A tense moment stretched between them. "We'll get the list of donor recipients," Norton said, "then we'll determine the killer's identity and figure out where he takes the victims."

Grady could not think of the word *victim* and Violet in the same sentence. Not while knowing the killer might already have her. But images flooded him. Violet having her blood drawn. Violet being wrapped in that sheet. Placed on the altar.

He had to stop this maniac. He couldn't let her die. Not without telling her he loved her.

CHAPTER TWENTY-SIX

GRADY BARRELED UP to the Black Mountain Research Hospital, tires squealing as he stopped at the wrought-iron security gate surrounding the property. He flashed his badge and explained he was there to meet Special Agent Nick Norton.

Huge old trees flanked the impressive two-story, stucco building, which had been built recently, partially funded by government grants, and subsidized by private investors. High tech genetic research was the main focus of the center, although other projects were carried out, as well.

Grady just prayed they had information on the fertility experiments that had taken place twenty years ago.

Five minutes later, after clearing inside security, he was escorted through another secured area to a set of offices. Behind double doors that required a key card, Grady finally came face-to-face with the director, a portly man in a three-piece suit with thick wire-rim glasses. The smell of strong coffee permeated the room, the desk was cluttered with papers and a state-of-the-art computer system occupied one corner.

Norton stood. "I've explained the circumstances to Dr. Ramsey. He's had a team searching files since we called a few days ago."

"It took some time," Dr. Ramsey explained. "But I believe we've located the information you need."

"Were you here during those fertility experiments?" Grady asked.

Ramsey nodded. "Yes, but I wasn't working with the fertility clinic. I had my own projects."

"Who was in charge of the clinic?" Norton asked.

"A doctor named Hadley. He retired years ago. Last I heard he's been very ill."

Norton took the files. "You have a list of all the women who received in vitro fertilization from the sperm donor we requested information on?"

"Yes. Their names are in there, as well as those of their offspring. Someone apparently thought they might need the information for follow-up purposes."

"Thanks." Agent Norton opened the file and read the names of the latter. "Darlene Monroe, Violet Baker, Amber Collins, Connie Allen, Kerry Cantrell, Lynnette Burgess, Minnie White, Rhoda Florence, Sandy Evans, Terry Yoder." He reached for his cell phone. "I'm calling this in. We'll assign agents to locate and warn the remaining victims."

Grady's eyebrows shot up. "And the name of the donor?"

"Actually, it was Dr. Hadley," Ramsey said.

"Where's Hadley now?" Grady asked.

"I'm not sure. Like I said, he's been ill these last few years." He snapped his fingers. "As a matter of fact, he had a rare autoimmune disease a long time ago. He chose to become one of the subjects in a gene replacement therapy we were working on back then."

"And the therapy worked?" Agent Norton asked.

"Yes. I don't know for sure if his current illness has to do with the disease or not."

Grady saw the pieces clicking into place. It fit with the information they'd learned from the victims' blood-work. "Does Hadley have children? A son who's a doctor or who works in health care, maybe?"

Ramsey's double chin sagged as he frowned. "Actually, he did have a son, but he's not a doctor. When the boy reached puberty, he had problems. I believe he was diagnosed with some kind of mental disorder. Dr. Hadley blamed himself—he thought the genetic therapy he'd undergone had adversely affected his son."

"But he still donated this sperm to have other children?" Grady asked, unable to hide disgust.

"He did that long before he knew his son had genetic problems. In fact, that may have been the reason Hadley asked for the names of the offspring. Maybe he wanted to follow up on them to verify that they were healthy."

"Or he needed their blood to help cure his illness," Norton said.

Grady nodded. "But his son used the names as his hit list."

A knot of apprehension tightened his belly. They had to find Hadley and his son. "Can you tell us if a man named Logan was here asking about this?" Grady inquired.

The doctor shook his head. "I don't recognize the name."

"We're still working on the list of all the doctors, nurses, lab techs, orderlies—anyone who worked here and at any neighboring hospitals," Norton said. "One of them is our man."

IT WAS TOO LATE. Lynnette knew it. He was getting ready to kill her.

Tears rolled down her cheeks. Her chest wrenched in spasm. Regrets screamed in her head.

The money no longer mattered. The baby she wanted did. The pregnancy test was on the counter. She hadn't even seen the results.

More tears trickled down her cheeks, cold and icy. They froze there, just like her limbs were frozen from whatever drug he'd given her.

And now he'd brought this other woman to join her. He'd said something about her sister. But he was crazy.

Lynnette didn't have a sister. She didn't have anyone except Ted. Why had she been so selfish? Demanding that everything be perfect before she conceived.

Her captor's footsteps clicked on the concrete floor. He was humming some stupid song under his breath. Some childhood song about angels. But he had it backward.

And he was no angel. He was the devil in disguise. A sicko. Someone she had trusted, though. Someone she had turned to for help.

But he was going to end her life, and if she was pregnant, her baby's....

VIOLET'S HEART WAS beating so rapidly she could hear it roaring in her ears. No, it wasn't hers. It was the other woman's. She was crying. And she was thinking about the baby she might be carrying.

No...

Violet felt her fear. There was so much the woman wanted to do before she died. Kiss her husband again. Make up for the fight they'd had that morning. Forgive him for letting their finances get in such a mess.

Violet slowly twisted her head sideways. Threads of reality interwove with the darkness. She wasn't in the hospital. But she was strapped onto a gurney.

The woman was in the same room with her. Her half sister. Lynnette.

Someone she had never met. Had never known existed. But Violet wanted desperately to save her.

She tried to move her hand. Her fingernails made a faint scratching sound against the stiff sheets.

"I'm here," she tried to say, but her vocal cords were immobilized from the drugs, just as her body was. Tears of rage and helplessness pressed against her eyelids. This woman might be pregnant; there was an innocent little baby's life to consider. But how could Violet save her if she couldn't free herself?

"Hello, Violet."

She blinked, searching for his face. But it was so dark, bathed in shadows. The inky blackness swallowed him completely.

"I know you can see me. You don't need light. You can see me in your mind, can't you?"

She closed her eyes. Willed the image to come. If he wanted to connect with her, then let him. Maybe she could talk some sense into him. At least stall him.

"I sent you the other half of Darlene's necklace. Now I want you to watch what I'm doing to our sister."

"No," she whispered, although no sound came out.

A nasty chuckle reverberated in the silence, echoed around the room. He shifted, just enough for her to see his hands.

And the needle. The syringe. Then she was in the other woman's mind again, connecting. Lynnette's arm jerked as the needle pricked her. Her blood began flowing slowly into the tube.

Violet's would be next.

"It has to be perfect," he said in that grating voice that sounded like sandpaper against rough wood. "It won't do for my father unless it is right."

Would he spare her if it was perfect?

No... The blood taking was only the beginning of the end. She would die like the others.

The other woman's fear bled into hers, nearly choking her.

Violet gritted her teeth, willed away the pain. Tried to shut out the terror and think of Grady.

The pleasure he'd given her. The warm presence of his body on top of hers. His fingers coaching her into the exhilarated feeling of arousal. His lips pressing against hers as he slid inside her...

A low sob tore from the other woman's throat, jerking Violet back to reality. The machine he used to test the blood rumbled in the silence.

Then the sharp crackle of bone breaking. He was carving again. Back and forth the knife went. Crafting the bone whistle he intended to play when he spread them on the altar.

"WE NABBED FARMER at the airport," Agent Adams said over the phone. "I'm still looking for your deputy."

Maybe Farmer had the answers. But where the hell was Logan? Norton's admission rang in Grady's ears. Logan was smart. He could have hidden Violet somewhere, then called in the accident. "Bring Farmer straight to the station."

"We'll meet you there," Agent Adams said.

Grady agreed, then disconnected the phone. His head was spinning. Suspecting everyone. Wheeler? Farmer? A stranger in town? The reports hadn't shown anything on that new doctor. Any one of them would be able to slip in and out of the community unnoticed. Trusted.

Grady wanted to scream. What if the killer was his deputy? The man he'd sent to guard Violet. The man who'd helped him find Baker's body and Kerry Cantrell's.

Grady was responsible….

He flashed the blue light on and tore down the mountain, oblivious to the rain. Thank God he and Norton were in separate cars. He didn't want anyone watching over his shoulder. If he got to the killer first, he'd forget his job. His badge.

He'd do whatever he had to do to save Violet.

Memories of the night they'd made love floated back. Violet offering herself so openly. The warm feel of her tender skin gliding against his. The beat of her heart as he'd suckled her nipples. The erotic feel of her naked heat closing around him.

He had been her first lover. He wanted to be her only one. Her last.

But not this way…

He shut out the thoughts. Tried to think optimistically. Tried to hold on to the fraying hope. But déjà vu flooded him. The night they'd searched for Darlene. The night he'd searched for Kerry Cantrell. He'd been too late both times.

This had to be different.

He accelerated, taking the curves at a dangerous speed, tires squealing on the asphalt. Recriminations screamed in his head. He hadn't even thanked Violet for the gift of her innocence. He would do it when he found her.

The rain pounded harder. Lightning cut through the trees. He didn't slow. He had to get to her.

A few minutes later, he raced up to his office and stalked inside. Agent Adams had Farmer locked in an interrogation room. Grady allowed his father to be in the room, hoping he could persuade Farmer to talk. "All right, Doc, spill it all."

Farmer dropped his head forward with a groan. "I need a lawyer."

"You need to give me some goddamn answers before I beat them out of you. Violet Baker is missing. The serial killer most likely has her. Now where the hell has he taken her?"

"Why do you think I know?" Farmer wailed.

"We found out about the sperm donor recipients. The victims were all bred from one donor. This Dr. Hadley, who had genetic replacement therapy, spawned them, and now his real son is killing them."

"Jesus Christ." He dropped his head forward. "My life, my reputation, everything will be ruined."

"Your lawyer is on his way." Grady propped his big body on the edge of the table, leaned into Farmer's face. "And I don't give a rat's ass about your reputation now, or the fact that you've been giving Mavis Dobbins drugs for her son, probably off the books. What I care about is saving lives. Unless you want to be charged for murder, you'd better tell me everything you know about Hadley and his son, including where to find them."

"I don't know."

Grady yanked him off the chair. "Where would he take these women?"

Walt Monroe cleared his throat. "For God's sake, Farmer, this has gone too far. Tell him."

"I was sending patients to the research center. Some of the women had no idea they received sperm from Hadley. They were just happy to conceive."

"Then Baker's wife had a reaction to the anesthesia, and went crazy. I think Hadley's son killed her, then later, Walt's wife."

"But you all kept this secret," Grady said. "Why?"

"To protect you and Violet," Walt said.

"Where the hell are Hadley and his son?" Grady bellowed.

"I don't know for sure," Farmer wheezed. "There's only two places I can think of—one of them his old estate home up in the Smoky Mountains. The other was the original research facility."

"I need exact locations."

Farmer sank back in the chair, sweating as he muttered some directions. Grady grimaced. Both places were isolated, remote. Would be difficult to locate. It would take time—time they didn't have.

"Who is Hadley's son?" Grady demanded.

Farmer swallowed, then looked at Grady's father.

"It's over, I tell you," Walt said. "We can't let anyone else die."

Farmer covered his eyes with his hands. "That's just it, I have no idea. Last I heard he'd been locked away as a teenager because of his psychosis. If he came to Crow's Landing, I don't know what name he's using."

Agent Norton glanced up from his computer. "I have

locations for his house and the old research center. Let's divide up."

Grady followed him into the outer office. Joseph Longhorse was standing in the doorway.

Norton glanced at Agent Adams. "I want you to stake out Wheeler's house, see if he returns."

"And keep trying to contact my deputy," Grady declared.

"I'll get a chopper," Agent Norton said, "and check the old estate."

Grady nodded. "I'll take the old research center."

Longhorse caught his arm. "This serial killer has Violet?"

"We think so," Grady said. "And I don't have time—"

"I heard the location," Longhorse said. "To reach it, you must hike in on foot."

"I know that. I'm prepared."

"Let me go with you," Joseph exclaimed. "I can lead you there. I know the woods well."

Grady's eyes connected with Longhorse. His half brother. They had always fought. Joseph hated him. Would he lead him astray to get revenge?

"Please," Longhorse insisted as if he'd read Grady's mind. "I am a good hunter. There are shortcuts that will save time, and some of the roads are washed out. We must work together."

"How do I know I can trust you?"

He frowned. "Violet is my friend. She should not suffer because of our differences."

Grady swallowed his pride. Violet had defended Longhorse. She had trusted him. Maybe he had to now, too. "All right. Then let's go."

Grady led the way to his car, his half brother following.

HE TWIRLED A STRAND of Violet's hair between his fingers, feeling its silky smoothness, damp with tears.

She had been such a scrawny kid when her little friend Darlene had taken her under her wing. He had almost felt sorry for her. Some kind of connection.

But now that connection could be his end.

If she somehow escaped, or connected with the others he hadn't yet caught, and revealed his location, the police would come after him. Then all his work for his father would be for nothing.

A frisson crawled up his spine He'd better hurry. The tests for Lynnette's blood were finished. It was worthless. Hers had the same abnormality as the first three.

His father's low moan echoed from the adjoining room. He was getting weaker. He needed the blood now.

Violet opened those iridescent eyes and gazed up at him. She had a way of looking into a man's soul. Could she see that he was special?

That he hated having to come to them to help his father? Because his own blood had not worked, either.

Anger flared, quickening his pulse and pounding in his temples, worsening the headache he lived with constantly. A side effect of neglecting his medicine.

But the rewards were worth it.

"The order is all wrong." Panic twisted inside him at the thought. "But Father cannot wait."

His fingers traced along Violet's arm. She lay motionless, staring up at him, trying to be brave. But the connection ran both ways now. Fear radiated between them.

"Relax, Violet, this part won't hurt."

Her pale cheeks were frozen, her dark lashes fluttering. He wound the tourniquet around her arm, raised the needle, tightened the rubber tubing. Then he pierced Violet's skin with the needle.

He needed more blood from her than the others. Then he would prepare for the bone marrow transplant. Poor Violet. That part would be painful, especially if he didn't anesthetize her.

But soon after, the pain would fade as she drifted up to heaven.

GRADY'S BODY ACHED as they climbed the foothills, the silent cries of the victims ringing in his mind. They had to hurry. Had to reach Violet in time.

"This way." Longhorse pointed to the east. The forest was thick, the vegetation appearing impassable. "It is the shortest way," he said.

Grady nodded.

Longhorse swung his machete, thrashing through the foliage, cutting his own path. His footsteps were determined and his pace steady. The stench of a dead animal filled the air—a deer carcass, rotting in the field. Moss, animal bones, the half-eaten remains of a predator's dinner were scattered along a decaying tree stump. They bypassed them, slogging through the muddy leftovers of a recent rain—the swampy part of the forest, Longhorse called it. Night was falling, thunderclouds rearing their heads again, the humidity creating a film of dampness on their skin.

Grady pushed forward, willing his legs not to give out. Willing Violet to be there, waiting.

He would take her in his arms, kiss her senseless. Carry her back to his place and help her forget this nightmare.

Yes, he had to make love to her one more time. Tell her with his body what his mouth refused to say.

It was the fantasy that kept him moving, kept him following Longhorse, who had the stealth of a wildcat and the instincts of a wolf.

"It is up there, on that ridge," Longhorse said.

Grady thought he detected a distant light burning in the old dilapidated building at the top of the mountain. He started running.

When they reached the clearing, he and Longhorse studied the aging brick and concrete structure. Shrouded in vines and surrounded by weeds, it appeared to be locked up and deserted, some of the windows boarded up.

Dammit. Despair and panic gripped him.

He punched in Norton's number, praying the agent had had better luck.

A DEEP CHILL ENGULFED Violet at the sound of a knife blade scraping against bone. Back and forth. Steady and rhythmic.

He would be carving two bone whistles. One for Lynnette. One for her.

Unless the other woman was already dead. Violet stilled, listening carefully. Nothing. No, a faint low cry.

She was alive.

Violet tried to turn her head. Her body was so heavy. Numb. Vulnerable. Finally, she twisted a fraction of an inch. The woman was staring at her, her green eyes filled with tears, begging for help.

Violet wiggled her fingers. The drug must be losing its effect. She had to get free before he injected her again.

Then she saw him in the shadows, watching. Wheeler? He had rescued her from the burning car. But this wasn't Wheeler, was it?

The scent of madness permeated the air. He saw the women connecting. *"Violet, there were ten, there were nine, there were eight little angels...."*

A sob caught in her throat. He was in her head. Whispering her name. Taunting her.

She wouldn't play his game. She would only connect with the other woman. Try to reassure her.

But he rose. Walked toward their half sister. His hands reached for the woman's neck and closed around it.

Tears rained down the woman's cheeks. Violet's own eyes flooded and overflowed. Lynnette would die. So would her baby. Violet squeaked out a scream of apology. Of sorrow.

The woman's gurgled cry echoed in reply.

CHAPTER TWENTY-SEVEN

"NO!" VIOLET CRIED.

Her scream rippled out in a whisper. But the killer heard.

He stalked toward her. Thunder rumbled. Rain splattered against the roof. Darkness cloaked the dimly lit room, turning it into a black inferno.

He took another hypodermic, tapped it above her face. The silver needle glinted in the darkness. She fought, but his hand clamped her arm. He tapped the needle again, traced an icy finger over her wrist. The needle slid into her skin, its devastating effects attacking her immediately. The numbness. The inability to move. The thousand prickles of life being stripped from her limbs. Her vocal cords being severed as if he'd cut them with a serrated knife.

"Why?" she mouthed.

He stopped and looked into her eyes. Felt the connection. Smiled.

"To save our father. I told you he is dying."

Her lips moved again, though no sound came out. *"You don't need to kill us."*

Laughter bubbled from his chest. He looked familiar yet different somehow. But he was still hidden in the murkiness. She couldn't see his face. Who was he?

"Yes, my sweetness. I am the chosen one. The only one."

"I don't understand."

"Years ago, Father was ill. He was a geneticist, and offered himself as the subject of a genetic experiment. The therapy worked and he was healed, but the mutated gene was passed on to me." He tsked. "Once he was healthy, he donated his sperm to be used in in vitro fertilization experiments. He didn't know yet about the side effects the treatment had on me. When he found out, he recovered the names of the recipients. He wanted to make sure you all were healthy." His voice hardened, filled with anger, bitterness. "I told him he didn't need you. He had me. I was his son. The only one."

Violet shuddered.

"But he wouldn't listen. So I showed him. I found Darlene."

"And you killed her?"

"And her mother. And yours. Then your father. They wanted to expose our secret. My father's work would have been finished. He's a genius. The world needs him…."

Emotions crowded Violet's chest. Her mother and Darlene's both had died to protect them.

"But now my…our father needs a bone marrow transplant. Because of the genetic treatment he received, finding a donor match has been impossible." He leaned closer. Alcohol scented his hands. She inhaled the sickening odor of his breath. Tasted the pleasure he found in frightening her. Saw the vials of blood with the names on them.

"It is yours, Violet. Your blood is the match that will save him."

"Why the bone whistle?" Violet mouthed.

"As a symbol of the sacrifice. *Pin peyeh obe,* look

toward the mountain, the bigger picture, the future. When Father is well again, he'll do wonderful things." His shoes clicked as he reached for his knife. "But you and the others, you are expendable."

"No," a gruff voice said from the corner, "it has to stop."

Violet tried to turn her head, but the drug held her captive. In her peripheral vision, she caught a movement. A frail-looking man in a wheelchair. A thin woman stood beside him, a hand on his shoulder.

"Father, you shouldn't be up now—you're too weak." He rushed to the man, his movements agitated. "I've found the donor, I'll prepare her soon. Mother can perform the transplant. Then you'll be better."

"It's over. I won't let you continue this," the older man said. "If it is my time, then so be it."

His wife was shaking her head. "Let us do the transplant," she whispered. "Then we'll put him back on medication. He won't go to trial." She turned to her son. "You won't," she told him. "They'll understand about your condition."

"No! I refuse to be locked up again." Rage exploded as he flew toward his mother, arms flailing. She pushed him back, but he struck her, and she fell to the floor. His father tried to stand, but he was too weak, and collapsed into the chair with a moan.

The killer stalked toward Violet again, this time wild-eyed and crazy.

"No!" She summoned all her will and screamed. But once again, her cry floated into the silence.

AGENT NORTON HAD FOUND nothing. Grady was just about to give up when Longhorse motioned toward the woods. Grady squinted and spotted a dark object. A car. A Jeep parked beneath some underbrush. He gestured to Longhorse that he understood, then they slowly circled the building. The door was locked. Longhorse pointed to a window with a missing pane. It had been boarded up, but the board was loose.

Grady withdrew his gun and motioned for Longhorse to wait.

"I am a fighter," Longhorse whispered. "You know that, my brother. I can help."

Grady hesitated. Joseph had proved himself fit in the brawls with the Barley boys. That, coupled with his size and agility, made him a worthy adversary.

It would also make him a worthy partner.

Grady nodded, then walked quietly through the brambles until they reached the space below the broken window. Grady yanked off the board, then climbed in, ignoring the glass that jabbed at his hands, wiping the blood on his jeans as he straightened. Longhorse followed, and they inched down a long dark hallway. The building smelled old and musty. The walls were faded, the offices and labs empty. But he spotted a faint light burning from a distant doorway.

"No, Son, stop it. It's too late!"

Grady hesitated at the sound of a voice. He turned to Longhorse and gestured for him to be silent. They crept slowly along the corridor, Grady taking the right side, Longhorse the left. A few feet farther, Grady spotted a room that had been newly furnished with modern hospital equipment. It looked as if it had been prepared for surgery. What exactly did this lunatic have planned?

His heart beating in a frenzy, Grady pressed himself against the wall, then slipped around the last corner. He quickly scanned the interior of the long room. Cold. Drab. Dark. It took a minute for his eyes to adjust. An elderly man was hunched over in a wheelchair. A gray-haired woman lay on the floor, groaning.

Another man stood near two gurneys. Not Logan or Wheeler. Dr. Gardener.

Jesus Christ. Gardener was the killer. Was Hadley's son. And he wasn't a doctor! How could Farmer not have known Gardener wasn't for real?

He'd been under their noses all the time. But everyone had accepted him because of Doc Farmer's recommendation. He was charming. Likable. Nice looking.

Someone a cop wouldn't suspect for a minute.

Someone a woman would trust. Until he injected her with drugs and killed her.

But why hadn't the federal agents turned up anything on him?

Panic stabbed at Grady's temples. His pulse clamored. He'd have to find that out later.

A blond-haired woman lay on one gurney. Her eyes were closed. Was she already dead?

Then he recognized Violet. Bile crowded his throat. He couldn't breathe for a moment. She was strapped down. Lying so still. Not making a sound. But her eyes were open.

His breath caught as he watched for movement. Her eyelids blinked.

Thank God. She was alive.

The killer moved closer. Hovered over her. His hands were encased in rubber gloves, a hypodermic clenched between his fingers.

Longhorse moved into position. Grady gestured that

he'd take the killer. The other man nodded, prepared for backup if the man in the wheelchair protested.

They burst into the room together, Grady leaping toward Gardener. Gardener howled, but Grady pointed his gun in his face. "Move and I'll kill you."

Blue eyes flared with fear; a childlike sound gurgled from his throat. Then a calmness washed over the man's features. "No, you can't. I am the chosen one. I must save my father."

"It's too late, Son," the old man said. Grady glanced sideways and saw Joseph standing over the old man and woman, daring them to move. "I tried to tell you. I gave myself a lethal injection." The old man coughed. "I won't let you take any more lives to save my own."

The woman began to cry, leaning against the old man's wheelchair and hugging him.

The scream that came from Gardener echoed off the walls, shrill and violent. Suddenly he jerked away, lunged at Violet, jammed the hypodermic needle into her arm. Grady vaulted forward, slammed the butt of his gun against Gardener's temple. The man howled again, fighting. Grady flipped him over and dragged his arms into handcuffs. Seconds later, he had him secure.

Then he ran to Violet.

VIOLET BLINKED to stem her tears, but they overflowed anyway. Then Grady was beside her, stroking her hair, wiping them away. His dark eyes flickered with emotions. Relief. Anger. Fear. Concern.

"Shh, it's okay," he whispered in a thick voice. "We'll get you to a doctor. You're going to be fine."

Violet moved her lips. "The other woman?"

Grady glanced toward the gurney. Joseph stood over

her, pressing two fingers to her throat. "She has a pulse. It's weak but she's alive," he said.

"Thank God," Violet whispered.

Grady nearly choked as he nodded, then he lowered his head and kissed her cheek.

Threads of despair rose inside Violet as she realized his lips were moving, but she couldn't feel them. Had Gardener given her too much of the drug?

Would she be paralyzed permanently?

THE NEXT FEW HOURS were grueling. Grady phoned for a chopper to airlift Violet, and Lynnette and Hadley to the hospital. Agents Norton and Adams flew over to take Hadley's son into custody. Apparently he'd assumed the name of one of his former doctors, which was why a red flag hadn't popped up when they'd plugged in the name Gardener. Hadley's wife was also arrested. The old man died on the way to the hospital.

Longhorse drove Grady's car back down the mountain, while Grady rode in the chopper with Violet. On the way, he explained their findings about the research work and Hadley, although he sensed she already knew some of it. He also relayed that their fathers and hers had kept silent to protect Grady and Violet. Doubts registered in her eyes there, and he couldn't blame her. But he reached out, took her hand in his and hugged it to his chest to reassure her.

In fact, he held her hand the entire way. Fear caught him in its clutches at the realization that she didn't feel his touch. He read that same fear in her eyes.

But Violet had been dealt some sharp blows over the past few weeks. She was tough. She had to survive.

He couldn't take it if she didn't.

His own selfish need wouldn't allow him to leave the waiting room in the hospital while she was treated. All during the search, he'd kept remembering the feel of her legs entwined with his. The touch of her skin hot against his own body. The heat radiating between them as he'd plunged inside her.

The tenderness she'd exuded when they'd made love.

"Sheriff." One of the nurses approached him. "You can go in and see her if you want. The doctor says she's stabilized now."

"Does she have feeling in her legs and arms?"

"Not yet. It may take time." She offered him a hopeful smile. "She'll probably sleep a lot over the next twenty-four hours. But that's the body's way of healing from trauma."

Physical and mental trauma. Violet had suffered both.

He thanked the nurse, then headed into the hospital room to wait beside Violet. Whatever the outcome, when she woke up he'd be with her to face it.

VIOLET SLEPT FITFULLY, nightmares tormenting her. A killer was on the loose, murdering women. Her sisters. No, she didn't have sisters. She was all alone. Except for her grandmother.

But her grandmother was in the hospital. She had to wake up and see her. Tell her that her father wasn't the killer.

And Grady...what about Grady?

She blinked and focused, seeing his handsome face come into view. He was slumped in the chair beside her, one hand resting on the sheet. She ached to reach over and touch him.

Pinpricks of fear stabbed at her. She'd lost all feeling....

More than anything, she wanted that numbness to dissipate. She wanted to feel the heat between them, the rough stubble of his beard as it glided over her belly. The hot molten lava flowing through her body as he came inside her.

She shifted. Realized her toe had actually moved. A slight tingling jabbed at her nerve endings, as if her foot had fallen asleep. But slowly, inch by inch, the prickly sensations increased.

She slid her hand a fraction of an inch. Then another. Emotions welled in her chest. The ache felt heavenly.

Then her fingers reached Grady's. He slowly opened his eyes. Began to smile as he felt her hand squeeze his.

"Oh, thank God," he whispered. "I was so afraid, Violet. When Darlene died, I felt so guilty. I couldn't live if you weren't okay."

Violet forced a smile. She wanted a declaration of love, not guilt. Then he bent his head, pressed his lips over hers. And she forgot everything as warmth spread through her.

THE NEXT DAY Grady left Violet visiting with Lynnette. The other woman was going to be okay, and so was her baby, although she would need counseling to recover from the trauma. She had thanked him and Violet for saving her life. Grady was relieved that Violet finally had someone else in the world, another family member, even though it was an awkward relationship.

Meanwhile, he had to follow up on the arrests. And he had to talk to his deputy.

His father had been released, and Farmer had made

a deal to testify about the past, so they could lock Hadley's wife and son away for a long time. Apparently, Hadley's son had been kept under strict lock and key and on medication since Darlene's death. During his stay in the hospital, he'd developed a fixation on Native American customs and had read everything he could get his hands on about the culture.

When Hadley grew ill, his son had stopped taking his medication. He'd resurfaced, intent on finding a donor to save his father. The mother had knowingly allowed him to hunt for the women, meaning she was just as responsible, maybe even more so. She was a doctor; she should have kept him confined.

In the hospital, Violet revealed that Ross Wheeler had carried her to Hadley's son. Grady had nearly come unglued. Logan had brought Wheeler in, the reverend on his heels. Grady had jumped on the deputy, demanding to know where he'd been, but Logan had claimed he'd had a hunch and had been checking out some isolated places in the mountains near where he lived. He'd been searching for Violet.

At first, Wheeler had denied knowing the killer's identity, but Grady had discovered the brake lines to Violet's car had been cut. Wheeler finally admitted that he had cut them, hoping to silence Violet forever. He'd also confided that he and Hadley's son had been lovers. Wheeler had also confessed to making the threatening calls and setting fire to the hospital, claiming he'd done so to protect his lover. He'd also been with Hadley when he'd kidnapped Kerry from her house.

It had taken all of Grady's self-restraint not to kill the man with his bare hands. In fact, his deputy had had to pull him off Wheeler, reminding him that he was a lawman.

Logan glared at him over an open file now. One that belonged to Grady. "I see you've been investigating me."

Grady clenched his teeth. "It was routine. I ran a background check on everyone new to the area. And since you were so secretive about your past, and you have a sealed file with a black mark on it, I figured I should follow up."

Logan gnawed his lip, then gave a clipped nod. "Fair enough, I guess." He paused. Fiddled with a paper clip. Adjusted his sunglasses. "All right, my file is closed because of the way I handled my last case in Nashville."

Grady arched a brow and waited.

"My wife…" He looked away, stared out the window for a long time. "She disappeared. I suspected she was murdered, but so far, her body hasn't been recovered. I thought I'd nailed the guy who did it…." He paused, pinched the bridge of his nose. "I almost killed him, but…but the police had evidence…evidence that said he was innocent." Logan grimaced. "But last week I got a note from her. She's happy and alive, cruising somewhere in the Caribbean with her new lover."

Grady's hand closed around the file. How could he question Logan, when he himself had craved revenge for so long he didn't know how to live without the anger? When he'd wanted to kill with his own bare hands the man who'd tied Violet down? In fact, he'd almost choked Ross Wheeler when he'd been brought in. Logan had stopped him…. "Sorry, man."

Grady reached out his hand to Logan. The deputy shook it, the bond between them silent but cemented.

WITH VIOLET'S RECOVERY, came a flood of emotions. The loneliness she'd experienced when she'd returned to Crow's Landing. The terror she'd felt at the sound of the women's cries. The guilt over not saving Darlene and the others.

Her blood sisters. She hadn't yet decided whether or not to contact the remaining ones. If they didn't know about their paternity, telling them might upset their lives completely. But she had a friend forever in Lynnette. And they'd both been relieved to learn the genetic abnormality wouldn't adversely affect them or their offspring.

At least Darlene's killer was behind bars. He would never hurt anyone else again.

The voices had all begun when the killings started. Now they had grown silent. All she had to listen to were her own thoughts. Her own worries. Her own need for Grady.

As if he realized that need, the doorbell rang. She practically ran to get it, then smoothed the folds of the pale blue sundress she'd slipped on. The purple smudges of her eyes couldn't be hidden.

When the door swung open, Grady raked his gaze over her. "You are so damn beautiful, Violet."

The air compressed in her lungs. A hunger unlike anything she'd ever known flared in her chest. Her body tingled from the raw passion that ignited in his eyes. Without another word, he shut the door, then hauled her into his arms and carried her to the bedroom. Her childhood bear lay on the bed, but she moved it aside. Made room for Grady.

His clothes hit the floor as he pulled them off. Then he stood before her, all raw, primal male, declaring his intentions. His need for her surged strong and bold in his sex. She reached out and cupped it, but he shook her hand away and reached for the straps of her dress, sliding them down effortlessly. He hadn't kissed her yet and she ached for his lips. For his touch. But he simply looked. Her nipples turn to hardened peaks as he unfastened her bra. The ceiling fan swirled lazily above, brushing her nakedness with cool air. But heat ignited in her belly. Warmth tingled down her legs. And her inner thighs quivered. He was only a breath away, and she desperately wanted him.

He dipped his fingers under the edge of her panties, and she smiled as he tugged them to the floor. He continued to stare at her, as if memorizing every inch.

"Do you know that fantasizing about this kept me going when you were missing?" His husky confession charged the air between them.

"I thought about you, too."

"What did you think, Violet?" He moved closer. She felt his breath on her cheek. Throbbed for his touch again. Wanted him inside her. Moving with her. Loving her.

A devilish look twinkled in his eyes. "What do you want me to do?"

She blushed, but she was tired of denying herself. She wanted to feel again. To have him erase the pain of the past.

"Violet?"

"Touch me," she whispered, her voice urgent. "I want you to touch me everywhere."

"Yes." He traced a finger over her lips. "Like this?"

Her nipples stiffened and a surge of sensations traveled down to her womb. "Yes."

He licked his lips. She could almost taste him on her. Suckling her. Licking her. Bringing her pleasure.

"That's what I thought about, too." His husky voice turned her inside out. "I imagined touching you like this, loving you." His sex brushed her belly. His hand moved lower. Teased the insides of her thighs. Spread her feminine folds and caressed her. "Being inside you."

"Grady."

A purely male smile filled his eyes as he slid one finger into her. She groaned, throwing her head back and offering herself in wild abandon.

He grabbed her, lowering his mouth to hers. Then he claimed her lips, plunged his tongue inside. He cupped her breast, and she cradled his jaw with her palm, dragging him closer.

Seconds later, his body moved above her. Big. Strong. Surging with hunger. His sex replaced his fingers. He licked those as she watched, his eyes primal. Then he thrust deeper inside her, pulled her hips upward. She wrapped her legs around him, groaned and skimmed her nails over his buttocks as he filled her.

Muttering her name in a tortured whisper, he rocked deeper, taking her with an intensity that seared her straight to her soul. His husky moan and the feel of his body joined with hers became imprinted on her being forever. And when twilight fell over the room, cloaking it in darkness, she was no longer alone. Or afraid of the darkness.

Because Grady was there beside her.

CHAPTER TWENTY-EIGHT

THEY MADE LOVE AGAIN and again through the night, the raw need between them palpable. The last time, just as dawn broke the darkness, a bitter sweetness filled Violet's chest. Unresolved emotions skittered through her. Questions about the future.

Was Grady telling her goodbye?

Inhaling his scent, she trailed a finger over his bare chest. "I need to see my grandmother today."

Grady nodded and hugged her tighter. She'd never been so close to a man. Never experienced love. Then Grady loosened his hold. Kissed her forehead. Stood. She felt him slipping away. She missed him already.

She wanted him back. Wanted him to whisper that he loved her. But she wouldn't beg, or act like a needy virgin.

"I'll drive you to the nursing home."

His muscular flanks bulged as he crossed the room to retrieve his clothes. Then he turned and his gaze floated over her, a myriad of emotions in his own eyes. Heat. Hunger. Regret that he couldn't make promises?

"Let me take a shower and then we'll go."

He nodded. She hoped he'd join her, but he pulled on his jeans instead and went to brew coffee.

GRADY DIDN'T UNDERSTAND this desperate need raging within him to be with Violet. To take her to bed and never let her go.

Because he sensed he was going to lose her.

Lose her because he had no idea how to be the man she wanted. How to commit or please a woman forever. How to give of himself when he'd been empty for so long.

For God's sake, all he wanted to do was take. Bury himself in her sweetness and drive the ache of loss and betrayal away with her innocent, sultry kisses.

Hating himself for not being able to say the words a woman wanted to hear, he poured coffee, splashing it on the counter when she entered the room. She smelled like sex and soap, and looked at him with those damn big eyes that were both wildly loving and forgiving.

She understood he was wrestling with demons. With his failures and inability to be the man she needed. Yet she had loved him through the night, anyway. Given herself to him without asking anything in return.

And here he was, hot and horny and wanting to rip off her clothes and sate himself with her again. Right on the kitchen floor, if she'd let him.

She deserved better.

He braced himself against the counter, then cupped the hot coffee in his hands to keep from reaching for her.

"Do you want breakfast?"

"No."

He saw the yearning in her eyes, and his body responded. But he couldn't continue taking without offering something more in return.

She headed to the door, and he followed like a love-sick puppy, too needy to do anything but cling to one more moment with her before she saw him for his real self and walked away.

VIOLET PUSHED OPEN the hospital room door, shocked to see her grandmother sitting up. Grammy's sister, Neesie, sat beside her, her gray hair pulled into a bun, her gnarled hands flicking a crocheting needle back and forth.

"Grammy?"

"Violet…"

Her grandmother's speech was slow, but steady. Tears filled her eyes as Violet rushed to her and hugged her. Weak hands rose and patted her back in return.

"It's so good to see you, darling."

Violet nodded, drinking in the sight of the rosy hue to her grandmother's cheeks. The nurse had assured her that her grandmother was doing better, making progress, but Violet hadn't believed it. Until now.

"You look great."

"And you look tired, but…something about you has changed."

A flush crept up Violet's cheeks. Could her grandmother possibly know that she'd given her virginity to Grady? That her childhood crush had stolen her heart years ago and had kept it forever?

That he would always hold it in his big hands?

"Tell me, are you all right?"

Violet's eyes jerked to Neesie. Apparently she'd heard about some of the events that had transpired, but wisely hadn't informed her grandmother of the details.

"I'm fine." She filled the two women in on the basics. Relief spread over her grandmother's face at the news of her son's innocence. Then Violet recounted the details of Darlene's real killer being caught, omitting the frightening ordeal of her own attack.

"Grammy, I found the scrapbooks of pictures," she told her. "Grady said that Dad and Mr. Monroe didn't come forward when they suspected Mom and Teresa Monroe were killed—"

"He did it to protect you, Violet." Grammy reached for her with a shaky hand, and Violet gently embraced her. "He sent you away because he thought one of those scientists had killed Darlene and might come looking for you."

An undeniable sadness engulfed Violet as the truth of her words registered. Relief and a newfound respect for her father followed. "Thank you for telling me, Grammy."

"It's true," her aunt Neesie said. "Jed was miserable after you left. He might have known that you weren't his blood relative, but, honey, that man loved you until the day he died."

Violet nodded, her chest tight. If only Grady loved her now… But he'd never said the words. And somehow she accepted that he couldn't. The tragedy that had happened years ago, the fact that Laney had given him up, even if it had been for unselfish reasons, had scarred him too deeply.

Violet couldn't place more pressure, responsibility, guilt on him.

She also couldn't stay here in town, seeing him every day, wanting him, yet knowing he could never love her.

"Grammy, I think I'm going to leave Crow's Landing," she said. "I have the shop in Savannah. My art there. And the voices in my head…they're gone."

Grammy patted her hand. "I know, dear. And I hope you don't mind, but I want to live here."

Violet nodded. She'd sensed that her grandmother had come home to stay. This morning, Violet had even bought some new bedspreads and sheets for the rooms, just in case. "Dad left you the house. But it needs some repairs and a woman's touch."

"That's okay. Neesie and I will have fun fixing it up together."

Her aunt's eyes twinkled. "We're two lonely old ladies, Violet. We need each other."

Violet nodded. She wanted her grandmother to be happy. Grammy had lived too long protecting her for Violet to deny her time now with her sister.

So she hugged them both, promising to write and to visit, then went to say goodbye to Grady.

THE RIDE BACK TO VIOLET'S was almost silent. She had informed Grady about her grandmother's decision to live with her sister. Then she'd announced that she planned to leave Crow's Landing.

For the first time in his life, Grady wished he had the courage to do the same thing. He'd felt drawn to Crow's Landing for so long. To the town. To the secrets.

To the guilt.

Trapped by it all, yet unable to break free.

And now he had just discovered his real mother was here. He had a half brother. So much unresolved. Could he just walk away?

Still, as Violet packed, he felt a lump the size of a baseball in his throat.

He stood ramrod straight, his heart banging mercilessly as she carried her suitcase to the den. Long-ago memories flooded back. The childhood ones. The brotherly instincts.

The night Violet had returned. The scent of her. Those big blue eyes taunting him with her innocence.

The incessant hunger that festered between them. The courage she'd had when facing the Bone Whistler. The sheer terror Grady had experienced when he thought she might die.

"Violet." Her name came out in a pained whisper.

She paused, then handed him a sketch. "I never draw people. Children." Her eyes clouded. "But I want you to have this."

His fingers shook as he studied the drawing. Darlene. Her small cherub face. Wisps of red hair feathering her cheeks. The marbles in her hand. Grady there on the dirt beside her, teaching her to play. Violet in the middle.

The one that had drawn them all together.

He opened his mouth to speak, but he was too raw inside to make a sound. She seemed to understand.

Then she brushed a kiss across his mouth, walked out the door and disappeared into the dusk. With her absence, she left the scent of her sweetness lingering behind, along with an aching emptiness that would never go away.

GRADY WAS NEARLY immobilized after Violet left. He drove into town, went to the jail. Everything was quiet. Then, for some reason that he couldn't understand, he drove to the Redbud Café.

His father's car was there. Laney was outside, a circle of children surrounding her. "Full circle," she said. "Look to the sun and the moon. It is as with nature."

Full circle. Had the circle brought him back to catch Darlene's killer? To find the little girl who'd brought them together in childhood, and now as adults? As lovers…

Laney's gray eyes shot up and acknowledged him. The children hugged her, and she returned the embrace before they dispersed, laughing and whispering. His anger rose again. How many times had he wanted a mother? Yearned for a hug like that? For the love she might have to offer? Yet Laney had been so close and had denied him.

"Violet left," he said.

"I know. I spoke to her."

Grady nodded. He figured she would have told Laney and Joseph goodbye. His family, and Violet had always been closer to them than he had. Because Laney had given him up.

So you would have a better life.

Only it hadn't worked out that way.

"I cannot change the past or my mistakes," Laney said, as if she'd read his mind.

He gave a clipped nod.

"But you can stop yourself from making the same ones your father and I did."

His eyes shot to hers, which were wise with age. With the pain of loss. "Violet did not want to leave you," she said.

His body jerked in response. He hadn't realized he'd felt abandoned again, but maybe that was the reason he hadn't gone after Violet. He'd wanted her to stay, to prove that she wouldn't leave him as his mother had, as Darlene had, as Violet herself had....

"She cannot make up for what I did to you, Son." Laney's fingers pulled at her long gray braid. "She did not abandon you. She has suffered herself and needs your love as much as you need hers."

He wanted to argue that he didn't need anyone. That

he wouldn't. He couldn't. Needing and loving meant getting hurt. Being abandoned.

But Laney was right.

Violet had been hurt as badly as he had been, shunned by his father as a child. She'd been sent away by her own.

But she'd still given herself to him. Had even whispered her love in the midst of the darkness, although she hadn't expected him to love her in return. The price her own childhood trauma had cost her.

"Violet encouraged me not to give up on you, my son. That one day you will forgive me."

His eyes met hers. He saw the regret. The pain she had suffered. The sacrifices she had made for him.

"I told her I could never give up on you. I love you, Grady." She paused, her voice not quite steady. "But Violet, she is the one I worry about. She is leaving something very important behind, and she will carry the ache forever."

He glanced around. Remembered his father threatening Violet right here in the café. "I know. All the bad memories of this place. Of the things I couldn't stop from happening."

Laney shook her head. "No, Grady. Those are things in their own right, not your fault. What she is leaving behind—it is the love of her life."

"I know nothing about love," he said.

"I didn't think I did, either. Even worse, I didn't think it mattered. But I'm learning." His father stepped from the shadows of the awning. He had been watching. "Laney's right, Son. Don't make the same mistake I did. I should have had the courage to admit my feelings for Laney a long time ago." He moved next to her,

curved an arm around her waist. "I'm not hiding anymore. And I'm sorry I failed you, that I acted as if I
blamed you for Darlene's death. I...that's unforgiva-
ble."

"Love is instinctual and forgiving," Laney said softly.
"Even though Darlene wasn't your blood relative, you
loved her, Grady. And you love Violet, even though you
are afraid of losing again. Let your heart open." She
swept her hands in an upward arc. "Our people have another belief—that we should not dwell on things of the
past, but look toward the future. Good things await you.
A life with Violet. A baby that will put the ache of loss
of your sister to rest."

Grady saw the knowledge in her eyes. He had never
believed in Laney's native sensitivities, but her wisdom
transcended time. And so had her unselfishness.

He reached out a hand to shake hers. It was a start.
Accepting and completely forgiving would take longer.
She smiled knowingly, then lifted her arms.

He went into them.

VIOLET BREATHED DEEPLY to control the pressure in her
chest. When she'd first driven into town in her Civic,
bad memories had assaulted her. Now, she was driving
a rental car out of town, hoping to leave those memories behind.

Only she was leaving behind something very precious, as well.

The love of her life.

But he hadn't wanted her....

The loss escalated into full-blown pain that throbbed
deep within her as she stopped at the cemetery to make
peace with her father. She knelt and spread the lilies

over his grave, her throat choking with emotions. "Dad, I know the truth now. It's all over—the secrets, the running…." she whispered. "Grammy said you sent me away to protect me." She paused and inhaled deeply. "I'm so sorry we never got to be together again. I wish I could have known you." She ran a finger over the tombstone, grateful that at least her parents were buried here together. A peace fell over her. They'd given her the greatest love of all—they'd died protecting her.

She bowed her head and murmured a prayer for both of them.

Unable to leave without visiting Darlene's grave, she walked to the site and filled the vase with the yellow roses she'd brought. Then she took the other half of the Best Friends necklace, Darlene's half, and hung it around the tombstone. "You'll always be my best friend, Darlene, and you'll always be with me."

The cluster of marbles that Grady must have left drew her eye. Made her smile. Maybe the ache would subside a little now, and the pain could give way to the good memories.

Everything would be all right, she told herself as she climbed back in the car. She would return to Savannah—the shop that she had bought, the little cottage. She'd sew those curtains. Make herself a new life. Turn back to her art.

But there would never be another Grady.

She stepped on the accelerator, the pressure in her chest building. She had to get out of town. Away from the memories.

A siren suddenly sounded, wailing behind her. She glanced in her rearview mirror. An emergency, maybe? She scanned the horizon for a fire or accident, but saw nothing. The police car soared up behind her. Moved closer, on her tail. The blue light swirled. The noise was deafening.

The officer was motioning for her to pull over.

She checked the speed limit. She had been pushing it, but not speeding. Panic jolted her. What if something had happened to her grandmother?

She swung to the curb and pulled on the brake, then vaulted from the car. It was Grady. Please, he couldn't have bad news! Grammy had been doing so much better.

He took his time getting out, then loped toward her. Violet's heart pounded relentlessly. She opened her mouth to ask about her grandmother, but lost her voice.

Something flickered in Grady's eyes. Need. Hunger. A desperate loneliness.

"Violet."

"Grady…is something wrong?"

He nodded, and her heart tripped in her chest.

"You can't leave like this. You…have something that belongs to me."

She frowned, not comprehending. Did he want the other half of Darlene's necklace?

"I'm not very good with words," he said, realizing her confusion. "But you stole something from me and I want it back."

She fingered the necklace. She couldn't let it go. It was all she had left. "What?"

He moved toward her. Gently lifted a strand of hair from her cheek. "My heart."

Relief rippled out with her breath. Then questions.

"I can't stay here," she whispered. "I…I love you, Grady, but I can't. This place has too many bad memories."

"I thought you told me that you couldn't escape them, even if you left town."

Sadness forced her to nod. "I can't. But I have a cabin on Tybee Island. The ocean there, my gift shop, my art… It's so peaceful. Beautiful, really."

"I see." The pad of his thumb stroked her cheek. "I was thinking. I've never been to Savannah. Never seen the ocean."

The sun drifted from behind the clouds. A breeze ruffled the air. Heat rippled between them. "You can visit."

"No."

Disappointment dried her mouth.

He closed his eyes, opened them. His throat worked as he swallowed. "I don't want to visit, Violet. I…want to go with you. Make a fresh start."

He was struggling. But so was she. She couldn't get her hopes up only to have them dashed again. And she needed the words, not just guilt or attraction. She needed love. "I don't understand, Grady."

"I loved Darlene, Violet, and when she died, I felt so guilty and alone. Then you came back and you reminded me of her. You made me want things…things I didn't know I wanted, things I didn't think I deserved."

Her resolve was melting.

"And then I fell in love with you," he said in a gruff voice, "but I was afraid of that, of losing you."

"You're never going to lose me," Violet whispered. "And we both have to stop blaming ourselves for Darlene's death. She would want us to be happy."

He captured her hand in his. "I love you, Violet. I'm only happy when I'm with you."

The air got trapped in her lungs.

"Marry me, Violet. Please say you'll marry me."

"Yes." She smiled and fell into his arms as he crushed her against him. "I love you, too, Grady."

He kissed her feverishly, then lowered his hand. Laid it over her stomach. "I want us to have kids, Violet," he whispered. "We'll celebrate their birthdays," he said gruffly. "And yours. We're going to make up for all those ones you missed."

She nodded. He understood about the loss, because he had been there with her. Even hundreds of miles apart, it was as if they had never been separated.

They would name their first girl after Darlene.

Then he lowered his mouth and captured her lips again, just as he'd captured her heart and soul years ago. They weren't running from their pasts anymore, they were running toward a future.

* * * * *

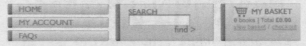

A SEARCH FOR SURVIVORS BECOMES A RACE AGAINST TIME – AND A KILLER

When a plane goes down in the Appalachian mountains, rescue teams start looking for the survivors and discover that a five-year-old boy and a woman are missing. Twenty miles from the crash site, Deborah Sanborn has a vision of two survivors, and she senses these strangers are in terrible danger.

With the snow coming down, not only are they racing against time and the elements – they're up against a killer desperate to silence his only living witness to murder.

Available 21st September 2007

A modern reconstruction of the crown of thorns

THE ROAD TO CALVARY
Jesus was flogged and mocked before his death. Because he had been called King of the Jews he was forced to wear a crown of thorns. He was made to carry his heavy cross along the steep road to Calvary, the place of crucifixion. Jesus tried but he was too weak, so a spectator, Simon of Cyrene, carried it for him.

Rosary medal showing Jesus wearing the crown of thorns

A CONDEMNED MAN
The council elders took Jesus to Pontius Pilate, the Roman governor, who had the power to impose the death penalty. Jesus was accused of setting himself up as King of the Jews but, when asked about this, Jesus simply said, "So you say". Pilate was unwilling to condemn Jesus, and said the crowd could choose one prisoner to be set free. But they refused to release Jesus.

IN DENIAL
Jesus was taken to the High Priest, Caiaphas, and was put before the supreme Jewish council. As the disciple Peter sat outside he was accused three times of being one of Jesus' followers, but he denied it each time. A cockerel crowed as Peter made his third denial. Jesus had told Peter that this would happen.

Many churches have a cockerel weather vane to remind us of the denial

THE LAST SUPPER
At the time of Jesus' arrest it was Passover – the festival that celebrates the freeing of the Jews from slavery and looks forward to the coming of the Messiah. Jesus told his disciples to arrange a Passover meal. He said that this would be the last meal he would share with them and that one of them would soon betray him.

The Kiss of Judas by Giotto di Bondone

13th-century Syriac manuscript

JUDAS KISS
After the last supper, Jesus went to the Garden of Gethsemane. His disciple Judas Iscariot arrived with Roman soldiers and the Jewish Temple guard. Judas greeted Jesus with a kiss – a signal he had agreed with the soldiers. The soldiers arrested Jesus, who told his disciples not to resist but to accept God's will.

The resurrection

CHRISTIANS BELIEVE that on the third day after his crucifixion Jesus rose from the dead. The Gospels (p. 21) describe how, when he appeared to his disciples after the resurrection, some of them did not recognize him. Jesus' body seemed to have changed, and he apparently was able to appear and disappear at will. Christians believe in the resurrection in different ways. Some are convinced that the risen Jesus was literally alive on Earth. Others believe his presence was a spiritual one, seen only in the ways in which his followers behaved. Most Christians believe that Jesus joined God in Heaven, where he will stay until the last judgement (p. 26).

STRONG SYMBOL
The resurrection is one of the most important parts of the Christian story. It is often depicted symbolically, as in the case of this embroidered decoration from a priest's clothing.

John, whose symbol is an eagle

Matthew, whose symbol is a man

THE EMPTY CROSS
An empty cross is a reminder of Jesus' resurrection. The lamb at the centre is a familiar symbol of Jesus, who is often referred to as the Lamb of God. The lamb is an innocent creature that is easily killed, so it reminds Christians of the sacrifice made by God in order to redeem humankind from sin.

Mark, whose symbol is a lion

ROCK TOMB
Joseph of Arimathea, a disciple of Jesus, offered his own tomb for Jesus' burial. This tomb was probably similar to the one above. Called an arcosolium, it has been cut into the rock of a cliff face and sealed with a large, round stone.

RISEN FROM THE DEAD
Pontius Pilate ordered soldiers to guard Jesus' tomb in case the disciples came to take away his body. But the Gospels tell how, on the third day after the crucifixion, Jesus rose from the dead while the guards slept. This set of three 15th-century Italian paintings (see also opposite) shows Jesus rising from a Roman-style sarcophagus, or tomb, set into the rocks.

SUPPER AT EMMAUS
Shortly after the resurrection, Jesus met two of his disciples near a village called Emmaus. The pair did not recognize him, but invited him to supper with other disciples. It was only when Jesus broke the bread and blessed it that they recognized him. Then he disappeared from their sight.

Illustration from a 15th-century Italian Bible

DOUBTING THOMAS
The disciple Thomas said that he would believe in Jesus' resurrection only if he saw the wounds that Jesus had received when he was crucified. John's Gospel recalls that, when Jesus met the disciples, he showed Thomas his wounds.

Mural from the Holy Trinity Church in Sopocani, Serbia, c. 1265

Jesus is shown surrounded by clouds and angels

"The Messiah must suffer and must rise from death three days later."

LUKE 24:46
Jesus to his disciples

THE ASCENSION
The Gospels and another New Testament book called Acts record that, after telling his disciples to spread the word (pp. 18–19), Jesus joined his Father in Heaven. He was raised up into the sky and then vanished behind a cloud.

12th-century stone relief from Saint Dominic's Abbey in Silos, Spain

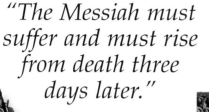

Luke, whose symbol is an ox

THE EMPTY TOMB
A group of women, probably including Jesus' follower Mary Magdalene, went to the tomb to anoint his body with spices. When they arrived, they found the tomb open and empty. An angel appeared to them and told them that Jesus had risen from the dead. In Matthew's account of this story, the amazing news was accompanied by an earthquake.

LOOKING FOR JESUS
John's Gospel contains a moving account of Mary Magdalene's search for Jesus' body. As she wept at his disappearance, a man appeared whom Mary believed to be a gardener. But when he spoke her name, she realized immediately that it was Jesus. He said, "Do not hold on to me, because I have not yet gone back up to the Father".

Spreading the word

In the decades following Jesus' crucifixion, his disciples continued his work of teaching and preaching. Saint Paul was the most important of these early preachers. He founded churches around the Mediterranean, and his letters to these and other churches make up many of the books of the New Testament. These letters have proved a source of inspiration to the countless others who have come after Paul and who have worked to spread Christianity around the world.

12th-century portrayal of Pentecost on the Verdun Altar in Austria

TONGUES LIKE FIRE
The Book of Acts describes how the disciples were gathered together for an ancient Jewish festival called Pentecost. There was a sound like a wind blowing through the room, and tongues like fire spread out and touched each disciple, filling them with the Holy Spirit. Pentecost took on a new significance to Christians after this day.

The seated disciples are surrounded by tongues like flame

Catacombs of Priscalla, Rome, Italy

PASSIONATE SAINT PETER
Peter, as pictured on this 1430s Italian prayer book, was one of the leaders of the disciples. At Pentecost, he spoke passionately to the others, telling them that they had been visited by the Holy Spirit and saying that Jesus had risen from the dead and was the Messiah promised by God.

PERSECUTED CHRISTIANS
After Pentecost, the Christian community started to grow, and Peter began to allow non-Jews to join the church. The Roman authorities did not approve of Christianity, however, and many believers were persecuted. When the faith spread to Rome itself, many Christians kept their beliefs secret, even going down into the catacombs (underground tombs) to worship.

Saint Paul

Saul was a Roman citizen and a Jew. He persecuted Christians and was present at the death of Stephen, the first Christian martyr (someone who dies for their faith). While on a journey to Damascus in Syria, Saul was temporarily blinded by a dazzling light, and he heard the voice of God asking him why he was attacking the church.

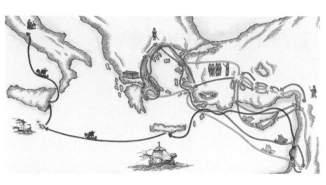

PAUL'S JOURNEYS
After his vision on the road to Damascus, Saul converted to Christianity and took the name Paul. He travelled around the Mediterranean, converting people to Christianity and setting up churches. As shown by this map, Paul's journeys took him to Cyprus, Turkey, Macedonia, and Greece.

ANCIENT EPHESUS
The ancient city of Ephesus (now in Turkey) was the site of one of the most important churches founded by Paul. His letter to the Ephesians encourages unity, and tells believers to follow the Christian path.

THE FIRST CHRISTIANS
For some time, Paul taught in the city of Antioch in Syria, where this church was built many years later. Paul sometimes referred to Jesus as Christ, meaning "the Anointed One", so from this time on believers became known as Christians.

EASTERN EMPEROR
Justinian I, a Christian emperor, ruled the eastern, or Byzantine, empire from 527 to 565. He encouraged religious tolerance, tried to make peace between the rival Christian sects that existed at the time, and built churches in his capital city of Constantinople (now Istanbul in Turkey).

Coin depicting Justinian I

CONSTANTINE THE CONVERT
In 312, Constantine I became emperor of Rome. The following year, he became a Christian and passed the *Edict of Milan*, which proclaimed that Christians should be tolerated not persecuted. The faith could now spread with ease across the vast Roman empire.

Coin depicting Constantine I

SAINT PAUL'S LEGACY
Ever since Saint Paul went on his journeys, Christians have travelled around the world preaching the faith. Much of this missionary activity took place in the 19th century, with Europeans like Charles Creed preaching in countries such as New Zealand, as pictured here.

God's book

WHO WROTE THE BIBLE?
The Bible was actually written by many different people. The books of the Old Testament were written by unknown scribes over hundreds of years. The authors of the New Testament were early Christians. Scribes later made copies of these original texts by hand using quill pens.

Quill pens and ink horns

THE CHRISTIAN BIBLE consists of more than 60 separate books written over many centuries. These books are divided into two main groups. The Old Testament contains the history and sacred writings of the Jewish people before the time of Jesus, which are sacred to Jews as well as to Christians. The New Testament deals mainly with Jesus and his early followers. The original texts (the Old Testament written in Hebrew and Aramaic, and the New in Greek) were translated into modern languages by biblical scholars in the 20th century (pp. 34–35).

Mosaic of the creation of the birds, Monreale Cathedral, Sicily

THE FIRST FIVE
The first five books of the Bible describe the creation of the universe and tell stories of the earliest Jewish ancestors. One of the most important stories relates how the Jewish leader Moses received the tablets of law, or ten commandments, from God. It is sometimes claimed that Moses was the author of these books.

GETTING HISTORICAL
Many of the Old Testament books are historical, following the fate of the Jewish people over hundreds of years. These historical writings describe events in the lives of notable kings, such as Solomon, who was famously visited from afar by the Queen of Sheba and her entourage.

HOLY PLACE
Built by King Solomon, the Temple in Jerusalem was the holiest of all places to the Jews. It was destroyed by the Babylonians, but the Jews eventually restored it. In the Roman period, the Temple was rebuilt again by Herod the Great. Luke's Gospel describes Jesus visiting this temple as a boy.

Artist's impression of Solomon's Temple in the time of Christ

2,500-year-old carved head of a woman from Sheba

13th-century illustration of David playing a harp

THE WORDS OF THE PROPHETS

A large number of Old Testament books contain the sayings of prophets, such as Jeremiah, Isaiah, and Ezekiel. These men brought messages from God, telling people about God's will in relation to everything from everyday life to the future of the Jewish people. To early Christians, many of the prophets' words seemed to predict the coming of Jesus.

Depiction of Jeremiah from a 12th-century wall painting from Cyprus

Illustration of Paul's death from a 12th-century manuscript

WORDS OF WISDOM

The wisdom books are a group of Old Testament books written in various styles and on a range of subjects. The Psalms (originally said to have been written by King David) contain poetry praising God; the Proverbs consist of pithy, instructive sayings; and other books, such as Job, discuss human suffering.

13th-century illustration of Jonah and the fish

STORY WITH A MORAL

God told the prophet Jonah to visit the city of Nineveh to persuade the people to repent their sins. When Jonah refused, God sent a storm. Jonah was thrown overboard from his ship, and was swallowed by a great fish. When the fish finally spewed Jonah onto dry land, the prophet went straight to Nineveh.

WORK OF GOD

The later books of the New Testament are concerned mostly with the work of Jesus' followers, who carried on his mission after the resurrection. This work is described both in the book of Acts and in the various epistles (letters) written by early church leaders such as Saint Paul.

SEEING TOGETHER

The first four books of the New Testament – the Gospels – tell the story of Jesus' life, crucifixion, and resurrection. The Gospels of Matthew, Mark, and Luke are very similar and are known as the "synoptic" (seeing together) Gospels. These were probably written soon after A.D. 65. John's Gospel is thought to have been written at the end of the 1st century.

Luke, the winged ox

John, the eagle

The symbols of the evangelists, or writers of the Gospels, by modern artist Laura James

Matthew, the angel

Mark, the lion

Continued on next page

Early Bible texts

The books of the Bible were first written down by hand in the local languages of the eastern Mediterranean – Hebrew, Aramaic, and Greek. When different scribes copied out the texts, small variations occurred. The books were then translated into other ancient languages, such as Syriac. As a result, scholars translating the Bible into modern languages have a range of different sources to refer to, which helps them to make their version as close as possible to the original.

GUIDANCE FROM GOD
The Hebrew Bible – the Torah plus other books of narrative, prophecy, and wisdom – also makes up the Old Testament of the Christian Bible. Jesus often referred to these ancient Jewish scriptures, calling them the Law or the Writings. The five books that make up the Torah are Genesis, Exodus, Leviticus, Numbers, and Deuteronomy. They are central to the Jewish faith, and Deuteronomy includes 613 commandments that Jews try to follow in their everyday lives.

Crown-like finials, or tips, indicate the importance of the Torah

Tik, or Torah case, commonly used by Spanish and eastern Jews

EARLIEST EXAMPLES
The Dead Sea Scrolls were found at Qumran in Jordan, on the edge of the Dead Sea, in 1947. They contain the earliest surviving manuscripts of most of the books of the Old Testament and also other texts in Hebrew, Greek, and Aramaic written down as early as the 2nd century B.C.

Pottery scroll jars

HIDDEN TREASURE
The original owners of the Dead Sea Scrolls were members of a Jewish group called the Essenes. They kept the texts in large pottery jars. When their area was overrun by the Romans, the Essenes hid the Scrolls, which lay undiscovered for almost 2,000 years. Most of the Scrolls were damaged, but they have helped modern Bible translators, and taught scholars much about life in the 1st century A.D.

COVER UP
In the west, the Torah is usually kept in a cloth covering called a mantle. This is often embroidered with religious symbols. On this mantle, the crown is the symbol of the Torah, the Hebrew writing reads "Crown of the Torah", and the lions represent Judah, one of the tribes of Israel.

Continued on next page

> *"What gives life is God's spirit; human power is of no use at all. The words I have spoken to you bring God's life-giving spirit."*
>
> JOHN 6:63
> Jesus to his followers

SIMPLY SYRIAC

Translations of the Bible into Syriac appeared very early – probably in the 1st or 2nd century A.D. Called the *Peshitta* (meaning "simple"), the Syriac Bible has been used ever since in churches in Syria and neighbouring areas, and was the basis for translations into Persian and Arabic.

ALL GREEK

The Gospels were written in the 1st century B.C. in Greek, a language shared by many early Christians. By this time, the Old Testament had been translated into Greek as well. The Greek Old Testament, called the *Septuagint*, was the version used by the earliest Christian communities and referred to in the Gospels.

The text of the Torah is written in Hebrew on a continuous scroll

4th-century Greek text of Saint John's Gospel

BOOK BINDER

Underneath the mantle, the Torah is bound with a cloth called a *mappah*. Beneath this band is the scroll containing the text of the Torah. This Hebrew text is read in all synagogues (Jewish places of worship) and Jews believe that, if they follow the Torah, they are following the guidance of God.

23

Continued from previous page

Later Bible texts

From the 4th to the 15th centuries, monks translated the Bible into Latin, the language of the western church. But the Reformation (pp. 34–35) brought a new demand for vernacular (local or current language) Bibles. People have been translating the Bible ever since, and today's translators try to be as accurate as possible while using words and phrases that are familiar to ordinary people.

Illuminated Bible with Latin text

THE ONE AND ONLY

Several Latin translations of the Bible were made, but the most famous was the one called the Vulgate, made by Saint Jerome in the late-4th century at the request of the pope. In 1546, the Council of Trent, a meeting of church leaders, declared the Vulgate to be the only authentic Latin text of the Bible.

The text of the Gutenberg Bible is the Latin Vulgate translation

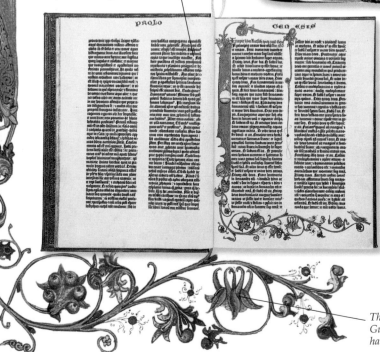

HANDY WORK

In the days before printing, monks wrote out the Latin texts of the books of the Bible by hand, often decorating the pages with beautiful illustrations. Psalters, which contain the words of the Psalms, were in great demand for use in services. This one includes an Old English translation between the lines of Latin text.

IN PRINT

Johannes Gutenberg (p. 34) produced the first printed edition of the entire Bible in Germany in 1455. Suddenly, it became possible to produce large numbers of Bibles quickly, bringing knowledge of the actual words of the Bible to more people than ever before.

WILLIAM TINDALL

The coloured decorations in the Gutenberg Bible were added by hand after the text was printed

Illustrations help bring the text to life

GOOD NEWS
By the 20th century, most translations of the Bible seemed old-fashioned, and demand for Bibles written in modern languages grew. The *Good News Bible* and the *New International Version*, translated into modern English from the best Hebrew and Greek sources, met this need and have sold millions of copies.

Modern German Bible

AHEAD OF THEIR TIME
German theologians translated parts of the Bible into their native language throughout the Middle Ages. The whole Bible was translated by about 1400, but the church frowned on vernacular Bibles, and these were not widely available until after the Reformation (pp. 34–35).

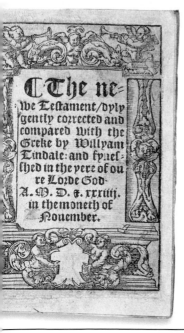

A GOOD INFLUENCE
In the early-16th century, reformer William Tyndale wanted to translate the Bible into English. The English church would not allow this, so Tyndale moved to Germany, where he published his New Testament in English in 1525. This copy is a revised version, printed in 1534. It greatly influenced later Bible translators.

The different languages are divided into columns and blocks

LOTS OF LANGUAGES
The interest in Bible translation, and the need to compare different texts, led to the production of polyglot Bibles, in which the text is printed side-by-side in several different languages. These pages come from an early polyglot Bible of 1516, with the text in Hebrew, Greek, Latin, and Arabic.

Heaven and Hell

ALL CHRISTIANS believe in one eternal and almighty God, who exists as three beings – the Father, the Son, and the Holy Spirit. They believe that Jesus is the Son of God, that he lived on Earth as the son of the Virgin Mary, and that he was crucified and rose from the dead. Christians have faith that if they follow the teachings of Jesus and repent their sins they will be rewarded after death with everlasting life in Heaven – the traditional name for God's eternal kingdom. Its opposite, the place or state without God, is known as Hell.

14th-century painting of the Holy Trinity by Andrei Roublev

THREE IN ONE
The idea of the Holy Trinity, the one God who exists as three beings, is one of the deepest mysteries of Christian faith. God the Father is the almighty creator of the universe. God the Son is Jesus, God made human. God the Holy Spirit is God's power on Earth. The Bible describes Jesus as sitting at God's right hand in Heaven.

This medieval illustration shows angels blowing their trumpets as the dead rise from their graves

LAST JUDGEMENT
Christians look forward to a time when Jesus will return to Earth. They believe that he will come again in glory to judge the living and the dead. Jesus will reward the righteous with eternal life, and the kingdom of God will truly exist and have no end.

Angel carrying a golden censer

Ivory counter showing human figures fighting off the demons of Hell to ascend to Heaven, 1120

IN HEAVEN
For some, Heaven is a literal place, a paradise where God dwells. Others emphasize that Heaven is not a place, but a state of being with God for ever. Catholics (pp. 28–31) believe that a person's soul goes first to a third place, called Purgatory, where it is purified before entering Heaven.

WINGED MESSENGERS
The Bible refers to angels as spiritual beings who live with God in Heaven. They act as messengers, bringing God's words and judgements to people on Earth and providing spiritual guidance. The Bible gives few clues about what angels look like, but they are traditionally portrayed as winged beings with human bodies.

JACOB'S LADDER

The life of Jacob, one of the ancestors of the people of Israel, is described in the Book of Genesis. Jacob had a dream in which he saw a ladder connecting Heaven and Earth. As Jacob watched angels passing up and down the ladder, God spoke and promised that the land where he slept would one day belong to him and his descendants.

Relief of Jacob's ladder, west front of Bath Abbey, England

Angel carrying a casket that may contain saintly relics (pp. 42–43)

Angel carrying a model church

Angels are often portrayed with shining, golden wings

THE FALL OF SATAN

According to the Book of Revelation, Satan – a member of the highest rank of angels, the archangels – started a war with God. As a result he was thrown out of Heaven and started his own evil kingdom in Hell. Some Christians believe Hell to be a place of pain, where Satan and his demons torture the souls of the damned, forcing them to endure everlasting fire.

DEVILISH DEPICTIONS

Since medieval times, artists have portrayed Satan and his demons as grotesque creatures, human in form but with horns, tails, and cloven hoofs. Most Christians today are less concerned with the appearance of Satan and Hell, and are more likely to think of the torture of Hell as the agony of an existence without the love of God.

Modern Mexican stamp depicting a devil

LOTERIA DE
MEXICO 1998-99
20¢
EL DIABLITO
G. NORMA / C. VERGARA T I E V

Catholicism

THE ROMAN CATHOLIC CHURCH is the largest of the Christian churches. Catholics place special stress on the Eucharist, or Mass (pp. 52–53), and are expected to go to Mass every Sunday. One distinctive feature of Catholic worship is commemoration of the saints. There is also a stress on devotional practices such as praying the rosary (p. 30) and making pilgrimages to shrines (pp. 42–43). In addition to the New Testament, Catholics are guided in their lives by the teachings of the church, which produces instruction on a range of topics from social justice to the church's contact with other faiths.

Golden angels face into the centre of the monstrance

Censer stand is shaped like a crozier (p. 31)

DISPLAY CASE
This vessel, known as a monstrance, is used to display the host (the consecrated bread used during Mass). It consists of a glass-covered compartment surrounded by a metal frame with outward-spreading rays. It is used when the host is carried in processions, during a service called Benediction, and when the host is displayed for the purposes of devotion.

CHARTRES CATHEDRAL
Combining magnificent Gothic and Romanesque features along with over 200 stained glass windows, Chartres cathedral is often called the greatest in Europe. The cathedral was begun in 1020, destroyed by fire in 1194, and rebuilt in the mid 13th century.

CREATING AN ATMOSPHERE
Incense is used widely in the Catholic church. It is burned in a vessel called a censer – a pierced metal container hung on chains. When the censer is swung gently from side to side, sweet-smelling smoke comes out of the holes in the top of the vessel.

Baroque confessional box from Vienna in Austria

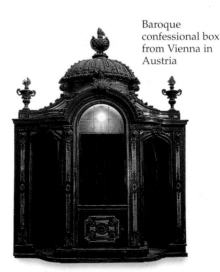

The lid lifts up so that the censer can be filled

CONFESSIONS
Catholics are expected to confess their sins regularly to a priest, who sits in a box-like structure called a confessional. The priest acts as an intermediary between God and the sinner, and pronounces God's willingness to forgive. The sinner may be asked to perform a penance – an action to show that they are truly sorry for their sin.

Bird's-eye view of an incense boat

Incense boat

Charcoal

Incense

Aspergillum

Benedictine monk sprinkling holy water

The pope

The Catholic church is led by the pope, whom Catholics believe to be the direct successor of the disciple Peter – the first pope. Because Peter's authority came direct from Jesus, Catholics believe the pope's decisions on faith and morality to be infallible. The pope's teachings, explained in his letters and other documents, therefore have a huge influence on Catholics all over the world.

BADGE OF OFFICE
The ring is one of the pope's badges of office. This one belonged to Eugenius IV (pope from 1431 to 1437). In those days, popes were famed for their fine robes and jewellery. Modern popes are more often known for their moral guidance and wide contacts with the world's churches.

TIME TO BURN
Incense, which may be kept in an incense boat, is burned by being put into a censer along with hot charcoal. Incense is often used in the procession during which the priest enters the church. It may also be used at other times, such as the elevation of the host during Mass.

SOLEMN RITES
Water that has been blessed may be sprinkled during solemn rites such as blessings, exorcisms (the banishing of evil spirits), and burials. People may also be sprinkled with holy water during Mass. The sprinkling device, called an aspergillum, is a rod tipped with a bulb or brush.

CATHOLIC HEADQUARTERS
As well as being leader of the church, the pope is the Bishop of Rome, and lives in the Vatican City – a tiny independent state within Rome itself. The Vatican City is the headquarters of the Catholic church and contains Saint Peter's Basilica, the main church in the Catholic world.

Continued on next page

Continued from previous page

Leadership and spirituality

The leadership of the Catholic church is provided by both the pope and by a hierarchy of clergy – archbishops, bishops, and priests. Bishops and priests lead by spiritual example, and also by teaching their flock about all areas of the Catholic faith. It is their job to educate members of the Catholic church on everything from the meaning of Mass (pp. 52–53) to the importance of prayer and reverence for the Virgin Mary.

14th-century bishops wearing full vestments

STATUS SYMBOLS
Mitres, pointed headdresses with two ribbons hanging at the back, are worn by bishops, archbishops, and abbots (p. 48). They are usually decorated with religious symbols or scenes. The mitre's tall shape is a sign of its wearer's status, the highest form of sacred ministry below that of the pope.

Depiction of the Annunciation

14th-century designs for mitres

Mary being crowned

A BISHOP'S WORK
A bishop oversees the churches and priests in his diocese. He preaches, writes advisory letters to the local clergy, and directs the training of priests and the religious instruction given in Catholic schools. Bishops also belong to local or national groups called Bishops' Conferences, which meet to discuss collective policies.

PRAYING THE ROSARY
Catholics use rosaries as an aid to prayer. Three different prayers – the *Hail Mary*, the *Our Father* or *Lord's Prayer*, and the *Glory to the Father* – are repeated as the person meditates on the key stages of the Christian story. The rosary beads are used to count the prayers.

Rosary with medals showing saints for contemplation

Jesus raising his hand in blessing

14th-century French mitre showing the coronation of the Virgin

PRIESTLY JEWELS
This chain was worn by a priest in 15th-century Italy. Modern priests rarely wear elaborate regalia like this, but they share the roles and values of their predecessors. Catholic priests must be male and are usually unmarried. They celebrate the sacraments, preach, provide instruction in the faith, and care spiritually for the people in their parish, or district.

Link made of gilded bronze

Sapphire mounted in chain

Pendant with nativity scene

Medieval crozier used by a bishop

Virgin Mary

Angel Gabriel

Enamelled and gilded decoration

THE BLESSED VIRGIN MARY
Catholics regard the Virgin Mary with special devotion, and scenes from her life appear on many works of religious art, as well as on vestments and everyday objects. The Catholic church teaches that Mary was free from original sin and that at the end of her life on Earth she was taken up, body and soul, into Heaven – an event referred to as the Assumption. Because Mary is so revered, several festivals associated with her are held throughout the church year.

White roses of the Virgin Mary

Madonna and Child, painted wood, c. 1320 Gothic

"Hail Mary, full of grace, the Lord is with you; blessed are you among women, and blessed is the fruit of your womb, Jesus."

THE HAIL MARY

31

The Orthodox church

THE FORM OF CHRISTIANITY that is strongest in eastern Europe and western Asia is known as the Orthodox church. It developed between the 9th and 11th centuries as a result of a split between eastern and western Christians, and claims to be closest to the faith as originally practised by Jesus' disciples. Like the Catholics, Orthodox Christians recognize several sacraments and venerate the Virgin Mary, but they do not recognize the authority of the pope. They place a heavy stress on holy tradition as revealed through the Bible and the collective decisions and teachings of the early church leaders.

ORTHODOX CHURCHES
The Orthodox church is a group of individual churches, each led by a patriarch, or senior bishop. Saint Basil's Cathedral in Moscow, Russia – with its striking onion domes – is under the leadership of the Patriarch of Moscow and all Russia.

Orthodox priests often have long beards and long hair

Greek icon showing three saints

HOLY FOCUS
Icons – usually small paintings of Jesus, Mary, or the saints – play a key part in Orthodox worship. Orthodox Christians see icons as reminders that God became human in the form of Jesus. They use them to help focus their prayers and devotions.

Russian annunciation icon

Portable icon designed to be worn as a pendant

The nails in Christ's hands are clearly visible

Crucifix icon from the Crimean War

THE HEART OF THE MATTER
Orthodox priests must be more than 30 years old, and they are allowed to be married. The celebration of Holy Communion (pp. 52–53), usually referred to as the Liturgy, is at the heart of their work. Orthodox Christians believe that, during the Liturgy, God is especially present in the wine.

ROYAL DOORS
In Orthodox churches, the sanctuary (the area containing the altar) is hidden by a screen called the iconostasis. The screen has a pair of doors called the royal doors, which are frequently beautifully decorated. These royal doors from the Russian Orthodox church in London, England, are decorated with images of the annunciation and the evangelists.

PORTABLE ICONS
Although the main place to display icons is in church, Orthodox Christians also use portable icons. These can be carried in processions, hung at shrines by the roadside, or used at home to help concentrate the mind during private prayer. Portable icons and similar items like this crucifix are especially popular in Russia.

OIL OF GLADNESS
When infants are baptized in the Orthodox church the priest immerses them three times in the font before anointing them with the "oil of gladness". The priest then performs the ceremony of chrismation, anointing the child on the head, eyes, nose, ears, and mouth. Chrismation in the Orthodox church is the equivalent to the western ceremony of confirmation (p. 58).

ORTHODOX MONASTICISM
Monasticism (pp. 44–47) began in the east, in areas such as Egypt and Syria, and is still an important part of Orthodox religious life. Orthodox Christians believe that the presence of the Holy Spirit is revealed in the lives of monks and nuns. The most famous Orthodox monasteries are on Mount Athos in Greece, a monastic republic where monks have lived since the 10th century.

Stoles were originally made of wool to symbolize the flock for which priests are responsible

The crozier symbolizes the priest's power over his flock

Cuff symbolizes the power of God's right hand

BISHOP'S BUSINESS
All bishops are equal in the Orthodox church. They do have an overall leader – the Patriarch of Constantinople (Istanbul) – but he has no authority over the others. The main authority comes from synods, or meetings, of bishops held in each of the Orthodox churches to make decisions on matters affecting the church as a whole. Orthodox bishops are not permitted to marry, so bishops begin their calling as monks not priests.

Orthodox bishop's vestments

The Reformation

DURING THE 14th and 15th centuries, many people in Europe were worried that the Catholic church was becoming corrupt. In the early-16th century three men – Martin Luther from Germany, Ulrich Zwingli from Switzerland, and John Calvin from France – spearheaded the reform of the church across Europe. In the movement now known as the Reformation, they and their followers founded new, Protestant churches. These churches rejected the control of the pope and bishops and stressed the importance of the Bible and preaching God's word.

Medal from the 1500s depicting the pope as Satan

CHURCH ABUSES
Reformers objected to several practices in the Catholic church. One of the most widespread abuses of the church was the use of indulgences – the payment of money instead of doing penance for sins. Even some popes were corrupt, and objectors often portrayed them as devil-like figures.

Bar, to screw down the platen

Platen, used to press the ink onto the paper

The coffin is pushed beneath the platen

AGAINST CORRUPTION
This coin was made in honour of Jan Hus, a Czech priest who became a reformer in the early-1400s. He spoke out against the corruption of the church but, despite support from ordinary people, was prevented from preaching, excommunicated, forced to leave Prague, and eventually burned at the stake.

Ink ball, to spread the ink evenly

EARLY IDEAS
Englishman John Wyclif, a theologian and politician, began to demand church reform in the late-14th century. Many of his ideas – such as the denial of the pope's authority and the call for the Bible to be translated into modern European languages – were taken up by later reformers all over Europe. In this painting by Ford Madox Brown, Wyclif is reading from his translation of the Bible.

PRINTING PRESS
In the 1450s, craftsman Johannes Gutenberg of Mainz in Germany invented a new method of printing. It enabled books to be printed quickly and cheaply. This major advance allowed the ideas of the Reformation to travel around Europe at great speed.

34

VOICE OF REASON
Education developed rapidly at the time of the Reformation through the work of teachers like Desiderius Erasmus, shown here in a painting by Hans Holbein. His methods were different from Luther's passionate, revolutionary approach – he hoped to reform the church through reason and scholarship. Erasmus edited the Greek New Testament, which was a great help to the scholars who would later translate the Bible into modern European languages.

MOTHER TONGUE
In 1549, the Archbishop of Canterbury, Thomas Cranmer, published the *Book of Common Prayer* – a church service book in English. It enabled English people to hold services in their own language for the first time. When England briefly returned to Catholicism, under Queen Mary I in 1553, Cranmer was executed.

FAMOUS THESES
In October 1517, Martin Luther posted 95 theses (arguments against indulgences) on a church door in Wittenberg, Germany. He followed this with several books about reform. He argued that salvation came from God's grace through the individual's faith in Christ, and could not be bought.

Full- and pocket-sized copies of the *Book of Common Prayer*

Tympan, where the paper is put

CHURCH LEADER
In 1534, King Henry VIII forced the English church to break from Rome because the pope would not allow him to divorce his wife, Catherine of Aragon. Henry himself became leader of the English church although, apart from his rejection of the pope, he remained Catholic in his beliefs. Despite this, he began the process that brought Protestantism to England.

Gallows, to support the tympan

Bolton Abbey, England

DISSOLUTION OF THE MONASTERIES
Henry VIII ordered his chief minister, Thomas Cromwell, to compile a report on the monasteries in England. Cromwell concluded that many were rich and corrupt, so Henry ordered all the monasteries to be dissolved (closed). He seized the wealth of the monasteries and gave many of their lands to his lords. Most of the monastery buildings, like Bolton Abbey, were left to become ruins.

16th-century portrait of Henry VIII by Hans Holbein the younger

Protestantism

SINCE THE REFORMATION, many different Protestant churches have been founded, all stressing the Bible as the source of their beliefs, and many advocating that salvation comes by God's grace, which is given to the believer through faith. Protestant churches range from huge international organizations, such as the Methodist, Anglican (p. 52), and Lutheran (pp. 34–35) churches to smaller groups like the Quakers, Shakers, and Seventh Day Adventists.

PURE AND SIMPLE
Protestant church buildings, like the one pictured above, tend to be plain with little of the decoration so common in Catholic and Orthodox interiors. The seats are arranged so that everyone can hear the sermons (p. 54) and readings.

Woman in 17th-century Puritan dress

PERSECUTED PURITANS
The Puritans were 17th-century English Protestants who wanted to cleanse the church of elements that they saw as Catholic, or "Popish" – such as vestments and bishops. Puritans, who stood out because of their plain clothes, were persecuted at home, so many moved abroad.

Model of the *Mayflower*

Quaker meeting house, Cornwall, England

17th-century Quaker

The ship was only 40 m (132 ft) long

MOVING MEETINGS
The Quakers worship in unadorned buildings called meeting houses. A typical Quaker meeting is simple and does not follow a set pattern. There are periods of meditation and silence until the Holy Spirit moves one or more of those present to speak or pray.

FRIENDS OF SOCIETY
The Quakers, originally called the Religious Society of Friends, were founded during the 17th century in England by George Fox. They have no Creed (p. 52), no sacraments, and their ministers are not ordained (pp. 48–49). Quakers are committed to peace, equality, and other social improvements, and played a major role in the abolition of slavery.

The cramped accommodation below deck was home to 102 pilgrims for 67 days

A Methodist Episcopal church, USA

Wesley preaching the gospel, Wesley's Chapel, London, England

Cross of Saint George – the English flag

WORLDWIDE WORSHIP
The first Methodist churches were founded by the British preacher John Wesley in the mid-18th century. Since then, Methodism has spread all over the world. With independent branches like the Methodist Episcopal church in North America, Methodism has grown to become one of the largest Protestant groups.

TOURING PREACHER
Wesley was originally an Anglican clergyman who preached outside so that large numbers of people could hear him. He toured widely, preaching in both Britain and North America. This led to the founding of Methodist churches – groups of Christians who aimed to achieve holiness through the "method" laid down in the Bible.

Methodist Communion in Harare, Zimbabwe

JOYFUL WORSHIP
Worship in Methodist churches follows a pattern similar to that in Anglican and other Protestant churches, with hymns, prayers, Bible-readings, a sermon, and the recital of the Creed. Within this framework, individuals in some churches stand up to affirm their faith with a joyful voice.

THE VOYAGE OF THE MAYFLOWER
In 1620, a group of Puritans from England and Holland sailed to America on the *Mayflower*. After a hard voyage, the group, later known as the Pilgrims, landed in Massachusetts, USA. Here they set up Plymouth Colony, a community where they could live and worship in their own way without fear of persecution.

Continued on next page

Shaker meeting with leader Mother Ann Lee, 1774

THE SIMPLE LIFE
The Shaker movement reached its peak in the 19th century, and now there are very few Shakers. Members follow a simple lifestyle; they dress plainly, avoid alcohol and tobacco, and live in communities set apart from the outside world. Shakers are famous for their simple, well-made furniture that seems to sum up their way of life.

Shaker table and sewing chair

Salvation Army badge

Member of the Salvation Army saluting God

SEEKING SALVATION
Methodist minister William Booth founded the Salvation Army in the late-19th century, and it has since become a worldwide organization. The Salvation Army is famous for its outdoor preaching, its tuneful music, and its work to help the poor and needy. It preaches a Bible-based Christianity centred on the immortality of the soul and salvation by faith through grace.

RESPECT YOUR ELDERS
There are a number of Presbyterian churches around the world, and they share one key feature – they are governed by presbyters, or elders, who may be either ministers or lay people. This kind of organization was based on the ideas of reformer John Calvin. Worship is simple and centres on preaching and – as shown in this 19th-century painting – study of the scriptures.

Salvation Army songster leader playing the cornet

Salvation Army tie

Modern Salvation Army man's hat

SOLDIERS OF GOD

The Salvation Army is organized along military lines. It is led by a "general", other church leaders are known as "officers", and members, or "soldiers", wear a distinctive uniform. Those who enroll sign a declaration of faith known as the "Articles of War". All members are entitled to bear the organization's red shield.

Victorian Salvation Army woman's bonnet

THE HOLY LIFE

Founded by a follower of the reformer Zwingli, Mennonites aim to live a life of holiness, set apart from the world in self-contained communities. They are pacifists, and they carry out relief work in many parts of the world.

Mennonite children in Belize

Red shield badge

Modern Salvation Army woman's hat

SEVENTH HEAVEN

Seventh Day Adventists, like this couple in Mozambique, believe that the time will come when they will be taken to Heaven for 1,000 years while Satan rules on Earth. At the end of this time, Jesus will return, destroy Satan, and create a new Earth. Adventists operate schools and a network of hospitals and clinics.

LIMITLESS WORSHIP

All Christians consider the work of evangelism, or spreading the Gospel, to be part of their faith. Many Protestants, like these in Guatemala, are very active evangelists. They often worship and preach outdoors, so their congregations are not limited by the size of a church building, and everyone who passes by can hear their message.

The Christian life

CHRISTIANS TRY TO FOLLOW Jesus' teachings and apply them to their own lives. All such believers are said to be part of the "community of saints". But some go to exceptional lengths for their faith, enduring suffering or persecution, or even becoming martyrs. Some of these men and women who have lived lives of special holiness are declared saints by the church. Saints are especially revered in the Catholic and Orthodox churches, where it is believed they can act as intermediaries between individual Christians and God.

The cross of Saint Brigid

FEEDING THE HUNGRY
Born in Ireland in the 6th century, Brigid became a nun and helped to spread Christianity by founding a monastery in Kildare. Brigid was famous for helping the poor, and was said to be able miraculously to make food multiply.

CHEATING DEATH
One of the many Christians who were persecuted by the Romans, Lucy remained true to her faith and gave away her possessions to the poor. The Romans were said to have tried to kill her by burning and by putting out her eyes. Lucy miraculously survived, and her eyes were restored. She was finally put to death by the sword.

Ivory relief of George and the dragon

Medieval gilded plaque of Saint Lucy

DRAGON SLAYER
George is thought to have been a 3rd-century soldier from the eastern Mediterranean. The best-known story about him tells how a dragon was terrorizing the neighbourhood and was about to devour the king's daughter. George said he would kill the monster if the people would believe in Jesus and be baptized. After killing the beast he would take no reward, but simply asked the king to help the church.

The palm is a symbol of the victory of the faithful over the enemies of the soul, and is often associated with martyrs

Eyes on a platter

SEEING THINGS

Hubert, the owner of this horn, lived in the 8th century and became a Christian after seeing a vision of the crucifixion between the antlers of a stag while out hunting. From then on he devoted himself to converting others to Christianity in his native Belgium. He eventually became Bishop of Maastricht and Liège.

Plaster statue of Saint Joseph

A MAN OF INFLUENCE

Born in Algeria in 354, Augustine became one of the most influential theologians of all time. He was a lawyer and teacher before converting to Christianity in his 30s. His many books on subjects such as the Holy Trinity, charity, and the Psalms are still read today. He was also Bishop of Hippo in North Africa, as shown in this 15th-century painting.

16th-century painting of Saints Erasmus and Maurice

POPULAR SAINTS

Maurice, a soldier from Egypt, and Erasmus, a Syrian bishop, were martyred in the late-3rd century. Although little is known of their lives, they were included in books of martyrs and became popular saints in the Middle Ages.

20TH-CENTURY SAINT

Italian Padre Pio was convinced of his "calling" as a child. When he became a Franciscan friar, he experienced visions of Jesus and received the stigmata – the miraculous appearance of wounds like those received by Jesus on the cross. Padre Pio endured his pain bravely, and devoted his life to prayer and serving God. He was declared a saint in 2002, 34 years after his death.

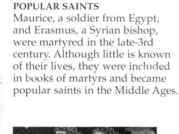

FAMILY LIFE

The family has a central role in Christian life. The Christian story begins with a family – Mary, Joseph, and Jesus – so it is seen by Christians as the ideal environment in which to raise children. This illustration shows a family walking to church on Christmas Eve.

HELPING HAND

Jesus told his followers to love their neighbours and give their wealth to the poor. Christians may follow these instructions through individual acts of kindness or through organizations that work to relieve suffering throughout the world.

Orphaned children helped by the Christian charity Tearfund

JOSEPH THE PROTECTOR

As protector of the holy family, Joseph plays a vital part in the Christian story, and is especially revered in the Catholic church. Joseph is celebrated as the patron saint of fathers, carpenters, the dying, social justice, and the universal church.

Santiago de Compostela

The Virgin Mary at Lourdes

PILGRIMAGE PLACES

Compostela in Spain and Lourdes in south-western France are two of Europe's best-known pilgrimage sites. Compostela is said to be the burial-place of Saint James, one of Jesus' disciples. Lourdes is a more recent shrine, the place where Saint Bernadette had a series of visions in the 19th century, and where many apparently miraculous healings have taken place.

Pilgrimages and relics

A pilgrimage is a journey to a place of religious significance. Many Christians, especially Roman Catholics, go on pilgrimages. They do so for various reasons – to visit places that are important for their faith, as an act of penance for their sins, to ask for help, or to give thanks to God. The most popular pilgrimage destinations are shrines. A shrine is a place linked to a particular saint, often housing their relics, or remains. Many sick people make pilgrimages to shrines such as Lourdes in the hope of a miraculous cure, but pilgrims are just as likely to travel in search of spiritual growth as physical healing.

Crown of semi-precious stones

Head is made of silver, but gilding gives it a golden colour

Ornate outer case for the relics of Saint Eustace

The base of the casket is decorated with holy figures

The top lifted off to reveal the remains stored within

Wooden inner case – the true receptacle for the relics of Saint Eustace

INSIDE STORY
This elaborate reliquary was made in about 1240 to hold remains. These included some of the bones of Saint Eustace, an early Christian who converted to the faith after seeing a vision of the crucifixion. The shining metal outer covering and wooden inner box did not contain Saint Eustace's whole skull, but held a number of bones, which were said to belong to several different saints.

CHAUCER'S PILGRIMS

In medieval England the shrine of Saint Thomas Becket at Canterbury was the most popular place of pilgrimage. The poet Geoffrey Chaucer wrote a long poem called *The Canterbury Tales*, made up of a series of stories told by a group of pilgrims as they travelled on horseback from London to Canterbury.

The Prioress   The Knight   The Man at Law   The Wife of Bath   The Squire

BECKET'S BONES

Thomas Becket was Archbishop of Canterbury in England during the reign of Henry II in the 12th century. When Becket fell out with the king, four of Henry's knights murdered him in Canterbury Cathedral. A shrine was soon built in the cathedral, and Becket's remains were kept in this beautiful casket.

Pewter badge of Saint Thomas Becket

Scallop-shaped ampulla, or flask, for holy water

One of the king's knights slices off Becket's head

MARK OF THE PILGRIM

In the Middle Ages, people often wore badges to show that they had been on a pilgrimage. The scallop shell, originally the badge of Compostela but later worn by pilgrims to any shrine, was the most common, but many places had their own badges.

INTO BATTLE

This reliquary, said to contain saintly bones, was carried into battle by the Abbot of Arbroath Abbey in Scotland. The occasion was the Battle of Bannockburn in 1314, when the Scots, under their leader Robert Bruce, defeated the English.

Fragments of bone, wood, and fabric are beautifully displayed

TREASURED REMAINS

Relics do not have to be actual human remains. Fragments of objects that played a part in the Christian story are also revered. This collection of tiny relics, kept at a British Benedictine abbey, is said to include fragments of the cross, Jesus' crib, and the veil of the Virgin Mary, as well as relics of several saints.

Cross surrounded by pearls

Pieces of bone set in gold

PORTABLE RELICS

In the Middle Ages, some people carried holy relics around with them, in the hope that the remains would bring them closer to God. This small reliquary holds tiny pieces of the bones of saints, together with a small cross set amongst pearls. The use of gold and pearls in the reliquary reflects the high value of the items it contains.

Monks and nuns

FOR HUNDREDS OF YEARS, some Christians have felt the need to live separately from the rest of society, in special communities devoted to serving God. Such communities are called monasteries, and their inhabitants – monks or nuns – live a life that is harsher and stricter than normal. They make solemn vows to God of poverty, chastity, and obedience – promising to give up personal possessions and sexual relations and to obey both the head of the monastery (the abbot or abbess) and the set of rules by which they live. Monasticism plays an especially important part in the Catholic and Orthodox churches.

Modern-day Coptic monk

NUN AND MONK
In the Middle Ages, new orders of monks and nuns were often founded because people felt the need to live by stricter rules than those governing other monasteries. Members of different orders, like this Servite nun and Slavonic monk, can often be distinguished by the colour of their clothes.

DESERT FATHERS
Monasticism began in Egypt in the 3rd century, when men such as Saint Antony withdrew to the desert to live as hermits. These "desert fathers" eventually joined to form monasteries, and their traditions are carried on today by members of the Coptic church.

A SIMPLE LIFE
Saint Benedict wrote his rule at the monastery of Monte Cassino, Italy, in the 6th century. The rule imposes a simple life dominated by worship, prayer, reading, and work. It was adopted widely, and there are still a number of Benedictine monasteries today.

Church

Cloister gives access to main buildings and provides space for private study

Chapter house, where regular meetings are held

Refectory, where meals are taken

Herb and vegetable gardens

Gatehouse provides an entrance to the monastery

Dormitory, where the monks or nuns sleep

Outer wall cuts off building from the outside world

Infirmary, where the sick are treated

INSIDE A MONASTERY
A monastery has to provide somewhere for its monks or nuns to live, work, and worship. Traditionally, the main buildings are arranged around a courtyard called the cloister to one side of the church. These main buildings include a place to sleep, a place to eat, and a place in which to hold meetings. Fields and gardens for growing food are usually situated beyond the main complex.

THE WORK OF GOD

The most important activity for a monk or nun is regular religious observance at set hours of the day. Saint Benedict called this the "Work of God", but it is also known as the divine office. Everyone in the monastery meets eight times every day to pray, read lessons from the Bible, and sing hymns and Psalms.

FIGHTING MONKS

In the Middle Ages there were specialized orders of "fighting monks", who lived by monastic rules and gave armed protection to pilgrims in the Holy Land. This gunpowder flask bears the emblem of one such order, the Knights of Saint John.

15th-century monastic service book

Poor Clares –
Franciscan nuns

PRIVATE PRAYER

Individual worship plays a vital part in the daily life of all monks and nuns. These Franciscan nuns – known as Poor Clares after their founder, Saint Clare – are praying the rosary. Some orders count their prayers using knots on a piece of rope instead of rosary beads.

DIVINE LIGHT

Several of the "hours" of the divine office are celebrated when it is dark. Mattins takes place at 2 am, vespers during the evening, and compline before bed-time. Traditionally, worship at such times had to be celebrated by candlelight. The candles would also have reminded those taking part of the idea of Jesus as a divine light shining in the world.

HOLY READING

Benedictine monks are encouraged to read the Bible (and other religious writings) in a devotional, contemplative way to bring them into close communion with God. This activity, known as *Lectio Divina* (holy reading), does not involve analysing the text, as some Bible-reading does. The reader should simply absorb the words and allow God's message to filter through.

Benedictine monk
in quiet
contemplation

Continued on next page

Continued from previous page

Lemon balm

Marjoram

Lungwort

Feverfew

HEALING HERBS
In the Middle Ages, monks grew plants like feverfew, lungwort, lemon balm, and marjoram to make medicines for ailments such as headaches and respiratory disorders. The monks wrote down their discoveries about the healing powers of plants in books called herbals. Herbs are still grown alongside other food plants in many monastery gardens today.

Everyday life and work
Although the divine office and prayer are at the heart of monastic life, monks and nuns are also expected to work hard to support themselves and their community. Monasteries often try to be as self-sufficient as possible, with many producing their own food, and some making items for sale. With their atmosphere of quiet contemplation, monasteries have always been centres of learning. In the Middle Ages, they provided Europe's only education and health services, and today many monks and nuns still teach in schools. They may also work in the wider community, giving aid to the sick, poor, and needy.

Benedictine monks in the refectory

FOOD FOR THOUGHT
In most monasteries, the monks or nuns eat together at long tables in a large communal refectory, or dining room. The food is simple but nourishing. Religious devotion even continues at meal times – everyone is expected to eat in silence while one of their number reads passages from the Bible.

SCENTED SERVICES
Incense – a substance that makes a sweet scent when it is burned – is used widely during services in both the Catholic and Orthodox churches. Some monasteries make incense, both for use in their own church and for sale to raise money.

Raw olibanum gum

Ground raw olibanum gum

Finished incense

Rubber gloves provide protection from the highly concentrated oil

1 NATURALLY SWEET
The naturally sweet-smelling raw olibanum gum is ground into smaller pieces. The monk then measures out a small amount of concentrated perfume oil and mixes this thoroughly with the ground gum.

2 DRYING OUT
The monk places shovels of the scented, ground gum into a large, wooden tray with a wire bottom and spreads it out evenly. He leaves the incense mixture until it is dry and then packs it up ready for sale.

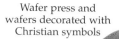

Wafer press and wafers decorated with Christian symbols

FLAT BREAD
In many churches, specially made wafers – traditionally manufactured in monasteries – are used instead of ordinary bread during Communion (pp. 52–53). The process starts with a bread dough mix. This is pressed into thin sheets, often marked with a Christian symbol, and cut into small discs. The finished wafers are then packaged and supplied to churches all over the world.

FAR FROM HOME
Many monks and nuns travel long distances to take part in aid programmes in areas that are affected by drought, war, famine, or other disasters. Members of monastic orders help to save lives and bring education to areas where there are no state schools.

Nun distributing cooking oil in Rwanda

The text is in Latin and is beautifully decorated

The desk slopes to make writing for long periods more comfortable

The nun studies the honeycomb to see if it is ready for harvesting

Monastic scribe's desk

WRITING FOR GOD
In the Middle Ages, monks and nuns were among the few people who produced books. They wrote out each page by hand and decorated them to produce results like this beautiful music manuscript. Today, some monks preserve these ancient skills, while others are notable scholars. They write books on subjects such as the Bible, theology, and the history of the church.

Wax tablet for writing holy passages on

SWEET AND SYMBOLIC
Honey is an ancient Christian symbol that reminds the faithful of the sweetness of Jesus' words. This Franciscan nun has learned the valuable skill of beekeeping, providing a nutritious food source for her sisters and beeswax for making candles. Many monks and nuns sell any honey and wax they do not use themselves to members of the public.

The angel's banner says "With the Lord a thousand years is a single day"

CHRISTIAN CROCKERY
The pottery founded by the Benedictine monks of Prinknash Abbey in England produces simple wares for everyday use, and more decorative ceramics that are especially attractive to visitors. Their millennium plate bears a picture of an angel, a reminder that the year 2000 was, above all, a Christian event – the 2,000th anniversary of Jesus' birth.

Plate made to commemorate the year 2000

The priesthood

PRIESTS, AND ministers – their equal in many Protestant churches, provide spiritual teaching, celebrate the sacraments, and play the leading role in rituals and worship. They also care for people in their parish, or area, for example by visiting the sick and caring for those with special needs. Being a priest is demanding, and most people who take on the role do so because they feel a spiritual "calling". In the Catholic and Orthodox churches, ordination, or admission, is a sacrament and is permanently binding, whereas in the Protestant churches it is not.

HOLY LEADERS
This ancient ivory chesspiece shows a bishop – a senior Catholic, Orthodox, or Anglican clergyman who oversees the work of other priests.

RELIGIOUS PRIESTS
An abbot is a priest who is the leader of a monastery. He and the monks in his charge are known in the Catholic church as "religious priests". The other members of the Catholic clergy – such as bishops and parish priests – are referred to as "secular priests".

Rear view of abbot's vestments

Mitre shows that the wearer is an abbot

Early-20th-century silver crozier, carried only by higher members of the clergy

Cowl, or hood

Red cope worn on major feast days, such as Pentecost, Easter, and Christmas

Ornamental cross

Surplice, or alb, worn beneath cope

Habit, or tunic, worn beneath vestments

Benedictine abbot in ceremonial vestments

SIMPLE STYLE

The Anglican church allows both men and women to become priests, or vicars, as they are often called. Much of the time vicars wear simple clothes, such as a round clerical collar and plain shirt. For services they may wear vestments, the style of which can vary according to the occasion and their own views.

Clerical collars are sometimes referred to as "dog collars"

Anglican vicar wearing everyday clothes

Anglican vicar dressed for Holy Communion

Confirmation

Eucharist

Baptism

Anointing the sick

SEVEN SACRAMENTS

The Catholic and Orthodox churches celebrate seven sacraments – rites that constitute a visible sign of the inward grace of God. The sacraments on this 15th-century altarpiece are ordination, confirmation, Eucharist, penance, anointing the sick, baptism, and marriage. Many Protestant churches recognize only two sacraments: baptism and Communion.

Gold trimmings add to the splendour of the outfit

Saint Ignatius of Loyola

TEACHING PRIESTS

The Society of Jesus, or Jesuits, are an order of Catholic priests founded in the 16th century by former soldier Ignatius of Loyola. The Jesuits have always been committed to missionary work and education, and priests often teach in schools or universities. After his death in 1556, Ignatius of Loyola was made a saint.

IN UNIFORM

When celebrating the sacraments, priests wear special clothes called vestments. These garments are similar in design to those worn by early Christians in ancient Rome. They consist of several layers, including a white tunic called an alb, a coloured over-garment called a chasuble, and a long, scarf-like stole.

The church

THE WORD CHURCH means a community of Christian believers, but it is also used to refer to a building in which Christians worship. Churches vary widely, but most have a large main space – often called the nave – for the congregation. Many churches also have a chancel or sanctuary, which houses the altar (p. 52); side chapels, used for private prayer; a vestry, where the priest prepares for services; and a space in which baptisms take place.

Ornate holy water stoup

HOLY WATER
In many churches there is a stoup, or basin, near the door. This contains holy water with which people can cross or sprinkle themselves as they enter the building, as a way of affirming their baptism (p. 58).

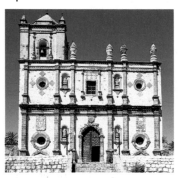

18th-century church, San Ignacio, Mexico

ALL SHAPES AND SIZES
There are many different church designs. The mission church at San Ignacio (above) and Saint George in the East (right) are in the baroque style, which uses decorative features adapted from buildings in ancient Rome. Both have a bell tower and a large door leading to the nave. Elaborate architecture like this is common in Catholic churches, but Protestant buildings tend to be plainer.

MAKING AN ENTRANCE
Church doorways are sometimes surrounded by statues of saints and biblical scenes, which remind people that they are entering a sacred building. This doorway is topped by a carving of the baby Jesus and the magi.

Doorway to a 12th-century church at Loches in France

Carving of a bishop

Carving of Saint Peter

Bell tower

Model of Saint George in the East church, London, England

Main entrance

A WORLD OF HORROR
In the Middle Ages, builders often placed carvings of ugly faces, monsters, and other weird beasts on the outside walls of churches. People looking at these grotesque carvings knew that when they went inside the church they were leaving behind the world of horror and the evil that went with it.

GOSPELS IN GLASS
In ancient churches, stained glass was a way of teaching Bible stories to ordinary people, most of whom were not able to read or write. Christian symbols like this fish from Prinknash Abbey in Gloucestershire, England, are particularly popular in modern churches.

15th-century German altarpiece

FOCAL POINT
Behind the altar in many churches there may be an altarpiece. This is a screen, painting, or carved relief that focuses attention on the altar itself. An altarpiece may be decorated with scenes from the Bible, images of saints, or representations of everyday life, as in this example that shows a family caring for a newborn child.

Lectern Bible

CHURCH READINGS
The word of God is central to the Christian faith and Bible-readings are part of almost every service. Most churches keep a large Bible open on a stand called a lectern. Lecterns are often made in the shape of an eagle, the emblem of Saint John the Evangelist.

Medieval lectern

ELEVATED POSITION
The structure in which the priest or minister stands to preach the sermon (p. 54) is called the pulpit. It is generally raised so the preacher can be seen and heard by everyone in the congregation. In Catholic churches the pulpit is usually set to one side, but in Protestant churches it is often central – reinforcing the emphasis on the importance of God's word.

SITTING COMFORTABLY
In a Catholic church like this English monastic chapel, the congregation sits in pews in front of the altar, which is the main focus. In Orthodox churches the altar is hidden behind a screen and there are few seats, so most of the worshippers stand. Congregations in Protestant churches tend to sit facing the pulpit.

Portuguese pulpit with a spiral stairway

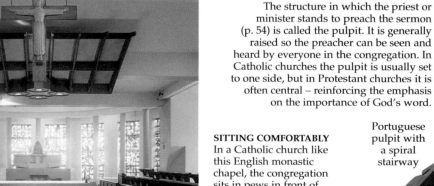

Holy Communion

The design on this kneeler combines the bread and wine with *chi* and *rho*, the first letters of the word Christ in Greek.

FOR MOST CHRISTIANS, the church's supreme rite is the re-enactment of the last supper, when participants receive the consecrated, or blessed, bread and wine. Catholics know this as the Mass or Eucharist, Orthodox Christians call it the Holy Liturgy, and Protestants may call it the Holy Communion or the Lord's Supper. In all churches, the bread and wine are identified with the body and blood of Jesus Christ. Protestants see the two elements as reminders of Jesus' sacrifice. Catholics believe that Christ's body and blood are actually present in the elements of the Mass.

THE ANGLICAN WAY
The various branches of the Christian church celebrate Holy Communion in different ways. These two pages show how Communion is celebrated in an Anglican church. The first part of the service focuses on the word (p. 54). It includes prayers, one or more Bible-readings, a sermon, the Creed (the statement of belief in God), and the Peace ("The Peace of the Lord be always with you").

1 TAKE THE BREAD
After the Peace, a hymn, and an offering, the priest's words recall the last supper. He takes the bread from the Communion table, which may also be referred to as the Lord's table or altar.

2 GIVE THANKS FOR THE BREAD
The priest gives thanks to God for the bread, echoing as he does so the description in the Gospels of how Jesus blessed the bread at the last supper.

3 BREAK THE BREAD
Again following the actions of Jesus at the last supper, the priest breaks the bread. This is so that those present may "share in the body of Christ".

4 RECEIVE THE BREAD
The priest invites the congregation to take Communion, and prays that their bodies will be cleansed through Jesus' body. The priest then takes and eats part of the consecrated bread. (Some priests receive the bread after blessing the wine.)

5 TAKE THE WINE
Next, the priest takes the wine from the Communion table. The wine is usually contained in a special goblet, or cup, called a chalice. The chalice represents the vessel that would have held the wine at the last supper.

The priest raises his right hand in a gesture of blessing

The priest offers the bread to the member of the congregation kneeling before him

9 GIVE THE WINE

Then members of the congregation take the wine from the chalice in turn. Afterwards, they say a further prayer of thanksgiving before the final hymn, prayer, and blessing bring the service of Holy Communion to an end.

6 GIVE THANKS FOR THE WINE

The priest blesses the wine. By giving thanks in this way, he has prayed that the souls of both clergy and congregation may be washed with Jesus' "most precious blood".

7 RECEIVE THE WINE

Raising the chalice to his lips, the priest receives the wine. He is now ready to offer Holy Communion to those members of the congregation who have come forwards to take it.

8 GIVE THE BREAD

When enough bread for the congregation to share has been broken, it is distributed to those present. In some churches, the bread may take the form of small, unleavened wafers.

Portable Communion set

Chalice

Bottle containing wine

Paten

Tin to hold Communion wafers

HOLY CUP
This 16th-century chalice is made of silver, and is beautifully decorated with the heads of saints. Although similar chalices are still used today, in some churches, especially those with large congregations, tiny individual cups are handed round instead.

PRECIOUS PLATE
The consecrated bread at Holy Communion is placed on a plate, known as a paten, which usually matches the chalice. Because the bread and wine are so important, both the paten and the chalice are often made of precious metals, such as silver or gold.

SMALL SCALE
Although the usual place to celebrate Holy Communion is in church, it may also take place elsewhere. If a priest or vicar is celebrating Holy Communion with a sick person, he or she will take a portable Communion set consisting of a box for consecrated bread or wafers, a bottle for wine, and a scaled-down paten and chalice.

THE WORD

Religious speeches known as sermons became popular in the Middle Ages, as shown by this 1491 woodcut, and are still a vital part of many church services. The preacher often takes a passage from the Bible as a starting point for the sermon, and uses it to explain a Christian message.

Ways to worship

COMMUNAL WORSHIP IS at the heart of the Christian faith, and many Christians come together regularly to praise God, confess their sins, and show that they are followers of Jesus Christ. Worship can involve all sorts of activities. Reading the Bible, singing hymns, songs and Psalms, praying, and listening to sermons are all aspects of Christian worship used in church services the world over. These services may vary widely in tone and mood, but most contain several of these key elements. For committed Christians, however, worship does not begin and end in church – they dedicate their whole life to God.

Medieval breviary

DAILY SERVICE

A breviary is a book used in the Catholic church that contains daily services for the canonical hours – services that are held at regular times each day. Each service consists of a short prayer, a hymn, three Psalms, a lesson, and final prayers. Modern breviaries contain services for morning, daytime, evening, and night time.

HOLDING CROSS

This simple cross is made of olive tree wood from the Holy Land, and is designed to be held in one hand during worship. Its rounded, smooth shape makes it comfortable and easy for a sick or elderly person to grip.

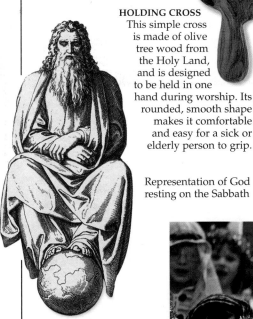

Representation of God resting on the Sabbath

THE SABBATH DAY

For thousands of years, the Jews have observed their Sabbath – a day set aside for rest and religious observance to mark God's day of rest after the creation – on a Saturday. The early Christians decided to make Sunday their Sabbath, and this day is still a day of rest in Christian countries.

POPULAR PSALMS

Books of Psalms called psalters, like this 700-year-old example, were some of the most beautiful volumes in the Middle Ages. Psalms are still sung, chanted, or spoken out loud today, and are widely used as the basis for popular hymns and prayers.

ANCIENT AND MODERN

Carols are songs that express religious joy, most widely sung at Christmas. Carols first became popular in the 15th century, but new ones are still being written, sung, and enjoyed alongside the old.

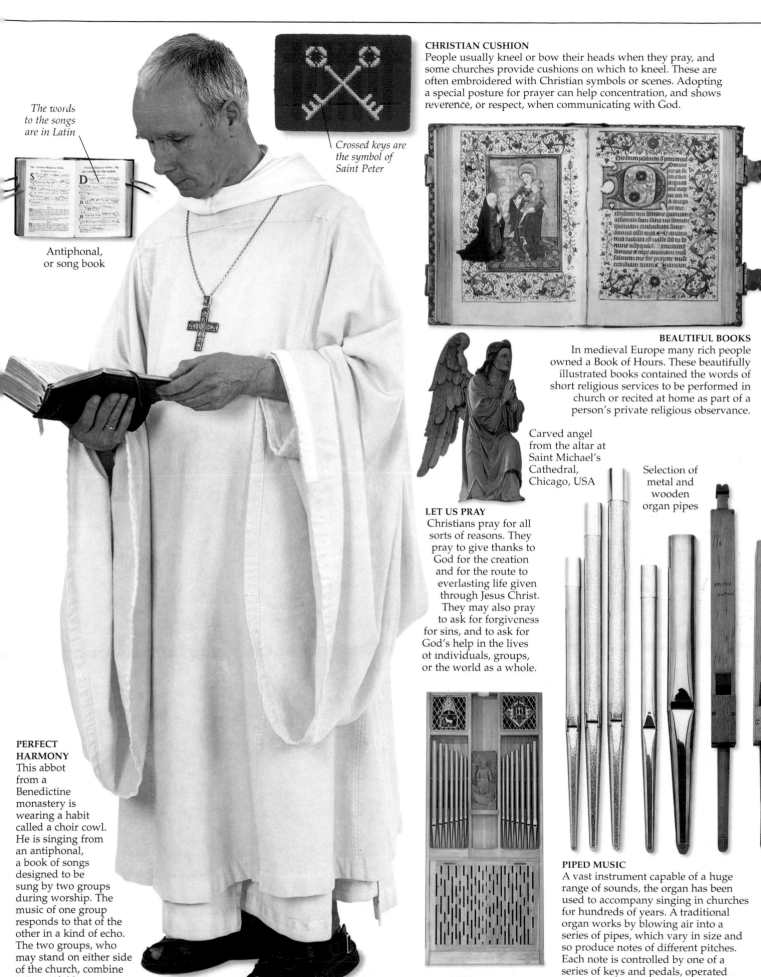

The words to the songs are in Latin

Antiphonal, or song book

CHRISTIAN CUSHION
People usually kneel or bow their heads when they pray, and some churches provide cushions on which to kneel. These are often embroidered with Christian symbols or scenes. Adopting a special posture for prayer can help concentration, and shows reverence, or respect, when communicating with God.

Crossed keys are the symbol of Saint Peter

BEAUTIFUL BOOKS
In medieval Europe many rich people owned a Book of Hours. These beautifully illustrated books contained the words of short religious services to be performed in church or recited at home as part of a person's private religious observance.

Carved angel from the altar at Saint Michael's Cathedral, Chicago, USA

Selection of metal and wooden organ pipes

LET US PRAY
Christians pray for all sorts of reasons. They pray to give thanks to God for the creation and for the route to everlasting life given through Jesus Christ. They may also pray to ask for forgiveness for sins, and to ask for God's help in the lives of individuals, groups, or the world as a whole.

PERFECT HARMONY
This abbot from a Benedictine monastery is wearing a habit called a choir cowl. He is singing from an antiphonal, a book of songs designed to be sung by two groups during worship. The music of one group responds to that of the other in a kind of echo. The two groups, who may stand on either side of the church, combine in beautiful harmony.

Modern organ

PIPED MUSIC
A vast instrument capable of a huge range of sounds, the organ has been used to accompany singing in churches for hundreds of years. A traditional organ works by blowing air into a series of pipes, which vary in size and so produce notes of different pitches. Each note is controlled by one of a series of keys and pedals, operated by the organist's hands and feet.

Christian calendar

THE CHRISTIAN YEAR is dominated by two major cycles, or groups of festivals. The first, at the beginning of the church year, starts with Advent and leads to Christmas. But, at the heart of the Christian calendar, is the observance of Jesus' crucifixion and resurrection. This begins with the period of Lent, followed by Holy Week, the mourning of Jesus' death on Good Friday, and the celebration of his resurrection on Easter Sunday. The other major Christian festival is Pentecost, which marks the gift of the Holy Spirit to Jesus' disciples.

Priest wearing coloured stoles

CALENDAR COLOURS
Many priests wear different coloured vestments at different times in the church calendar. The colours vary, but red is often worn for Pentecost and green for the Sundays after Epiphany and Trinity, when the Holy Trinity is honoured.

Satsumas and walnuts

Coal sweets

GIFTS FOR THE GOOD
Epiphany, on 6 January, marks the visit of the magi to Bethlehem – the first time that Jesus was revealed to non-Jews. In Spain, children believe that the magi come to give them presents. They put out fruit and nuts for "the magi", who leave behind gifts for well-behaved children and sweets that look like coal for those who have misbehaved.

Spanish girl with chocolate models of the magi

German Advent calendar

"This very day in David's town your Saviour was born – Christ the Lord!"

LUKE 2:11
Angel of the Lord to the shepherds

COUNTDOWN TO CHRISTMAS
To most Christians, Advent is the period leading up to Christmas, including the four Sundays before 25 December. During this season, Christians celebrate the arrival of John the Baptist, the coming of the Messiah, and Jesus' future second coming. Calendars offering a treat to eat on each day of Advent are traditional in many homes.

American Christmas meal

FESTIVE FUN
Jesus' birth is celebrated on 25 December in most branches of the Christian church. People attend joyful services, decorate their homes, exchange presents, and eat festive meals. In the west, a traditional Christmas dinner consists of roast turkey with a selection of vegetables and sauces.

VISUAL REMINDER
A crib is a model of the stable where Jesus was born, featuring the holy family, shepherds, animals, and magi. This example comes from El Salvador. Cribs are a good visual aid for teaching children about the Christmas story – and are a reminder to all of the Christmas message.

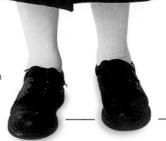

16th-century Italian
Lent parade helmet

A SOLEMN TIME

Shrove Tuesday is traditionally a time for people to confess their sins and use up rich foods before Lent – the 40-day period preceding Easter. Lent is a time of solemnity, penance, and devotion to God. It was originally a time of fasting, but today most Christians fast only on Ash Wednesday and Good Friday.

Jesus reigning from the cross

A NEW LIFE

Easter is the feast of Jesus' resurrection. In church, priests read the Gospel story of the resurrection and lead joyful prayers, hymns, and processions to celebrate the risen Christ. Eggs are seen as symbolic of Jesus' new life, and many people eat chocolate eggs or decorate real eggs at Easter time.

Palm leaf crown

PALM SUNDAY

On the Sunday before Easter, Christians commemorate Jesus' entry into Jerusalem. People take part in processions carrying, wearing, and waving palm leaves and palm crosses. Palm Sunday marks the beginning of Holy Week, the time when people remember the events that led up to the crucifixion.

Benedictine monk taking part in an Easter procession

Pumpkin – a traditional harvest vegetable

GIVING THANKS

Harvest festival is not part of the official church calendar, but Christians in many places get together each year to give thanks for the produce of the land. People sing special hymns and bring produce to churches to be distributed to the poor and needy. Some seaside towns celebrate the "harvest of the sea" brought in by local fishermen.

Palm ring

LIFE AND DEATH

All Soul's Day, on 2 November, is a popular Catholic festival. It is a day when people pray for the souls of the dead and put flowers on family graves. People in Mexico celebrate two Days of the Dead at this time of year. They exchange gifts like this sugar skull as reminders of death and the continuity of life.

Ethiopian boy in Palm Sunday dress

The cycle of life

As a Christian passes through the key stages of life, their relationship with the church develops. This development is marked with rites such as baptism (when a person enters into the church), confirmation (when they confirm their faith), marriage (when a couple are united in the eyes of the church), and funeral services (when a person dies). Baptism, together with confirmation and marriage in the Catholic church, is a sacrament, an outward sign of God's inward and spiritual grace.

Kneeling cushion with a design for a confirmation service

MAKING A COMMITMENT
When an infant is baptized, the parents and godparents make a commitment to Christianity on the baby's behalf. When old enough, the child confirms their faith. After a preparatory course, the candidate for confirmation vows to leave evil behind and to be a committed Christian. The bishop lays his hands on the candidate's head and blesses them.

The baby is dressed in white as a symbol of purity

Anglican priest baptizing a baby

Portable font filled with holy water

BORN AGAIN
In the Baptist church, and some other churches, people are baptized only when they are old enough to decide for themselves that they believe in God. In this "believer's baptism", the person confesses their faith and is completely immersed in water. The baptism symbolizes being washed clean and born again in Jesus.

THE BAPTISM OF JESUS
It is the baptism of Jesus by John the Baptist in the River Jordan that has led several Protestant churches to follow this practice. The total immersion is considered to be symbolic of Jesus' death, burial, and resurrection.

BABY BAPTISM
When an Anglican priest baptizes a baby, she brings the child to the font, reads from the Gospels, says a prayer, and addresses its carers about its Christian upbringing. She then baptizes the child, pouring holy water over its head and saying, "I baptize you in the name of the Father, and of the Son, and of the Holy Spirit". In the Catholic church, the baby is also anointed with consecrated oil, called chrism.

The bride traditionally wears a veil, a symbol of chastity

'TIL DEATH US DO PART

Christians see marriage as a lifelong partnership and some churches, such as the Catholic church, do not recognize divorce. A wedding is therefore both a happy event and a serious one. Weddings are full of symbolism. Orthodox couples, for example, are crowned with wreaths to show that they are rulers of their kingdom – the family.

Lilies are symbols of purity: they also represent the Virgin Mary

WEDDING CEREMONIES

Churches all over the world hold wedding ceremonies. These are joyful occasions often attended by many guests. The priest establishes that the couple are free to marry, vows and rings are exchanged, and the union is blessed.

The dove reminds couples of the presence of the Holy Spirit

Wedding kneeler

Mourning brooches from the mid-1800s

CELEBRATING A LIFE

When someone dies, their body is placed in a coffin and taken to church, where mourners gather to celebrate the life of the deceased. Prayers, readings, and hymns remind mourners that the soul of the dead person will live on, and give thanks for this. Finally the body is either cremated or buried in a consecrated graveyard.

Ivory counter showing burial scene

White wedding dresses have been popular since the 19th century

DEATH CEREMONIES

Funerals vary widely in style, from solemn and contemplative to noisy and expressive. Protestant funerals include prayers, Bible-readings, hymns, and a eulogy, or speech, commemorating the deceased before the burial or cremation. Catholics pray for the soul of the dead person and may hold a special Requiem Mass in their honour.

Jazz funeral, New Orleans, USA

Continued from previous page

ACTING WITH PASSION

In some parts of Europe, local people put on traditional plays enacting the story of the Passion – the events leading up to Jesus' crucifixion. In the village of Oberammergau in southern Germany, the Passion play has been staged regularly ever since the people escaped the plague in 1633. The play is now produced every ten years.

This scene is set in the disciple Simon's house

The performing arts

Music has been a part of Christian worship for centuries, and many composers in the Middle Ages were monks who spent their lives writing and singing church music. But from the beginning, religious music influenced other types of music, from extravagant choral pieces to dances and popular songs. Drama has also been influenced by Christianity for hundreds of years, and there are numerous famous films and plays with religious themes.

The parting of the Red Sea

Moses

Rameses II

FROM STAGE TO SCREEN

The "rock opera" *Jesus Christ Superstar* was first staged in 1970, and made into a film in 1973. With music by Andrew Lloyd Webber and words by Tim Rice, the production was one of the most popular 20th-century treatments of the Christian story.

"Sing to the Lord, all the world! Worship the Lord with joy; come before him with happy songs!"

PSALM 100:1–2
A hymn of praise

EPIC MOVIE

The Ten Commandments – a film created in 1956 by Hollywood director Cecil B. de Mille – tells how Moses led his people out of slavery in Egypt to their promised homeland. It features a huge cast, with Charlton Heston as Moses and Yul Brynner as Rameses II, and spectacular special effects, such as the parting of the Red Sea to let the Israelites pass.

SACRED SONGS

Sacred oratorios (a blend of solo and choral music) became popular in the 18th century. Among the most famous are J. S. Bach's two settings of the Passion story and G. F. Handel's *Messiah*. Handel wrote the piece in less than four weeks in 1741, and its portrayal of Jesus' life is still enjoyed by audiences today, especially around Christmas time.

Handel's original score of *Messiah*

Gospel choir performing in Washington D.C. in the USA

GRACEFUL GOSPEL

Soul singer Aretha Franklin is the daughter of a preacher and a gospel singer from Detroit in the USA. She sang with her father's choir before starting to make her own records. Her music is powerfully emotional and full of strong vocal effects, showing her roots in gospel music. Her album *Amazing Grace* is a collection of reworked gospel songs.

MUSICAL CONVERSATION

Baptist churches in the USA are the original home of gospel music, in which the preacher and congregation create an emotional musical conversation. The excitement of gospel music – with its sliding melodies, joyful shouts, and other vocal effects – has had a huge influence on singers in many diverse areas of modern music, from soul to rock.

THE KING

Rock and roll legend Elvis Presley learned to sing in his local church choir, and was influenced by gospel music. He combined this with rhythm and blues and country music to create a unique style. Later in his career, he recorded unique versions of a number of hymns and carols.

Did you know?

AMAZING FACTS

There have been 266 popes of the Roman Catholic Church. They include 205 Italians, 19 Frenchmen, 14 Greeks, 8 Syrians, 6 Germans, 3 Africans, 2 Spaniards, an Austrian, a Palestinian, an Englishman, a Dutchman, and a Pole.

Benedict XVI

Many popular children's books are based on the Christian story, including C. S. Lewis's *Chronicles of Narnia* series. Aslan the lion symbolizes Christ, while his adversary, the evil White Witch, symbolizes the forces of evil. The stories contain many allusions to Christ's sacrifice and the constant struggle between good and evil.

The Vatican City in Rome, Italy, is the world's smallest independent state, with a population of just over 900.

Many of the world's most important civil rights leaders have begun as Christian ministers – including Reverend Martin Luther King Jr, who led the Civil Rights Movement in the United States, and Archbishop Desmond Tutu, who won the Nobel Peace Prize in 1984 for his work against apartheid in South Africa.

Archbishop Desmond Tutu

Charles Darwin was training to be a priest before a scientific fact-finding trip around the world on HMS *Beagle* led him to develop his theory of evolution. By the time he finally published *The Origin of Species* in 1859, he had lost his faith and become agnostic. His theories were greeted with much controversy at the time but are now widely accepted. However, they are still rejected by fundamentalist Christians known as Creationists.

ΙΧΘΥϹ

The fish symbol and *ichthys* label

Early Christians used secret symbols to help them communicate and worship without persecution. One way of encoding Jesus's name was the fish symbol – the Greek word for fish, *ichthys*, can also stand for "Jesus Christ, Son of God, Saviour". After AD 313, Christians were allowed to worship in public by imperial decree, yet many of these coded signs are still used in Church iconography today.

Martin Luther (1483–1546), renowned for igniting the Protestant movement, also contributed to the popularization of the Church by translating the Bible into his native German (at a rate of more than 1,500 words per day) and writing some of Christianity's most popular hymns.

In the 2001 UK census, 72 per cent of Britons identified themselves as Christian, although only 7 per cent are regular church-goers. Anglicans and Catholics make up the two largest groups.

Since the 4th century, bishops have worn purple as a symbol of their status. Purple, made from an expensive dye, was once worn only by the Roman emperor and senators. The bishops' purple sash showed that they had the same status as Roman senators.

Mary in blue robes

In the 5th century, the monk Dionysius the Short introduced a new Christian calendar centred around the date of Jesus's birth, using the terms AD (*Anno Domini* or Year of our Lord) and BC (Before Christ). This calendar is still used today, even though Dionysius had Jesus's birthday wrong by at least three years. Sometimes BCE (Before the Common Era) and CE (Common Era) are used instead.

Roughly two billion Christians make up a third of the world's population. As the number of practising Christians in Europe and America (mostly Protestant) declines, Christianity's centre is shifting to the Southern hemisphere of Africa, Latin America, and Asia (mostly Catholic and Pentecostal).

St Pius I (AD 140–155) was the first bishop of Rome to exercise sole authority over the Church. Before this, the Church was governed by a council of elders or deacons. Until 1073, all bishops had the title "pope".

The Catholic Church divides holy relics into three categories. A first-class relic is part of a saint's body or an object directly relating to the events of a saint's life. A second-class relic is an object or article of clothing owned by a saint. A third-class relic is a piece of cloth touched to the body of a saint after death, or else brought to a saint's shrine.

St Peter's chains are a first-class relic

An important duty of early monks was to copy the scriptures by hand onto illuminated (or illustrated) pages. The detailed artwork used pigments made from precious metals and stones, such as gold and lapis lazuli – a stone so rare that its rich blue was reserved for the robes of the Virgin Mary.

QUESTIONS & ANSWERS

Q What denominations make up Christianity?

A Christianity is the world's largest religion, followed by Islam and Hinduism. The major Christian denominations include Roman Catholics, Orthodox Christians, Baptists, Anglicans (or Episcopalians), Presbyterians, Lutherans, Pentecostalists, and Methodists. Most share a belief in the Trinity of Father, Son, and Holy Spirit. Many of the smaller Protestant sects, such as Jehovah's Witnesses, are centred around their founder's unique interpretation of Jesus's teachings.

Jerry Falwell, a leader of the Christian Right

Q What is the "Christian Right"?

A The Christian Right is an umbrella term for the American supporters of a fundamental brand of Christianity, which holds very conservative social and political views. They oppose any policies that they see as un-Christian, such as the right to abortion and the teaching of evolution in schools. Through their churches, they influence large numbers of voters to elect and put pressure on governments to turn their values and beliefs into official policy.

White smoke at the Vatican

Q How is the pope chosen?

A After a pope's death, cardinals gather at the Vatican to elect a new pope. They cast their votes on paper ballots, which are counted and burned. Black smoke from the chimney signals that no candidate has received a two-thirds majority and the votes are recast. White smoke marks the election of a new pope.

Q What are the sacraments?

A A sacrament is a Christian rite intended to confer God's grace on the recipient. Seven sacramental rites have been used since the earliest days of the Church. Protestants regard only baptism and the Eucharist (or communion) as sacramental rites. The Catholic and Orthodox churches also consider confirmation, ordination, marriage, confession, and holy unction (or anointing the sick) as sacramental rites.

Q How long did it take to build a Gothic cathedral?

A The Gothic cathedrals that came into fashion in the 12th century were so massive and ornate that funds often ran out before they could be finished. For this reason, and because of the sheer amount of labour required, a church could take centuries to build. Cologne Cathedral in Germany took more than 700 years to complete.

Q Why do the colours on the altar and on a priest's vestments change?

A Every season has its own colour, chosen to suit the mood of the events it commemorates. For example, during Lent, purple is used to remind Christians that they are being asked to make sacrifices and prepare for Easter. On Easter Sunday, white is used to reflect the joyfulness of Christ's resurrection.

Q What are the core beliefs?

A Most denominations agree that a list of core beliefs should include the Trinity (God, Jesus, and Holy Spirit), the deity (godlike nature) of Jesus, his resurrection from the dead, his death as atonement for our sins, and salvation through faith or grace alone. Catholics also stress the sacred nature of Jesus's mother, the Virgin Mary.

Q Who becomes a saint?

A A saint or holy person is someone who after their death is recognized as having achieved, through their virtuous behaviour or deeds, the right to be worshipped or held up by the community as a role model. Canonization is the process of officially recognizing a person as a saint.

Flying buttresses support much of the weight

Cologne Cathedral

Communion wafers

Q Can any bread become communion?

A A priest's blessing makes any bread suitable for communion. However, most churches choose to use simple, unleavened bread, which is what Jesus would have blessed at the Last Supper.

Record Breakers

LARGEST CATHEDRAL
The Cathedral of St John the Divine in New York City measures 36,880 sq m (121,000 sq ft) – the size of two football pitches.

LONGEST-REIGNING POPE
Some Christians consider St Peter, one of Christ's apostles, to be the longest-reigning pope. He supervised the early Church for over 34 years. Others give the title to Pius IX, who held office for 31 years during the 19th century.

OLDEST CHURCH
The earliest known church built specifically as a Christian place of worship was found in Aqaba, Jordan. It dates from the late 3rd century.

MOST POPULAR HYMN
According to an online poll, the most popular hymn is *Amazing Grace*, which was composed in the 18th century by John Newton.

LARGEST BIBLE
The world's largest Bible is 110 cm (43 ½ in) tall, has a spine that is 86 cm (34 in) wide, and weighs 496 kg (1,094 lb).

Timeline

CHRISTIANITY HAS ITS ROOTS in the Old Testament books of the Bible with their stories of creation and God's special relationship with the Jewish people. The pivotal event, however, is the birth of Christ. Documents from the early years disagree about some of the dates, so it is not always possible to pin them down exactly. But as this timeline shows, Christianity has helped to shape much of the history of the Western world.

Constantine

C. 2100 BC

Birth of Judaism. According to the Bible's Book of Genesis, God made a Covenant with Abraham, promising him a new land in Canaan where he would found a great nation, and that the Jews would be God's "chosen people" if they agreed not to worship any other god.

C. 1250 BC

Moses leads the Jewish people out of Egypt in the Exodus. He receives the Ten Commandments from God on Mt Sinai, en route to Canaan.

Moses with the Ten Commandments

37 BC

King Herod is appointed ruler of Judaea, where Jesus will be born. This small province in the Roman Empire includes what is now Israel and the Palestinian territories. Many of Herod's subjects are unhappy with his reign.

31 BC

Octavian, Julius Caesar's adopted son, becomes Augustus, emperor of Rome. Jesus's parents, Joseph and Mary, will travel to Bethlehem for Augustus's census.

C. 4 BC

Birth of Jesus in Bethlehem.

The Holy Family

4 BC

Herod dies and his kingdom is divided among his sons.

C. AD 26

John the Baptist, Jesus's cousin, begins his ministry, at the age of 27. Living in the desert, he performs mass baptisms and tries to prepare the people of Jerusalem for the coming of a new Christ, or Messiah.

C. AD 27

Jesus is baptized by John the Baptist and begins his ministry. He travels around Galilee and Judaea, preaching a gospel of faith and salvation with the help of his 12 apostles, or disciples.

C. AD 30

Jesus is crucified on the orders of the Roman governor, Pontius Pilate, having been charged with sedition (inciting rebellion against the state).

C. AD 49

The Council of Jerusalem, presided over by Peter, decides that many Jewish laws, such as circumcision and dietary restrictions, do not apply to Christian converts.

AD 64–311

Persecution of Christians in the Roman Empire starts with Emperor Nero, who finds them useful scapegoats for the Great Fire of Rome. Their active proselytization (looking for new converts) and allegiance to Christ are seen as a threat to the emperor's authority, since emperors are held up as gods themselves. Many Christians are martyred (killed for their faith), and some will become saints.

AD 70

A fierce Jewish rebellion against Roman rule ends with the Fall of Jerusalem and the destruction of the Temple. About 600,000 people are killed.

AD 313

Emperor Constantine converts to Christianity. His Edict of Milan decrees freedom of worship for all Roman subjects.

AD 325

Constantine summons 300 bishops to a Council at Nicaea to draw up the statement of Christian beliefs known as the Nicene Creed. It promotes the idea of the Trinity, or God as three beings in one: Father (God), Son (Jesus), and Holy Spirit (God's continuing presence in the world).

AD 367

Bishop Athanasius authorizes 27 books to be included in the New Testament.

AD 380

Christianity is made the official religion of the Roman Empire.

AD 382–405

Jerome works on the Vulgate, a translation of the Bible from its Hebrew, Aramaic, and Greek parts into a single Latin volume.

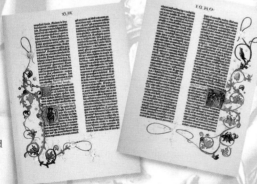

Pages from a 15th-century Vulgate

AD 430

Death of Saint Augustine of Hippo, one of the most important figures in the development of Christian beliefs. Author of many works, he promotes key doctrines, such as salvation, grace, and original sin.

AD 432

Saint Patrick brings Christianity to Ireland. It later spreads to Scotland with Saint Columba, who founds a community on the island of Iona. This marks the beginning of Celtic Christianity.

1054

Disagreements between the heads of the Western and Eastern churches lead to the split known as the Great Schism, when Pope Leo IX and Patriarch Michael Cerularius excommunicate each other. The Western church, based in Rome, becomes known as Roman Catholic, and the Eastern church, based in Constantinople (capital of the Byzantine empire), as Orthodox.

1095

Pope Urban II calls for a crusade to defend Christian lands in the East against the Turks. In response, European rulers raise armies for the First Crusade and take Jerusalem in 1099, massacring its Muslim population. Eight more Crusades follow, after losing Jerusalem, but fail to retake it. The last is in 1271.

1215

The Fourth Lateran Council is the most important church council of the Middle Ages. Amongst other decrees, it promotes the doctrine of transubstantiation.

1378–1423

Disagreements over the election of Urban VI lead to a new election of a second pope, who is installed in Avignon, France. The Western Schism brought about by these events is finally resolved when the papacy is re-established in Rome.

1431

After responding to divine inspiration and leading the armies of France, Joan of Arc becomes a martyr when she is burned at the stake for witchcraft.

Joan of Arc

Creationist Christians selling literature at the Scopes trial

1478–1834

The Spanish Inquisition, founded by Ferdinand and Isabella of Castile, becomes an institution notorious for its use of torture and execution to suppress heresies within the Catholic Church. Historians estimate that between 2,000 and 30,000 people were killed during this period.

1517

Martin Luther nails his 95 Theses to a church door in Wittenberg, Germany, in protest against the Church's corrupt practices, including the sale of Indulgences. Intended as a call for reform, their unexpected consequence wil be to split the Church in two and start the Protestant Reformation.

1534

After the pope refuses to allow Henry VIII to divorce his wife, the king forces the English Church to break from Rome and make him its new leader. This starts the process that brings Protestantism to England. In 1559, his daughter Elizabeth I establishes the Reformed Church of England, also known as the Anglican or Episcopalian Church.

1536

French theologian John Calvin publishes his defence of Protestant ideas and is forced into exile. The city-state of Geneva invites him to put his ideas into practice, setting an influential example and becoming a renowned sanctuary for religious refugees.

1791

Death of John Wesley, founder of the Methodist Church and famed for his open-air preaching among the poor. His teachings will inspire the 20th-century Charismatic Movement.

1841

David Livingstone, a Scottish missionary, starts to set up missions across Africa.

1869

The First Vatican Council announces the Dogma of Papal Infallibility, which states that certain decrees are inherently correct.

1925

The "Scopes Monkey Trial" in Tennessee, USA, draws widespread attention to the opposition of Christian fundamentalists to Charles Darwin's theory of evolution, published 65 years earlier.

1948

The World Council of Churches holds its first meeting. Part of the ecumenical movement, its main aim is to promote unity between the different Christian Churches.

1962–65

The Second Vatican Council calls for a spiritual renewal of the Catholic Church and greater accommodation with the modern world. Reforms include making Mass more accessible by replacing Latin with the local language.

1989

Barbara Harris of Massachusetts, USA, is ordained the first female Anglican bishop.

Bishop Harris

2005

Benedict XVI, a German, is elected the 266th pope.

Find out more

WHETHER YOU LIVE IN A BIG CITY WITH ACCESS to top museums or a small community with a single church, there are plenty of opportunities to learn more about Christianity. Often the best place to start is your local church. Many churches run youth programmes, social activities, and performances of devotional music. You can also find many examples of Christian art in galleries and museums. The Internet is full of resources and information that are only a click away.

VISIT MUSEUMS
Most major museums or galleries have permanent exhibits of religious art and artefacts. Look for paintings and statues of Jesus, stained glass, and even richly decorated chalices.

Playing an angel in the Nativity, a re-enactment of Christ's birth

PARTICIPATE IN YOUTH GROUPS
Local churches can help you find Christian youth groups in your area – or you can try the Internet. Many youth groups spend time reading the scriptures together or discussing the readings and sermons from that week's service. Some also put on special holiday programmes and are active volunteers in their communities.

READ THE BIBLE
There are many different versions of the Bible, so if you find yours difficult to understand, visit a Christian bookstore for help in finding one that is more accessible. Some come with illustrations, background information, or study guides to help you get the most out of your reading.

USEFUL WEBSITES

• To find statistics on the world's religions, including every Christian denomination; also lists the religious affiliations of famous people:
www.adherents.com
• For information on the popes, biographies of the saints, news updates from Rome, and a map of Vatican City:
www.vatican.va
• For explanations of different religions, including plenty of history and facts about Christianity:
www.religionfacts.com
• For a good example of a Christian youth site full of useful links and information:
www.kernowyouth.co.uk

Cathedral of Our Lady of the Angels, Los Angeles, USA

VISIT A CHURCH

Visit churches in your community to see different styles of architecture and worship. Regular services are open to everyone, but be sensitive – if the service is not of your faith, you may want to stay seated during the communion or other blessings.

LISTEN TO CHURCH MUSIC

If your church has a resident choir, find out when they perform and drop by to listen. You can find out about other choirs or performances of religious works by renowned composers by checking the listings in your local newspaper. You will find that different churches use different styles of music – Latin Masses in Catholic churches, celebratory hymns in Anglican churches, or gospel music in Pentecostal churches.

WATCH FILMS

Cinema has often borrowed Christian themes and stories to draw in audiences. Musicals, such as *Jesus Christ Superstar*, treat Jesus's story with a light touch, in contrast with more dramatic re-enactments, such as *The Passion of Christ*. This created controversy with its graphic portrayal of Jesus's suffering in the period before and during his Crucifixion.

Places to visit

WESTMINSTER ABBEY, LONDON

This largely Gothic church, built on the scale of a cathedral, is the traditional place of coronation for English monarchs. The original Abbey was built by the Saxons. Many famous people, such as Isaac Newton, Charles Darwin, and Dr Johnson, lie buried within its walls.

ROSSLYN CHAPEL, EDINBURGH

The 15th-century Rosslyn Chapel was originally intended as part of a larger building. A visit is a thrilling experience as almost every surface is covered in detailed carvings of biblical scenes or vivid symbolic imagery. The Chapel featured in the bestselling book *The Da Vinci Code*.

SKELLIG MICHAEL, COUNTY KERRY

This mysterious barren rock rises 213 m (700 ft) out of the sea 13 km (8 miles) off the Irish west coast. Now a World Heritage Site, during the 1st century it was home to a community of 12 monks for over 200 years until disruption by Viking raids. Today, the tiny monastery is a place of pilgrimage and can be reached by a steep stairway of 600 stone steps.

ST PETER'S BASILICA, ROME

Conceived as the "greatest church in Christendom" and completed in 1590, St Peter's dominates the tiny Vatican state. Designed in the form of a cross with a huge dome over its centre, it is built on the legendary tomb of St Peter, Christ's disciple and the first pope. Many important architects and artists worked on it, including Bramante and Michelangelo, who designed the dome and painted the Sistine Chapel ceiling. The world's largest church, in Yamassoukro, Ivory Coast, is modelled on St Peter's.

SANTIAGO DI COMPOSTELA CATHEDRAL

Santiago di Compostela in northwest Spain once marked the destination of an important medieval pilgrimage route and is still walked today. A mixture of Romanesque and baroque styles, the cathedral is built over the remains of Saint James, one of Christ's disciples. Those who completed the trail wore a white cockleshell as a badge of honour.

Glossary

ABBOT/ABBESS The head of a community of monks or nuns.

ALTAR A raised structure at the east end of a church, where bread and wine are consecrated.

ANGEL A spiritual being who may act as a messenger from God or as a guardian to humans.

ANNUNCIATION An announcement, specifically the announcement that Mary would bear the Son of God.

ANOINTING The act of conferring a blessing, typically by making the sign of the cross over a person's head with oil or water.

APOSTLE A missionary, a supporter, or a person sent to spread the word of Christ; specifically, one of Jesus's 12 disciples during his lifetime.

ASPERGILLUM A small, perforated ball or brush used for sprinkling holy water during church services.

ASSUMPTION The taking of a soul into Heaven. The religious holiday called the Feast of the Assumption celebrates the taking of Mary's soul into Heaven.

BAPTISM A sacrament in which holy water is used to bless a new member of the church and "wash away" his or her original sin.

BISHOP A high-ranking member of the clergy with spiritual and administrative powers over a diocese or group of churches.

CARDINAL Senior official in the Roman Catholic Church, ranking just below the pope. Duties include advising the pope and electing new popes. Most also lead a diocese or archdiocese.

CATACOMBS Underground cemeteries made up of cavelike hallways. During the 300 years after Christ's death when Christianity was illegal, many Christians used the catacombs to worship in secret.

Angel

CATHEDRAL The pricipal church of a diocese, often large and ornate. The name is derived from *cathedra,* which is the Latin word for "throne", or the official seat of a bishop.

CHALICE A ceremonial cup from which communion wine is taken.

CONFESSION A sacrament in which a person confesses their sins in order to be absolved or forgiven. In the Catholic tradition, a priest hears confession before granting absolution. In the Protestant tradition, the sincere act of confession through prayer is believed to achieve absolution.

COWL The hood or hooded cloak worn by a monk.

CROZIER A tall staff shaped like a shepherd's crook that symbolizes a bishop's or abbot's office.

CRUCIFIXION The act of executing a person by hanging them on a cross; specifically, Jesus's death on the cross.

DENOMINATION An organized group of Christians that adheres to a certain set of practices and beliefs.

DOGMA A decree handed down as an absolute truth from the pope.

ENCYCLICAL An official letter from the pope to all Roman Catholic bishops.

EPISTLE A letter, especially a formal or official letter.

Chalice

EUCHARIST Another word for communion; the re-enactment of Christ's sharing of bread and wine as his body and blood at the Last Supper.

EXCOMMUNICATE To expel from membership of the Church.

GOOD SAMARITAN Like the character in Jesus's parable, someone who is willing to help another person, even if the person is an enemy or stranger.

GOSPEL One of the first four books of the New Testament, by Matthew, Mark, Luke, and John. Each gospel presents the story of Jesus Christ from his birth to his death and resurrection. A gospel reading is included in most church services.

GRACE The spiritual state of being close to God; a short prayer recited before or after a meal to invoke a blessing on the food.

HABIT A nun's or monk's uniform.

HERETIC A baptized person who holds beliefs contrary to Church teachings.

HOLY ORDERS The sacrament of being ordained as a priest, nun, or other minister of the Church.

HOLY WATER Water that has been blessed by a priest for use in church services.

ILLUMINATED MANUSCRIPT A handwritten book whose pages are illustrated with colourful, intricate artwork, usually by scribes in a monastery.

INDULGENCE A "credit" for grace or absolution (forgiveness of sins) that was once sold to parishioners by Catholic Church officials.

Catacomb

70

MAGI Wise men from the East, often referred to as the three kings, who visited the baby Jesus in Bethlehem.

Magi

MANGER A trough from which animals eat; specifically, used as a "cradle" for the baby Jesus.

MANTLE A loose, sleeveless overgarment worn by priests during church services.

MARTYR A person who suffers death rather than renounce their religious beliefs.

MESSIAH One of Christ's titles; specifically, the long-awaited saviour of the Jews.

MIRACLE An occurrence that cannot be explained by the laws of nature and is attributed to God or a saint.

MITRE A tall, pointed headdress worn by bishops and abbots.

MONASTERY A place where monks live and worship together as a community.

MONK A male member of a religious community who has taken a vow of poverty, chastity, and obedience.

MYRRH A kind of fragrant resin; one of the gifts brought to the baby Jesus by the magi.

NUN A female member of a religious community who has taken a vow of poverty, chastity, and obedience.

ORTHODOX Relating to the Eastern branch of Christianity.

PAGAN A person who worships many gods or any religion other than Christianity, Judaism, or Islam.

PARABLE A story told to teach a lesson.

PATEN A ceremonial plate used to carry bread for the Eucharist.

PIETÀ A scene, often depicted in religious art, of Mary holding the dead Jesus after he has been taken down from the cross.

PILGRIM A person who travels to a sacred place as an act of religious devotion.

POPE The elected head of the Catholic Church.

PRIEST A person ordained to lead church services and perform sacraments.

PSALM A sacred song or poem.

PSALTER A book of psalms for devotional use.

PULPIT A podium in a church from which readings or sermons are delivered.

PURGATORY According to Catholic belief, a place between Heaven and Hell, where one may have to wait for sins to be absolved before being admitted into Heaven.

RELIC A scrap of clothing, bone, or other artefact from the life of a saint, which is believed to help its holder in understanding the scriptures and often to have healing properties as well.

RESURRECTION Jesus's coming back to life from death.

RITUAL A prescribed form of religious ceremony.

ROSARY A circular string of beads with a crucifix attached, used as a devotional aid in Catholic prayer.

SABBATH A day of rest and worship: Sunday for Christians, Saturday for Jews.

Pulpit

SACRAMENT A formal religious ceremony conferring God's grace on those who receive it. All denominations recognize baptism and the Eucharist as sacramental rites.

SACRIFICE An offering of something valued to a god or for the sake of a higher consideration.

SAINT A person whose good works on Earth have earned them official recognition as holy beings from the Church after his or her death.

SCHISM One of two major breaks in the Christian Church – between the Eastern and Western churches in the 11th century, or between the papal seats of Rome and Avignon during the 14th and 15th centuries.

Pietà

SCRIPTURE The writings of the Bible, also known as Holy Writ.

SECT see DENOMINATION.

SHRINE A place or object of worship.

SOUL The spiritual part of a person as opposed to the physical body.

SPIRE A vertical, pointed structure that rises above a church's roofline.

STOLE A long, thin band worn over the shoulders of a priest.

TRANSUBSTANTIATION The Catholic doctrine that bread and wine changes into the body and blood of Christ when blessed during the Eucharist.

TRINITY The three aspects of God, consisting of the Father, Son, and Holy Spirit.

VESTMENTS Ceremonial clothing.

VESTRY A room in a church where vestments are kept and parochial meetings are held.

Vestments

Index

A

abbots, 30, 31, 44, 48, 54
Abraham, 7, 66
Acts, Book of, 17, 18, 21
Advent, 56
All Souls Day, 57
altars, 50, 51, 52, 65
angels, 8, 17, 26–27, 55, 60
Anglicanism, 35, 36, 48, 49, 52–53, 58, 67
annunciation, 8, 32
Antony, St, 44
Aramaic, 20, 22
art, 60–61, 68
ascension, 17
assumption, 31
Athos, Mount, 33
Augustine, St, 41, 67

B

baptism, 8, 10, 33, 50, 58
Baptist church, 58, 63
Becket, Thomas, St, 43
Benedictines, 44, 46, 48
Benediction, 28
Bernadette, St, 42
Bethlehem, 8, 56, 66
Bible, 20–25, 32, 34, 36
  Gospels, 8–9, 11, 16–17, 20, 21, 23, 52
  Latin, 24
  modern, 25
  New Testament, 17, 18, 20–21
  Old Testament, 6–7, 20–23
  polyglots, 25
  texts, 22–25
  translations, 20, 34–35, 64
bishops, 30, 31, 33, 36, 48, 64
Book of Common Prayer, 35
Book of Hours, 55
Booth, William, 38
breviaries, 54
Brigid, St, 40
Byzantine empire, 19, 67

C

Caiaphas, 15
Calvary, 15
Calvin, John, 34, 38, 67
carols, 54, 63
cathedrals, 29, 32, 43, 61
Catholicism, 26, 28–31, 34, 40, 42, 44, 46, 48, 49, 64, 65
censers, 28,–29
chalices, 52–53
Chaucer, Geoffrey, 43
Christmas, 48, 54, 56, 63
churches, 36, 50–51, 69
Compostela, 42, 43, 69
confession, 28, 65
confirmation, 33, 58, 65
Constantine I, Emperor, 19, 66
Constantinople, 19, 33, 67
Coptic church, 44
Cranmer, Thomas, 35
creation, 6, 20, 54, 55
Creed, Charles, 19
crib, 56
Cromwell, Thomas, 35
crosses, 16, 32, 54
croziers, 31, 33, 48
Crucifixion, 10, 14–15, 26, 56, 66

D

Daniel, 7
David, King, 21
Dead Sea Scrolls, 22
desert fathers, 44
devils, 27
Deuteronomy, Book of, 22
disciples, 10, 12, 17, 18, 32
divine office, 45, 46

EF

Easter, 48, 56, 57
Eden, Garden of, 6
Emmaus, 17
Ephesus, 19
Epiphany, 56
Epistles, 18, 21
Erasmus, Desiderius, 35
Erasmus, St, 41
Essenes, 22
Eugenius IV, Pope, 29
Eustace, St, 42
evangelism, 39
festivals, 31, 56–57
films, 60, 62, 69
Fox, George, 36
funerals, 58, 59

G

Gabriel, Angel, 8, 31
Galilee, Sea of, 10, 11
Genesis, Book of, 6, 7, 22, 27
George, St, 40
Gethsemane, Garden of, 15
God, 6, 7, 9, 12, 26, 54
Good Samaritan, 12
Greek, 20, 22, 23, 35
Gutenberg, Johannes, 24, 34

H

Hail Mary, 30, 31
Heaven, 6, 16, 26–27, 39
Hebrew, 6–7, 20, 22–23
Hell, 6, 26–27
Henry II, King, 43
Henry VIII, King, 35, 67
Herod, King, 9, 20, 66
Holy Communion, 14, 32, 47, 52–53
Holy Spirit, 8, 10, 18, 26, 33, 56, 58
Holy Trinity, 26, 41, 56
holy water, 29, 43, 50
honey, 47
Host, 28, 29, 47
Hubert, St, 41
Hus, Jan, 34

IJ

icons, 32
Ignatius, St, 49
incarnation, 8
incense, 28–29, 46
Isaac, 7
Isaiah, 7
Jacob, 27
James, St, 42, 69
Jeremiah, 21
Jerome, St, 24, 66

Jerusalem, 14, 20, 57, 66, 67
Jesuits, 49
Jesus, 29, 60
  baptism, 8, 10, 58
  life, 8–10, 63
  death and resurrection, 10, 14–17
  teachings, 10–13
Jews, 6–7, 14, 20, 22–23, 54, 66
Job, Book of, 21
John the Baptist, 8, 56, 58
Jonah, 21
Jordan River, 8
Joseph, 8, 9, 41
Joseph of Arimathea, 16
Judas Iscariot, 15
Justinian I, Emperor, 19

KL

Knights of St John, 45
Lamb of God, 16
Last Judgement, 16, 26
Last Supper, 14, 15, 52
Lent, 56, 57
Lord's Prayer, 13, 30
Lourdes, 42
Lucy, St, 40
Luther, Martin, 34, 35, 64, 67
Lutheran church, 36

M

Madonna, see Mary
Magi, 9, 50, 56
Mardi Gras, 57
marriage, 58, 59
martyrs, 19, 40–41, 66
Mary, 8, 9, 26, 30, 31, 32, 41, 58
Mary I, Queen, 35
Mary Magdalene, 10, 17
Mass, 28, 29, 30, 52, 67
Maurice, St, 41
Mayflower, 36–37
Mennonites, 39
Messiah, 7, 15, 18, 56
Methodism, 36, 37, 67
Michael, St, 6
Middle Ages, 25, 50, 54
miracles, 10–11
missionaries, 19
mitres, 30, 48
monasticism, 33, 35, 44–47, 62, 64

monks, see monasticism
monstrance, 28
Moses, 7, 20, 62, 66
music, 55, 59, 60, 62–63, 69

NO

nativity, 8–9
Noah, 7
nuns, see monasticism
original sin, 6, 31, 67
Orthodox church, 32–33, 40, 44, 46, 48, 49, 65, 67

PQ

Palm Sunday, 57
parables, 12–13
Passion plays, 62
patriarchs, 32, 33
Paul, St, 18, 19, 21
penance, 28, 42
Pentecost, 18, 48, 56
Peter, St, 15, 18, 29, 55, 69
Pharisees, 11
pilgrimage, 28, 42–43
Pilgrims, 37
Pio, St, 41
Pontius Pilate, 15, 16, 66
Poor Clares, 45
popes, 28, 29, 30, 32, 34, 64, 65
prayer, 13, 28, 30, 45, 55, 60
preaching, 37, 38
Presbyterianism, 38
Presley, Elvis, 63
priests, 28, 30–32, 48–49
prophets, 7, 8, 14, 21
Protestantism, 34, 35, 36–39, 48, 65, 67
Proverbs, Book of, 21
Psalms, Book of, 21, 24, 41, 54, 62
Purgatory, 26
Puritans, 36, 37
Quakers, 36

R

Reformation, 24, 25, 34–35, 67
relics, 42–43, 64
Resurrection, 16–17, 26, 56, 65

Revelation, Book of, 27
Roman Catholics, see Catholicism
Romans, 14, 18, 19, 22, 40
rosaries, 28, 30, 45

S

Sabbath, 54
sacraments, 49, 58, 65
saints, 28, 30, 40–43, 61, 65
Salvation Army, 38–39
Satan, 6, 27, 39
Saul, 19
second coming, 12, 26, 56
Sermon on the Mount, 12–13
sermons, 36, 51, 54
Seventh Day Adventists, 39
Shakers, 36, 38
Sheba, Queen of, 20
shrines, 28, 42
Simon of Cyrene, 15
sin, 6, 8, 16, 26, 28, 42, 54
Solomon, King, 20
stained glass, 7, 10–11, 50, 61
Stephen, St, 19
stigmata, 41
synods, 33

TU

Ten Commandments, 20
Thomas, 17
Torah, 22–23
Trent, Council of, 24
Tyndale, William, 25
Urban VIII, Pope, 29

VWZ

Vatican, 29, 64, 67
vestments, 30, 33, 36, 48–49, 56
vicars, 49
Virgin, see Mary
Vulgate, 24
wafers, 47, 53
Wesley, John, 37, 67
wise men, see Magi
Wyclif, John, 34
Zechariah, 14
Zwingli, Ulrich, 34, 39

Acknowledgements

The publisher would like to thank models: Father Francis Baird, Father Stephen Horton, Julian Brand, Valerie Brand, Sister Susanna Mills, Sister M. Anthony, Sister Irene Joseph, Rev. Malcom Allen, Rev. Stephen Tyrrell, Rev. Felicity Walters, and Amber Mullins. With special thanks to: the monks of Prinknash Abbey, Cranham, UK, and the nuns of the Convent of Poor Clares, Woodchester, UK. Index: Chris Burnstein.

Scripture taken from the HOLY BIBLE, NEW INTERNATIONAL VERSION®. NIV®. Copyright© 1973, 1978, 1984 by International Bible Society. Used by permission of Zondervan. All rights reserved.

The publishers would like to thank the following for their kind permission to reproduce their photographs:
a=above; b=below; c=centre; l=left; r=right; t=top

AKG London: 6br, 17tr, 19cb, 20bl, 21tl, 26tr, 33tl, 35tc, 36bc, 38tl, 38tc, 43t, 43t; British Library 63t; Erich Lessing 6tl, 7bc, 7cbr, 7r, 11bl, 15C, 18tr, 20tr; alamy.com: 28bc; Brian Harris 54b; All Saints Church: 2tl, 26br, 27tr,
27cl; Ancient Art & Architecture Collection: 10clb, 14r, 17tl, 61br; R. Sheridan 26tl, 27cr; Arcaid: Alex Bartel 32tl; Bridgeman Art Library, London/New York: 12cr, 21b, 25br, 35bc, 35br, 38c, 41clb, 41bcl, 61bl; Alte Pinakothek, Munich, Germany 41cla; American Museum, Bath, Avon 38cl; Bibilioteque Mazarine, Paris 21cr; Bible Society, London, UK 23tr, 23br; Biblioteca Publica Episcopal, Barcelona 49bc; Bradford Art Galleries and Museums 34bl; British Library, London, UK 24br; The Fine Art Society 38bl; Instituto da Biblioteca Nacional, Lisbon 21cl; Koninklijk Museum voor Schone Kunsten, Antwerp 49tr; Musee Conde, Chantilly, France 26cl; Museo di San Marco dell' Angelico, Florence, Italy 18bl; Museum of the City of New York, USA 37tl; National Museum of Ancient Art, Lisbon, Portugal 41c; Private Collection 27br; Rafael Valls Gallery, London, UK 36cal; Richardson and Kailas Icons, London 32cal; Sixt Parish Church, Haute-Savoie, France 30c; Victoria and Albert Museum, London 26bc; Wesley's Chapel, London, UK 37tr; British Library: 24tr, 24bl, 54c; British Museum: 1c, 16r, 22ca, 29tr, 29tr, 42ca, 43br, 48tl, 59cr; Corbis: 61tl; Dallas and John Heaton 29br; Peter Turnley 63cr; Philip Gould 59br; Danish National Museum: 14t; DK Picture Library: Barnabas Kindersley

56tr, 56tr, 56tr, 56cl, 56br, 57bl; Mary Evans Picture Library: 12tr; Florence Nightingale Museum: 32bc; Getty Images: Allsport 60tl; Sonia Halliday Photographs: 10c, 16bc, 19cla, 21c; Laura Lushington 9br, 12cl; Jewish Museum: 22b, 23bl; Museum of London: 39ca, 39cra, 43cra; Museum of Order of St John: 45tr, 53bc, 54tl; National Gallery, London: 16bl, 17bl, 17br; National Maritime Museum: 2b, 36br; National Museums of Scotland: 43bl; Christine Osborne: 42tcl, 58bl; Liam White 47tr; Panos Pictures: Adrian Evans 36cl; Alain le Garsmeur 39cra; Jan Hammond 39c; Eric Miller 60br; Chris Sattlberger 37cr, 59tr; Paul Smith 39br; The Picture Desk: Art Archive Monastery of Santo Domingo de Silas, Spain/ Dagli Orti (A) 17ca; Diocesan Museum,Vienna/ Dagli Orti 31br; Pictorial Press Ltd: 62bl, 62br; Powerstock Photolibrary: 33tr; Prinknash Abbey, Gloucestershire, UK: 44cr, 50br, 51bl; Robin W. Symons 46c; Zev Radovan, Jerusalem: 10br, 20r, 22r, 22c; Royal Museum of Scotland: 51tl; Russian Orthodox Church, London: 32c, 33c; Saint Bride Printing Library: 34c; Scala Group S.p.A.: 8bl, 10tl, 10tr, 14bl, 15br, 18br, 19tr, 20cl, 35tl, 42tl; Pierpont Morgan Library/Art Resource 10cl; Science Museum: 40c; Sir John Soane's Museum: 4cal, 50cbr; South of England Rare Breeds Centre: 7bl; Tearfund: Jim Loring 41br; Topham Picturepoint: 19bc, 60tr, 60cl, 62t; Image Works 63bl; UPPA Ltd 63br; Wallace Collection: 28tl, 28l, 34cl, 40cl, 41t; Warburg Institute: 54t;

York Archaeological Trust: 20tl.

AKG Images: 66br
Alamy: Christine Osbourne 65br; Chad Ehlers 69cl; V&A Images 71br
AP Wideworld Photos: 64tl, 64bl
Bridgeman Art Library: 1448.5 The Annunciation, illuminated manuscript page, 1498 (vellum), French School, (15th century) / © Lambeth Palace Library, London, UK / Bridgeman Art Library 64br; Moses with the Tablets of the Law, 1663 (oil on canvas), Champaigne, Philippe de (1602-74) / Musee de Picardie, Amiens, France, Giraudon / Bridgeman Art Library 66tl; Emperor Constantine I (c.274-337) the Great (mosaic), Byzantine / San Marco, Venice, Italy, Lauros / Giraudon / Bridgeman Art Library 66tr
Corbis: Bettman 67tr; David Lees 65bl; Wally McNamee 65tl; Gianni Dagli Orti 66bl, 67br; Reuters 67br, 69tr; Ariel Skelley 68b
Getty Images: 64tr
Kobal Collection: Icon Prod. / Marquis Films / The Kobal Collection / Antonello, Phillipe 69br

All other images © Dorling Kindersley
For further information see:
www.dkimages.com